About the Authors

Sharon Kendrick started storytelling at the age of eleven and has never stopped. She likes to write fast-paced, feel-good romances with heroes who are so sexy they'll make your toes curl! She lives in the beautiful city of Winchester – where she can see the cathedral from her window (when standing on tip-toe!). She has two children, Celia and Patrick and her passions include music, books, cooking and eating – and drifting into daydreams while working out new plots.

Abby Green spent her teens reading Mills & Boon romances. She then spent many years working in the Film and TV industry as an Assistant Director. One day while standing outside an actor's trailer in the rain, she thought: *there has to be more than this*. So she sent off a partial to Mills & Boon. After many rewrites, they accepted her first book and an author was born. She lives in Dublin, Ireland and you can find out more here: www.abby-green.com

In 2002 **Janice Maynard** left a career as a primary teacher to pursue writing full-time. Her first love is creating sexy, character-driven, contemporary romance. She has written for Kensington and NAL, and is very happy to be part of the Mills & Boon family – a lifelong dream. Janice and her husband live in the shadow of the Great Smoky Mountains. They love to hike and travel. Visit her at www.JaniceMaynard.com

D0419998

Christmas with the Billionaire

SHARON KENDRICK

ABBY GREEN

JANICE MAYNARD

MILLS & BOON

All rights reserved including the right of reproduction in whole or in part in any form. This edition is published by arrangement with Harlequin Books S.A.

This is a work of fiction. Names, characters, places, locations and incidents are purely fictional and bear no relationship to any real life individuals, living or dead, or to any actual places, business establishments, locations, events or incidents. Any resemblance is entirely coincidental.

This book is sold subject to the condition that it shall not, by way of trade or otherwise, be lent, resold, hired out or otherwise circulated without the prior consent of the publisher in any form of binding or cover other than that in which it is published and without a similar condition including this condition being imposed on the subsequent purchaser.

® and TM are trademarks owned and used by the trademark owner and/or its licensee. Trademarks marked with ® are registered with the United Kingdom Patent Office and/or the Office for Harmonisation in the Internal Market and in other countries.

First Published in Great Britain 2020
By Mills & Boon, an imprint of HarperCollins*Publishers*
1 London Bridge Street, London, SE1 9GF

CHRISTMAS WITH THE BILLIONAIRE © 2020 Harlequin Books S.A.

Christmas in Da Conti's Bed © 2014 Sharon Kendrick
A Christmas Bride for the King © 2017 Abby Green
A Billionaire for Christmas © 2013 Janice Maynard

ISBN: 978-0-263-28219-1

MIX
Paper from responsible sources
FSC™ C007454

This book is produced from independently certified FSC™ paper to ensure responsible forest management.

For more information visit: www.harpercollins.co.uk/green

Printed and bound in Spain
by CPI, Barcelona

CHRISTMAS IN DA CONTI'S BED

SHARON KENDRICK

This book lovingly acknowledges the feisty and wonderful McCormick women – and most especially, Joan and Eileen.

CHAPTER ONE

NICCOLÒ DA CONTI hated marriage, Christmas and love—but most of all he hated it when people didn't do what he wanted them to.

An unfamiliar feeling of frustration made him bite back a graphic expletive as he paced the floor of the vast New York hotel suite. Outside, skyscrapers and stars glittered against the deepening indigo sky, though not nearly as brightly as the Christmas lights which were already adorning the city.

But Niccolò was oblivious to the party atmosphere, or even to the onset of this most hated time of year. All he could think about was his only sister and wondering why she was being so damned *disobedient*.

'I do not want,' he said, sucking in a ragged breath in an attempt to control his rapidly spiralling temper, 'some tacky topless model acting as your bridesmaid. I have worked long and hard to establish a degree of respectability in your life, Michela. Do you understand what I'm saying? It cannot be allowed to happen, and what is more—I will not allow it to happen.'

From the other side of the glitzy New York hotel penthouse suite, Michela's expression remained unchanged as she looked at him.

'But you can't stop me from having her, Niccolò,' she said stubbornly. 'I'm the bride and it's my decision. That's the thing.'

'You think so?' His mouth hardened and he felt another hot flicker of rage. 'I could refuse to pay for this wedding for a start.'

'But the man I'm marrying is rich enough to carry the cost of the marriage if you decide to take such drastic action.' Michela hesitated. 'Though I'm sure you wouldn't want the world to know that Niccolò da Conti had refused to finance his only sister's wedding, just because he doesn't approve of her choice of bridesmaid. Wouldn't that be a step too far in the modern world—even for a man as old-fashioned as you?'

Niccolò flexed and then relaxed his fingers, wishing there were a nearby punch-bag on which he could vent his mounting frustrations. The world usually ran according to his wishes and he was not used to having them questioned. Bad enough that Alekto Sarantos was acting like some kind of prima donna…without having to cope with the bombshell that Alannah Collins was here.

His mouth tightened with anger as he thought about his sister and the sacrifices he had made. For too long he had fought to keep their tiny family unit intact and he was not prepared to relinquish control over her just yet. Because old habits died hard. He had faced shame and tragedy and had seen them off. He had protected Michela as much as was within his power to do so, and now she was about to enter into marriage, which would see her secure for life. His careful vetting of would-be suitors had paid dividends and she was about to marry into one of the most powerful Italian-American families in New York. She would have the sanctity he had always wished for her and nothing would be allowed to tarnish the occasion. Nothing and no one.

Especially not Alannah Collins.

Even the *thought* of the minxy little tramp made his body react in a complicated way he found difficult to control—and he was a man who prided himself on control. A powerful combination of lust and regret flooded over him, although his overriding emotion was one of rage, and that was the one he hung onto.

'I cannot believe that she has had the nerve to show her face,' he bit out. 'I can't believe she's even here.'

'Well, she is. I invited her.'

'I thought you hadn't seen her since I withdrew you from that appalling school.'

Michela hesitated. 'Actually, we've…well, we've stayed in touch over the years,' she said. 'We emailed and phoned—and I used to see her whenever I was in England. And last year she came to New York and we took a trip to the Keys and it was just like old times. She was my best friend at school, Niccolò. We go back a long way.'

'And yet you told me nothing of this before?' he demanded. 'You maintain a secret friendship and then spring it on me on the eve of your marriage? Didn't you stop to consider how it might look—to have someone as notorious as this tawdry exhibitionist playing a major role in your wedding?'

Michela lifted her hands up to the sides of her head

in a gesture of frustration. 'Are you surprised I didn't tell you, when this is the kind of reaction I get?'

'What does Lucas say about your connection with her?' he demanded.

'It happened a long time ago. It's history, Niccolò. Most people in the States haven't even heard of *Stacked* magazine—it folded ages ago. And yes, I know that a video of the original shoot seems to have found its way onto YouTube—'

'What?' he exploded.

'But it's really quite tame by modern standards,' said Michela quickly. 'If you compare it to some of the music videos you see these days—well, it's almost suitable for the kindergarten! And Alannah doesn't do that kind of stuff any more. You've got her all wrong, Niccolò, she's—'

'She is a tramp!' he gritted out, his Sicilian accent becoming more pronounced as his temper rose once again. 'A precocious little tramp, who shouldn't be allowed within ten feet of decent society. When will you get it into your head, Michela, that Alannah Collins is—'

'Whoops!' A cool voice cut into his angry tirade and Niccolò turned to see a woman strolling into the room without bothering to knock and suddenly his words were forgotten. If somebody had asked him his name right then, he thought he might have trouble remembering it. And yet for a moment he almost didn't recognise her—because in his memory she was wearing very little and the woman in front of him had barely an inch of flesh on show. It was the sound of her naturally sultry voice which kick-started his memory and his libido. But it didn't take long for his eyes to reacquaint themselves with her magnificent body—nor to acknowledge the natural sensuality which seemed to shimmer from it in almost tangible waves.

She was wearing jeans and a white shirt with a high collar, but the concealing nature of her outfit did nothing to disguise the luscious curves beneath. Thick black hair like lustrous jet hung over her shoulders, and eyes the colour of denim were studying him with a hint of mockery in their depths. Niccolò swallowed. He had forgotten the pale creaminess of her complexion and the rosiness of her lips. He had forgotten that this half-Irish temptress with an unknown father could burrow underneath his skin, without even trying.

As she moved he could see the glitter of a little blue dragonfly brooch gleaming on her shirt-collar, which matched the amazing colour of her eyes. And even though he despised her, he could do nothing about the leap of desire which made his body grow tense. She made him think of things he'd rather not think about—but mostly she made him think about sex.

'Did I just hear my name being taken in vain?' she questioned lightly. 'Would you like me to walk back out and come in again?'

'Feel free to walk out any time you like,' he answered coldly. 'But why don't you do us all a favour, and skip the second part of the suggestion?'

She tilted her chin in a way which made her black hair ripple down her back, like an ebony waterfall. But the smile she slanted at him didn't quite reach her eyes.

'I see you've lost none of your natural charm,

Niccolò,' she observed acidly. 'I'd forgotten how you could take the word "insult" and give it a whole new meaning.'

Niccolò felt a pulse begin to pound in his temple as his blood grew heated. But much worse was the jerk of lust which made his groin feel unbearably hard. Which made him want to crush his mouth down over her lips and kiss all those insolent words away and then to drive deep inside her until she screamed out his name, over and over again.

Damn her, he thought viciously. Damn her, with all her easy confidence and her louche morals. And damn those sinful curves, which would compel a grown man to crawl over broken glass just to have the chance of touching them.

'Forgive me,' he drawled, 'but for a moment I didn't recognise you with your clothes on.'

He saw the brief discomfiture which crossed her face and something primitive gave him a heady rush of pleasure to think that he might have touched a nerve and hurt her. Hurt her as she had once hurt his family and threatened to ruin their name.

But she turned the look into a bright and meaningless smile. 'I'm not going to rise to that,' she said as she turned instead to his sister. 'Are you ready for your fitting, Michela?'

Michela nodded, but her eyes were still fixed nervously on Niccolò. 'I wish you two could be civil to each other—at least until the wedding is over. Couldn't you do that for me—just this once? Then you never need see one another again!'

Niccolò met Alannah's speculative gaze and the thought of her smiling serenely in a bridesmaid gown made his blood boil. Didn't she recognise that it was hypocritical for her to play the wide-eyed innocent on an important occasion such as this? Couldn't she see that it would suit everyone's agenda if she simply faded into the background, instead of taking on a major role? He thought of the powerful bridegroom's elderly grandparents and how they might react if they realised that this was the same woman who had massaged her own peaking nipples, while wearing a dishevelled schoolgirl hockey kit. His mouth hardened. How much would it take to persuade her that she was persona non grata?

He flickered his sister a brief smile. 'Why don't you let Alannah and I have a word or two in private, *mia sorella*? And let's see if we can sort out this matter to everyone's satisfaction.'

Michela gave her friend a questioning look, but Alannah nodded.

'It's okay,' she said. 'You're quite safe to leave me alone with your brother, Michela—I'm sure he doesn't bite.'

Niccolò stiffened as Michela left the suite and his unwanted feeling of desire escalated into a dark and unremitting tide. He wondered if Alannah had made that remark to be deliberately provocative. He would certainly like to bite *her*. He'd like to sink his teeth into that slender neck and suck hungrily on that soft and creamy skin.

Her eyes were fixed on him—with that infuriating look of mild amusement still lingering in their smoky depths.

'So come on, then, Niccolò,' she said insouciantly. 'Do your worst. Why don't you get whatever is bugging you off your chest so that we can clear the air and give your sister the kind of wedding she deserves?'

'At least we are agreed on something,' he snapped. 'My sister does deserve a perfect wedding—one which will not involve a woman who will attract all the wrong kind of publicity. You have always been wild—even before you decided to strip for the cameras. And I don't think it's acceptable for every man at the ceremony to be mentally undressing the bridesmaid, instead of concentrating on the solemn vows being made between the bride and groom.'

'For someone who seems to have spent all his life avoiding commitment, I applaud your sudden dedication to the marriage service.' Her cool smile didn't slip. 'But I don't think most men are as obsessed with my past as you are.'

'You think I'm obsessed by your past?' His voice hardened. 'Oh, but you flatter yourself if you imagine that I've given you anything more than a fleeting thought in the years since you led my sister astray.' His gaze moved over her and he wondered if the lie showed in his face because he had never forgotten her, nor the effect she'd had on him. For a long time he had dreamt of her soft body and her sweet kiss—before waking up in a cold sweat as he remembered what he had nearly done to her. 'I thought you were out of her life,' he said. 'Which is where I would prefer you to stay.'

Calmly, Alannah returned his stare and told herself not to react, no matter what the provocation. Didn't matter how angry he got, she would just blank it. She'd seen enough of the world to know that remaining calm—or, at least, *appearing* to—was the most effective weapon in dealing with an adversary. And Niccolò da Conti was being *very* adversarial.

She knew he blamed her for being a bad influence on his beloved sister, so maybe she shouldn't be surprised that he still seemed to bear a grudge. She remembered reading something about him in the press—about him not being the kind of man who forgot easily. Just as he wasn't the kind of man who was easily forgotten, that was for sure. He wore his wealth lightly; his power less so. He could silence a room by entering it. He could make a woman look at him and want him, even if he was currently staring at her as if she were something which had just crawled out from underneath a rock. What right did he have to look at her like that, after all these years? Because she'd once done something which had appalled his straight-laced sensibilities—something she'd lived to regret ever since? She was a different person now and he had no right to judge her.

Yet it was working, wasn't it? The contempt in his eyes was curiously affecting. That cold black light was threatening to destabilise a poise she'd spent years trying to perfect. And if she wasn't careful, he would try to crush her. *So tell him to keep his outdated opinions to himself. Tell him you're not interested in what he has to say.*

But her indignation was beginning to evaporate, because he was loosening the top button of his shirt and drawing attention to his body. Was he doing that on purpose? she wondered weakly, hating the way her stomach had suddenly turned to liquid. Was he deliberately reminding her of a potent sexuality which had once blown her away?

She became aware that her heart was pounding like mad and that her cheeks had grown hot. She might not like him. She might consider him the most controlling person she'd ever met—but that didn't stop her from wanting him in a way she'd never wanted anyone else. Didn't seem to matter how many times she tried to block out what had happened, or tried to play it down—it made no difference. All they'd shared had been one dance and one kiss—but it had been the most erotic experience of her life and she'd never forgotten it. It had made every other man she'd met seem as insubstantial as a shadow when the fierce midday sun moved over it. It had made every other kiss seem about as exciting as kissing your teddy bear.

She ran her gaze over him, wishing he were one of those men who had developed a soft paunch in the intervening years, or that his jaw had grown slack and jowly. But not Niccolò. No way. He still had the kind of powerful physique which looked as if he could fell a tree with the single stroke of an axe. He still had the kind of looks which made people turn their heads and stare. His rugged features stopped short of being classically beautiful, but his lips looked as if they had been made with kissing in mind—even if their soft sensuality was at odds with the hostile glitter in his eyes.

She hadn't seen him for ten years and ten years could be a lifetime. In that time she'd achieved a notoriety she couldn't seem to shake off, no matter how much she tried. She'd grown used to men treating her as an object—their eyes fixed firmly on her generous breasts whenever they were talking to her.

In those ten years she'd seen her mother get sick

and die and had woken up the day after the funeral to realise she was completely alone in the world. And that had been when she'd sat down and taken stock of her life. She'd realised that she had to walk away and leave the tawdry world of glamour modelling behind. She had reached out to try something new and it hadn't been easy, but she had tried. She was still trying—still dreaming of the big break, just like everyone else. Still trying to bolster up her fragile ego and hold her head up high and make out she was strong and proud, even if inside she sometimes felt as lost and frightened as a little girl. She'd made a lot of mistakes, but she'd paid for every one of them—and she wasn't going to let Niccolò da Conti dismiss her as if she were of no consequence.

And suddenly, she was finding it difficult to do 'calm', when he was staring at her in that contemptuous way. A flicker of rebellion sparked inside her as she met his disdainful gaze.

'While you, of course, are whiter than the driven snow?' she questioned sarcastically. 'The last thing I read was that you were dating some Norwegian banker, who you then dumped in the most horrible way possible. Apparently, you have a reputation for doing that, Niccolò. The article quoted her as saying how cruel you'd been—though I guess that shouldn't have really surprised me.'

'I prefer to think of it as honesty rather than cruelty, Alannah,' he answered carelessly. 'Some women just can't accept that a relationship has run its natural course and I'm afraid Lise was one of them. But it's interesting to know you've been keeping tabs on me all this time.' He gave her a coolly mocking smile. 'I guess single billionaires must have a certain appeal to women like you, who would do pretty much anything for money. Tell me, do you track their progress as a gambler would study the form of the most promising horses in the field? Is that how it works?'

Alannah tensed. Now he'd made it sound as if she'd been *stalking* him. He was trying to make her feel bad about herself *and she wasn't going to let him.* 'Now who's flattering themselves?' she said. 'You're best friends with the Sultan of Qurhah, aren't you? And if you go out for dinner with royalty, then the photos tend to make it into the tabloids—along with speculation about why your date was seen sobbing outside your apartment the following morning. So please don't lecture me on morality, Niccolò—when you know nothing of my life.'

'And I would prefer to keep it that way,' he said. 'In fact, I'd like to keep you as far away from any member of the da Conti family as possible. So why don't we get down to business?'

She blinked at him, momentarily disconcerted. 'Business?'

'Sure. Don't look so startled—you're a big girl now, Alannah. You know how these things work. You and I need to have a little talk and we might as well do it in some degree of comfort.' He waved his hand in the direction of the cocktail cabinet which stood at the far end of the glittering hotel suite. 'Would you like a drink? Don't good-time girls always go for champagne? I can't guarantee a high-heeled shoe for you to sip it from, but I can vouch for an extremely good vintage.'

Don't rise to it, she told herself, before fixing a

weary smile to her lips. 'I hate to challenge your stereotype, but I'm not crazy about champagne and even if I was I certainly wouldn't want to drink it with you. That might imply a cordiality we both know doesn't exist. So why don't you say whatever it is you're determined to say? And then we can end this conversation as quickly as possible so that I can concentrate on fitting Michela's wedding gown.'

He didn't answer for a moment, but instead leaned back against one of the giant sofas and looked at her, his arms folded across his broad chest. Yet for all his supposedly casual stance, Alannah felt a chill of foreboding as his eyes met hers. There was a patina of power surrounding him which she hadn't noticed in that long-ago nightclub. There was a hardness about him which you didn't find in your average man. Suddenly he looked formidable—as if he was determined to remind her just who she was dealing with.

'I think we both know a simple way to resolve this,' he said softly. 'All you have to do is step out of the spotlight right now. Do that and there will be no problem. Michela is about to marry a very powerful man. She is about to take on an important role as a new wife. In time, she hopes to have children and her friends will be role models to them. And…'

'And?' she questioned, but she knew what was coming. It was crystal clear from the look on his face.

'You are not an appropriate role model,' he said. 'You're not the kind of woman I want fraternising with my nephews and nieces.'

Her heart was beating very fast. 'Don't you dare judge me,' she said, but her voice wasn't quite steady.

'Then why not make it easy for yourself? Tell Michela you've changed your mind about acting as her bridesmaid.'

'Too late!' Forcing herself to stay strong, she held up her palms in front of her, like a policeman stepping into the road to stop the traffic. 'I've made my own dress, which is currently swathed in plastic in my room, waiting for me to put it on just before noon tomorrow. I'm wearing scarlet silk to emphasise the wedding's winter theme,' she added chattily.

'But it's not going to happen,' he said repressively. 'Do you really think I would let it?'

For a moment Alannah felt another shimmer of doubt flicker into the equation. The quiet resolution of his voice scared her and so did the forthright expression in his eyes. Somehow he was making her feel…vulnerable. *And she wasn't going to let that happen.* Because she didn't do vulnerable. Not any more. Vulnerable got you nowhere. It made you fall down when life landed one of its killer punches and think you'd never be able to get back up again. It made you easy prey to powerful predators like Niccolò da Conti. 'How wicked you make me sound,' she said.

'Not wicked,' he corrected silkily. 'Just misguided, out-of-control and sexually precocious. And I don't want any publicity generated by the presence of *Stacked* magazine's most popular pin-up.'

'But nobody—'

'Michela has already mistakenly tried to tell me that nobody will know,' he interrupted impatiently. 'But they will. The magazines you stripped for have become collectors' items and back issues now change hands for thousands of dollars. And I've just been informed that a film of you has made its way onto YouTube, raising your public profile even further. It doesn't matter what you wear or what you don't wear—you still have the kind of body which occupies a fertile part of the male imagination. Men still look at you and find themselves thinking of one thing—and only one thing.'

Alannah tried not to cringe, but unfortunately his words struck home. Clever, cruel Niccolò had—unwittingly or not—tapped into her biggest insecurity. He made her feel like an object. Like a *thing*. Not a woman at all, but some two-dimensional image in a magazine—put there simply for men to lust over.

The person she was now wouldn't dream of letting her nipples peek out from behind her splayed fingers, while she pouted at the camera. These days she would rather die than hook her thumbs in her panties and thrust her pelvis in the direction of the lens. *But she'd needed to do it, for all kinds of reasons. Reasons the uptight Niccolò da Conti wouldn't understand in a million years.*

'You were *notorious*, Alannah,' he continued. 'And that kind of notoriety doesn't just go away. It sticks like mud.'

She looked at him in despair. He was telling *her* that? Didn't he realise that she'd been living with the consequences of that job ever since? No, of course he didn't. He saw what he wanted to see and no more—he didn't have the imagination to put himself in someone else's shoes and think what their life might be like. He was protected by his wealth and position and his arrogance.

She wanted to go up and shake *him* and tell him

to think outside the box. To wipe that judgemental look from his face and to start seeing her as a person, instead of someone who'd once behaved rashly. She could see exactly why Michela had been so scared of him when they'd been at school together. Was it any wonder that the Italian girl had rebelled from the moment he'd dropped her off at the exclusive Swiss finishing school where Alannah's mother had worked as school matron?

'The most important thing for me,' she said slowly, 'is that Michela wants me there. It's her day and she's the bride. So, short of tying me up and kidnapping me—I intend to be there tomorrow.'

'Unless we come to some kind of mutually beneficial arrangement,' he said.

'Oh?' She tilted her head. 'Tell me more.'

'Oh, come on, Alannah.' He smiled. 'You're a streetwise woman. You've been around. There must be something in your life that you'd…*like*.'

'Something in my life that I'd like?' she repeated. 'You mean like a cure for the common cold, or an alarm that doesn't make you want to smash the phone every time you hear it?'

'Very amusing. No, nothing like that.' He paused, and his black eyes glittered. 'I am a very wealthy man—and I'm willing to make it worth your while to tell Michela that you've changed your mind.'

She stared at him in disbelief.

'Let me get this straight,' she said. 'You're offering me *money* to stay away from your sister and not be her bridesmaid?'

'Why not?' He gave a cold smile. 'In my experience, if you want something badly enough you can usually get it. The tricky thing is negotiating the right price—but that is something I should imagine you're very good at.'

'But that's...bribery.'

'Try thinking of it as common sense,' he suggested softly.

She was shaking her head. 'You know, Michela used to tell me how unbelievably controlling you were,' she said. 'And part of me thought she might have been exaggerating. But now I can see that every word was true.'

'I am not seeking your approval of my character,' he clipped out. 'Just think why I'm making you this offer.'

'Because you're a control freak?'

'Because Michela means everything to me,' he said, and suddenly his voice grew harsh as he remembered how he'd fought to protect his sister from the sins of their father. *And their mother.* He thought of their flight from Sicily—his mother pregnant with Michela and not knowing what lay ahead. Niccolò had been only ten, but he had been the one everyone had relied on. He had been the man around the house. And it was hard to relinquish that kind of role or those kinds of expectations...

'Michela is the only family I have left in the world and I would do anything for her,' he ground out.

'Except give her the freedom which a woman of her age has the right to expect?' she retorted. 'Well, I'm *glad* she's had the courage to stand up to you. To maybe make you realise that you can't keep snapping your fingers and expecting everyone else to just leap to attention. I'm not going anywhere until after the wedding. Better deal with it, Niccolò.'

Their gazes clashed and Niccolò felt the flicker of something unknown as he returned her stare. Oh, but she was a one-off. She took defiance to a whole new level and made it seem erotic. She made him want to take her in his arms and dominate her—to show her that he could not and would not be thwarted. He took a step towards her and a primitive surge of pleasure rippled over him as he watched her eyes darken. Because she still wanted him, he realised. Maybe not quite as much as he wanted her—but the desire he could read in her eyes was unmistakable.

And couldn't desire be the most powerful weapon of all? Didn't sex give a man power over a woman who wanted it?

'Why don't you think about what I've said?' he suggested. 'So that by the time I see you at the pre-wedding dinner later, you'll have had the sense to change your mind about my offer.'

Her eyes narrowed. 'But…'

He raised his eyebrows. Suddenly, she didn't look quite so defiant. Suddenly she looked almost unsure of herself. 'But?'

'I…' She shrugged her shoulders. 'It's just that… well, Michela said you were probably going to skip the dinner and that we wouldn't see you until tomorrow. Something to do with a business deal. Some new apartment block you've recently built in London.'

'Is that what she said?' He smiled. 'Well, not any more. I've decided business can wait, because something much more important has come up.' There was a pause as he looked at her and suddenly it was easy to forget the pressing needs of his billionaire clients and friends. 'What is it they say? Keep your friends close but your enemies closer. And I want you *very* close for all kinds of reasons, Alannah. You'd better believe that.'

CHAPTER TWO

ALANNAH PULLED UP the zip of her cocktail dress and stared at her pale-faced reflection in the mirror. She'd tried deep breathing and she'd done a quick bout of yoga, but her hands were still trembling and she knew why. Slipping on a pair of high-heeled shoes, she felt a wave of self-recrimination washing over her.

She thought about the things Niccolò had said to her earlier. The way he'd insulted her and looked down his proud, patrician nose. He'd been judging her in the most negative way possible, but that hadn't stopped her wanting him. She shuddered. Where was the self-respect she'd worked so hard to get back? She wondered what had happened to the cool, calm Alannah who wasn't going to let him get under her skin. How had he managed to puncture her self-possession with nothing more than a heated ebony gaze, which reminded her of things she'd rather forget?

Because memory was a funny thing, that was why—and sometimes you had no control over it. It flipped and jerked and jumped around like a flapping fish on the end of a hook. It took you to places you didn't want to visit. It could make ten years seem like a minute, or a minute seem like an hour.

It could put you back inside the skin of the person you'd once been.

And suddenly she was a teenager again. Seventeen years old and about to break the rules. Off to a party wearing the make-up which her Swiss finishing school strictly forbade, when really she should have been tucked up in bed in the dormitory. Wearing a tiny little micro-mini because she had been young and carefree—because back then she hadn't realised that a woman's body could become her enemy, instead of her friend…

By rights, someone like her shouldn't have been a pupil at the exclusive all-girls academy, tucked high in the beautiful mountains of Switzerland. She wasn't rich. She wasn't well-connected. She was just the illegitimate daughter of a single-parent mother who happened to be Matron at the fancy boarding school. And while this meant that Alannah got herself a great education, her 'charity' status meant that most of the girls simply tolerated her.

Michela da Conti was different. She was the only one who had held out the hand of genuine friendship—maybe because they had something in common, despite their rich-girl/poor-girl pairing. Alannah had spent her life rebelling against her super-strict mother while Michela had known real tragedy in her short life, plus she wanted to escape the strictures of her controlling brother, Niccolò.

Their youthful rebellion usually stretched no further than going out for illicit under-age drinks in one of the nearby bars after lights-out, or hanging out of the dormitory window, trying to inhale cigarettes without being sick.

But one night they heard about a party. A glitzy twenty-first birthday celebration for one of Niccolò's godsons—which was being held in one of the neighbouring mountain valleys.

'And we're going!' declared Michela excitedly.

Alannah remembered frowning. 'But what about your brother? Won't he be there?'

'You're kidding.' Michela had given a smile of satisfaction. 'Apparently, he's miles away in some obscenely expensive resort in Barbados, with his latest ghastly supermodel girlfriend. So we're safe.'

Alannah remembered walking into the crowded room, where coloured lights were flashing and music was blaring out loudly. Her borrowed silver minidress was clinging to her body like honey and she was getting lots of requests to dance, but she turned down every one because all the boys seemed too loud and too brash to be interesting.

She did her best to enjoy herself. She sipped a soft drink and admired the snowy view. Found a sleeping kitten on her way back from the loo and spent an enjoyable ten minutes stroking its furry tummy and wishing she could go home. When eventually she went back into the main room to find Michela to suggest they got a cab back to school, she couldn't find her anywhere. So she went and stood in a quiet corner of the room, losing herself in the shadows while everyone else partied—and that was when she saw him.

Him.

She had never forgotten that moment. It was like being struck by something with no sense of warning that it was coming. As if a velvet sledgehammer had hit her very hard. She was aware that he was tall and his hair was as black as the night sky. His eyes were black too—even from this distance she could see that. He was dressed in a dark suit, which made him look outwardly sophisticated, but she could sense something *primitive* about him. There was something predatory in the gleam of his eyes, which should have scared her as he began to walk towards her, with a sense of purpose in his step.

But she wasn't scared.

It was the most illogical thought she'd ever had, but at that moment she felt as if she'd been waiting all her life for him to arrive, and here he was.

Here he was.

He looked her up and down—as if it was his right to study a strange woman as he might study a car he was thinking of buying. But surely no car would make him smile like that—a smile which seemed to come from somewhere deep inside him, one that pierced her heart and made her knees feel as if they might have difficulty supporting her.

'I think you need to dance,' he said.

'I'm not a very good dancer.'

'That's because you've never danced with me. So come here and let me teach you how.'

Later, she would remonstrate with herself at the eagerness with which she fell into his arms. At the way she let him slide his hands around her back as if she'd known him for years. His hand moved to her hair and he started stroking it and suddenly she wanted to purr as loudly as that kitten had done earlier.

They said very little. The party was too loud for conversation and, anyway, it didn't seem to be conversation which was dominating Alannah's thoughts right then. Or his. Words seemed superfluous as he pulled her closer and, although the music was fast, they danced so slowly that they barely moved. Their bodies felt as if they were glued together and Alannah almost wept with the sheer pleasure of it all. Did he sense her enjoyment? Was that why he dipped his mouth to her ear, so that she could feel the warmth of his breath fanning her skin?

'You,' he said, his velvety voice underpinned with an accent which she recognised as Sicilian, 'are very beautiful.'

Wasn't it funny how some people you just seemed to spark off? So that she—inexperienced and raw as she was—didn't respond in a conventional way. She didn't blush and tell him she wasn't beautiful at all—but instead came out with something which sounded almost slick.

'And you,' she cooed back, looking straight into his black eyes, 'are very handsome.'

He smiled. 'A perfect match, then?'

She tipped her head back. 'Aren't you getting a little ahead of yourself?'

'Probably.' He leaned forward, so that her face was bathed in the dark spotlight of his gaze. 'Especially as we haven't even kissed. Don't you think that's a shocking omission, my beauty? So shocking that I think we ought to remedy it right now.'

She remembered the way her heart had crashed loudly against her ribcage. The way her mouth had dried with anticipation and the words had just come tumbling out of her mouth. 'Who says I'm going to kiss you?'

'I do.'

And he did.

In that shadowy corner of some anonymous house in the Swiss mountains, while outside flakes of snow floated past the window like big, white feathers, he kissed her.

He kissed her so intensely that Alannah thought she might faint. He kissed her for so long that she wanted him never to stop. It was like that pile of bone-dry sticks she'd once built on a long-ago holiday to Ireland—she remembered the way they'd combusted into flames the moment her aunt had put a match to them. Well, it was a bit like that now.

She was on fire.

His thumb brushed over her breast and Alannah wriggled with excitement. Because surely this was what she had been made for—to stand in this man's arms and be touched by him. To have him look at her as if she were the most beautiful woman in the world. He deepened the kiss to one of added intimacy and as he pushed his thigh between hers the atmosphere suddenly changed. It became charged. She could feel the flood of liquid heat to her groin and the sudden, almost painful hardening of her nipples as they pushed insistently against his chest. His breath was unsteady as he pulled away from her and there was a primitive emotion on his face which she didn't recognise.

'We'd better think about moving somewhere more comfortable,' he said roughly. 'Somewhere with a bed.'

Alannah never had a chance to reply because suddenly the mood was broken by some kind of commotion at the door. She felt him tense as Michela burst into the room with snow melting on her raven hair, and the guilty look on her friend's face when she saw Niccolò told its own story.

It was unfortunate that Michela was surrounded by the miasma of sickly-sweet marijuana smoke—and even more unfortunate when Niccolò's discreet enquiries the next day yielded up the information that both girls were already on a formal warning from the school. A small matter of the building's elaborate fire-alarm system having been set off by the two of them hanging out of a dormitory window, smoking.

Alannah would never forget the look of passion dying on Niccolò's face, only to see it being replaced with one of disgust as he looked at her. She remembered wanting to wither beneath it.

'You are my sister's friend?' he questioned incredulously. 'Her *school friend*?'

'Y-yes.'

'How old are you?'

'Seventeen.'

All the colour drained from his face and he looked as if she'd hit him. 'So Michela associates with a *puttana*, does she?' he hissed. 'A cheap little tart who puts out for strangers at parties.'

'I d-don't remember you objecting,' she stammered, stung into defending herself, even if deep down she felt she had no real defence to offer.

'No man objects when a woman offers herself to him on a plate like that,' he snapped.

The following day he had withdrawn Michela from the school and shortly afterwards the head teacher had summoned Alannah and her mother to her office. The head had clearly been furious at the prospect of having to say goodbye to Niccolò da Conti's generous donations to the school. She had told Alannah that her behaviour was unacceptable and her mother had pre-empted the inevitable expulsion by offering up her resignation.

'I'm not having my girl scapegoated by some rich financier,' she'd said fiercely. 'If you're going to heap all the blame on her, then this is not the kind of school for her.'

Of course, that was not an end to it—merely the beginning of a nightmare which put the whole Niccolò incident to the back of her mind.

But she'd never grassed up Michela and Michela had remained loyal to her ever since.

Her thoughts cleared and she saw her friend looking at her in the dressing-table mirror, her face still glowing from her pre-wedding facial, and Alannah sighed as she met Michela's questioning gaze. 'Maybe it would be better if I just bowed out, if it's going to cause a massive row between you and your brother. I'll just stand at the back like everyone else and throw rose petals. I can live with that.'

Michela glared as she put her hairbrush down.

'And let Niccolò have his own way? I don't think so. You've been the best of friends to me, Alannah—and I want you there. In fact, it'll probably do Niccolò good on all kinds of levels. I've never heard *anyone* speak to him the way you do.' She smirked. 'Nobody else would dare.'

Alannah wondered what Michela would say if she realised how much of her reaction to her powerful brother was bravado. That her feelings for him were… *complicated.* Would she be shocked if she knew the truth? That she only had to look at him to want to rip the shirt from his body and feast her eyes on all that silken olive flesh? That somehow he brought out a wildness in her which frightened her. Which she knew was wrong. And not only wrong…she knew only too well that those supposedly seamless sexual fantasies were nothing but an illusion.

She forced a smile. 'Okay, if you insist…it'll be business as usual. In which case, we'd better get going. I know it's traditional for the bride to keep her groom waiting on the big day, but not on the eve-of-wedding dinner!'

They took the elevator down to the iconic Midnight Room, where a large clock was set permanently at the witching hour. It was a spectacular party room designed by Emma Constantinides, the hotel owner's wife—and had won countless industry prizes since its opening. Circular tables had been set for dinner and the dark velvet ceiling was punctured with tiny lights, so that it resembled a star-filled sky. In the silvery light from hundreds of candles, people in evening dress stood drinking champagne as the scent of dark blue hyacinths wafted through the air.

A roar of delight greeted the bride-to-be's appearance and Alannah leaned forward to whisper in Michela's ear as people began to surge towards them. 'You go and sparkle,' she said. 'Anything you need me to check?'

Michela shook her head. She had already spotted Lucas on the opposite side of the room, talking to his mother. 'No. You go and sparkle too,' she said. 'And for goodness' sake, have a very large cocktail before we sit down to dinner. You look completely washed out, Alannah.'

But Alannah refused a drink. A drink on an empty stomach was a recipe for disaster and hers was already in knots. All she had to do was to get through the next thirty-six hours without crumbling, and surely she could do that.

And then she looked around the room and saw Niccolò—and every empowering thought flew straight from her mind as her gaze focused on him.

He was standing talking to a blonde whose sequined dress left little to the imagination and Alannah found herself thinking that he didn't seem to have a problem with *that*. The woman was gazing up at him and nodding intently, as if nothing but pearls of wisdom were falling from those cruel and kissable lips. There were other women clustering nearby, too—as if he were a dark shark and they were all hungry little pilot fish, just waiting for whatever scraps he cared to leave for them.

He lifted his head as if he had sensed her watching him—glancing across the room to where she stood. And suddenly it was too late to look away. His gaze captured hers and held it and it felt as if some fierce dark light were piercing through her skin. She felt sensitive. Exposed and raw. Terrified he would see through to the dark mass of insecurities hidden beneath her cool exterior, she tried to look away, but she couldn't. *She couldn't.* He seemed to be drawing her in by the force of his formidable will.

Desperately, she tried to compose herself. To concentrate on something other than how beautifully the dark suit caressed his hard body, but she failed at that, too. Instead she found herself staring at the snowy edge of his dinner-shirt and the way his olive skin gleamed like burnished gold above it.

He bent his head to say something to the blonde, who turned to look at her, and Alannah thought she saw faint surprise clouding the other woman's eyes. Had her uncomfortable stance given her away—making the woman guess that she was the outsider here?

She forced herself to turn away to talk to some of the other guests, who seemed genuinely charmed by her English accent, and for a while she allowed herself to relax before the bell rang for dinner. But a glance at the seating plan showed her that she was next to Niccolò—*of course she was,* for hadn't Michela made it clear that she wanted the two of them to get along better? She wondered when her friend was going to realise that it simply wasn't going to happen. Or at least, not in this lifetime. Her heart began thumping painfully as she made her way towards the top table.

She felt his presence behind her even before his shadow fell over the table. The palms of her hands were clammy and the race of her heart was thready, but somehow she managed to fix a wide smile to her lips as she turned to look at him.

'Niccolò!' she said brightly.

'Just the person you wanted to sit beside, right?'

'How did you guess?' Solely for the benefit of the other guests, she maintained that brittle rictus of a smile. 'You were right at the top of my list.'

But Alannah tensed as he leaned forward to kiss her on both cheeks, just as he would have done to any other female guest. She wondered if any other female guest would have reacted the way she did, with a pulse which was threatening to rocket out of control and a desire to tip her head up so that his mouth would meet hers, instead of grazing the innocent surface of her cheek. She found herself longing to reach up to touch that hard, chiselled jaw and to feel it scrape against her fingertips. She wanted to press her lips against his ear and kiss it. And how crazy was that? How could you want a man so much when you didn't even *like* him?

Stop it, she told herself as he pulled out her chair with an exaggerated courtesy, which seemed to be at odds with the mockery gleaming from his eyes. Did he know what kind of effect he had on her? Did he realise that her legs were weak and her breasts growing heavy? He sat down next to her and she could smell his warm, male flesh—as subtle and spicy as sandalwood—and all she wanted to do was to breathe it in. Reaching out, she picked up her champagne flute and took a gulp.

She could feel him watching as she drank the cold, fizzy wine but the champagne tasted as sour as a remedy you might take for an upset stomach. She put down her glass and looked at him, because they couldn't go on like this. Not with a whole day and a half to get through.

'I think Michela has sat us together deliberately,' she said.

He raised his eyebrows. 'Because?'

'I think she's hoping that we're going to declare some sort of truce.'

'Why—are we engaged in some sort of battle?'

'Please don't be disingenuous, Niccolò. You know we are. We've done nothing but argue since we reconnected.' She shrugged. 'And while that seems to be what you seem to want—I'd prefer it, and your sister would prefer it, if we could manage to be non-confrontational. At least, in public.'

Niccolò met her denim-blue eyes and gave a small dissenting shake of his head—thinking how wrong she'd got it. Because battle was the last thing he wanted. His needs around Alannah Collins were much more fundamental. He might even have contemplated a more conventional route by asking her out on a date, if she hadn't been the kind of woman he despised.

Yet there was nothing of the precocious teenager or sexy glamour model about her tonight. The image she presented was almost *demure*. Her navy silk dress was high-necked and the hemline showed nothing more than an couple of inches of slender knee. A small, glittering brooch in the shape of a fluttering moth was her only jewellery. Her most magnificent assets—the breasts which had once so captured the imagination of the British public—were only hinted at and certainly not on show. All he could see was the occasional glimpse of a soft curve as the material brushed against them. He swallowed. Was she aware that it was just as provocative to conceal something, as to reveal it?

Of course she was.

Trading on her own sexuality had been her stock-in-trade, hadn't it? She knew everything there was to know about how to pull in the punters and leave them slavering for more.

Shaking out his napkin, he placed it in his lap and scowled, recalling the first time he'd seen her at his godson's birthday party.

He remembered looking in amazement at the silver dress, which had clung to her curvy body like melted butter, and thinking that he'd never seen anyone looking quite so alluring. Had he been frustrated? Too long without a woman? Unlikely. All he knew was that he hadn't been able to tear his eyes away from her.

The look which had passed between them had been timeless. The lust which had overwhelmed him had been almost tangible. He had never experienced anything like it in his life—not before, nor since. The hardness at his groin had been almost unbearable as he had danced with her. Something elemental had caught him in its grip and he'd felt almost…*lost.* The dance had been simply a formality—paving the way for their first kiss. He had kissed her for a long time, tempted by a need to pull her into a dark and anonymous corner and just *take* her. And even though he detested being out of control…even though his own history had warned him this was not the way to go—it hadn't been enough to deter him from acting on it.

He had been just about to drive her back to his hotel, when there had been some sort of commotion by the door. He remembered turning to see Michela giggling as she'd entered the room, accompanied by a group of boys. His *sister.* Large flakes of snow had been melting on her raven hair and her look of guilt when she had seen him had told its own story.

And that was when Niccolò had discovered that Alannah Collins wasn't some twenty-something party guest, but the teenage best friend of his only sister. A wild-child who had been threatening to ruin Michela's reputation and bring shame on the da Conti name, after he'd spent years meticulously dragging it from the mud.

Was it any wonder that he despised her?

Was it any wonder that he despised himself, knowing what he had nearly done to her?

What he still wanted to do to her.

He leaned back in his chair, paying little attention to the plates of smoked salmon which were being placed in front of them. 'Did you ever tell Michela what happened between us?' he questioned suddenly.

She stiffened a little before turning to look at him, her eyes narrowing warily. 'But nothing did happen.'

'Oh, come on.' He gave a harsh laugh. 'It might as well have done. It would have done, if my sister hadn't arrived. I've never had a dance quite so erotic as the one I had with you. It was a dance which was headed straight for the bedroom.'

'Oh, for heaven's sake—'

'Does Michela realise that you would have spent the night with me if she hadn't turned up when she did?'

'You can't know that.'

'Yes, I can. And so can you. Why don't you try being honest with yourself for once, Alannah?' He leaned forward and his voice roughened. 'I know enough about women to realise when they want a man to make love to them—and you were screaming out to have me do it to you that night.'

'Really?' She took a nervous sip of her drink.

'And you've avoided answering my question,' he persisted. 'What exactly did you tell Michela?'

There was a pause. 'I didn't tell her anything.'

'Why not?'

Alannah shrugged, reluctant to admit the truth—that she'd been too ashamed of her own reaction to want to acknowledge it to anyone and certainly not to her best friend. That she'd felt dirty and cheap. Michela had warned her that her big brother was a 'player'. That he changed his women nearly as often as he changed his shirts. She remembered the two of them agreeing that any woman who went out with a man like him was *sad*. But she'd nearly been one of those women, hadn't she? Because he was right. If Michela hadn't walked in right then, she would have…

Briefly, she let her eyes close. She'd been so in thrall to him that he probably could have taken her outside and taken her virginity pressed up against a cold and snowy tree. She had certainly been up for going back to his hotel with him.

She opened her eyes and looked at him. 'Why not? Because even though Michela has always thought you a total control freak, she absolutely idolised you—and I knew you were the only family she had. It wasn't for me to disillusion her by telling her that you'd been hitting on her best friend.'

'Hitting on her best friend?' He gave a cynical smile. 'Oh, please. Unfortunately, I didn't realise I was dealing with *jailbait* at the time. You kept that one crucial fact to yourself.'

'Is that why you got me expelled?' she said, without missing a beat.

He shook his head. 'I didn't mention your name when I withdrew Michela from the school.'

Her eyes narrowed. 'Are you serious?'

He shrugged. 'There was no need. I thought I was removing Michela from your bad example—what I didn't realise was that you were going to continue the friendship behind my back.'

Alannah ran her fingertip down over her champagne glass, leaving behind a transparent stripe in the condensation. 'But all that happened a long time ago,' she said slowly.

'I guess it did.' He leaned back in his chair. 'And since your role seems to be non-negotiable, I guess I'm just going to have to be nice to you.'

'Is that possible?'

'Me being nice?' He watched the golden flicker of candlelight playing on her pale skin. 'You don't think so?'

'Not really. I think it would be like someone hand-rearing a baby tiger and then expecting it to lap contentedly from a saucer of milk when it reaches adulthood. Naïve and unrealistic.'

'And nobody could ever accuse you of that.'

'Certainly not someone with as cutting a tongue as you, Niccolò.'

He laughed, his gaze drifting over fingers which he noticed were bare of rings. 'So what has been happening to you in the last ten years? Bring me up to speed.'

Alannah didn't answer for a moment. He didn't want to know that her life had imploded like a dark star when her mother had died and that for a long time she had felt completely empty. Men like Niccolò weren't interested in other people's sadness or ambition. They asked polite questions at dinner parties because that was what they had been taught to do—and all they required was something fairly meaningless in response.

She shook her head at the waitress who was offering her a basket heaped with different breads. 'I'm an interior designer these days.'

'Oh?' He waited while the pretty waitress stood close to him for slightly longer than was necessary, before reluctantly moving away. 'How did that happen? Did you wake up one morning and decide you were an expert on soft furnishings?'

'That's a very patronising comment.'

'I have experience of interior designers,' he said wryly. 'And of rich, bored women who decide to set themselves up as experts.'

'Well, I'm neither rich, nor bored. And I think you'll find there's more to the job than that. I studied fashion at art school and was planning to make dresses, but the fashion world is notoriously tough—and it's difficult to get funding.' Especially when you had the kind of past which meant that people formed negative judgements about you.

'So what did you do?'

'I worked for a big fashion chain for a while,' she continued, pushing her fork aimlessly around her plate. 'Before I realised that what I was best at was putting together a "look". I liked putting colours and fabrics together and creating interesting interiors. I spent a few years working for a large interiors company to gain experience and recently I took the plunge and set up on my own.'

'And are you any good?' he questioned. 'How come I've never heard of you?'

'I think I'm good—have a look at my website and decide for yourself,' she said. 'And the reason you haven't heard of me is because there are a million other designers out there. I'm still waiting for my big break.'

'And your topless modelling career?' he questioned idly. 'Did that fall by the wayside?'

Alannah tried not to flinch, terrified he would see how much his question had hurt. For a minute back then she'd actually thought they were sticking to their truce and talking to each other like two normal human beings. 'This is you being "nice", is it, Niccolò? Behaving as if I was something you'd found on the sole of your shoe?'

His eyes didn't leave her face. 'All I'm doing is asking a perfectly legitimate question about your former career.'

'Which you can't seem to do without that expression of disgust on your face.'

'Wouldn't anyone be disgusted?' he demanded hotly. 'Isn't the idea of a woman peddling her flesh to the highest bidder abhorrent to any man with a shred of decency in his bones? Although I suspect the end-product must have been spectacular.' There was a pause before he spoke. 'Alannah Collins *shaking her booty.*'

His last few words were murmured—and Alannah thought how unexpected the colloquialism sounded when spoken in that sexy Sicilian accent of his. But his words reminded her that what you saw wasn't necessarily what you got. Despite his cosmopolitan appearance and lifestyle, Niccolò da Conti was as traditional as they came. His views and his morals came straight from another age. No wonder his sister had been so terrified of him. No wonder she'd gone off the rails when she had been freed from his claustrophobic presence and judgemental assessment.

'Those photographs were stills,' she said tonelessly. 'I never *shook* anything.'

'Ah, but surely you're just splitting hairs.' He gave a dangerous smile, his finger idly circling the rim of his untouched champagne glass. 'Unless you're trying to tell me that cupping your breasts and simulating sexual provocation for the camera while wearing a school uniform is a respectable job for a woman?'

Alannah managed to twist a sliver of smoked salmon onto the end of her fork, but the food never made it to her mouth. 'Shall I tell you why I did that job?'

'Easy money, I'm guessing.'

She put the fork back down. Oh, what was the point? she thought tiredly. He didn't *care* what had motivated her. He had judged her—he was still judging her—on the person she appeared to be. Someone who had danced too intimately with a stranger at a party. Someone who had gone off the rails with his beloved sister. Someone who had discovered that the only way to keep hope alive had been by taking off her clothes…

Who could blame him for despising her—for not realising that she was so much more than that?

She dabbed at her lips with her napkin. 'On second thoughts, I don't think polite interaction is going to be possible after all. There's actually too much history between us.'

'Or not enough?' he challenged and suddenly his voice grew silky. 'Don't you think it might be a good idea to forge some new memories, Alannah? Something which might cancel out all the frustrations of the past?'

Alannah stiffened. Was he suggesting what she *thought* he was suggesting? Was he *flirting* with her? She swallowed. And if he were? If he were, she needed to nip it in the bud. To show him she respected herself and her body.

She slanted him a smile. 'I don't think that's going to happen. I think we need to avoid each other as much as possible. We'll support Michela all the way and try not to let our mutual animosity show, but nothing more than that. So why don't you do me a favour and talk to the woman on your other side? She's been trying to get your attention since you first sat down and she's very beautiful.' She picked up her wine glass and took a sip, her eyes surveying him coolly over the rim. 'I'm surprised you hadn't noticed that, Niccolò.'

CHAPTER THREE

IT WAS THE worst night he'd had in a long time, or maybe it was just that Niccolò couldn't remember ever losing sleep over a woman before. He lay tossing and turning in the king-size bed of his hotel room, trying to convince himself that Alannah had been right and the less time they spent together, the better. But every time he thought about distancing himself from those denim-blue eyes and that pouting, provocative mouth he felt an uncomfortable ache deep inside him.

What was the matter with him?

Kicking away the rumpled sheet, he told himself she wasn't his kind of woman—that she represented everything he despised in a sometimes trashy and disposable society.

Abandoning all further attempts to sleep, he dealt with his emails and spoke to his assistant in London, who informed him that Alekto Sarantos was still unhappy with the interior of the penthouse suite. The Greek billionaire had let it be known that the apartment's design was too 'bland' for his tastes and, despite a close association going back years, he was now considering pulling out of the deal and buying in Paris instead. Niccolò silently cursed his temperamental friend as he terminated the phone-call and wondered how soon he could decently leave after the wedding to return to work.

Pulling on his gym gear, he went for a run in Central Park, where the bare trees were etched dramatically against the winter sky. Despite his restless night and the fact that little was in bloom, his senses seemed unusually receptive to the beauty which surrounded him on this cold winter morning. There were ducks and gulls on the lakes and woodpeckers were tapping in the trees. Other runners were already out pounding the paths and an exquisite-looking blonde smiled hopefully at him, slowing down as he approached. But he didn't even bother giving her a second look. Her eyes were glacial green, not denim blue—and it was that particular hue which had been haunting his sleep last night.

The run took the edge off his restlessness, even if it didn't quell it completely, and after he'd showered and dressed he found a series of increasingly frantic texts from his sister queuing up on his smartphone. The final one was followed by a wobbly voicemail message, demanding to know where he was.

He went along the corridor and knocked at her door—stupidly unprepared for the sight of Alannah opening the door, even though he'd known she was sharing a suite with his sister. He felt almost *high* as he looked at her and could feel the aching throb of longing which stabbed at his groin. She was wearing a denim shirt-dress which matched her eyes and a tiny ladybird brooch which twinkled red and black on the high collar. For a moment it occurred to him that she was dressed as sedately as a schoolteacher and he watched as a complicated series of expressions flitted across her face as she looked at him, before producing a smile which was clearly forced.

'Hi,' she said.

'Hi.' He tried his own version of that fake smile. 'Sleep well?'

She raised her eyebrows. 'You're here to enquire how I slept?'

No, I'm here because I'd like to take your panties down and put my tongue between your thighs. He shrugged. 'Michela has been bombarding my phone with texts. Is she here?'

'She's…' cocking her head in the direction of one of the closed doors behind her, she pulled a face '…in the bathroom.'

'Is something wrong?'

'She's broken a nail.'

He frowned. 'Is that supposed to be some kind of a joke?'

'No, Niccolò, it's not a joke. It's the finger her wedding ring will go on and everyone will notice. To a bride who's just hours away from the ceremony, something like this is nothing short of a catastrophe. I've called the manicurist, who's on her way up.'

'First World problems,' he said caustically. 'So everything is under control?'

'Well, that depends how you look at it.' She met his gaze and seemed to be steeling herself to say something. 'Her nerves aren't helped by the worry that you're going to lose your temper at some point today.'

'What makes her think that?'

'Heaven only knows,' she said sarcastically, 'when you have a reputation for being so mild-mannered and accommodating. Could it have something to do with the fact that you and I were at loggerheads throughout dinner last night, and she noticed?'

He raised his eyebrows. 'So what does she want us to do—kiss and make up?'

'Hardly,' she snapped. 'That might be stretching credibility a little too far.'

'Oh, I think I could manage to put on a convincing enough performance,' he drawled. 'How about you?'

So she *hadn't* been imagining it last night. Alannah stiffened. He really *was* flirting. And she was going to have to put on the performance of a lifetime if she wanted to convince him that it wasn't working.

She raised her eyebrows. 'So can I tell Michela that you're planning to be a good boy today? Do you think you're a competent enough actor to simulate enjoyment and behave yourself for the duration of the wedding?'

'I don't usually have to simulate anything—and I've never been called a *good boy* in my life,' he answered softly. 'But if Michela wants reassurance that I'm going to behave myself, then tell her yes. I will be extremely virtuous. And I will be back here at three, to take you both down to the wedding.'

Alannah gave a brief nod and her cool, careful smile didn't slip until she had shut the door on him, though her pulse was pounding loudly.

At least an air of calm had descended by the time the manicurist arrived to repair the tattered nail and the mood was elevated still further as Alannah helped Michela slide into her delicate white gown. Because this was *her* territory, she reminded herself fiercely.

She was proud of the dress she'd made for the bride and she wasn't going to let Niccolò da Conti whittle away at her confidence.

Her movements became sure and confident as she smoothed down the fine layers of tulle and soon she felt like herself again—Alannah Collins, who was living life according to her own rules, and ignoring the false perceptions of other people.

But the moment Niccolò arrived all that composure deserted her. She was aware of his piercing gaze as he watched her adjusting the floral circlet which held Michela's veil in place and it was difficult to keep her fingers steady. She could feel his dark eyes moving over her and the only comfort she got was by reminding herself that after this day was over, she need never see him again.

So why did that make her heart plummet, as if someone had dropped it to the bottom of a lift-shaft?

'You look beautiful, *mia sorella*,' he said, and Michela gave a smile of delight as she did a twirl.

'*Do* I?'

'Indeed you do.' His voice was indulgent. 'Lucas is a very lucky man.'

'Well, I have Alannah to thank for my appearance,' said Michela brightly. 'She's the one who made the dress. It's gorgeous, isn't it, Niccolò?'

Alannah wanted to tell her friend to stop trying so hard. To tell her that she and her brother were never going to achieve anything more than a forced civility. But she maintained the fiction necessary to soothe the bride's frazzled nerves by smiling at him in what she hoped looked like a friendly way.

'It is indeed a very beautiful dress,' he agreed

softly, his eyes gleaming out a silent message which she didn't dare analyse.

Alannah tried to relax as she handed Michela her bouquet and the three of them made their way to the Pembroke's celebrated wedding room, where the assembled guests were waiting. A harpist began to play and Alannah saw the sudden look of tension which hardened Niccolò's features into a grim mask as he gave his sister away to be married.

Maybe he just didn't like weddings, she thought.

She tried not to stare at him as the vows were made and to ignore the women who were clearly trying to catch his eye. And after the rings had been exchanged, Alannah tried to be the best guest she possibly could. She chatted to the groom's sister and offered to suggest some new colour schemes for her house in Gramercy Park. After the wedding breakfast, she took time to play with several of the frilly-dressed little girls from Lucas's huge extended family. And when they were all worn out, she lined them all up to twist their long hair into intricate styles, which made them squeal with delight.

By the time the tables had been cleared and the band had struck up for the first dance, Alannah felt able to relax at last. Her duties had been performed to everyone's satisfaction and the wedding had gone off without a hitch. Drink in hand, she stood on the edge of the dance-floor and watched Michela dancing in the arms of Lucas—soft white tulle floating around her slender body and a dreamy smile on her face as she looked up at her new husband.

Alannah felt her heart contract and wished it wouldn't. She didn't want to feel *wistful,* not today—

of all days. To wonder why some people found love easy while others seemed to have a perpetual struggle with it. Or to question why all that stuff had never happened to her.

'How come I always find you standing alone on the dance-floor?'

Alannah's heart clenched at the sound of Niccolò's Sicilian accent, but she didn't turn round. She just carried on standing there until he walked up to stand beside her.

'I'm just watching the happy couple,' she said conversationally.

He followed the direction of her gaze and for a moment they stood in silence as Lucas whirled Michela round in his arms.

'Do you think they'll stay happy?' he asked suddenly.

The question surprised her. 'Don't you?'

'If they are contented to work with what they've got and to build on it, then, yes, they have a chance. But if they start to believe in all the hype…' His voice grew hard. 'If they want stardust and spangles, then they will be disappointed.'

'You obviously don't rate marriage very highly.'

'I don't. The odds against it are too high. It's a big gamble—and I am not a gambling man.'

'And love?' she questioned as she turned at last to look at him. 'What about love?'

His mouth hardened and for a moment she thought she saw something bleak flaring at the depths of his black eyes.

'Love is a weakness,' he said bitterly, 'which brings out the worst in people.'

'That's a little—'

'Dance with me,' he said suddenly, his words cutting over hers, and Alannah tensed as his fingers curled over her bare arm.

They were a variation on the words he'd spoken all those years ago. Words which had once turned her head. But she was older now and hopefully wiser—or maybe she was just disillusioned. She no longer interpreted his imperious command as masterful—but more as an arrogant demonstration of the control which was never far from the surface.

She lifted her face to his. 'Do I get a choice in the matter?'

'No.' Removing the glass from her hand, he placed it on the tray of a passing waitress, before sliding his hand proprietorially around her waist and propelling her towards the dance floor. 'I'm afraid you don't.'

She told herself that she didn't have to do this. She could excuse herself and walk away. Because he was unlikely to start behaving like a cave-man by dragging her onto the dance-floor—not with all his new in-laws around.

Except that she left it a split second too long and suddenly it was too late for objections. Suddenly, she was on the dance-floor and his arms were round her waist and the worst thing of all was that she *liked* it. She liked it way too much.

'You can't do this, Niccolò,' she said breathlessly. 'It's over-the-top alpha behaviour.'

'But I just can't help myself,' he said mockingly. 'I'm an over-the-top alpha man. Surely you knew that, Alannah.'

Oh, yes. She knew that. A block of stone would

have known that. Alannah swallowed because his hands were tightening around her waist and making her feel there was no place else she would rather be. She told herself it would cause a scene and reflect badly on both of them if she pulled away from him. *So endure it. One dance and it will all be over.*

She tried to relax as they began to move in time with the music and for a while they said nothing. But it wasn't easy to pretend that it meant nothing to be wrapped in his arms again. Actually, it was close to impossible. His body was so hard and his arms were so strong. His unique scent of sandalwood and raw masculinity seemed to call out to something deep inside her—to touch her on a subliminal level which no one else had even come close to. She could hear the thunder of her heart as he lowered his head to her ear and even his voice seemed to flood over her like velvety-dark chocolate.

'Enjoying yourself?' he said.

She swallowed. 'I was before you forced me into this farce of pretending we have a civilised enough relationship to be dancing together.'

'But surely you can't have any complaints about what we're doing, *mia tentatrice*. Aren't I behaving like a perfect gentleman?'

'Not with…' Her words tailed away, because now he had moved his hands upwards and his fingers were spanning her back. She could feel their imprint burning through the delicate material of her bridesmaid dress and her throat constricted.

'With what?'

'You're holding me too tightly,' she croaked.

'I'm barely holding you at all.'

'You are a master of misinterpretation.'

'I am a master of many things,' came the silken boast, 'but misinterpretation wouldn't have been top of my list.'

She looked up from where she had been staring resolutely at his black tie and forced herself to meet the mocking light in his eyes. 'Why are you doing this?' she whispered.

'Dancing with you? Isn't it customary for the brother of the bride to dance with the bridesmaid at some point—particularly if both of them are single? Or were you holding out for the best man?'

'I'm not holding out for anyone. And I don't remember telling you I was single.'

'But you are, aren't you? And if you're not, then you might as well be.' He met her eyes. 'Because you are responding like a woman who hasn't been touched by a man for a very long time.'

She was tempted to snap back at him with indignation, but how could she? Because he was right. It *was* a long time since she had been touched by a man. It was a long time since she had danced with a man too, and it had never felt like this. Not with anyone. *It had only ever felt like this with him.*

'I don't understand what it is you want,' she said. 'Why you're dancing with me. Taunting me. Trying to get underneath my skin. Especially when you don't even *like* me—and the feeling is mutual.'

He pulled her closer. 'But not liking doesn't stop us *wanting*, does it, Alannah? Desire doesn't require affection in order to flourish. On the contrary, sometimes it works better without it. Don't you find that, *mia tentatrice*?' He stroked a reflective finger along her waist. 'That sex can be *so* much more exciting when there is a frisson of animosity between a man and a woman?'

Her skin still tingling from the lazy caress of his finger, she pulled away from him, trying to focus on the presumptuous things he was saying, rather than the way her body was reacting. 'Stop it,' she said weakly.

'But you haven't answered my question.'

'And I don't have to. Just as I don't have to stand here and take any more provocative comments. My duty dance is over.' With a monumental effort, she pulled away from him. 'Thanks for reminding me what a consummate player you are, Niccolò. And thanks for reminding me that ten years might have passed but you don't seem to have changed. You still treat the opposite sex as if—'

'I wouldn't generalise if I were you,' he interjected and now his voice was edged with steel. 'Because you have no idea how I treat women. And believe me when I tell you that I've never had any complaints.'

The sexual boast was blatant and Alannah suddenly felt as if her skin were too tight for her body. As if her flesh wanted to burst out of her bridesmaid dress. Her breasts were tingling and she knew she had to get away from him before she did something she regretted—or said something she would never live down. 'Goodnight, Niccolò,' she said, turning away and beginning to walk across the dance-floor. 'I think we can officially declare our truce to be over.'

Niccolò watched her go and felt frustration mount inside him, along with an even greater feeling of disbelief. She had gone. She had walked away with her head held high and her shoulders stiff and proud, and all his hunter instincts were aroused as he watched the retreating sway of her silk-covered bottom.

He swallowed.

He had played it wrong.

Or maybe he had just read her wrong.

She had been right. He didn't particularly like her and he certainly didn't *respect* her. But what did that have to do with anything? He still wanted her in a way he'd never wanted anyone else.

And tomorrow she would be gone. Leaving New York and going back to her life in London. And even though they lived in the same city, their paths would never cross, because their two lives were worlds apart. He would never know what it was like to possess her. To feel those creamy curves beneath his fingers and her soft flesh parting as he thrust deep inside. He would never know what sound she made when she gasped out her orgasm, nor the powerful pleasure of spurting his seed deep inside her. She might be the wrong type of woman for him on so many levels—but not, he suspected, in bed.

Still mesmerised by the sway of her bottom, he began to follow her across the dance-floor, catching up with her by one of the bars, where she was refusing a cocktail.

She barely gave him a glance as he walked up beside her.

'You're not leaving?' he said.

'I can't leave. At least, not until Michela has thrown her bouquet and driven off into the night with Lucas. But after that, you won't see me for dust, I promise.'

'Before you make any promises—I have a proposition you might like to hear.'

'I don't need to hear it,' she said flatly. 'I wouldn't need to be a genius to work out what you might have in mind, after the things you said on the dance-floor and the way you were holding me. And it doesn't make any difference.' She sucked in a deep breath and met his gaze. 'I'm not interested in having sex with you, Niccolò—got that?'

Niccolò wondered if she knew how blatantly her nipples were contradicting her words—but maybe now wasn't the time to tell her.

'But what if it was a business proposition?' he questioned.

Her eyes narrowed. 'What kind of business proposition?'

He looked at the waxy white flowers which were woven into her hair and he wanted to reach out and crush them between his fingers. He wanted to press his lips on hers. He wanted to undress her and feast his eyes on that soft, creamy body. In a world where he had managed to achieve every single one of his objectives, he suddenly recognised that Alannah Collins had been a residual thorn in his flesh. A faint but lingering memory of a pleasure which had eluded him.

But not for much longer.

He smiled. 'You said you were an interior designer and suggested I have a look at your website, which I did. And you *are* good. In fact, you are very good. Which means that you have a skill and I have a need,' he said.

Her mouth thinned into a prudish line. 'I don't think that your needs are the kind I necessarily cater for.'

'I think we're talking at cross purposes, Alannah. This has nothing to do with sex.' He slanted her a thoughtful look. 'Does the name Park View ring any bells?'

'You mean that enormous new apartment block overlooking Hyde Park which has been disrupting the Knightsbridge traffic for months?'

'That's the one.'

'What about it?'

'It's mine. I own it. I built it.'

Alannah blinked. 'But it's the most…'

'Don't be shy, Alannah,' he said softly as her voice tailed off. 'One should never be shy when talking about money. It's the most expensive building of its kind in the world—isn't that what you were going to say?'

She shrugged. 'I fail to see how your property portfolio could possibly interest me.'

'Then hear me out. A friend of mine—a brilliant Greek named Alekto Sarantos—is about to complete one of the penthouse apartments.'

She lifted her hand to adjust a stray petal on her headdress. 'And is there a problem?'

'*Sì*. Or at least—he certainly seems to think there is.' A note of irritation entered his voice. 'The problem is that Alekto doesn't like the décor, even though it has been overseen by one of the most popular designers in the city.'

'Let me guess.' She raised her eyebrows. 'Cream walls? Bowls of big pebbles lying around the place? Lots of glass and neutral-coloured blinds?'

He frowned. 'You must have seen photos.'

'I don't need to, but I'd recognise a bandwagon

anywhere—and every interior designer in the business seems to be jumping on it. Presumably this friend of yours doesn't do bland and that's why he doesn't like it.'

'No, Alekto doesn't do bland—in fact, he is the antithesis of bland. He described the décor to my assistant as a "tsunami of beige" and unless I can transform the place to his satisfaction before the Greek new year, then he says he'll pull out of the deal and go to Paris instead. It has become a matter of pride for me that he chooses London.' He gave a hard smile. 'And maybe that's where you could come in.'

'Me?'

'You want a break, don't you? I don't imagine they get much bigger than this.'

'But…' Somehow she managed to keep the tremble of excitement from her voice. 'Why me? There must be a million other designers itching to accept a job like this.'

His gaze swept over her like an icy black searchlight—objective, speculative and entirely without emotion.

'Because I like your style,' he said unexpectedly. 'I like the way you dress and the way you look. I always have. And if you can satisfy my exacting friend with your designs—then the job is yours.'

Alannah felt ridiculously thrilled by his praise, yet she didn't want to be thrilled. She wanted to feel nothing. To give nothing and take nothing. She met his dark gaze. 'And the fact that you want to go to bed with me has nothing to do with your offer, I suppose?'

He gave a soft laugh. 'Oh, but it has everything to do with it, *mia sirena*,' he said. 'As you said yourself, there are a million interior designers out there, but your desirability gives you a distinctive edge over your competitors. I cannot deny that I want you or that I intend to have you.' His black eyes gleamed. 'But I wouldn't dream of offering you the job unless I thought you were capable of delivering.'

CHAPTER FOUR

'NICCOLÒ WILL SEE you in just a moment, Alannah.' The redhead sitting outside Niccolò's office wore a silk blouse the colour of the lilies on her desk and when she smiled her lips were a neat coral curve. 'My name's Kirsty, by the way—and I'm one of Niccolò's assistants. Take a seat over there. Can I get you a coffee? Some tea perhaps?'

'No. I'm fine, thanks.' Carefully putting down her mood-boards, Alannah sank onto a seat, wondering if any of her reservations showed in her face. Whether her nerves or sick dread were visible to the impartial observer.

Ever since she'd left New York, she had listed all the reasons why she should say no to Niccolò's offer of work and during the cramped flight she had checked them off on her fingers. He was arrogant. Tick. He was dangerous. Double tick. He was also completely unapologetic about wanting to take her to bed. Only he hadn't even said *that* in a flattering way. He'd made it sound as if she was just something he needed to get out of his system. Like an itch. Or a fever. She bit her lip because his attitude brought too many memories flooding back. She hated men who regarded a woman as some kind of *object*, so surely self-respect and pride should have made her turn his offer down, no matter how lucrative?

But he was offering her work—legitimate work. His proposition had been like a cool drink when your throat was parched. Like finding a crumpled ten-pound note in your jeans before you washed them. She thought about the scarcity of jobs in her highly competitive field, and the ridiculously high mortgage on her tiny bedsit. She couldn't *afford* to turn him down—which was why she'd spent all weekend coming up with ideas she thought might appeal to a Greek billionaire who didn't like beige. And through it all she had realised that this was the vital springboard her career needed and she was going to grab at it with both hands.

She stared at the cream lilies on Kirsty's desk, trying to concentrate on their stark beauty, but all she could think about was the way Niccolò had stroked his finger over her when they'd been dancing at the wedding. Her heart began to pound. It had been an almost *innocent* touch and yet her response had been anything but innocent. The intensity of her feelings had shocked her. She had wanted him to peel the bridesmaid dress from her body and touch her properly. She had wanted him to kiss her the way he'd done all those years before—only this time not to stop.

And that was the problem.

She still wanted him.

She had done her best to quash that thought when she'd emailed him some suggestions. And had attempted to ignore her spiralling feeling of excitement when his reply came winging into her inbox late last night.

These are good. Be at my offices tomorrow at 7p.m.

It hadn't been the most fulsome praise she'd ever received, but it was clear he considered her good enough for the job and that pleased her more than it should have done. And hot on the heels of professional pride came a rather more unexpected feeling of gratitude. She had stared at his email and realised that, no matter what his motives might be, Niccolò was giving her the chance to make something of herself.

So she'd better show him that his faith had not been misplaced.

A buzzer sounded on Kirsty's desk and she rose to her feet, opening a set of double doors directly behind her.

'Niccolò is ready for you now, Alannah.' She smiled. 'If you'd like to come this way.'

Alannah picked up her mood-boards and followed Kirsty into a huge and airy office, blinking a little as she looked around her, because she'd never been anywhere like this before. She gulped. It was...*spectacular.* One wall consisted entirely of glass and overlooked some of London's more familiar landmarks and Alannah was so dazzled by the view that it took a moment for her to notice Niccolò sitting there and to realise that he wasn't alone.

Her first thought was how at home he looked in the luxury of his palatial surroundings. Long legs stretched out in front of him, he was reclining on a large leather sofa in one corner of the vast office—and opposite him was a man with black hair and the bluest eyes she'd ever seen. This must be Alekto Sarantos, Alannah thought, but she barely noticed him. Despite his unmistakable gorgeousness, it was Niccolò who captured her attention. Niccolò whose outwardly relaxed stance couldn't quite disguise the tension in his powerful body as their gazes clashed and held. She could read the mockery in his eyes. *I know how much you want me,* they seemed to say. And suddenly she wished that the floor could swallow her up or that the nerves which were building up inside her would show her some mercy and leave her alone.

'Ah, Alannah. Here you are.' Black eyes glittered with faint amusement as he looked her up and down. 'Not jet-lagged, I hope?'

'Not at all,' she lied politely.

'Let me introduce you to Alekto Sarantos. Alekto—this is Alannah Collins, the very talented designer I was telling you about.'

Alannah gave an uncertain smile, wondering exactly *what* he'd said about her. They were friends, weren't they? And didn't men boast to their mates about what they'd done with a woman? She could feel her cheeks growing slightly warm as she looked at Alekto. 'I'm very pleased to meet you.'

'Do sit down,' he said, in a gravelly Greek accent.

Alannah saw Niccolò pat the space beside him on the sofa—and she thought it looked a bit like someone encouraging a dog to leap up. But she forced herself to smile as she sat down next to him, unwinding the vivid green pashmina which was looped around her neck.

Alekto turned his startling blue gaze on her. 'So…

Niccolò assures me that you are the person who can replace the existing décor with something a little more imaginative.' He grimaced. 'Although frankly, a piece of wood could have produced something more eye-catching than the existing scheme.'

'I'm confident I can, Mr Sarantos.'

'No. *Parakalo*—you must call me Alekto,' he said, a hint of impatience hardening his voice, before giving a swift smile. 'I always like to hear a beautiful woman saying my name.'

Beautiful? No woman ever thought she was beautiful and that certainly hadn't been the effect Alannah had been striving for today. She'd aimed for a functional, rather than a decorative appearance—tying her hair back in a thick plait to stop it being whipped up by the fierce December wind. She had wanted to project style and taste as well as hoping her clothes would be like armour—protecting her from Niccolò's heated gaze.

Her Japanese-inspired grey dress bore the high neckline which had become her trademark and the fitted waist provided structure. A glittering scarab beetle brooch and funky ankle-boots added the unconventional twists which she knew were necessary to transform the ordinary into something different. It was the detail which counted. Everyone knew that.

'If you insist,' she said, with another polite smile. 'Alekto.'

Niccolò raised his eyebrows. 'Perhaps you'd like to show *Alekto* what ideas you have in mind for his apartment, while he concentrates on your undoubted beauty,' he suggested drily.

Trying to ignore the sarcasm in his voice, Alannah

spread out the mood-boards she'd been working on and watched as Alekto began to study them. Squares of contemporary brocade were pasted next to splashes of paint colour, and different swatches of velvet and silk added to the textural diversity she had in mind.

'We could go either traditional or contemporary,' she said. 'But I definitely think you need something a little bolder in terms of colour. The walls would work well in greeny-greys and muted blues—which would provide a perfect backdrop for these fabrics and textiles and reflect your love of the sea.'

'Did Niccolò tell you that I love the sea?' questioned Alekto idly.

'No. I searched your name on the Internet and had a look at your various homes around the world. You do seem rather fond of sea views and that gave me a few ideas.'

'Enterprising,' Alekto commented, flicking through each page, before lifting his head. '*Neh.* This is perfect. All of it. You have chosen well, Niccolò. This is a huge improvement. You have pleased me, Alannah—and a woman who pleases a man should always be rewarded. I think I shall take you out for dinner tonight, to thank you.'

'I'm sure Alannah would love nothing more,' interjected Niccolò smoothly, 'but, unfortunately, she is already committed this evening.'

'Really?' Alekto raised dark and imperious brows. 'I'm sure she could cancel whatever it is she is *committed* to.'

'Possibly.' Niccolò shrugged. 'But only if you are prepared to wait for your apartment to be completed, my friend. Time is of the essence if you expect it to be ready for your new year party. Isn't that what you wanted?'

The gazes of the two men clashed and Alekto's eyes suddenly hardened with comprehension.

'Ah,' he said softly as he rose to his feet. 'Suddenly, I begin to understand. You have always been a great connoisseur of beauty, Niccolò. And since good friends do not poach, I shall leave you in peace.' His blue eyes glittered. 'Enjoy.'

Alekto's chauvinistic innuendo took Alannah by surprise but she reminded herself that she was simply working for him—she wasn't planning on having him as her friend. Keeping her lips clamped into a tight smile, she stood up to let him shake her hand, before Niccolò led him into the outer office.

She waited until the Sicilian had returned and closed the door behind him before she turned on him.

'What was that all about?' she questioned quietly.

'What?' He walked over to his desk, stabbing at a button on his telephone pad, so that a red light appeared. 'The fact that your designs pleased him? Alekto is one of the wealthiest men I know. You should be delighted. The patronage of a man like that is more priceless than rubies.' He looked at her, his eyes curiously flat and assessing. 'Who knows what kind of opportunities could now come your way, Alannah. Especially since he clearly finds you so attractive.'

'No, none of that!' She shook her head—hating the way he was looking at her. Hating the way he was talking about her. 'I don't care that he's rich—other than it means I will have a very generous budget to work with. And I don't care whether or not he finds me attractive. I'd like it if for once we could keep my looks out of it, since I'm supposed to be here on merit.' She stared at him. 'What I'm talking about is you telling him I was busy and couldn't have dinner with him tonight.'

'Did you want to have dinner with him?'

'That's beside the point.'

He slanted her a look. 'I'm not sure what your point is.'

'That I don't want you or anyone else answering for me because I like to make my own decisions. And…' she hesitated '…you have no right to be territorial about me.'

'No,' he said slowly. 'I realise that.'

She narrowed her eyes warily. 'You mean you're agreeing with me?'

He shrugged. 'For a man to behave in a territorial way towards a woman implies that she is his. That she has given herself to him in some way. And you haven't, have you, Alannah?' The eyes which a moment ago had looked so flat now gleamed like polished jet. 'Of course, that is something which could be changed in a heartbeat. We both know that.'

Alannah stiffened as his gaze travelled over her and she could feel her throat growing dry. And wasn't it crazy that, no matter how much her mind protested, she couldn't seem to stop her body from responding to his lazy scrutiny. She found herself thinking how easy it would be to go along with his suggestion. To surrender to the ache deep inside her and have him take all her frustration away. All she had to do was smile—a quick, complicit smile—and that would be the only green light he needed.

And then what?

She swallowed. A mindless coupling with someone who'd made no secret of his contempt for her? An act which would inevitably leave him triumphant and her, what? *Empty*, that was what.

A lifetime of turning down sexual invitations meant that she knew exactly how to produce the kind of brisk smile which would destabilise the situation without causing a scene. But for once, it took a real effort.

'I think not,' she said, scooping up her pashmina from the sofa. 'I have a self-protective instinct which warns me off intimacy with a certain kind of man, and I'm afraid you're one of them. The things I require from you are purely practical, Niccolò. I need a list of craftsmen—painters and decorators—who you use on your properties and who I assume will be available to work for me—and to work very quickly if we're to get this job in on time.'

The impatient wave of his hand told her that painters and decorators were of no interest to him. 'Speak to Kirsty about it.'

'I will.' She hitched the strap of her bag further over her shoulder. 'And if that's everything—I'll get going.'

He nodded. 'I'll drive you home.'

'That won't be necessary.'

'You have your own car?'

Was he kidding? Didn't he realise that car parking costs in London put motoring way beyond the reach of mere mortals? Alannah shook her head. 'I always use public transport.'

'Then I will take you. I insist.' His eyes met hers

with cool challenge. 'Unless you'd prefer to travel by train on a freezing December night, rather than in the warm comfort of my car?'

'You're boxing me into a corner, Niccolò.'

'I know I am. But you'll find it's a very comfortable box.' He took his car keys from his jacket pocket. 'Come.'

In the elevator, she kept her distance. Just as she kept her gaze trained on the flashing arrow as it took them down to the underground car park, where his car was waiting.

He punched her postcode into his satnav and didn't say another word as they drove along the busy streets of Knightsbridge, where Christmas shoppers were crowding the frosty pavements. Alannah peered out of the window. Everywhere was bright with coloured lights and gifts and people looking at the seasonal displays in Harrods's windows.

The car turned into Trafalgar Square and the famous Christmas tree loomed into view and suddenly Alannah felt the painful twist of her heart. It was funny how grief hit you when you least expected it—in a fierce wave which made your eyes grow all wet and salty. She remembered coming here with her mother, when they were waiting for the result of her biopsy. When standing looking up at a giant tree on an icy winter night had seemed like the perfect city outing. There'd been hardly any money in their purses, but they'd still had hope. Until a half-hour session with a man in a white coat had quashed that hope and they'd never been able to get it back again.

She blinked away the tears as the car began to speed towards West London, hoping that Niccolò's concentration on the traffic meant he hadn't noticed. He reached out to put some music on—something Italian and passionate, which filled the air and made her heart clench again, but this time with a mixture of pleasure and pain.

Closing her eyes, she let the powerful notes wash over her and when she opened them again the landscape had altered dramatically. The houses in this part of the city were much closer together and as Niccolò turned off the main road a few stray traces of garbage fluttered like ghosts along the pavement.

'Is this where you live?' he questioned.

She heard the faint incredulity in his voice and realised that this was exactly why she hadn't wanted this lift. *Because he will judge you. He will judge you and find you wanting, just as he's always done.* 'That's right,' she said.

He killed the engine and turned to look at her, his dark features brooding in the shadowed light.

'It's not what I expected.'

Her question was light, almost coquettish. She wondered if he could tell she'd been practising saying it in her head. 'And what *did* you expect?'

For a moment Niccolò didn't answer, because once again she had confounded his expectations. He had imagined a pricey location—a fortified mansion flat bought on the proceeds of the money she'd earned from *Stacked* magazine. Or a cute little mews cottage in Holland Park. Somewhere brimming with the kind of wealthy men who might enjoy dabbling with a woman as beautiful as her.

But *this*…

The unmistakable signs of poverty were all around

them. The rubbish on the pavement. A battered car with its wing-mirror missing. The shadowy group of youths in their hoodies, who stood watching their car with silent menace.

'What happened to all your money?' he questioned suddenly. 'You must have earned—'

'Stacks?' she questioned pointedly.

His smile was brief as he acknowledged the pun. 'A lot.'

She stared down at her handbag. 'It was a short-lived career—it didn't exactly provide me with a gold-plated pension.'

'So what did you do with it?'

I paid for my mother's medical bills. I chased a miracle which was never going to happen. I chased it until the pot was almost empty though the outcome hadn't changed one bit. She shrugged, tempted to tell him that it was none of his business—but she sensed that here was a man who wouldn't give up. Who would dig away until he had extracted everything he needed to know. She tried to keep her words light and flippant, but suddenly it wasn't easy. 'Oh, I frittered it all away. As you do.'

Niccolò looked at the unexpected tremble of her lips and frowned, because that sudden streak of vulnerability she was trying so hard to disguise was completely unexpected. Was she regretting the money she had squandered? Did she lay awake at night and wonder how the hell she had ended up in a place like this? He tried and failed to imagine how she fitted in here. Despite all her attempts to subdue her innate sensuality and tame her voluptuous appearance, she must still stand out like a lily tossed carelessly into a muddy gutter.

And suddenly he wanted to kiss her. The streetlight was casting an unworldly orange light over her creamy skin, so that she looked like a ripe peach just begging to be eaten. He felt temptation swelling up inside him, like a slow and insistent storm. Almost without thinking, he found himself reaching out to touch her cheek, wondering if it felt as velvety-soft as it appeared. And it did. Oh, God, it did. A whisper of longing licked over his skin.

'What…what do you think you're doing?' she whispered.

'You know damned well what I'm doing,' he said unsteadily. 'I'm giving into something which has always been there and which is refusing to die. Something which gets stronger each time we see each another. So why don't we just give into it, Alannah—and see where it takes us?'

She knew it was coming. Of course she did. She'd been kissed by enough men to recognise the sudden roughening of his voice and opaque smoulder of his black eyes. But no man had ever kissed her the way Niccolò did.

Time slowed as he bent his face towards hers and she realised he was giving her enough time to stop him. But she didn't. How could she when she wanted this so much? She just let him anchor her with the masterful slide of his hands as they captured the back of her head, before he crushed his lips down on hers.

Instantly, she moaned. It was ten long years since he'd kissed her and already she was on fire. She felt *consumed* by it. Powered by it. Need washed over her as she splayed her palms against his chest as his tongue licked its way into her mouth—her lips opened greedily, as if urging him to go deeper. She heard his responding murmur, as if her eagerness pleased him, and something made her bunch her hands into fists and drum them against his torso—resenting and wanting him all at the same time.

He raised his head, dark eyes burning into her like fire. But there were no subtle nuances to his voice now—just a mocking question in an accent which suddenly sounded harsh and *very* Sicilian. 'Are you trying to hurt me, *bella*?'

'I—yes! *Yes!*' She wanted to hurt him first—before he had the chance to do it to her.

He gave a soft laugh—as if recognising his own power and exulting in it. 'But I am not going to let you,' he said softly. 'We are going to give each other pleasure, not pain.'

Alannah's head tipped back as he reached down to cup her breast through the heavy silk of her dress. And she let him. Actually, she did more than let him. Her breathless sighs encouraged him to go even further, and he did.

He kissed her neck as his hand crept down to alight on one stockinged knee. And wasn't it shameful that she had parted her knees—praying he would move his hand higher to where the ache was growing unbearable? But he didn't—at least, not at first. For a while he seemed content to tease her. To bring her to such a pitch of excitement that she squirmed with impatience—wriggling restlessly until at last he moved his hand to skate it lightly over her thigh. She heard him suck in a breath of approval as he encountered the bare skin above her stocking top and she shivered as she felt his fingers curl possessively over the goose-pimpled flesh.

'I am pleased to see that despite the rather staid outfits you seem to favour, you still dress to tantalise underneath,' he said. 'And I need to undress you very quickly, before I go out of my mind with longing. I need to see that beautiful body for myself.'

His words killed it. Just like that. They shattered the spell he'd woven and wiped out all the desire—replacing it with a dawning horror of what she'd almost allowed to happen.

Allowed?

Who was she kidding? She might as well have presented herself to him in glittery paper all tied up with a gift ribbon. He'd given her a lift home and just assumed…*assumed*…

He'd assumed he could start treating her like a pin-up instead of a person. Somewhere along the way she had stopped being Alannah and had become a body he simply wanted to ogle. Why had she thought he was different from every other man?

'What am I doing?' she demanded, jerking away from him and lifting her fingertips to her lips in horror. 'What am I *thinking* of?'

'Oh, come on, Alannah.' He began to tap his finger impatiently against the steering wheel. 'We're both a little too *seasoned* to play this kind of game, surely? You might *just* have got away with the outraged virgin scenario a decade ago, but not any more. I'm pretty sure your track record must be almost as extensive as mine. So why the sudden shutdown at exactly the wrong moment, when we both know we want it?'

It took everything she had for Alannah not to fly at him until she remembered that, in spite of everything, he was still her boss. She realised she couldn't keep blaming him for leaping to such unflattering conclusions, because why *wouldn't* he think she'd been around the block several times? Nice girls didn't take off their clothes for the camera, did they? And nice girls didn't part their legs for a man who didn't respect them.

'You might have a reputation as one of the world's greatest lovers, Niccolò,' she said, 'but right now, it's difficult to see why.'

She saw his brows knit together as he glowered at her. 'What are you talking about?'

Grabbing the handle, she pushed open the car door and a blast of cold air came rushing inside, mercifully cooling her heated face. 'Making out in the front of cars is what teenagers do,' she bit out. 'I thought you had a little bit more finesse than that. Most men at least offer dinner.'

CHAPTER FIVE

EVERY TIME NICCOLÒ closed his eyes he could imagine those lips lingering on a certain part of his anatomy. He could picture it with a clarity which was like a prolonged and exquisite torture. He gave a groan of frustration and slammed his fist into the pillow. Was Alannah Collins aware that she was driving him crazy with need?

Turning onto his back, he stared up at the ceiling. Of course she was. Her *profession*—if you could call it that—had been pandering to male fantasy. She must have learnt that men were turned on by stockings—and socks. By tousled hair and little-girl pouts. By big blue eyes and beautiful breasts.

Had she subsequently learnt as she'd grown older that teasing and concealment could be almost as much of a turn-on? That to a man used to having everything he wanted, even the *idea* of a woman refusing sex was enough to make his body burn with a hunger which was pretty close to unbearable. Did she often let men caress the bare and silky skin of her thigh and then push them away just when they were in tantalising reach of far more intimate contact?

Frustratedly running his fingers through his hair, he got out of bed and headed for the bathroom.

If she hadn't been such a damned hypocrite when she'd slammed her way out of his car last night, then he wouldn't be feeling this way. If she'd been honest enough to admit what she really wanted, he wouldn't have woken up feeling aching and empty. She could have invited him in and turned those denim-blue eyes on him and let nature take its course. They could have spent the night together and he would have got her out of his system, once and for all.

He turned on the shower, welcoming the icy water which lashed over his heated skin.

True, her home hadn't looked particularly *inviting.* It didn't look big enough to accommodate much more than a single bed, let alone any degree of comfort. But that was okay. His mouth hardened. Mightn't the sheer *ordinariness* of the environment have added a piquant layer of excitement to a situation he resented himself for wanting?

Agitatedly, he rubbed shampoo into his hair, thinking that she made him want to break every rule in the book and he didn't like it. The women he dated were chosen as carefully as his suits and he didn't do *bad girls.* His taste tended towards corporate bankers. Or lawyers. He liked them blonde and he liked them cool. He liked the kind of woman who never sweated…

Not like Alannah Collins. He swallowed as the water sluiced down over his heated skin. He could imagine *her* sweating. He closed his eyes and imagined her riding him—her long black hair damp with exertion as it swung around her luscious breasts. He turned off the shower, trying to convince himself that the experience would be fleeting and shallow. It would be like eating fast food after you'd been on a health kick. The first greasy mouthful would taste like heaven but by the time you'd eaten the last crumb, you'd be longing for something pure and simple.

So why not forget her?

He got ready for the office and spent the rest of the week trying to do just that. He didn't go near Alekto's apartment, just listened to daily progress reports from Kirsty. He kept himself busy, successfully bidding for a new-build a few blocks from the Pembroke in New York. He held a series of back-to-back meetings about his beach development in Uruguay; he lunched with a group of developers who were over from the Middle East—then took them to a nightclub until the early hours. Then he flew to Paris and had dinner with a beautiful Australian model he'd met at last year's Melbourne Cup.

But Paris didn't work and neither did the model. For once the magic of the city failed to cast its spell on him. Overnight it had surrendered to the monster which was Christmas and spread its glittering tentacles everywhere. The golden lights which were strung in the trees along the Champs Élysées seemed garish. The decorated tree in his hotel seemed like a giant monument to bad taste and the pile of faux-presents which rested at its base made his mouth harden with disdain. Even the famous shops were stuffed with seasonal reminders of reindeer and Santa, which marred their usual elegance.

And all this was underpinned by the disturbing fact that nothing was working; he couldn't seem to get Alannah out of his mind. *Even now.* He realised that something about her was making him act out of character. There were plenty of other people whose style he liked, yet he had hired her without reference and only the most cursory of glances at her work. Governed by a need to possess her, he had ignored all reason and common sense and done something he'd sworn never to do.

He had taken a gamble on her.

He felt the icy finger of fear whispering over his spine.

He had taken a gamble on her and he never gambled.

He ordered his driver to take him to the towering block which rose up over Hyde Park. But for once he didn't take pride in the futuristic building which had been his brainchild, and which had won all kinds of awards since its inception. All he could think about was the slow build of hunger which was burning away inside him and which was now refusing to be silenced.

His heart was thudding as he took the elevator up to the penthouse, his key-card quietly clicking the door open. Silently, he walked through the bare apartment, which smelt strongly of paint, and into the main reception room where he found Alannah perched on a stepladder, a tape measure in her hand.

His heart skipped a beat. She wore a loose, checked shirt and her hair was caught back in a ponytail. He didn't know what he'd been planning to say but before he had a chance to say anything she turned round and saw him. The stepladder swayed and he walked across the room to steady it and some insane part of him wished it would topple properly, so that he could catch her in his arms and feel the soft crush of her breasts against him.

'N-Niccolò,' she said, her fingers curling around one of the ladder's rungs.

'Me,' he agreed.

She licked her lips. 'I wasn't expecting you.'

'Should I have rung to make an appointment?'

'Of...of course not,' she said stiffly. 'What can I do for you?'

His eyes narrowed. She was acting as if they were strangers—like two people who'd met briefly at a party. Had she forgotten the last time he'd seen her, when their mouths had been hot and hungry and they'd been itching to get inside each other's clothes? Judging from the look on her face, it might as well have been a figment of his imagination. He forced himself to look around the room—as if he were remotely interested in what she was doing with it. 'I thought I'd better see how work is progressing.'

'Yes, of course.' She began to clamber down the ladder, stuffing the tape measure into the pocket of her jeans. 'I know it doesn't look like very much at the moment, but it will all come together when everything's in place. That...' Her finger was shaking a little as she pointed. 'That charcoal shade is a perfect backdrop for some of the paintings which Alekto is having shipped over from Greece.'

'Good. What else?' He began to walk through the apartment and she followed him, her canvas shoes squeaking a little on the polished wooden floors.

'Here, in the study, I've used Aegean Almond as a colour base,' she said. 'I thought it was kind of appropriate.'

'Aegean Almond?' he echoed. 'What kind of lunatic comes up with a name like that?'

'You'd better not go into the bathroom, then,' she warned, her lips twitching. 'Because you'll find Cigarette Smoke everywhere.'

'There's really a paint called Cigarette Smoke?'

'I'm afraid there is.'

He started to laugh and Alannah found herself joining in, before hurriedly clamping her mouth shut. Because humour was dangerous and just because he'd been amused by something she'd said it didn't mean he'd suddenly undergone a personality transplant. He had an *agenda*. A selfish agenda, which didn't take any of *her* wishes into account and that was because he was a selfish man. Niccolò got what Niccolò wanted and it was vital she didn't allow herself to be added to his long list of acquisitions.

She realised he was still looking at her.

'So everything's running according to schedule?' he said.

She nodded. 'I've ordered velvet sofas and sourced lamps and smaller pieces of furniture.'

'Good.'

Was that enough? she wondered. How much detail did he need to know to be convinced she was doing a good job? Because no matter what he thought about her past, he needed to know she wasn't going to let him down. She cleared her throat. 'And I've picked up some gorgeous stuff on the King's Road.'

'You've obviously got everything under control.'

'I hope so. That is what you're paying me for.'

Niccolò walked over to the window and stared out at the uninterrupted view of Hyde Park. The wintry trees were bare and the pewter sky seemed heavy with the threat of snow. It seemed as if his hunch about her ability had been right. It seemed she was talented, as well as beautiful.

And suddenly he realised he couldn't keep taking his anger out on her. Who *cared* what kind of life she'd led? Who cared about anything except possessing her? Composing his face into the kind of expression which was usually guaranteed to get him exactly what he wanted, Niccolò smiled.

'It looks perfect,' he said. 'You must let me buy you dinner.'

She shook her head. 'Honestly, you don't have to do that.'

'No?' He raised his eyebrows in mocking question. 'The other night you seemed to imply you felt short-changed because I'd made a pass at you without jumping through the necessary social hoops first.'

'That was different.'

'How?'

She lifted her hand to fiddle unnecessarily with her ponytail. 'I made the comment in response to a situation.'

'A situation which won't seem to go away.' His black eyes lanced into her. 'Unless something has changed and you're going to deny that you want me?'

She sighed. 'I don't think I'm a good enough actress to do that, Niccolò. But wanting you doesn't automatically mean that I'm going to do anything about it. You must have women wanting you every day of the week.'

'But we're not talking about other women. What if I just wanted the opportunity to redeem myself?

To show you that I am really just a…what is it you say?' He lifted his shoulders and his hands in an exaggerated gesture of incomprehension. 'Ah, yes. A regular guy.'

'Of course you are.' She laughed, in spite of herself. 'Describing you as a regular guy would be like calling a thirty-carat diamond a trinket.'

'Oh, come on, Alannah,' he urged softly. 'One dinner between a boss and his employee. What's the harm in that?'

Alannah could think of at least ten answers, but the trouble was that when he asked her like that, with those black eyes blazing into her, all her reservations slipped right out of her mind. Which was how she found herself in the back of a big black limousine later that evening, heading for central London. She was sitting as far away from Niccolò as possible but even so—her palms were still clammy with nerves and her heart racing with excitement.

'So where are we going?' she questioned, looking at the burly set of the driver's shoulders through the tinted glass screen which divided them.

'The Vinoly,' Niccolò said. 'Do you know it?'

She shook her head. She'd heard about it, of course. Currently London's most fashionable venue, it was famous for being impossible to get a table though Niccolò was greeted with the kind of delight which suggested that he might be a regular.

The affluence of the place was undeniable. The women wore designer and diamonds while the men seemed to have at least three mobile phones lined up neatly beside their bread plates and their gazes kept straying to them.

Alannah told herself she wasn't going to be intimidated even though she still couldn't quite believe she'd agreed to come. As she'd got ready she had tried to convince herself that exposure to Niccolò's arrogance might be enough to kill her desire for him, once and for all.

But the reality was turning out to be nothing like she'd imagined. Why hadn't she taken into account his charisma—or at least prepared herself for a great onslaught of it? Because suddenly there seemed nothing in her armoury to help her withstand it.

She had never been with a man who commanded quite so much attention. She saw the pianist nodding to him, with a smile. She saw other diners casting surreptitious glances at him, even though they were pretending not to. But it was more than his obvious wealth which drew people's gaze, like a magnet. Beneath the sophisticated exterior, he radiated a raw masculinity which radiated from his powerful body like a dark aura.

They sat down at a discreet table but suddenly the complex menu seemed too rich for a stomach which was sick with nerves. Alannah found herself wishing she were eating an omelette at her own kitchen table rather than subjecting herself to a maelstrom of emotions which were making her feel most peculiar.

'What are you going to have?' asked Niccolò as the waiter appeared.

The words on the menu had blurred into incomprehensible lines and she lifted her gaze to him. 'I don't know. You order for me,' she said recklessly.

He raised his eyebrows before giving their order but once the waiter had gone he turned to study her, his black eyes thoughtful. 'Are you usually quite so accommodating?'

'Not usually, no.' She smoothed her napkin. 'But then, this isn't what you'd call *usual*, is it?'

'In what way?'

'Well.' She shrugged. 'You made it sound like a working dinner, but it feels a bit like a date.'

'And what if we pretended it was a date—would that help you relax a little more?'

'To be honest, it's been so long since I've been on a date that I've almost forgotten what it's like,' she said slowly.

He took a sip of water which didn't quite disguise the sudden cynicism of his smile. 'I find that very difficult to believe.'

She laughed. 'I'm sure you do—given your apparent love of stereotypes. What's the matter, Niccolò—doesn't that fit in with your image of me? You think that because I once took off my clothes for the camera, that I have men queuing up outside the bedroom door?'

'Do you?'

'Not half as many as you, I bet,' she said drily.

They were staring at one another across the table, their eyes locked in silent battle, when suddenly he leaned towards her, his words so low that only she could hear them.

'Why did you do it, Alannah?' he questioned roughly. 'Wasn't it bad enough that you were kicked out of school for smoking dope and playing truant? Why the hell did you cheapen yourself by stripping off?'

The waiter chose precisely that moment to light the

small candle at the centre of the table. And that short gap provided Alannah with enough time for rebellion to flare into life inside her.

'Why do you think I did it?' she demanded. 'Why do people usually do jobs like that? Because I needed the money.'

'For what?' His lips curled. 'To end up in a poky apartment in one of the tougher ends of town?'

'Oh, you're so quick to judge, aren't you, Niccolò? So eager to take the moral high ground, when you don't have a clue what was going on in my life and you never did! Did you know that when my mother handed in her notice, she never found another job to match that one—probably because the reference the school gave her was so grudging. Did you know that they got all their clever lawyers to pick over her contract and that she lost all her rights?'

His eyes narrowed. 'What kind of rights?'

'There was no pension provision made for her and the salary she got in lieu of notice was soon swallowed up by the cost of settling back in England. She couldn't find another live-in job, so she became an agency nurse—with no fixed contract. I had to go to a local sixth-form college to take my exams and at first, I hated it. But we were just beginning to pick ourselves up again when…'

Her voice tailed off and his words broke into the silence.

'What happened?' he demanded.

She shook her head. 'It doesn't matter.'

'It *does*.'

Alannah hesitated, not wanting to appear vulnerable—because vulnerability made you weak. But wasn't anything better than having him look at her with that look of utter *condemnation* on his face? Shouldn't Niccolò da Conti learn that it was wise to discover all the facts before you condemned someone outright?

'She got cancer,' she said baldly. 'She'd actually had it for quite a long time but she'd been ignoring the symptoms so she didn't have to take any unnecessary time off work. By the time she went to see the doctor, the disease was advanced and she was scared,' she said, swallowing down the sudden lump in her throat. They'd both been scared. 'There was nobody but me and her. She was only a relatively young woman and she didn't want…' The lump seemed to have grown bigger. 'She didn't want to die.'

'Alannah—'

But she shook her head, because she didn't want his sympathy. She didn't *need* his sympathy.

'Our doctor told us about an experimental drug trial which was being done in the States,' she said. 'And early indications were that the treatment was looking hopeful, but it was prohibitively expensive and impossible to get funding for it.'

And suddenly Niccolò understood. Against the snowy tablecloth, he clenched his hands into tight fists. *'Bedda matri!'* he said raggedly. 'You did those photos to pay for your mother to go to America?'

'Bravo,' she said shakily. 'Now do you see? It gave me power—the power to help her. The thought of all that money was beyond my wildest dreams and there was no way I could have turned it down.' *No matter how many men had leered in her face afterwards. No matter that people like Niccolò judged her and looked down their noses at her or thought that she'd be up for easy sex because of it.* 'My unique selling point was that I'd left one of the most exclusive Swiss finishing schools under rather ignominious circumstances and I guess I can't blame them for wanting to capitalise on that. They told me that plenty of men were turned on by girls in school uniform, and they were right. That's why that issue became their best-seller.'

Alarmed by the sudden whiteness of her face, he pushed the wine glass towards her, but she shook her head.

'It wasn't narcissism which motivated me, Niccolò—or a desire to flash my breasts like the exhibitionist you accused me of being. I did it because it's the only way I could raise the money. I did it even though I sometimes felt sick to the stomach with all those men perving over me. But I hid my feelings because I wanted to bring a miracle to my mother, only the miracle never happened.' Her voice wavered and it took a moment or two before she could steady it enough to speak. 'She died the following spring.'

She did pick up her glass then, swilling down a generous mouthful of red wine and choking a little. But when she put the glass back down, she had to lace her fingers together on the table-top, because she couldn't seem to stop them from trembling.

'Alannah—'

'It's history,' she said, with a brisk shake of her head. 'None of it matters now. I'm just telling you what happened. I used the rest of the money to put myself through art school and to put down a deposit on a home. But property is expensive in London.

That's why I live where I do. That's why I chose to live in one of the "tougher" parts of London.'

Niccolò put his glass down with a hand which was uncharacteristically unsteady as a powerful wave of remorse washed over him. It was as if he was seeing her clearly for the first time—without the distortion of his own bigotry. He had judged her unfairly. He saw how she must have fought against the odds to free herself from a trap from which there had been no escaping. He'd fought against the odds himself, hadn't he? Though he realised now that his own choices had been far less stark than hers. And although he hated the solution she had chosen, he couldn't seem to stop himself from wanting to comfort her.

'I'm sorry,' he said huskily. 'For what happened and for the choices you had to make.'

She shrugged. 'Like I said, it's history.'

'Your mother was lucky to have a daughter like you, fighting for her like that,' he said suddenly. He found himself thinking that anyone would be glad to have her in their corner.

Her head was bent. 'Don't say any more,' she whispered. 'Please.'

He stared down at the plateful of cooling risotto which lay before him. 'Alannah?'

'What?'

Reluctantly, she lifted her head and he could see that her eyes were unnaturally bright. He thought how pale and wan she looked as he picked up his fork and scooped up some rice before guiding it towards her mouth. 'Open,' he instructed softly.

She shook her head. 'I'm not hungry.'

'Open,' he said again.

'Niccolò—'

'You need to eat something,' he said fiercely. 'Trust me. The food will make you feel better. Now eat the risotto.'

And although Alannah was reluctant, she was no match for his determination. She let him feed her that first forkful—all warm and buttery and fragrant with herbs—and then another. She felt some of the tension seep away from her, and then a little more. She ate in silence with his black eyes fixed on her and it felt like a curiously intimate thing for him to do, to feed her like that. Almost *tender*. Almost *protective.* And she needed to remember it was neither. It was just Niccolò appeasing his conscience. Maybe he'd finally realised that he'd been unnecessarily harsh towards her. This was probably just as much about repairing his image, as much as trying to brush over his own misjudgement.

And he was right about the food. Of course he was. It *did* make her feel much better. She could feel warmth creeping through her veins and the comforting flush of colour in her cheeks. She even smiled as he swopped plates and ate some himself while she sat back and watched him.

He dabbed at his lips with a napkin. 'Feel better now?'

'Yes.'

'But probably not in the mood to sit here and make small talk or to decide whether or not your waistline can cope with dessert?'

'You've got it in one,' she said.

'Then why don't I get the check, and we'll go?'

She'd assumed he would take her straight back to

Acton but once they were back in the car he made the driver wait. Outside, fairy lights twinkled in the two bay trees on either side of the restaurant door, but inside the car it was dark and shadowy. He turned to study her and all she could see was the gleam of his eyes as his gaze flickered over her face.

'I could take you home now,' he said. 'But I don't want the evening to end this way. It still feels…unfinished.'

'I'm not in the mood for a nightcap.'

'Neither am I.' He lifted his hand to her face and pushed back a thick strand of hair. 'I'm in the mood to touch you, but that seems unavoidable whenever you're near me.'

'Niccolò—'

'Don't,' he said unsteadily. 'Don't say a word.'

And stupidly, she didn't. She just sat there as he began to stroke her cheek and for some crazy reason she found that almost as reassuring as the way he'd fed her dinner. Was she so hungry for human comfort that she would take anything from a man she suspected could offer nothing but heartbreak?

'Niccolò—'

This time he silenced her protest with the touch of his lips against hers. A barely-there kiss which started her senses quivering. She realised that he was teasing her. Playing with her and tantalising her. And it was working. Oh, yes, it was working. She had to fight to keep her hands in her lap and not cling onto him like someone who'd found themselves a handy rock in a rough sea.

He drew away and looked into her face and Alannah realised that this was a Niccolò she'd never seen before. His face was grave, almost…assessing. She imagined this was how he might look in the boardroom, before making a big decision.

'Now we could pretend that nothing's happening,' he said, as calmly as if he were discussing the markets. 'Or we could decide to be very grown-up about this thing between us—'

'Thing?' she put in indignantly, but his fingers were still on her face and she was shivering. And now the pad of his thumb had begun to trace a line across her lower lip and that was shivering, too.

'Desire. Lust. Whatever you want to call it. Maybe I just want to lay to rest a ghost which has haunted me for ten long years, and maybe you do, too.'

It was his candour which clinched it—the bald truth which was her undoing. He wasn't dressing up his suggestion with sentimental words which didn't mean anything. He wasn't insulting her intelligence by pretending she was the love of his life or that there was some kind of future in what he was proposing. He was saying something which had been on her mind since Michela's wedding. Because he was right. This *thing* between them wouldn't seem to go away. No matter how much she tried, she couldn't stop wanting him.

She wondered if he could read the answer in her eyes. Was that why he leaned forward to tap briefly on the glass which separated them from the driver, before taking her in his arms and starting to kiss her?

And once he had done that, she was left with no choice at all.

CHAPTER SIX

HE DIDN'T OFFER her a coffee, nor a drink. He didn't even put the lamps on. Alannah didn't know whether Niccolò had intended a slow seduction—but it didn't look as if she was going to get one. Because from the moment the front door of his Mayfair apartment slammed shut on them, he started acting like a man who had lost control.

His hands were in her hair, he was tugging her coat from her shoulders so that it slid unnoticed to the ground and his mouth was pressing down on hers. It was breathless. It was hot. It was…*hungry.* Alannah gasped as he caught her in his arms. He was burying his mouth in her hair and muttering urgent little words in Sicilian and, although her Italian was good, she didn't understand any of them. But she didn't need to. You wouldn't have to be a linguist to understand what Niccolò was saying to her. The raw, primitive sounds of need were international, weren't they?

He placed his hands on either side of her hips and drew her closer, so that she could feel the hard cradle of him pressing against her. He kissed her again and as the kiss became deeper and more urgent she felt him moving her, until suddenly she felt the hard surface of the wall pressed against her back and her eyelids flew open.

He drew back, his eyes blazing. 'I want you,' he said. 'I want to eat you. To suck you. To bite you. To lick you.'

She found his blatantly erotic words more than a little intimidating and momentarily she stiffened—wondering if she should confess that she wasn't very good at this. But now his palms were skating over her dress to mould the outline of her hips and the words simply wouldn't come. She felt his hand moving over her belly. She heard him suck in a ragged breath of pleasure as he began to ruck up her dress.

'Niccolò,' she said uncertainly.

'I want you,' he ground out. 'For ten years I have longed for this moment and now that it is here, I don't think I can wait a second longer.'

Niccolò closed his eyes as he reached her panties and impatiently pushed the flimsy little panel aside, because she was wet. She was very wet. He could detect the musky aroma of her sex as he slid his fingers against her heated flesh and began to move them against her with practised ease.

'Niccolò,' she whispered again.

'I want to see your breasts,' he said, moving his shaking fingers to the lapels of her silky dress and beginning to unbutton it. Within seconds two luscious mounds were revealed—their creamy flesh spilling over the edge of her bra. He narrowed his eyes to look at them. *'Madre di Dio,'* he breathed, his fingertips brushing over the soft skin. 'In the flesh it is even better. You have the most beautiful body I have ever seen.'

And suddenly he knew he really couldn't wait a second longer. Besides, she seemed more than ready for him. He felt as if something had taken hold of him and made him into someone he didn't recognise. As if this wasn't him at all but an imposter who'd entered his body. Unsteadily, he unzipped himself and he wanted to explode even before he positioned himself against her honeyed warmth.

She went very still as he entered her and for a moment he paused, afraid that he might come straight away—and when had *that* ever happened? But somehow he managed to keep it together, drawing in a deep breath and expelling it on another shuddering sigh as he began to move.

One hand was spread over her bare bottom as he hooked her legs around his hips and drove into her as if there were no tomorrow. As if there had been no yesterday. Her nails were digging into his neck as he kissed her, but he barely noticed the discomfort. He tried to hold back—to wait for her orgasm before letting go himself—but suddenly it was impossible and he knew he was going to come.

'Alannah!' he said, on a note of disbelief—and suddenly it was too late.

Wave after wave took him under. His frame was racked with spasms as he gasped out her name, caught up in a feeling so intense that he thought he might die from it. It felt like the first orgasm he'd ever had. He closed his eyes. The only orgasm he'd ever had. And it wasn't until his body had grown completely still that he noticed how silent and how still she was.

He froze.

Of course she was.

Remorse filled him as she put her hand against his chest and pushed him away. And although withdrawing from her succulent heat was the last thing he felt like doing he could see from the tight expression on her face that she wanted him to. And who could blame her?

There had been no answering cry of fulfilment from her, had there? He had given her no real *pleasure.*

With a grimace, he eased himself from her sticky warmth, bending to pull up his trousers before carefully zipping them up. 'Alannah?'

She didn't answer straight away—she was too busy fastening her dress, her fingers fumbling to slide the buttons back in place. He went to help her, but her voice was sharp.

'Don't.'

He waited until she'd finished buttoning and whatever little insect brooch she was wearing was surveying him with baleful eyes, before he lifted her chin with his finger, so that their eyes were locked on a collision course. 'I'm sorry,' he said.

She shook her head. 'It doesn't matter.'

'It does.' He heard the flatness in her voice. 'I'm not usually so…out of control.'

She gave a wry smile. 'Don't worry, Niccolò. I won't tell anyone. Your reputation is safe with me.'

His mouth hardened and his body tensed. It was her cool response which made something inside him flare into life—a feeling of anger as much as desire. A feeling set off by wounded male pride and an urgent need to put things right. This had never happened to him before. He was usually the master of control. He had always prided himself on his lovemaking skills; his ability to give women physical pleasure—even if he could never satisfy them emotionally.

A shudder of comprehension made his blood run cold.

Did he really want her to walk away thinking of him as a selfish lover? As a man who took, but gave nothing back? Was that how he wanted her to remember him?

'Let's hope you don't have to,' he said, his voice full of sudden resolution as he bent down to slide his arm behind her knees and then lifted her up.

'What…what the hell do you think you're doing?' she spluttered as he began to carry her along the wide corridor.

'I'm taking you to bed.'

'Put me down! I don't want to go to bed. I want to go home.'

'I don't think so,' he said, kicking open his bedroom door and walking over to the vast bed, before setting her down in the centre of the mattress. His knees straddling her hips, he began to unbutton her dress, but she slapped his hand away and he realised that his normal methods of seduction weren't going to work with her. Come to think of it, nothing felt remotely normal with her—and right now, this felt a million miles away from seduction.

He smoothed the tousled hair away from her face, staring down into the reproachful belligerence of her blue eyes, before slowly lowering his head to kiss her.

It wasn't a kiss, so much as a duel.

For a few seconds she held back, as if he were kissing some cold, marble statue. She lay there like a human sacrifice. He could sense her anger and frustration, so he forced himself to take it slowly—so slowly that it nearly killed him. He explored her lips with a thoroughness which was new to him—until he felt he knew them almost better than his own. And as she gradually opened them up to him—when she had relaxed enough to let his tongue slide inside her mouth—it felt like one of the most intimate acts he'd ever taken part in.

Her hands reached for his shoulders and he took the opportunity to press his body close to hers, but the shudder of delight as their bodies crushed against each other was entirely new to him. And still he took it slowly—still feasting on her lips until he was certain that her own desire was strong enough to make her wriggle against him with a wordless message of frustration.

He didn't speak. He didn't dare. Something told him that she didn't want him to undress her and he suspected that doing so would shatter a mood which was already dangerously fragile. His hands were trembling as they slid beneath her dress to reacquaint themselves with the hot, moist flesh beneath her panties. He heard her give a little moan—a sound of pleasure and submission—and his heart hammered as he unzipped himself and tugged her panties down over her knees.

He was only vaguely aware of the awkward rumpling of their unfastened clothing, because by then he was caught up with a hunger so powerful that he groaned helplessly as he slid inside her for a second time. It felt… For a moment he didn't move. It felt out of this world. He looked down to see an unmistakable flare of wonder in her eyes as he filled her, but just as quickly her dark lashes fluttered down to veil them. As if she was reluctantly granting him access to her body—but not to her thoughts.

He moved slowly. He kept her on the edge for a long time—until she was relaxed enough to let go. She wrapped her legs and her arms around him and held him close and Niccolò thought he'd never been quite so careful before. He'd learnt a lot about women's bodies during a long and comprehensive sexual education, but with Alannah it became about much more than technique.

Her body began to change. He could feel the tension building until it was stretched so tightly that it could only shatter—and when it did, she made a series of gasping little sighs, before she started to convulse helplessly around him. He was dimly aware of the groan he gave before he too let go, his every spasm matching hers, and he could feel her heart beating very fast against his as his arms tightened around her.

He must have fallen asleep, because when he next became aware of his surroundings it was to feel her shifting out from under him. His fingers curled automatically around her waist. 'What are you doing?' he questioned sleepily, moving his head so that her lips were automatically redirected to his and his voice was indistinct as his tongue slid into her mouth. 'Mmm?'

She let him kiss her for a moment before putting distance between them. He felt her lips ungluing themselves from his as she moved away.

'It's late, Niccolò—and this is a school night.'

He knew what she was doing. She was giving him

the opportunity to end the evening now, without either of them losing face. He wondered if this was what she normally did—give into a hot and mindless lust without much forethought, before following it up with a cool smile as if nothing had happened?

Without much forethought.

The words struck him and imprinted themselves on his consciousness. Suddenly he went hot and then cold as he realised their implication and he stared at her with growing horror.

'You know what we've just done?' he questioned and there was a note in his voice he'd never heard before.

She tilted her chin, but he could see the way she had instinctively started to bite her lip. 'Of course. We've just had sex. Twice.'

His fingers dug into her forearms, his voice suddenly urgent. 'Are you on the pill?'

He saw the exact moment that it registered. That would be the moment when her blue eyes widened and her lips began to tremble.

'We...' she whispered. 'We've...'

'Yes,' he completed grimly. 'We've just had unprotected sex.'

She swallowed. 'Oh, God,' she breathed. 'What are we going to do?'

He didn't answer at once. It was pointless to concentrate on the anger and frustration which were building up inside him, because he could see that harsh words of recrimination would serve no useful purpose. His mouth hardened. He should have known better. How could he have failed to take contraception into account?

'I think that there is only one thing we can do,' he said. 'We wait.'

'I…guess so.'

He frowned as he noticed that her teeth had started to chatter. 'You're shivering. You need to get into bed.'

'I don't—'

'I'm not listening to any objections,' he said emphatically. 'I'm going to undress you and put you to bed and then I'm going to make you tea.'

She wriggled. 'Why don't you go and make the tea and I'll undress myself?'

He frowned, and there was a heartbeat of a pause. 'Alannah, are you *shy*?'

She attempted a light little laugh, which didn't quite come off. 'Me? Shy? Don't be ridiculous. How could I possibly be shy when I've exposed my body to the harsh glare of the camera?'

Placing his palms on either side of her face, he stared down into her wide blue eyes. 'But stripping for a camera is a very anonymous thing to do,' he said slowly. 'While stripping for a man is intensely personal.'

She pulled a face. 'Stick with the day job, Niccolò—I don't think analysis is really your thing.'

Niccolò frowned. No, it wasn't his thing at all. Normally he ran a million miles from trying to work out what was going on in a woman's head. But most women weren't perplexing enigmas, were they? They didn't answer one question and immediately make you want to ask them a hundred more.

'You're shy,' he repeated. 'Are you going to tell me why?'

Alannah stifled a sigh as she looked at him, because telling Niccolò anything was the last thing she wanted. His lovemaking had left her feeling soft and vulnerable enough to have her defences weakened. And she wasn't stupid. She might despise the men who persisted in thinking of her as nothing but a body—yet surely that was the main attraction for Niccolò, no matter how much he might try to deny it. Wouldn't he be disappointed to discover the mundane truth about her?

Because iconic glamour models were supposed to typify sexuality, not belong to a band of women who had always found sex rather overrated until now.

'Yes, I'm shy,' she admitted grudgingly. 'I don't really like men looking at my body. I'm hung up about it. I hate being thought of as nothing but a pair of gravity-defying breasts. That's probably why I'm not usually able to relax very much. Why my sex life has been…'

Her words tailed off as she became aware that she'd said too much and she braced herself as she waited for him to distance himself, like a man who thought he'd bought a racy sports-car—only to find that he'd landed himself with a second-hand model which kept breaking down.

'Why your sex life has been, what?' he prompted softly.

She pulled a face. 'You really want me to spell it out for you? Isn't your ego healthy enough already without the added boost of me telling you how good you are in bed?'

He took her hand and lifted it to his lips, unable to hide his slow, curving smile of satisfaction. 'Am I?'

'You know you are.' She pulled her hand away. 'I'm sure I'm not the first woman to tell you that.'

'No, but you're the first woman who is such a mass of contradictions that you have my head spinning. You have a wildness…'

'Niccolò—'

He silenced her with a long kiss and when he finally raised his head, it was to subject her to a look of narrow-eyed thoughtfulness. 'I think we've done the subject to death for tonight,' he said. 'You're tired and so am I, and you're right—it *is* a school night. Bedtime,' he added firmly.

'I'm not sure,' she said.

'Well, I am. Relax, *mia tentatrice*.'

He was unbuttoning her dress again and suddenly Alannah had no desire to stop him. She lay there as he slid the silky garment from her body until she was left in just her hold-ups and her bra and, automatically, her palms moved towards her breasts—to protect them from his seeking gaze. But to her surprise he wasn't even looking at her breasts. He was sliding down her hold-ups as impersonally as if he'd been undressing a child who had been caught in a storm. Even her bra was removed with nothing but deft efficiency, so that she was naked and snuggled beneath the warm duvet almost before she'd realised it.

She blinked as he captured her in that searing ebony gaze.

'Now…was that so traumatic?' he questioned silkily.

She shook her head. 'I wasn't expecting…' Her words tailed off.

'You thought I would be unable to resist drooling

as I ogled your breasts? That you find yourself surprised by my sensitivity?'

'Something like that,' she mumbled.

He smiled, the pad of his thumb trailing a path over her bottom lip and causing it to tremble. 'You and me both,' he said drily, before getting up to let himself quietly out of the room.

While he was gone, Alannah took the opportunity to look around what was one of the most impersonal bedrooms she'd ever seen. There were no photos on display. No real hints as to what kind of man Niccolò really was. She knew his parents were dead—but there was no misty-eyed memorial of their wedding day. She remembered Michela clamming up whenever anyone had asked her about her folks—and hadn't she been a bit like that herself if people wanted to know about *her* father? It had seemed too crass to tell them the truth. *Oh, my mother was fresh out of Ireland and she had her drink spiked...*

She hadn't found out the whole story until three days before her mother had died. That Bridget Collins had woken up in her dingy hostel room with a splitting headache and vague, shifting memories of what had happened the night before—as well as a terrible soreness between her legs. She'd never seen the man again and the shame of it was that she didn't even know his surname. Nine months later Alannah had been born and her mother's over-protectiveness had kicked in.

Alannah stared at the photograph opposite the bed—a smoky, atmospheric monochrome study of a brooding Mount Vesuvius. If she'd known all that stuff before...if she'd been able to make sense of why her mother had been so unbelievably strict with her—would it have changed anything?

Probably not. And even if it had—it was all irrelevant now. Because you could never go back. You could never wipe out the things you'd done. Everyone knew that.

She was almost asleep by the time Niccolò returned, carrying a tray of camomile tea. Her eyelashes fluttered open as he sat down and the bed sank beneath his weight.

'This will help you sleep,' he said.

She didn't think she needed any help, but she drank the flower-filled brew anyway and then settled back down against the bank of pillows while Niccolò gently stroked her hair.

She wriggled her bare toes and stretched out her body and at that precise moment she didn't think she'd ever felt quite so blissfully content. Until a dark memory flickered into her mind like an evil imp—reinforcing the disturbing thought that they hadn't remembered to use protection....

CHAPTER SEVEN

'ANYONE WOULD THINK,' said Niccolò slowly, 'that you were trying to avoid me.'

Alannah looked up to find herself caught in the spotlight of a pair of ebony eyes, which cut into her like dark twin lasers. Winter light was flooding into the main reception room of the still bare Sarantos apartment, emphasising its vast and elegant dimensions. She had been there all morning, sitting on the newly upholstered window seat and sewing tassels onto a cushion, but the sight of the Sicilian standing in the doorway made her suspend her needle in mid-air.

She tried to compose herself and to say the right thing. Just as she'd been trying to do the right thing, ever since she'd crazily decided to have sex with him. She needed to treat what had happened as a one-off, and keeping their relationship on a purely professional footing was the only sane solution.

For both of them.

She put the needle down and pushed her empty coffee mug along the floor with the tip of her sneaker. 'Of course I'm not trying to avoid you,' she said lightly. 'You're my boss—I wouldn't dare.'

'Is that so?' He walked towards her. 'So why wouldn't you have dinner with me last night?'

'I explained that,' she protested. 'I had to travel to Somerset to buy some paintings and the man who owned the shop was just about to close up for the holidays, so it was the only day I could go. And then on the way back, there were loads of leaves on the line so the train was delayed. Didn't you get my voicemail message?'

'Oh, yes, I got your voicemail message,' he said impatiently. He stood looking down at her, feeling perplexed and more than a little frustrated. This had never happened to him before. Usually he had to barricade his bedroom once a woman had been granted access to it—he couldn't remember a lover ever being so reluctant to return. His mouth tightened. 'But the fact remains that on Tuesday we had sex and I've barely seen you since.'

She shrugged. 'That's just the way it's worked out. You're employing me to get this apartment done in a hurry and that's what I'm trying to do. That's my primary role, isn't it? You're not paying me to keep appearing at your office door and haunting you.'

Niccolò felt his mouth dry. He wouldn't mind her appearing at his office door. She was making him think of a few very creative uses for his desk… He swallowed. 'Am I going to see you later?'

Alannah sucked in a breath, trying not to be flattered at his persistence, but it wasn't easy. Because she had been dreading this meeting. Dreading and yet longing for it, all at the same time. Ever since she'd slipped out of his Mayfair apartment on Tuesday she'd told herself that it would be safer to stay away from Niccolò and not pursue the affair any further. She liked him. She liked him way more than was sensible for what she was sure he'd only ever intended to be a casual hook-up. And she didn't do casual. Just as she didn't do the kind of affair which would end up with her getting her heart smashed into a hundred little pieces.

'You're my boss, Niccolò,' she said.

'I haven't lost sight of that fact, *mia tentatrice*. But what does that have to do with anything?'

'You know very well. It's...unprofessional.'

He gave a soft laugh. 'You don't think we might already have crossed that boundary when you lay gasping underneath me for most of the night?' He narrowed his eyes. 'And on top of me at one point, if my memory serves me well.'

'Stop it,' she whispered, feeling colour flooding into her cheeks. 'That's exactly what I'm talking about. It blurs the lines and confuses things. I'm trying to concentrate on my work and I can't when you—'

'Can't stop wanting a rerun?'

'A rerun is what you do with movies. And it's a bad idea.'

'Why?'

She sighed. 'What happened last week was...' Her words tailed off. How best to describe it? The most amazing sex she'd ever had? Well, yes. She had certainly never realised it could be so intense, or so powerful. But there had been another blissful side to that night which was far more worrying. She'd realised that she could get used to waking up with Niccolò lying asleep beside her, his arms wrapped tightly around her. Just as she could get used to thinking about him at odd moments of the day and wishing he were there to kiss her. And those kind of daydreams would get her nowhere.

Because where would that leave her when the whole thing imploded? She'd just be another heart-broken woman crying into her gin and tonic, trying to resist the urge to send him a 'casual' late-night text. She would run the risk of making herself vulnerable and she wasn't going to let that happen. She felt a new resolve steal over her. 'A mistake,' she said.

'A mistake,' he repeated.

'Maybe that's a bad way to put it. It was obviously very enjoyable.' She pushed the cushion away and forced herself to face the truth, no matter how un-palatable it was. 'But the fact remains that you don't really like me. You told me that.'

He smiled. 'I like you a lot more now.'

'You described what you felt for me as, and I quote—"a wildness". You made me sound like a mild version of the bubonic plague.'

'I don't think any plague feels quite like this—except maybe for the fever in my blood when I close my eyes at night and find it impossible to sleep because I can't get you out of my mind.' His eyes gleamed. 'And you look incredibly beautiful when you're being defiant. Do you do it because you know how much it turns me on?'

'It's not defiance for the sake of it,' she said. 'It's defiance for a reason. I'm not doing it to try to entice you.' She forced herself to say it. To put the words out there instead of having them nagging away inside her. 'This relationship isn't going anywhere. We both know that.'

'So you're not pregnant?'

His words completely shattered her fragile façade and she stared at him, her heart pounding. During the day, when she was busy working, it was easy to push that thought to the back of her mind. It was at night-time when it became impossible. That was when the fear flooded through her body as she tried to imagine just how she would cope with having Niccolò da Conti's baby. That was when she had to fight to stop herself imagining a downy little black head, glugging away contentedly at her breast.

'I don't know,' she said. 'It's too early to do a test.'

'Which means we may be about to be parents together, *sì*? I think that constitutes some sort of relationship, don't you?'

'Not the best kind,' she said.

'Maybe not. But I need to know that if you are pregnant—*if you are*—whether I am the only man in the frame who could be the father.' His black eyes burned into her, but he must have seen her flinch because his voice softened by a fraction. 'Is that such an unreasonable request?'

She met his gaze, telling herself that in the circumstances he had every right to ask. But that didn't make it hurt any less and some of that hurt came spilling out.

'Yes. You are the only man in the frame. Did you think that because of my previous line of work that there would be a whole load of contenders?' She shook her head in despair. 'You really are fond of stereotypes, aren't you, Niccolò? Well, for your information, there isn't. If you really must know, I could count my previous lovers on one hand and still have some fingers free—and there's been no one in my life for the last three years.'

Niccolò let out the breath he'd been holding, unprepared for the powerful hit of pleasure which flooded through his body in response to her words. *He was the only man in the frame. There had been no one else in her life for the past three years.*

He stared at her, his eyes taking in the way she was illuminated in the harsh winter light. Her thick hair looked blue-black, like the feathers of a raven. He swallowed. *Dai capelli corvini.*

In her jeans and loose shirt she shouldn't have looked anything special, but somehow she looked unbelievably beautiful. Against her hair, her skin was creamy and her pallor emphasised the dramatic blue of her eyes. A little brooch in the shape of a dragonfly glittered on her lapel and suddenly he found himself envying the proximity of that worthless piece of jewellery to her body.

What if there were a baby?

His mouth hardened.

He would cross that bridge when he came to it.

The shrill sound of the doorbell shattered the silence.

'That'll be one of the painters,' she said. 'He rang up to say he'd left his keys behind.' Rising to her feet, she walked over and picked up a shoal of silver keys from where they lay on another window seat. 'I won't be long.'

Alannah was aware of his eyes burning into her as she left the room. Her shoes were squeaking as she went to open the front door where one of the painters stood. There were four of them in total and they'd been working around the clock—and although she'd stopped short of making cups of tea for them, she'd been friendly enough. This one had plaster dust in his hair and he was grinning.

She forced a smile as she held out the clump of keys. 'Here you go, Gary.'

But after he'd taken them and shoved them into his dust-covered jeans, he caught hold of her wrist. His big, calloused fingers curled around her skin and his face had suddenly gone very pink. 'I didn't realise you were *the* Alannah Collins,' he said suddenly.

Her heart sank as she snatched her hand away because she knew what was coming next. She wondered if it would be better to call his bluff or to slam the door in his face. But there were only a few days of the project left and it *was* nearly Christmas...why alienate one of the workforce unless it was absolutely necessary?

'Will there be anything else?' she questioned pointedly. 'Because I have work to do.'

'The schoolgirl,' he said thickly. 'With the big—'

A figure seemed to propel itself out of nowhere and it took a moment for Alannah to realise it was Niccolò and he was launching himself at Gary with a look of undiluted rage on his face.

Grabbing hold of the workman's shirt collar, he half lifted him from the ground and shoved his face very close.

'Che talii bastardu?' he spat out. *'Ti scippo locchi e o core!'*

'Niccolò!' protested Alannah faintly, but he didn't seem to be listening.

'How dare you speak to a woman like that?' he demanded. 'What's your name?'

The man blanched. 'G-Gary.'

'Gary what?'

'G-Gary Harkness.'

'Well, take it from me that you won't ever work in this city again, Gary Harkness—I shall make sure of that.' Releasing the shirt collar, Niccolò pushed him away and the man staggered a little. 'Now get out of here—get out before I beat your worthless body to a piece of pulp.'

Alannah didn't think she'd ever seen anyone look so petrified as the workman turned and ran down the corridor towards the elevator.

She lifted her gaze to Niccolò and met the furious blaze firing from his eyes as he clicked the door shut.

'What was that you said to him in Sicilian?'

'I asked him what he was looking at.' He paused as he steadied his breath. 'And I told him I would wrench out his eyes and his heart.'

Alannah gulped. 'You don't think that was a little…over the top?'

'I think he's lucky he didn't end up in hospital,' he ground out and his jaw tightened as he stared at her. 'How often does that happen?'

'Not much. Not these days.' She shrugged as she began to walk back into the main reception room, aware that he was following her. Aware that her heart was pounding. This wasn't a conversation she usually had—not with anyone—but maybe Niccolò was someone who needed to hear it. She turned to look at him. 'It used to be a lot worse. People only ever seemed able to have a conversation with my breasts—

or think that I would instantly want to fall into bed with them.'

Guilt whispered over his skin and Niccolò swallowed down the sudden dryness in his throat. Because hadn't he done something very similar? Hadn't he judged her without really knowing the facts and assumed a promiscuity which simply wasn't true?

'And I did the same,' he said slowly.

Her gaze was fearless. 'Yes, you did.'

'That was why you suddenly froze in the hallway of my house when I was making love to you, wasn't it?' he questioned suddenly.

His perception was nearly as alarming as the realisation that the conversation had taken an even more intimate twist. Despite her determination to stay strong, Alannah couldn't prevent the rush of heat to her cheeks. 'Yes,' she said quietly.

She started to turn her head away, but suddenly he was right there in front of her and his fingers were on her arm. They felt good on her arm, she thought inconsequentially.

'Tell me,' he urged.

It was hard to get the words out. Baring her soul wasn't something she normally did—and she had never imagined herself confiding in Niccolò da Conti like this. But for once his gaze was understanding and his voice was soft and Alannah found herself wanting to analyse the way she'd reacted—not just because he'd asked, but because she needed to make sense of it herself. 'I just remember you saying something about my body being even better in the flesh and I started to feel like an object. Like I wasn't a real person—

just a two-dimensional image in a magazine, with a staple in her navel. Like I was *invisible*.'

'That was not my intention,' he said slowly. 'I think I found myself overwhelmed by the realisation that I was finally making love to you after so many years of thinking about it.' There was a pause as he looked at her. 'Do you think you can forgive me for that, *mia tentatrice*?'

She studied him, and the flicker of a smile nudged at her lips because it was strange seeing him in this conciliatory mood. 'I'll think about it.'

Niccolò pulled her into his arms and she didn't object. She didn't object when he bent his head to kiss her either. Her breath was warm and flavoured with coffee and he wanted to groan with pleasure. She tasted as good as he remembered—in fact, she tasted even better—and there seemed something awfully decadent about kissing her in the near-empty apartment. This wasn't the kind of thing he usually did between meetings, was it? His heart skipped a beat as his fingertips skated over her breast, feeling it swell as he cupped it, and he heard her breath quicken as he began to unbutton her shirt.

It pleased him that she let him. That she really did seem to have forgiven him for his out-of-control behaviour of the other night. That she was relaxed enough not to freeze again.

He deepened the kiss, rubbing at her taut nipple with his thumb, and she gave a little sigh of pleasure. He kissed her for a long time until she was squirming impatiently and kissing him back. Until he forced himself to pull away from her, his voice unsteady as he looked into the darkening of her denim eyes and he felt a rush of triumph fuse with the headiness of sexual hunger.

'I would like to lay you down on the bare floor and make love to you, but I am short of time and must go straight from here to a meeting. And I don't feel it would do my reputation much good if I walked in so dishevelled.' He grimaced as he remembered that time in the hallway of his apartment, when he had shown all the finesse of a teenage boy. 'And I am aware that perhaps you like your lovemaking to be a little more slow and considered.'

'I…thought I did.'

He heard the reluctance in her voice but noticed she was still gripping tightly onto his arms. Her lips were trembling, even though she was biting down on them in an effort to stop it—and he realised just how turned on she was.

'Of course…' He moved his hand down to the ridge of hard denim between her legs. 'I probably do have enough time for other things. Things which you might enjoy.'

'Niccolò,' she said breathlessly.

'What do you think?' he said as he edged his middle finger forward and began to stroke her. 'Yes, or no?'

'Y-yes,' she gasped.

'Keep still,' he urged—but to his delight she didn't obey him. Or maybe she just couldn't. Her head was tipping back and suddenly she didn't look remotely shy…she looked *wild.* Beautiful. He felt her thighs part and heard her moaning softly as he increased the relentless pressure of his finger.

She came very quickly, tightening her arms around

his neck and making that shuddering little crescendo of sighs with which he'd become so familiar on Tuesday night. As he kissed her again her fingers began to claw at his shirt, as if she wanted to tear it from his chest, and for a moment he thought about changing his mind and taking her in the most fundamental way possible.

Temptation rushed over him in a dark wave. Impatiently, his hand strayed to the belt of his trousers, until some remaining shred of reason forced him to play out the ensuring scene. What did he have in mind? Rushing into his meeting with his shirt creased and a telltale flush darkening his skin? Using Alekto's apartment to have sex with a woman—wouldn't that be kind of *cheap*? On every single level, it wouldn't work—but that didn't make it any easier to pull away from her.

She started buttoning her shirt back up with trembling fingers and he walked over to the window to compose himself, willing his frustration to subside.

Outside, a light flurry of snowflakes was whirling down and he felt a sudden sense of restlessness. He thought about the impending holiday and what he would be forced to endure, because one thing he'd learned was that unless you were prepared to live in a cave—it was impossible to ignore Christmas. Already there was a glittering tree which he'd been unable to ban from the main reception of his offices. He thought about the horrendous staff party he'd been forced to attend last night, with those stodgy mince pies they were so fond of eating and several drunken secretaries tottering over to him with glassy smiles and bunches of mistletoe.

He turned round. Alannah had finished buttoning up her shirt, though he noticed her hands were shaking and her cheeks still flushed.

'What are you doing for Christmas?' he questioned suddenly.

'Oh, I'm wavering between an invitation to eat nut roast with some committed vegans, or having an alternative celebration all of my own.' She glanced over his shoulder at the snowflakes. 'Like pretending that nothing's happening and eating beans on toast, followed by an overdose of chocolate and trash TV. What about you?'

He shrugged. 'I have an invitation to ski with some friends in Klosters, but unfortunately my schedule doesn't allow it. I hate Christmas. What I would really like is to fast-forward the calendar and wake up to find it was the new year.'

'Oh, dear,' she said softly.

His eyes met hers and another wave of desire washed over him. 'But since we are both at a loose end, it seems a pity not to capitalise on that. We could ignore the seasonal madness and just please ourselves.'

She opened her eyes very wide. 'Are you asking me to spend Christmas with you, Niccolò?'

There was a pause. 'It seems I am.' He gave a cool smile. 'So why don't you speak to Kirsty and have her give you one of my credit cards? You can book us into the best suite in the best hotel in the city—somewhere you've always wanted to stay. Forget the nut roast and the beans on toast—you can have as much caviar and champagne as you like.' He gave a slow smile as he touched his fingertips to her raven hair. 'Maybe I can make some of your Christmas wishes come true.'

* * *

Alannah felt like taking her sharpest pair of scissors and snipping the small square of plastic into tiny pieces. She thought about what Niccolò had said to her. Make her wishes come true. *Really?* Did he honestly think that staying in a fancy hotel suite was the sum total of her life's ambition, when right now her biggest wish would be to tell him that she didn't need his fancy platinum credit card and she'd rather spend Christmas day alone than spend it with him?

Except that it wouldn't be true, would it? She might *want* it to be true, but it wasn't. Why else would she be sitting hunched in front of her computer, about to book a two-night break in a London hotel? She wondered what had happened to her determination to forget the night she'd spent with him and maintain a professional relationship.

She bit her lip. It had been shattered by Niccolò's resolve—that was what had happened. She had been lost the moment he'd kissed her. A single touch had been enough to make all her good intentions crumble. All her silent vows had been a complete waste of time—because she'd gone up in flames the moment he'd taken her in his arms.

She remembered the way his fingertip had whispered over the crotch of her jeans and her face grew hot. She hadn't been so shy then, had she? He'd soon had her bucking beneath him, and he hadn't even had to remove a single item of clothing. And still in that dreamy, post-orgasmic state she had agreed to spend Christmas with him.

That was something it was hard to get her head round. There must be millions of things he could be doing for the holiday—but he wanted to spend it with her. *Her.* Didn't that mean something? Her mouth grew dry. Surely it *had* to.

She stared at the credit card, which Kirsty had crisply informed her had no upper limit. Imagine that. Imagine having enough money to buy whatever you wanted. *The best suite in the best hotel.* How fancy would a hotel have to be for Niccolò not to have seen it all before, and be jaded by it? She ran through a list of possibilities. The Savoy. The Ritz. The Granchester. London had heaps of gorgeous hotels and she'd bet that he'd stayed in all of them. Had constant exposure to high-end affluence helped contribute to his inbuilt cynicism?

She was just about to click onto the Granchester when something made her hesitate. Perhaps it was a desire to shift him out of his comfort zone—away from the usual protective barriers which surrounded him. He had knocked down some of her defences, so why shouldn't she do the same with him? Why *shouldn't* she try to find out more about the real Niccolò da Conti?

She thought of a fancy hotel dining room and all the other people who would be congregated there. People who had no real place to go, who just wanted the holiday to be over. Or even worse—the wink-wink attitude of Room Service if they started asking for turkey sandwiches and champagne to be brought to their room.

An idea popped into her mind and it started to grow more attractive by the minute. She stared at the long number on the credit card. She might not have much money of her own, but she did have her imagination. Surely she was capable of surprising him with something unexpected. Something simple yet meaningful, which would incorporate the true meaning of Christmas.

His power and privilege always gave him an edge of superiority and that couldn't be good for him. An expensive tab in a smart hotel would only reinforce the differences between them. Wouldn't it be great to feel more like his *equal* for a change?

Because what if she *was* pregnant? She was going to have to get to know him better, no matter what the outcome. Her heart gave a painful lurch as she waited for that intrusive yet strangely compelling image of Niccolò da Conti's baby to subside.

She waited a minute before typing *cute Christmas cottage* into her browser. Because cute was exactly what she needed right now, she told herself. Cute stood a chance of making a cynical man melt so you might be able to work out what made him tick. Scrolling down, she stared at the clutch of country cottages which appeared on the screen.

Perfect.

CHAPTER EIGHT

THE FLURRIES WERE getting stronger and Niccolò cursed as he headed along the narrow country lane.

Why could nothing ever be straightforward? Glancing in his rear-view mirror at the swirl of snowflakes which was obscuring his view, he scowled. He'd given Alannah a credit card and told her to book a hotel in town and she'd done the exact opposite—directing him to some godforsaken spot deep in the countryside, while she went on ahead earlier.

Well, in terms of distance he wasn't actually *that* far from London but he might as well be in middle of his friend Murat's Qurhahian desert for all the sense he could make of his bearings. The sudden onset of heavy snow had made the world look like an alien place and it was difficult to get his bearings. Familiar landmarks had disappeared. The main roads were little more than white wastelands and the narrow lanes had begun to resemble twisting snakes of snow.

Glancing at his satnav, he could see he was only four minutes away, but he was damned if he could see any hotel. He'd passed the last chocolate-boxy village some way back and now an arrow was indicating he take the left fork in the road, through an impenetrable-looking line of trees.

Still cursing, he turned off the road, his powerful headlights illuminating the swirling snowflakes and turning them golden. Some people might have considered the scene pretty, but he wasn't in the mood for pretty scenery. He wanted a drink, a shower and sex in exactly that order and he wanted them now.

Following the moving red arrow, he drove slowly until at last he could see a lighted building in the distance, but it looked too small to be a hotel. His mouth hardened. Something that small could only ever be described as a cottage.

He could see a thatched roof covered with a thick dusting of snow and an old-fashioned lamp lit outside a front door, on which hung a festive wreath of holly and ivy. Through latticed windows a woman was moving around—her fall of raven hair visible, even from this distance. His hands tightened around the steering wheel as he brought the car to a halt and got out—his shoes sinking noiselessly into the soft, virgin carpet.

He rang the bell—one of those old-fashioned bells you only ever saw on ships, or in movies. He could hear the sudden scurrying of movement and footsteps approaching and then the door opened and Alannah stood there, bathed in muted rainbow light.

His body tensing, he stepped inside and the door swung violently shut behind him. His senses were immediately bombarded by the scene in front of him but, even so, the first thing he noticed was her dress. Who could fail to notice a dress like that?

It wasn't so much the golden silk, which skimmed

her curves and made her look like a living treasure, it was the scooped neck showing unfamiliar inches of creamy skin and the soft swell of her breasts. She had even positioned the glittery grasshopper brooch so that it looked poised to hop straight onto her nipple. Had she started to relax enough to stop covering her body up in that old puritanical way? he wondered.

But even this wasn't enough to hold his attention for long. His gaze moved behind her, where a fire was blazing—with two wing chairs on either side. Sprigs of holly had been placed above the paintings and, yes, there was the inevitable sprig of mistletoe dangling from the ceiling. On a low table a bowl was filled with clementines and in the air he could scent something cooking, rich with the scent of cinnamon and spice. But it was the Christmas tree which jarred most. A fresh fir tree with coloured lights looped all over the fragrant branches from which hung matching baubles of gold.

He flinched, but she didn't seem to notice as she wound her arms around his neck and positioned her lips over his. 'Merry Christmas,' she whispered.

Like a drowning man he fought against her feminine softness and the faint drift of pomegranate which clung to her skin. Disentangling her arms, he took a step back as he felt the clutch of ice around his heart.

'What's going on?' he questioned.

She blinked, as if something in his voice had alerted her to the fact that all was not well. 'It's a surprise.'

'I don't like surprises.'

Her eyes now held a faint sense of panic. Was she realising just how wrong she'd got it? he wondered grimly. He could see her licking her lips and the anger inside him seemed to bubble and grow.

'I thought about booking a hotel in London,' she said quickly. 'But I thought you'd probably stayed in all those places before, or somewhere like them. And then I thought about creating a real Christmas, right here in the countryside.'

'A *real* Christmas,' he repeated slowly.

'That's right.' She gestured towards a box of truffles on the table, as if the sight of chocolate were going to make him have a sudden change of heart. 'I went online at Selfridges and ordered a mass of stuff from their food hall. It was still much cheaper than a hotel. That's a ham you can smell cooking and I've bought fish too, because I know in Europe you like to eat fish at Christmas. Oh, and mince pies, of course.'

'I hate mince pies.'

'You don't…' Her voice faltered, as if she could no longer ignore the harsh note of censure in his voice. 'You don't *have* to eat them.'

'I hate Christmas, full stop,' he said viciously. 'I already told you that, Alannah—so which part of the sentence did you fail to understand?'

Her fingers flew over her lips and, with the silky dress clinging to her curves, she looked so like a medieval damsel in distress that he was momentarily tempted to pull her into his arms and blot out everything with sex.

But only momentarily. Because then he looked up and saw the Christmas angel on top of the tree and something about those gossamer-fine wings made his heart clench with pain. He felt the walls of the tiny cottage closing in on him as a dark tide of unwanted emotion washed over him.

'Which part, Alannah?' he repeated.

She held out the palms of her hands in a gesture of appeal. 'I thought—'

'What did you think?' he interrupted savagely. 'That you could treat me like your tame puppet? Playing happy couples around the Christmas tree and indulging in some happy-ever-after fantasy, just because we've had sex and I asked to spend the holidays with you, since we were both at a loose end?'

'Actually,' she said, walking over to the blaze of the fire and turning back to stare at him, 'I thought about how soulless it might be—having a corporate Christmas in some horrible anonymous hotel. I thought that with the kind of life you lead, you might like some home cooking for a change.'

'But I don't *do* home. Don't you get that?' he questioned savagely. He saw a small, rectangular present lying on the table and realised he hadn't even bought her a gift. *It wasn't supposed to be that kind of Christmas.* He shook his head. 'I can't stay here, Alannah. I'm sorry if you've gone to a lot of trouble but it's going to be wasted. So pack everything up while I put out the fire. We're going back to town.'

'No,' she said quietly.

His eyes narrowed. 'What do you mean…*no*?'

'You go if you want to, but I'm staying here.'

There was a pause. 'On your own?'

Alannah felt a sudden kick of rebellion as she met the incredulity in his eyes. 'You find that so surprising?' she demanded. 'You think I'm scared? Well, think again, Niccolò. I live on my own. I've spent pretty much the last seven years on my own. I don't need a man to protect me and look after me—and I certainly don't want to drive back to London with someone who can misinterpret a simple gesture with your kind of cynicism. So go to your anonymous hotel and spend the next few days splashing your cash and telling yourself how much you hate Christmas. I'll be perfectly happy here with my chocolate and mulled wine.'

His black eyes glittered. 'I'm telling you now that if you're calling my bluff, it won't work. I'm not staying here, but I'm not leaving without you, either.'

'I'm afraid you don't have a choice,' she said, walking across to the cocktail cabinet and pouring herself a glass of wine with a trembling hand. 'Like I said, I'm not going anywhere—and I don't imagine that even you are macho enough to drag me out by my hair. So leave. Go on. Just *leave*!'

Silently, they faced each other off before he pulled open the door and a fierce gust of wind brought a great flurry of snowflakes whirling into the room, before it slammed shut behind him.

Alannah didn't move as she heard the sound of his car starting up and then slowly pulling away on the snowy path. Her fingers tightened around her wine glass as she wondered how she could have judged him so badly. Had she thought that, because he'd murmured soft words in Sicilian when he'd been deep inside her, he'd lost the elements of ruthlessness and control which defined him?

Or was he right? Had she been naïve enough to imagine that a homespun meal might make him crave an intimacy which extended beyond the bedroom?

Her heart pounded.

Yes, she had.

Walking over to the sink, she threw away the wine, washing out the glass and putting it on the side to dry. She drew the curtains on the snowy darkness of the night and switched on the radio, just in time to hear the traditional Christmas service being broadcast from King's College, Cambridge. And as soon as the sound of carols filled the room she felt tears spring to her eyes, because it was so heartbreakingly beautiful.

She thought about the nativity scene—the helpless little child in a manger, and briefly she closed her eyes. She'd got it so wrong, hadn't she? She had taken him as her lover and ignored all the warning bells which had sounded so loudly in her ears. She had conveniently forgotten that everything was supposed to be on *his* terms and she'd tried to turn it into something it wasn't. Something it could never be. What had she been thinking of? She'd even bought herself a new and more revealing dress to send out the silent message that he had liberated her from some of her inhibitions. And she was almost as grateful to him for that as she was about the job he'd given her.

But he had thrown the offer back in her face.

She was cold now and ran upstairs to find a sweater, her heart contracting painfully as she looked around the bedroom. She had thought he would be charmed by the antique iron bedstead and the broderie-anglais linen. She'd imagined him picking up that old-fashioned jug and studying it—or telling her that he liked the view out into the snow-covered woods at the back of the house. She had planned to run him a bath when he arrived, and to light some of the scented candles she'd had delivered from London. She had pictured washing his back. Maybe even joining him, if he could persuade her to do so. She'd never shared a bath with anyone before.

What a fool she was, she thought viciously, dragging a mismatched blue sweater over the golden dress, and shaking her hair free. It wasn't as if she'd had no experience of life and the cruel lessons it could teach you. Hadn't she learnt that you had to just accept what you were given—warts and all? She should have taken what was already on the table and been satisfied with that. But she had been greedy, hadn't she? Niccolò had offered her something, but it hadn't been enough. She had wanted more. And still more.

The sound of the front door clicking open and closing again made her heart race with a sudden fear which made a mockery of her defiant words to Niccolò. Why the hell hadn't she locked it after he'd left—or was she hoping to extend an open invitation to any passing burglar? Except that no self-respecting burglar would be out on a snowy Christmas Eve like this. Even burglars probably had someone to share the holiday with.

'Who is it?' she called.

'Who do you think it is? Father Christmas?'

The sardonic Sicilian voice echoed round the small cottage and Alannah went to the top of the stairs to see Niccolò standing in the sitting room, snow clinging like frozen sugar to his black hair and cashmere coat. He looked up.

'It's me,' he said.

'I can see that. What happened?' she questioned

sarcastically as she began to walk downstairs. 'Did you change your mind about the mince pies?'

He was pulling off his coat and snow was falling in little white showers to the ground. She reached the bottom stair just as the poignant strains of 'Silent Night' poured from the radio. Quickly, she turned it off, so that all she could hear was the crackling of the fire and the sound of her own heartbeat as she stared at him. 'Why did you come back?'

There was a pause. His black eyes became suddenly hooded. 'It's a filthy night. I couldn't face leaving you here on your own.'

'And I told you that I would be fine. I'm not scared of the dark.' *I'm much more scared of the way you make me feel when you kiss me.*

'I'm not about to change my mind,' he said. 'I'm staying, and I need a drink.'

'Help yourself.'

He walked over to the bottle she'd opened earlier. 'You?'

A drink would choke me. 'No, thanks.'

She went and sat by the fire, wondering how she was going to get through the next few hours. How the hell did you pass the time when you were stuck somewhere with someone who didn't want to be there? After a couple of moments Niccolò walked over and handed her a glass of wine, but she shook her head.

'I said I didn't want one.'

'Take it, Alannah. Your face is pale.'

'My face is always pale.' But she took it anyway and drank a mouthful as he sat down in the other chair. 'And you still haven't really told me why you came back.'

Niccolò drank some of his wine and for a moment he said nothing. His natural instinct would be to tell her that he didn't have to justify his actions to her. To anyone. But something strange had happened as he'd driven his car down the snowy lane. Instead of the freedom he'd been expecting, he had felt nothing but a heavy weight settling somewhere deep in his chest. It had occurred to him that he could go and stay in a hotel. That if the truth were known, he could easily get a flight and join his friends and their skiing party. He could pretty much get a plane to anywhere, because the hosts of the many parties he'd declined would have been delighted if he'd turned up unexpectedly.

But then he'd thought of Alannah. Curled up alone by the fire with her raven hair aglow, while beside her that corny Christmas tree glittered. All that trouble she'd taken to create some sort of occasion and he'd just callously thrown it back in her face. What kind of a man did that? He thought of how much he'd anticipated making love to her again. How he'd spent the day aching to possess her and wanting to feel her arms wrapped tightly around him. What was *wrong* with him?

He put down his glass and his face was sombre as he turned to look at her.

'I came back because I realised I was behaving like an idiot,' he said. 'I shouldn't have taken it out on you and I'm sorry.'

Alannah sensed that sorry wasn't a word which usually featured highly in his vocabulary, but she wasn't letting him off that lightly. Did he think that a single word could wash away all the hurt he'd inflicted? 'But you did.'

'Yes. I did.'

'Because you always have to be in charge don't you, Niccolò?' she demanded, her anger starting to bubble up. 'You decided how you wanted Christmas to play out and that was it as far as you were concerned. What *you* want is paramount, and everyone else's wishes can just go hang. This is exactly what happened at Michela's wedding, isn't it? Niccolò wants it this way—so this is the way it must be.'

'That was different.'

'How?' she demanded. 'How was it different? How did you ever get to be so damned...*controlling*?'

The flames were flickering over his brooding features and illuminating his ebony hair, so that it glowed like fire-touched coal.

'How?' He gave a short laugh. 'You don't have any ideas?'

'Because you're Sicilian?'

'But I'm not,' he said unexpectedly. 'I'm only half Sicilian. My blood is not "pure". I am half Corsican.' He frowned. 'You didn't know that?'

She shook her head and suddenly his almost swashbuckling appearance made sense. 'No. I had no idea. Michela never really talked about that kind of thing. Boarding school is about reinvention—and escape. About painting yourself in the best possible light so that nobody feels sorry for you. All we knew was that you were unbelievably strict.' She put her glass down. 'Although you did used to take her to the Bahamas for Christmas every year, and we used to get pretty jealous about that.'

'She never told you why?'

'I knew that your parents were dead.' She hesitated. 'But nobody wants to talk about that kind of stuff, do they?'

Niccolò felt his mouth dry. No, they didn't. They definitely didn't. And when death was connected with shame, it made you want to turn your back on it even more. To keep it hidden. To create some kind of distance and move as far away from it as you could. He'd done that for Michela, but he'd done it for himself, too. Because some things were easier to forget than to remember.

Yet even though she was doing her best to disguise it, Alannah was looking at him with such hurt and confusion on her face that he felt it stab at his conscience. All she'd done was to try to make his Christmas good and he had thrown it back in her face in a way she didn't deserve. He'd given her a lot of stuff she didn't deserve, he realised—and didn't he owe her some kind of explanation?

'Mine was a very…unusual upbringing,' he said, at last. 'My mother came from a powerful Sicilian family who disowned her when she married my father.'

She raised her eyebrows. 'Wasn't that a little… dramatic?'

He shrugged. 'Depends which point of view you take. Her family was one of the wealthiest on the island—and my father was an itinerant Corsican with a dodgy background, who worked in the kitchens of one of her family hotels. It was never going to be thought of as an ideal match—not by any stretch of the imagination.' His gaze fixed on the flames which danced around one of the logs. 'My father was completely uneducated but he possessed a tremendous charisma.' He gave a bitter laugh. 'Along with a massive gambling addiction and a love of the finer things in life. My mother told me that her parents did everything in their power to prevent the marriage and when they couldn't—they told her she would only ever be welcome if she parted from him. Which for a strictly traditional Sicilian family was a pretty big deal.'

Alannah stared at him. 'So what did she do?'

'She defied them and married him anyway. She loved him. And she let that *love—*' His voice took the word and distorted it—so that when it left his lips it sounded like something dark and savage. 'She let it blind her to everything. His infidelity. His habitual absences. The fact that he was probably more in love with her inheritance, than with her. They took the boat to Italy when my mother was pregnant with me and we lived in some style in Rome—while my father flew to casinos all over the world and spent her money. My mother used to talk to me all the time about Sicily and I guess I became a typical immigrant child. I knew far more about the place of my birth than I did about my adopted homeland.'

Alannah leaned forward to throw another log on the fire as his words tailed off. 'Go on,' she said.

He watched the flames leap into life. 'When I was old enough, she used to leave me in charge of Michela so she could go travelling with him. She used to sit in casinos, just watching him—though I suspect it was mainly to keep the other women at bay. But he liked the attention—the idea that this rich and wealthy woman had given up everything to be with him. He used to tell her that she was his lucky charm. And I guess for a while that was okay—I mean, the situation certainly wasn't perfect, but it was bearable. Just that beneath the surface everything was crumbling and there was nothing I could do to stop it.'

She heard the sudden darkness in his voice. 'How?'

Leaning his head back against the chair, he half closed his eyes. 'My mother's inheritance was almost gone. The rent on our fancy apartment in Parioli was due and the creditors were circling like vultures. I remember her mounting sense of panic when she confided the bitter truth to me. I was eighteen and working towards going to college, though something told me that was never going to happen. My father found out about a big tournament in Monaco and they drove to France so that he could take part in it.' There was a pause. 'It was supposed to be the solution to all their problems.'

She heard the sudden break in his voice. 'What happened?'

'Oh, he won,' he said. 'In fact, he cleaned up big time. Enough to clear all his debts and guarantee them the kind of future my mother had prayed for.'

'But?' She sensed there was a *but* coming. It hung in the air like a heavy weight about to topple. He lowered his head to look at her and Alannah almost recoiled from the sudden bleakness in his eyes.

'That night they celebrated with too much champagne and decided to set off for Rome, instead of waiting until the morning. They were driving through the Italian alps when they took a bend too fast. They hit the side of the mountain and the car was destroyed.' He didn't speak for a moment and when he did, his words sounded as if they had been carved from stone.

'Neither of them would have known anything about it. At least, that's what the doctors told me.'

'Oh, Niccolò,' she breathed. 'I'm so sorry. Michela told me they'd died in a car crash, but I didn't know the background to the story.'

'Because I kept as much from her as I could. The post-mortem was inconclusive.' His voice hardened. 'Determining the level of alcohol in a…cadaver is always difficult. And no child should have the shame of knowing her father killed her mother because he was on a drunken high after winning at cards.'

She thought how *cold* he sounded—and how ruthless. But that was his default position, wasn't it—and wasn't it somehow understandable in the circumstances? Wasn't much of his behaviour explained by his dreadful legacy? 'You still must have been devastated?' she ventured.

He gave a bitter laugh. 'Do you want the truth? The real and shocking truth? My overriding emotion was one of relief that my father had won so big and that somehow the money got to me intact. It meant that I could pay the rent and clear the debts. It meant that I could send Michela away to school—at thirteen she was getting too much for me to handle. And it meant that I could live my own life. That I could capitalise on his win and make it even bigger. And that's what I did. I bought my first property with that money and by the end of that first year, I had acquired three.'

Alannah nodded. It was funny how when you joined up the dots the bigger picture emerged. Suddenly, she realised why he'd always been so strict with his sister. She saw now that his own controlling nature must have developed as an antidote to his father's recklessness. Financial insecurity had led him to go on and make himself a colossal fortune which nobody could ever bleed away. His wealth was protected, but in protecting it he had set himself in a world apart from other men.

'And did this all happen at Christmas?' she questioned suddenly. 'Is that why you hate the holidays so much?'

'No. That would have been neat, wouldn't it?' He gave a wry smile. 'It's just that Christmas came to symbolise the bleak epicentre of our family life. For me, it was always such an empty festival. My mother would spend vast amounts of money decking out the rooms of our apartment, but she was never there. Even on Christmas Eve she would be sitting like some passive fool on the sidelines while my father played cards. Supposedly bringing him luck, but in reality—checking out that some buxom hostess wasn't coming onto him.'

She winced at the phrase, but suddenly she could understand some of his prejudice towards her, too. For him, buxom women in skimpy clothes were the ones who threatened his parents' relationship. Yet in the end, his puritanical disapproval of her chosen career had done nothing to destroy his powerful lust for her, which must have confused him. And Niccolò didn't do confusion. She'd always known that. Black and white, with nothing in between.

'To me, Christmas always felt as if I'd walked onto a stage set,' he said. 'As if all the props were in place, but nobody knew which lines to say.'

And Alannah realised that she'd done exactly the same. She had tried to create the perfect Christmas.

She'd bought the tree and hung the holly and the mistletoe—but what she had created had been no more real than the empty Christmases of his past.

'Oh, Niccolò—I'm sorry,' she said. 'I had no idea.'

He looked at her and some of the harshness left his face. 'How would you have done? I've never talked about it. Not to anyone.'

'Maybe some time, it might be good to sit down and discuss it with Michela?' she ventured.

'And destroy her memories?'

'False memories are dangerous. And so are secrets. My mother waited until she was dying to tell me that her drink had been spiked and she didn't even know my father's name. I wish she'd shared it with me sooner. I would have liked to have let her know how much I admired her for keeping me.'

His eyes narrowed. 'She sounds an amazing woman.'

'She was.' His words pleased her but she felt vulnerable with his black eyes looking at her in that curiously assessing way. In an effort to distract herself, she got up and went to look out of the window. 'I'm afraid the snow shows no sign of melting?'

'No.'

She turned round. 'I suppose on a practical level we could take down all the decorations if that would make you feel better—and then we could watch that programme on TV which has been generating so much publicity. Have you heard about it? It's called "*Stuff Christmas*".'

Without warning, he rose from the chair and walked over to her, his shadow enveloping her and suddenly making her feel very small. His ebony gaze flickered over her and she saw that the bitterness in his eyes had been replaced by the much more familiar flicker of desire.

'Or we could do something else, *mia fata*,' he said softly. 'Something much more appealing. Something which I have been aching to do since I walked back in here. I could take you upstairs to bed and make love to you.'

His features were soft with lust and Alannah thought she'd never seen him looking quite so gorgeous. She wanted him just as she always wanted him, but this time her desire was underpinned with something else—something powerful and inexplicable. A need to hold him and comfort him, after everything he'd told her. A need to want to reach out and protect him.

But he'd only told her because of the situation in which they found themselves and she needed to face the truth. He wanted her for sex—*that was all*—and she needed to protect her own vulnerable heart. Maybe it was time to distance herself from him for a while. Give them both a little space.

But by then he was kissing her and it was too late to say anything. Because when he kissed her like that, she was lost.

CHAPTER NINE

SLOWLY, NICCOLÒ LICKED at the delicious rosy flesh of Alannah's nipple until eventually she began to stir. Raising her arms above her head, she stretched languorously as the silky tumble of her hair rippled over the pillow like a black banner.

'Niccolò,' she murmured, dark lashes fluttering open to reveal the sleepy denim eyes beneath.

He gave a smile of satisfaction as she somehow turned his name into a breathy little sigh—a variation of the different ways she'd said it throughout the night. She had gasped it. Moaned it. At one point she had even screamed it—her fingernails clawing frantically at his sweat-sheened body as she'd bucked beneath him. He remembered her flopping back onto the pillow afterwards and asking if was it always like this. But he hadn't answered her. He hadn't dared. For once there had been no words in his vocabulary to describe a night which had surpassed any other in his experience. He had come over and over again… in her and on her. And this time he'd remembered to use protection. Hell. Even doing *that* had felt as if it should be included in the pages of the Kama Sutra. He swallowed as he felt the renewed jerk of desire just from thinking about it. No orgasm had ever felt more powerful; no kisses that deep.

He was still trying to work out why. Because he had allowed her to glimpse the bleak landscape of his past—or because he had waited what seemed like a whole lifetime to possess her? He gave another lick. Maybe it was simply that he was discovering she was nothing like the woman he'd thought her to be.

'Niccolò?' she said again.

'Mmm?'

'Is it morning?'

'I think so.' His tongue traced a sinuous path over the creamy flesh and he felt her shiver. 'Though right now I don't really care. Do you?'

'I don't…' He could hear the note of dreamy submission in her voice. 'I don't think so.'

'Good.' He moved his tongue down over her body, feeling himself harden as it trailed a moist path to her belly. But the anatomical significance of that particular spot suddenly began to stab at his conscience and the thought he'd been trying to block now came rushing into his mind. *Was* she pregnant? He felt the painful contraction of his heart until he reminded himself that was a possibility, not a fact—and he only ever dealt with facts. There was nothing he could do about it right now—so why not continue tracking his tongue down over her salty skin and obliterating the nagging darkness of his thoughts with the brief amnesia of pleasure?

He wriggled down the bed and knelt over her, his legs straddling her as he parted her thighs and put his head between them. The dark triangle of hair at their apex was soft and for a moment he just teased at the curly strands with his teeth. She began to writhe as he flickered his tongue with featherlight accuracy against her clitoris, and the fingernails which had begun to claw restlessly at the sheet now moved to grip his shoulders.

She tasted warm and wet against his mouth and her urgent little cries only increased when he captured her circling hips and pinned them firmly against the mattress, so that he could increase the unremitting pressure of his tongue. He could hear her calling his name out. He could feel her spiralling out of control. And suddenly he felt her begin to spasm helplessly against his mouth.

'N-Niccolò!' she breathed. 'Oh, Niccolò.'

His mind and his body were at such a fever-pitch of hunger that he couldn't speak and, urgently, he reached for a condom and eased himself into her slick warmth.

He groaned. She felt so *tight*. Or maybe it was because he felt so big—as if he wanted to explode from the moment he thrust inside her. As if he wanted to come, over and over again. And yet surely she had drained every seed from his body, so that there was nothing left to give?

It seemed she had not. He drove into her until he didn't know where he ended and she began. Until her back began to arch and her eyes to close—each exquisite spasm racking through his body as time seemed to suspend itself, leaving him dazed and breathless.

The silence of the room was broken only by the sound of his own muffled heartbeat.

'I don't know how much more pleasure I can take,' she said eventually and he felt her face pressing against his shoulder.

He turned his head and blew a soft breath onto her cheek. 'Don't you know that you can never have too much pleasure, *mia tentatrice*?'

But Alannah wrinkled her nose as she stared up at the ceiling because she didn't agree. You could. You definitely could. There was always a snake in the garden of Eden—everyone knew that. She thought about all the things he'd confided in her last night. Her heart had softened when she'd heard his story. She'd felt so close to him—and flattered that he had trusted her enough to tell her all that stuff about his past. But that was dangerous, too. If she wasn't careful she could start weaving hopeless fantasies about something which was never intended to last.

She looked over at the window where bright light was shining against the closed curtains. And she realised that it was Christmas morning and last night he'd wanted to leave. She watched as he got out of bed and walked over to the window to pull back the curtains and she blinked as she gazed outside. Thick snow lay everywhere. Branches and bushes were blanketed with the stuff. Against a dove-grey sky the world looked blindingly white and not a sound could be heard and Alannah knew she mustn't let the fairy-tale perfection of the scene in front of her blind her to the reality of their situation.

She put her hands beneath the duvet, her warm belly instinctively recoiling from the icy touch of her fingers.

'We haven't really discussed what's going to happen if I'm pregnant.'

The words hung and shimmered in the air, like the baubles on the unwanted Christmas tree downstairs.

He seemed to choose his words carefully, as if he was walking through a minefield of possibilities.

'Obviously, if such a situation arises—then I will be forced to consider marrying you.'

Alannah did her best not to recoil because he made it sound like someone being forced to drink a bitter draught of poison. She didn't say anything for a moment and when she did, she chose her words as carefully as he had done.

'Before you do, I think there's something you should take into account,' she said quietly. 'Gone are the days when women could be forced to marry against their will—because there's a baby on the way. If I *am* pregnant, then I want my baby to have love—real love. I would want my baby to put contentment before wealth—and satisfaction before ambition. I would want my baby to grow up to be a warm and grounded individual—and, obviously, none of those things would be possible with you as a cynical role model. So don't worry, Niccolò—I won't be dragging you up the aisle any time soon.'

She had expected anger, or a righteous indignation—but she got neither. Instead, his expression remained cool and non-committal. She almost thought she saw a flicker of amusement in those ebony eyes.

'Have you finished?' he said.

She shrugged, wishing she didn't want him so much. 'I guess.'

'Then I'll make coffee.'

He didn't just make coffee. After a bath which

seemed to take for ever to fill, Alannah dressed and went downstairs to find him deftly cracking eggs into a bowl with one hand.

He glanced up. 'Breakfast?'

She grimaced. 'I don't know if I can face eggs.'

'You really should eat something.'

'I suppose so.' She sat down and took the cup of coffee he poured for her and, after a couple of minutes, a plate of scrambled eggs was pushed across the table. She must have been hungrier than she'd thought because she ate it all, before putting her fork down and watching while he finished his own. She thought how he could even make eating look sexy. *Keep your mind fixed on practicalities,* she told herself. 'We ought to investigate the roads,' she said. 'Maybe we can dig ourselves out.'

'Not yet.' His eyes were thoughtful as they surveyed her over the rim of his coffee cup. 'I think we should go for a walk. You look as if you could do with some colour in your cheeks.'

'That's what blusher is supposed to be for.'

He smiled. 'There's a cupboard below the stairs packed with boots and waterproof jackets—why don't we go and investigate?'

They found coats and wrapped up warm and as Niccolò buttoned up her coat Alannah kept reinforcing the same mantra which had been playing in her head all morning. That none of this meant anything. They were just two people who happened to be alone at Christmas, who happened to enjoy having sex with each other.

But the moment they stepped out into the snow, it

was impossible to keep things in perspective. It felt as if nature were conspiring against her. How could she not be affected when it felt as if she'd been transplanted into a magical world, with a man who made her feel so *alive*?

They walked along, their footsteps sinking into the virgin tracks, and she was surprised when he took her hand as they walked along. Funny how something so insignificant could feel so meaningful—especially when she thought about the many greater intimacies they'd shared. Because holding hands could easily masquerade as tenderness and tenderness was shot with its own special kind of danger…

As occasional stray flakes drifted down on their bare heads they talked about their lives. About the reasons he'd come to live in London and her summer holidays in Ireland. She asked how he'd met Alekto Sarantos, and he told her about their mutual friend Murat, the Sultan of Qurhah, and a long-ago skiing trip, when four very alpha men had challenged each other on the slopes.

'I didn't realise you knew Luis Martinez,' she said. 'That *is* Luis Martinez the world-champion racing driver?'

'Ex world champion,' he said, a little testily—and Alannah realised how competitive the four friends must have been.

He told her he hated litter and cars which hogged the middle lane of the motorway and she confided her dislike of drugs and people who ignored shop assistants by talking on their mobile phones. It was as if they had made an unspoken decision to keep the conversation strictly neutral and, unexpectedly, Alannah found herself relaxing. To anyone observing them, they probably looked like an ordinary couple who'd chosen to escape the mad rush of the city to create a dream holiday for themselves. And that was all it was, she reminded herself fiercely. A dream.

'Are you finding this…impossible?' she said. 'Being stuck here with this manufactured Christmas everywhere, when last night you were desperate to leave?'

He kicked at some snow, so that it created a powdery white explosion before falling to the ground. 'No,' he said eventually. 'It's easier than I imagined. You're actually very good company. In fact, I think I enjoy talking to you almost as much as I enjoy kissing you.' His eyes gleamed. 'Although, on second thoughts…'

She turned away, blinking her eyes furiously because kindness was nearly as dangerous as tenderness in helping you to distort reality. But he was getting to her—even though she didn't want him to. Wasn't it funny how a few kind words had the power to make everything seem different? The world suddenly looked bright and vivid, even though it had been bleached of colour. The snow made the berries on the holly bushes stand out like drops of blood and Alannah reached up to bend back a tree branch, watching as it sent a shower of snow arcing through the air, and something bubbled up inside her and made her giggle.

She turned around to find Niccolò watching her, his eyes narrowed against the bright light, and her mouth grew dry as she saw an instantly recognisable hunger in their black depths.

'What…what are we going to do if it doesn't melt?' she said, suddenly breathless.

He leaned forward to touch a gloved finger to her lips. 'Guess,' he said, and his voice was rough.

CHAPTER TEN

HE MADE LOVE to her as soon as they got back—while her cheeks were still cold from the snowy air and her eager fingers icy against his chest as she burrowed beneath his sweater. Alannah lay on the rug in front of the fire, with her arms stretched above her head, wearing nothing but a pair of knickers. And all her shyness and hang-ups seemed like a distant memory as he trailed his lips over every inch of her body.

His fingertips explored her skin with a curiously rapt attention and she found herself reaching for him with a sudden urgency, drawing in a shuddering breath as he eased into her and letting the breath out again like a slow surrender as he lowered his mouth to hers. She loved the contrast of their bodies—his so olive-skinned and dark against her own milky pallor. She liked watching the flicker of flames gilding his flesh and the way his limbs interlocked so perfectly with her own. She loved the way he tipped his head back when he came—and made that low and shuddered moan of delight.

Much later, he pulled his sweater over her head and set about cooking lunch, while she curled up on the sofa and watched him, and suddenly she felt relaxed.

Really and properly relaxed. The cushion behind her back was soft and feathery and her bare toes were warm in the fire's glow.

'It seems *weird*,' she said as he tipped a pile of clean vegetables from the chopping board into a saucepan, 'to see you in the kitchen, looking like you know exactly what you're doing.'

'That's because I do. It isn't exactly rocket science,' he answered drily. 'Unless you think cooking is too complicated for a mere man and that women are naturally superior in the kitchen?'

'Women are naturally superior at many things,' she said airily. 'Though not necessarily at cooking. And you know what I mean. You're a billionaire businessman who runs an international empire. It's strange to see you *scraping carrots*.'

Niccolò gave a soft laugh as he grabbed a handful of fresh herbs, though he recognised that she'd touched a nerve. Just because he *could* cook, didn't mean he did—and it was a long time since he'd done anything like this. Yet wasn't there something uniquely *comforting* about creating a meal from scratch? He'd cooked for his sister in those early days of loss but as she'd got older his responsibilities towards her had lessened. When he had sent her away to school, only the vacations had required his hands-on guardianship. But he had enjoyed his role as quasi-parent and he'd made sure that he carried it out to the best of his ability—the way he tackled everything in his life.

He remembered the trips to the famous Campagna Amica market, near the Circus Maximus. He had taken Michela with him and shown the sulky teenager how to select the freshest vegetables and the finest pieces of fruit. And all the stall-owners had made a fuss of her—slipping her a ripe pear or a small bunch of perfect grapes.

When Michela had finally left home, he had filled every available hour with work—building up his property portfolio with a determination to underpin his life with the kind of security he'd never had. And as his wealth had grown, so had his ability to delegate. These days he always ate out, unless a woman was trying to impress him with her culinary repertoire. His Mayfair fridge was bare, save for coffee and champagne. His apartment was nothing but a base with a bed. It wasn't a home because he didn't *do* home. But as he squeezed lemon juice over the grilled fish he realised how much he had missed the simple routine of the kitchen.

He glanced up to find Alannah still watching him, her bare legs tucked up beneath her. His sweater was much too big for her and it had the effect of making her look unbelievably fragile. Her black hair was spilling down over her shoulders and her blue eyes were shining and something about that almost innocent look of eagerness made his heart contract.

Deliberately, he turned away, reaching for a bottle of prosecco and two glasses. *She's just someone you're trying to get out of your system,* he reminded himself grimly.

His face was composed by the time he handed her a glass. 'Happy Christmas,' he said.

They drank prosecco, lit candles and ate lunch. Afterwards, he made love to her again and they fell asleep on the sofa—and when they awoke, the candles were almost burnt down and outside the starry sky was dark and clear.

Alannah walked over to the window and he wondered if she was aware that her bare bottom was revealed with every step she took.

'I think the snow might be melting,' she said.

He heard the unmistakable note of disappointment in her voice and something inside him hardened. Did she think they could exist in this little bubble for ever, and pretend the rest of the world wasn't out there?

He insisted on loading the dishwasher and making tea to eat with their chocolate. Because any kind of activity was better than sitting there letting his mind keep working overtime.

But action couldn't permanently silence the nagging thoughts which were building inside him and he thought about what she'd said earlier. About putting contentment before wealth and satisfaction before ambition. About not wanting to drag him up the aisle.

Because that was not a decision she alone could make. And if there *was* a baby, then surely there was only one sensible solution, and that solution was marriage.

His jaw tightened. Obviously it was something he'd thought about, in the same way that the young sometimes thought about getting old—as if it would never happen to them. He liked children—and was godfather to several. Deep down, he'd recognised that one day he wanted to be a father and would select a suitable woman to bear his child.

He'd imagined she would be blonde and slightly aloof. Maybe one of those American women who had been brought up on milk and honey and could trace their roots back over generations. The type who kept their emotions on an even keel. The type who didn't believe in fairy tales. The type he felt safe with. It wasn't their trust funds which excited him, but the satisfaction of knowing that they would unknowingly welcome the son of a Corsican bandit into their rarefied drawing rooms.

He stared across the room at Alannah. In no way was she aloof; he had never seen a woman looking quite so accessible. Even with her fingers wrapped chastely around a mug of herb tea, she looked…wild. He felt his throat dry. She touched something deep inside him, something which felt…*dangerous.* Something which took him to the very edges of his self-control. She always had. She spoke to him as nobody else did. She treated him in a way which no one else would dare try.

But the fact remained that she had a background even more unsettled than his own. He had already taken a gamble on her—but surely there was no need to take another. He might not have learnt many lessons at the knee of his father, but one thing he knew was that the more you gambled—the greater your chance of losing. The most sensible thing he could do would be to walk away from her. To keep on walking, without looking back.

He swallowed. Yet if she carried his child—he could walk nowhere. What choice would he have other than to stay with her? To tie himself to someone who no way fitted the image of the kind of woman he wanted to marry. Two mismatched people united by a single incident of careless passion. What future was there in that?

She looked up and her expression grew wary.

'Why are you frowning at me?'

'I didn't realise I was.'

'Actually, frowning isn't really accurate. You were glaring.'

'Was I?' He leaned back in his chair and studied her. 'I've been thinking.'

'Sounds ominous,' she said.

'You do realise that despite all your words of rebellion this morning—I'm going to marry you if you're having my baby?'

Her creamy skin went pink. He saw her fingertips flutter up to touch the base of her neck.

'What…what made you suddenly think of that?'

He saw the flare of hope in her eyes and knew he mustn't feed it, because that wasn't fair. He had a responsibility to tell her the truth and the last thing he wanted was her thinking he was capable of the same emotions as other men. He mustn't fool her into thinking that his icy heart might be about to melt. His mouth hardened. Because that was never going to happen.

'I suddenly realised,' he said slowly, 'that I could never tolerate my son or daughter growing up and calling another man Father.'

'Even though I am the last kind of person you would consider marrying under normal circumstances.'

He met her eyes—but hadn't he always been completely honest with her? Wouldn't she see through a placatory lie to try to make her feel better? 'I guess.'

She put her cup down quickly, as if she was afraid she was going to spill it. 'So this is all about possession?'

'Why wouldn't it be? This child is half mine.'

'*This child* might not even exist!' she choked out. 'Don't you think we ought to wait until we know, before we start having arguments about parental rights?'

'When *can* you find out?'

'I'll do the test when I get back to London,' she said, jumping up from the sofa and dabbing furiously at her eyes with shaking and fisted hands.

The warm and easy atmosphere of earlier had vanished. And how.

Alannah stormed upstairs to splash cold water onto her face and to try to stem the hot tears from springing to her eyes, and yet all she could feel was a growing sense of frustration. She didn't *want* to be like this. She couldn't blame him for what he'd said, just because it didn't fit in with her fantasies. He was only being straight with her. So maybe this was a wake-up call to start protecting herself. To start facing up to facts.

Their fairy-tale Christmas was over.

She went back downstairs and turned on the TV, giving an exaggerated sigh of relief when she heard the weatherman announce that a warm weather front was pushing up from Spain, and the snow was expected to have thawed by late morning.

'Great news,' she said. 'London here we come.'

Niccolò watched as she stomped out of her chair to throw away the untouched mince pies and chocolates and every attempt he made to start a conversation was met with a monosyllabic response. He realised that he'd never been given such cool treatment by a woman before.

But that didn't stop them having sex that night. Very good sex, as it happened. Their angry words momentarily forgotten, he reached for her in the darkness with a passion which she more than matched. In a room washed silver by the full moon, he watched as she arched beneath him and called out his name.

He awoke to the sound of dripping outside the window to find the weatherman's predictions had been accurate and that the snow was melting. Leaving Alannah sleeping, he packed everything up, made a pot of coffee, then went along the lane to find his car.

By the time he drove back to the cottage, she was up and dressed, standing in the middle of the sitting room, clutching a mug—her face pale and her mouth set. He noticed she'd turned the tree lights off and that the room now looked dull and lacklustre.

'Christmas is over,' she said brightly, as if he were a stranger. As if she hadn't been going down on him just a few sweet hours before.

'What about the tree?'

'The woman I hired the cottage from supplied it. She said she'll take it away.'

'Alannah—'

'No,' she said quietly. 'I don't want any protracted stuff, or silly goodbyes. I just want to get back to London and finish up the job you've employed me to do.'

Niccolò felt a flicker of irritation at her suddenly stubborn and uncompromising attitude, but there didn't seem to be a damned thing he could do about it. She was almost completely silent on the journey back as the car slushed its way through the unnaturally quiet streets and, for some reason, the passionate opera he usually favoured while driving now seemed completely inappropriate.

He drove her to Acton and parked up outside her

home, where most of the small nearby houses seemed to be decked with the most garish tinsel imaginable. Someone had even put an inflatable Santa in their cramped front yard.

'Thanks for the lift,' she said, as she reached for the door handle.

'Aren't you going to invite me in?'

She gave him a steady stare. 'Why would I do that?'

'Maybe because we've been sleeping together and I might like to see where you live?'

Alannah hesitated and hated herself for that hesitation. She wondered if secretly she was ashamed of her little home and fearful of how judgemental he might be. Or was it simply an instinctive reaction, because she was unwilling to expose any more of herself to him?

'Okay, come in, then,' she said grudgingly.

'Grazie,' came his sardonic reply.

It was shiveringly cold as she unlocked the door. She'd turned the heating down low before the taxi had arrived to take her to the cottage and now the place felt like an ice-box. Niccolò stood in the centre of her small sitting room as she adjusted the thermostat, looking around him like a man who had just found himself in a foreign country and wasn't quite sure what to do. She wondered how he managed to make her furniture look as if it would be better suited to a doll's house.

'Would you like a guided tour?' she said.

'Why not?'

The cramped dimensions meant she needed to be vigilant about tidiness and Alannah was glad there were no discarded pieces of clothing strewn around her bedroom and that the tiny bathroom was neat. But it still felt excruciating as she led him through an apartment in which she'd tried to maximise all available light in order to give an illusion of space. She'd made all the drapes herself from sari material she'd picked up at the local market, and the artwork which hung on the walls was her own. A friend from college had feng-shuied every room, there were pots of herbs lined up on the window sill in the kitchen, and she found the place both restful and creative.

But she wondered how it must seem through Niccolò's eyes, when you could practically fit the entire place into his downstairs cloakroom back in Mayfair.

They walked back into the sitting room and, rather awkwardly, she stood in front of him. He really did seem like a stranger now, she thought—and a terrible sense of sadness washed over her. How weird to think that just a few hours ago he was deep inside her body—making her feel as if she was closer to him than she'd ever been to anyone.

'I would offer you coffee,' she said. 'But I really do want to get on. If Alekto is going to have the apartment ready for his New Year's Eve party, then I need to get cracking.'

'You're planning to work *today*?'

'Of course. What did you think I'd be doing?' she questioned. 'Sobbing into my hankie because our cosy Christmas is over? I enjoyed it, Niccolò. It was an… interesting experience. And you're a great cook as well as a great lover. But you probably know that.'

She made a polite gesture in the direction of the door but he suddenly caught hold of her wrist, and all pretence of civility had gone.

'Haven't you forgotten something?' he iced out, his eyes glittering with unfeigned hostility.

She snatched her hand away, swallowing as she met his gaze. 'No, I haven't. It's not the kind of thing you can easily forget, is it? Don't worry, Niccolò. I'll let you know whether I'm pregnant or not.'

CHAPTER ELEVEN

'I'M NOT PREGNANT.'

Alannah's voice sounded distorted—as if it were coming from a long way away, instead of just the other side of his desk—and Niccolò didn't say anything—at least, not straight away. He wondered why his heart had contracted with something which felt like pain. Whether he'd imagined the cold taste of disappointment which was making his mouth bitter. He must have done. Because wasn't this the news he'd been longing for? The only sane solution to a problem which should never have arisen?

He focused his eyes to where Alannah sat perched on the edge of a chair opposite him and thought how pale she looked. Paler than the thick white lanes through which they'd walked on Christmas Day, when the snow had trapped them in that false little bubble. Her blue eyes were ringed with dark shadows, as if she hadn't been sleeping.

Had she?

Or had she—like he—been lying wide-eyed in the depths of the night, remembering what it had felt like when they'd made love and then fallen asleep with their limbs tangled warmly together?

He flattened the palms of his hands flat on the surface of his desk. 'You're sure?'

'One hundred per cent.'

He wondered why she had chosen to tell him here, and now. Why she had come to his office after successfully negotiating a ten-minute slot in his diary with Kirsty. And Kirsty hadn't even checked with him first!

'Couldn't you have chosen a more suitable time and place to tell me, rather than bursting into my office and getting my assistant to collude with you?' he questioned impatiently. 'Or is it just a continuation of your determination to keep me at arm's length?'

'I've been busy.'

That was usually *his* excuse. He leaned back in his chair and studied her. 'You won't even have dinner with me,' he observed coolly.

'I'm sure you'll get over it,' she said lightly.

His gaze didn't waver. 'I thought you said you'd enjoyed our "experiment" over Christmas—so why not run with it a little longer? Come on, Alannah.' A smile curved his lips. 'What harm could it do?'

Alannah stared at him. What *harm* could it do? Was he serious? But that was the trouble—he was. Unemotional, cynical and governed by nothing but sexual hunger—Niccolò obviously saw no reason why they shouldn't continue with the affair. Because it meant different things to each of them. For him, it was clearly just an enjoyable diversion, while for her it felt as if someone had chipped away a little bit of her heart every time she saw him. *It was being chipped away right now.*

She had chosen his office and a deliberately short

appointment in which to tell him her news in order to avoid just this kind of scene. She'd actually considered telling him by phone but had instinctively felt that such a move would have been counterproductive. That he might have insisted on coming round to confront her face to face and her defences would have been down.

It was bad enough trying to stay neutral now—even with the safety of his big oak desk between them. Sitting there in his crisp white shirt and tailored suit, Niccolò's face was glowing with health and vitality and she just wanted to go and put her arms around him. She wanted to lean on him and have him tell her that everything was going to be okay. But he didn't want a woman like her leaning on him and anyway—she was independent and strong. She didn't need a man who could never give her what she wanted, and what she wanted from him was love. *Join the queue,* she thought bitterly.

'You haven't *done* anything,' she said. 'You haven't made or broken any promises. Everything is how it's supposed to be, Niccolò. What happened between us was great but it was never intended to last. And it hasn't.'

'But what if…?' He picked up the golden pen which was lying on top of the letters he'd been signing and stared at it as if he had never really seen it before. He lifted his gaze to hers. 'What if I wanted it to last—at least for a little while longer? What then?'

Alannah tensed as fear and yearning washed over her—yet of the two emotions, the yearning was by far the deadlier.

'And how long did you have in mind?' she questioned sweetly. 'One week? Two? Would it be presumptuous to expect it might even continue for a *whole month*?'

He slammed the pen down. 'Does it matter?' he demanded. 'Not every relationship between a man and a woman lasts for ever.'

'But most relationships don't start out with a discussion about when it's going to end!' She sucked in a breath and prayed she could hold onto her equilibrium for a while longer. 'Look, nothing has changed. I'm still the same woman I always was—except that I have you to thank for helping me lose some of my inhibitions. But I still don't know who my father was and I still have the kind of CV which would make someone with your sensitive social antennae recoil in horror. Appearances matter to you, Niccolò. You know they do. So why don't you just celebrate the fact that you had a lucky escape and that we aren't going to be forced together by some random act of nature.' She rose to her feet. 'And leave me to finish off Alekto's apartment in time for his party. The caterers are arriving tomorrow, and there are still some last-minute touches which need fixing.'

'Sit down,' he said. 'I haven't finished yet.'

'Well, I have. We've said everything which needs to be said. It's over, Niccolò. I'm not so stupid that I want to hang around having sex with a man who despises everything I stand for!'

'I don't despise what you stand for. I made a lot of judgements about you and some of them were wrong.'

'Only *some* of them?' she demanded.

'Why can't you just accept what I'm offering? Why do you have to want more?'

'Because I'm worth it.' She hitched the strap of her handbag over her shoulder. 'And I'm going now.'

He rose to his feet. 'I don't want you to go!' he gritted out.

'Tough. I'm out of here. *Ciao.*'

And to Niccolò's amazement she picked up her handbag and walked out of his office without a backward glance.

For a moment he stood there, stunned—as the door slammed behind her. He thought about rushing after her, about pulling her into his arms and kissing her and *then* seeing whether she was so damned certain their relationship was over. But that would make it all about sex, wouldn't it? And sex had always been the least troublesome part of this equation. Besides, Kirsty was buzzing through to tell him that his eleven o'clock had arrived, so he was forced to concentrate on listening to what his architect was saying, rather than on a pair of stubborn pink lips he still wanted to crush beneath his own.

By seven o'clock that evening, he decided that Alannah had been right. Better to end it now, before she got in too deep—because it wouldn't be fair to break her heart as he had broken so many others. She would start falling in love with him. She would want more from him than he was capable of giving. Better they both recognised his limitations now.

He glanced up at the clock again. Maybe he should start as he meant to go on. Dinner with someone new would surely be the way to go. A civilised dinner with someone who didn't get under his skin the way she did.

He flicked through his address book, but none of the long list of names excited him enough to pick up the phone. He had his driver drop him home and worked in his study until way past midnight. But still he couldn't sleep. He kept remembering when Alannah had spent the night with him there and, even though the linen had been laundered, he thought he could still detect the unique scent of her skin on his sheets. He thought about the cottage. About the tree-lights and the snow. About that unreal sense of quiet satisfaction as he had cooked her Christmas lunch. The way they had fallen asleep on the sofa after they'd made love. Hadn't that been like the closest thing to peace he'd felt in a long, long time?

And that was all make-believe, he told himself fiercely. As insubstantial as Christmas itself.

He lay and watched the luminous numbers on his clock changing slowly and just before his alarm was due to go off a text arrived from Alekto Sarantos.

Don't be late for my party! Beautiful women and a beautiful apartment—what better way to see in the new year? A

Niccolò stared blankly at the screen of his mobile phone, telling himself that a party was exactly what he needed, and didn't Alekto throw some of the best parties he'd ever been to? But just the thought of it left him cold. Tugging on his running gear, he got ready for the gym and wondered why his eyes looked so shadowed and haunted.

But deep down, he knew exactly why.

'It is *spectacular.*' Alekto Sarantos smiled as he looked around the main reception room, his blue eyes gleaming. 'You have transformed my apartment, Alannah—and you have worked against the clock to get it done in time for my party. *Efkaristo poli.* I thank you.'

Alannah smiled back, even though just smiling seemed to take a massive effort these days. It was true that the place *did* look pretty amazing—especially when she thought back to the sea of beige it had been before. The woman who had made the curtains had got very excited about it and she had told someone, who had told someone else. Even during the short period between Christmas and new year, word had soon got round in an industry which survived by constantly seeking out new ideas and new faces. Already Alannah had received a phone call from one of the big interior magazines, asking if they could do a photo shoot there. She doubted whether Alekto would agree, since she got the idea he was very hot on privacy. Still, she could *always ask* him. And even if he didn't give his permission, she sensed that she had turned a corner—because this was the big break she had been waiting for. *And she had Niccolò to thank for it.*

Security and creative fulfilment were lying within her grasp. So why did it all feel so empty? Why was she having to force herself to look and sound enthusiastic about something she'd always dreamed of?

She sighed. She knew *exactly* why. *Because she'd made the fundamental mistake of falling in love with a man who had never offered her anything but sex.*

'I hope you're coming to my new year's party?' Alekto was saying. 'You really ought to be the guest of honour, after what you've achieved here. Unless, of course, you have already made plans?'

Alannah glanced out at the late afternoon sky, which was now almost dark. The only plans she had made were to buy the TV guide and turn up the central heating, while she waited for Big Ben to chime in a new year she couldn't seem to get worked up about. She thought about getting dressed up for a party attended by Alekto Sarantos and his glamorous friends, and how any sane person would leap at such an opportunity.

But what if Niccolò was there?

Her heart pounded. The possibility was high. It was more than high. They were best mates, weren't they? She shook her head. 'It's very sweet of you—but I think I'll just have a quiet evening in,' she said.

'Up to you.' Alekto shrugged. 'But if you change your mind…'

Alannah went home, bathed and washed her hair—before pulling on her dressing gown and a pair of slouchy socks and switching on the TV. She flicked channels. Crowds of people were already flocking into Trafalgar Square, even though it was still early. People were being interviewed, swigging from beer bottles and giggling—and Alannah suddenly saw herself as a fly on the wall might see her. A woman sitting on her own at nine o'clock on New Year's Eve, wearing a dressing gown and a pair of old socks.

What had she become?

She swallowed. She had become a cliché, that was what. She had fallen in love with someone who had always been out of reach. And yet, instead of accepting that and holding her head up high and just getting on with her life, the way she'd always done, she had caved in. She was like some sort of mole, living in darkness—cowering inside her own safe little habitat, because she was afraid to go out. It was the worst night of the year to be home alone—especially if your stupid heart was heavy and aching—and yet here she was. *Mole.*

What was she so worried about? That she might see Niccolò with another woman? Surely that would be the best of all possible outcomes—it would remind her of how easily he could move on. It would make her accept *reality*, instead of chasing after rainbows.

Tearing off her slouchy socks, she pulled out the gold dress she'd worn at Christmas and slithered into it. Then she slapped on a defiant amount of make-up, her highest heels—and a warm, ankle-length coat. People were milling outside pubs as she made her way to the station and more snow was falling as she caught the underground and got out at Knightsbridge.

It was much quieter in this part of town. There were few revellers out and about around here—this was the world of the private, rather than the street party. But by the time she reached Park View other partygoers were milling around in the foyer and the party atmosphere was contagious. She shared the elevator up to Alekto's apartment with several stunning women and a man who kept surreptitiously glancing at his phone.

The elevator pinged to a halt and the door to the penthouse was opened by a waitress dressed as a flamingo, a tray of exotic-looking cocktails in her hand. Alannah went off to hang up her coat and then wandered along the corridors she knew so well, back towards the sitting room. It was strange seeing the place like this—full of people—when she had only ever seen it empty. Most of the furniture she'd installed had been pushed back against the walls to maximise the space—but the room still looked spectacular. Even she could see that. The colours worked brilliantly—providing the perfect backdrop for Alekto's extensive art collection—and she was particularly proud of the lighting.

In spite of everything, she knew Niccolò would be pleased with her work. He might regret some things, but he would never regret giving her the job and she should take pride in that. A horrible dark pain washed over her, only this time it was underpinned with reproach. She wasn't supposed to be thinking about Niccolò. Wasn't that going to be her one and only new year resolution? That part of her life was over. She had to cut her losses and move on. And it was a waste of time to wonder what it would have been like if she *had* been pregnant. Or to dwell on that irrational and sinking sense of disappointment when she had stared at the test result and it had been negative.

A woman masquerading as a bird of paradise offered her a drink and Alannah took one, but the sweet concoction tasted deceptively powerful and she put the glass down as Alekto Sarantos came over to talk to her.

'You made it, then,' he said, with a smile. '*Thavmassios.* If I had a Euro for every person who has asked me who is responsible for the design of this apartment, then I would be a very rich man.'

'But I thought you *were* a very rich man,' she said, and he laughed, before giving her a thoughtful look. 'I might have some work for you in Greece, if you're interested?'

Alannah didn't even need to think about it. 'I'd be very interested,' she said immediately, because a different country might be just what she needed. What was it they said? A new year and a new start.

'Why don't you call my office on Monday?' he suggested, pulling out a business card and handing it to her.

'I will,' she said, putting it into her handbag as he walked away.

'Alannah?'

A familiar voice curled over her skin like dark velvet and she turned to see Niccolò standing there. His hair and shoulders were wet with melting snow and he was wearing a dark cashmere coat, which made him stand out from all the other guests. Alannah stiffened as his shadow fell over her and her heart began to hammer as she looked up into his shuttered features.

The knot of tension in her stomach grew tighter. But she had come here tonight to hold her head high, hadn't she? Not to hang it in shame. Nor to waste time wishing for something which could never be.

'Niccolò,' she said coolly. 'Fancy seeing you here.'

'What were you saying to Alekto?'

'That's really none of your business.'

'You do know he is world-famous for breaking women's hearts?'

'Why, has he lifted the crown from you?' she questioned acidly. 'And what are you doing still wearing your overcoat?'

'Because I have driven halfway across London looking for you,' he growled.

She frowned. 'Why?'

'Why do you think?' he exploded. 'I went round to your apartment, only you weren't there.' He had spent the afternoon psyching himself up, making careful plans about what he was going to say to her. He had decided to surprise her, because he…well, because he wanted to—and that in itself was uncharacteristic. He had naturally made the assumption that she would have been home alone, only when he'd got there Alannah's apartment had been shrouded in darkness and his heart had sunk. The sight of all those empty windows had suddenly seemed like a metaphor for his life and they had confirmed the certainty which had been growing inside him for days.

Instinct had made him pull out his telephone to speak to Alekto and his hunch was proved right. His friend had coolly informed him that, yes, Alannah *had* been invited to the party and although she'd told him she wasn't coming, she seemed to have changed her mind. In fact, she had just walked in, looking like a goddess in a spectacular golden dress.

Niccolò had turned his car around and driven from Acton, getting snarled up in the new-year traffic—his nerves becoming more and more frayed as an unfamiliar sense of agitation nagged away at him. And now he was here standing in front of her and nothing was as he thought it would be. He had not intended to launch into a jealous tirade because he'd seen her being chatted up by one of the world's biggest players.

Wasn't he supposed to be a 'player' himself?

His mouth hardened.

Not any more.

He was in a roomful of some of the most beautiful

women in the world and yet he could see only one. One who was staring at him with hostility and suspicion and, in his heart, he knew he couldn't blame her.

So why the hell was he demonstrating an arrogance which might cause her magnificent pride to assert itself, and tell him to take a running jump? He needed to keep her onside. To placate her. To make her realise why he had come here. *And to make her realise that it was the only possible solution.*

'I need to talk to you,' he said.

'Talk away.' She gave a careless shrug. 'I'm not stopping you.'

'In private.'

'I'd prefer to stay here, if you don't mind.'

'Unfortunately, *tentatrice*, I do mind.'

Without warning, he caught hold of her hand, his fingers enclosing her hammering pulse as he led her through the throng of partygoers until they had reached one of the bedrooms. He shut the door, just as she shook her hand free and glared at him.

'What do you think you're doing?' she demanded. 'You can't just waltz up to someone in the middle of a party and *manhandle* them like that! You can't just drag a woman from a room because you've decided you want a private word with her. Oh, sorry—I'd forgotten.' She slapped her palm against her brow. 'You can—and you do. Well, you might be Tarzan but I am not your Jane. I don't *do* Neanderthal and I don't *do* arrogant men who think they can just blaze into other people's lives doing exactly what they want. So will you please step aside and let me pass?'

'Not until you've heard me out,' he said, as a strange sense of calm washed over him. 'Please.'

She looked at him for a moment before pointedly glancing at her watch. 'You've got five minutes.'

Niccolò sucked in a breath but for a moment he couldn't speak. His calmness seemed to be deserting him as he realised that this wasn't going to be easy. He was going to have to do something unheard of—something he had instinctively always shied away from. He was going to have to pull out his feelings from the dark place where he'd buried them and he was going to have to admit them. To her. And even when he did, there was no guarantee that it might not be too late.

He looked into the wary blue of her eyes and his heart pounded. 'I need to ask your forgiveness,' he said. 'For all the unjust accusations I hurled at you. For my bull-headedness and my lack of compassion. For taking so long to realise the kind of woman you really are. Strong and proud and passionate and loyal. I've missed you, Alannah, and I want you back. Nobody talks to me the way you do, or makes me feel the way you do. Nobody else makes my heart skip a beat whenever I see her. I want to spend the rest of my life with you. To one day make the baby we didn't have this time. I want to make a real home—with you. Only with you.'

She took a step back, as if she'd just seen a ghost, and she started shaking her head. 'You don't want me,' she said in a hoarse voice. 'You only think you do, because I'm the one who walked away and that's probably never happened to you before. You want someone respectable, who is as pure as the driven snow—because that's the sort of thing you care about. Someone *suitable*. You didn't want me as bridesmaid because you were worried about what other people would think. Because you're hung up on appearances and how things look from the outside, no matter what you say.'

'I used to be,' he said savagely. 'But you have made me realise that appearances and social position don't matter. It's what's underneath which counts. And you have everything that counts. You are soft and smart and funny. You are kind and caring and talented. You didn't even smoke dope at school, did you—even though you were accused of it?'

Startled by this sudden conversational twist, Alannah narrowed her eyes suspiciously. 'Did Michela tell you that?'

He shook his head. 'She didn't have to. I worked it out for myself. I think you may just have covered up for my sister all this time.'

'Because that's what friends do,' she said fiercely. 'That's called loyalty.'

'I realise that now,' he said. 'It's just taken me a long and very circuitous route to get here. But I don't want to talk about the past any more… I want to concentrate on the future.'

He reached within the pocket of his snow-covered overcoat and pulled out a little box. 'This is for you,' he said, and his voice was slightly unsteady.

Alannah watched as he opened it and she was shamefully aware of a sinking sense of disappointment as she looked inside. Had she really thought it was an engagement ring? Was she really that fickle? Because glittering against the background of dark velvet was a brooch shaped like a little honey-bee. Its back was covered with yellow, black and white stones and she found herself thinking that she'd never seen anything so sparkly. She looked up at him, still disorientated.

'What's this?' she said.

'You collect insect brooches, don't you? They're diamonds. The black ones are quite rare. It's for you,' he said again. 'Because I didn't buy you a Christmas present.'

But Alannah felt a terrible lump in her throat as she began to blink her eyes rapidly. 'You just don't get it, do you?' she whispered. 'The brooches I have are all worth peanuts. I wear them because my mother gave them to me—because they *mean* something to me. I don't care if they're diamonds or paste, Niccolò. I don't care how much something is *worth*.'

'Then what if I tell you this is worth what I feel for you, and that is everything. *Everything*.' He moved closer. 'Unless you want me to go to a flea-market to find you something cheaper? Tell me, Alannah—are you going to set me a series of challenges before you will accept me?'

She almost laughed, except that now hot tears were springing to her eyes and she couldn't seem to stop them. 'I don't know what I'm going to do,' she whispered. 'Because I'm scared. Scared because I keep thinking this is all a dream and that I'm going to wake up in a minute.'

'No, not a dream,' he said, taking the brooch from the box and pinning it next to the little grasshopper which already adorned her golden dress. 'I bought you this because I love you. This is the reality.'

Her lips parted. 'Niccolò,' she said again, and now her voice was shaking. 'If this isn't true—'

He halted her protest by placing his finger over her lips. ‘It *is* true. It has always been true. The first time I set eyes on you, I was hit by a thunderbolt so powerful that I felt as if you’d cast some kind of spell on me. And that spell never really faded. I love you, Alannah—even though I’ve been running away from the idea of love all my life. I saw what it did to my mother. I saw it as a weakness which sucked the life from everything in its path. Which blinded her even to the needs of her children.’

She bit her lip. ‘I can understand that.’

He sensed her absolution, but he was not finished. ‘But what I feel for you does not feel like weakness. I feel strong when I am with you, Alannah. As strong as a mountain lion. As if I could conquer the world.’

She let him put his arms around her and her head rested against his chest. ‘That’s funny, because right now I feel as weak as a kitten.’

His black eyes burned into her as he gently levered her face up so that she was looking directly at him. ‘The only thing I need to know is whether you love me?’

‘Of course I love you.’ The words came tumbling out as if she’d been waiting all her life to say them. She thought about the first time she’d seen him, when they’d just clicked. It had been a thunderbolt for her, too, and she had never been able to forget him. She thought about how empty her life seemed when he wasn’t there. He wasn’t the man she’d thought him to be—he was so much more. ‘I think I’ve always loved you.’

‘Then kiss me, my beautiful Alannah,’ he said softly. ‘And let me show you my love.’

Slowly and tenderly, he traced his fingertip along the edges of her lips before lowering his head towards hers and Alannah's heart filled up with so much happiness that she felt as if she might burst with it.

EPILOGUE

'I USED TO think you hated weddings.'

Niccolò looked down into Alannah's face as he closed the door to their honeymoon suite, and smiled at her. 'I did. But that was before I found the woman I wanted to marry. Now it seems that I'm their biggest fan.'

'Mmm. Me, too.' She looped her arms around his neck. 'You did like the dress?'

'You looked beautiful. The most beautiful bride in the world. But then, you could wear a piece of sacking and I still wouldn't be able to tear my eyes away from you.'

'Oh, Niccolò.' She slanted him a look from between her lashes. 'Whoever would have guessed that beneath that cynical exterior beat the heart of a true poet?'

'It's true,' he said, mock-seriously. 'Though I must be careful not to lose my edge. If my competitors find out how much I'm softening, then I will soon be toast in the world of finance.'

'You?' She laughed easily. 'Yeah, sure. Like *that's* ever going to happen!'

He began to unzip her dress. 'Are you tired?'

'Not a bit. Even though it's been a very long day.'

She closed her eyes as the costly gown pooled to the ground around her feet. She had thought he would want a quiet wedding—something discreet, even a little hushed-up. Hadn't she thought he'd want to keep the risk of press interest to a minimum, despite his protestations that her past no longer bothered him? Probably. But once again he had surprised her. It was funny how love had the power to change people and to alter their views on what was important. He had told her that he was going to announce their engagement to the world's press and then he had gone out and bought her an enormous sapphire ring, which he said was the closest colour he could get to the denim-blue of her eyes.

Predictably, some of the old photos from *Stacked* magazine had made an appearance in the papers—but suddenly, they didn't seem to matter. It was slightly surreal to hear Niccolò echoing his sister's words—*and believing them*—by saying really they were very tame in comparison to a lot of the stuff you saw in contemporary music videos.

'I am proud of you, *tentatrice*,' he had murmured, crumpling the newspaper into a ball and hurling it into the bin. 'Proud of all you have achieved and how you have kept your dignity intact. Most of all, I am proud that you have consented to be my wife.'

And she had smiled. 'Oh, darling.'

The wedding was held in London's oldest Italian church, in Clerkenwell, and there was a stellar number of guests. A fully recovered Luis Martinez was there—as was the Sultan of Qurhah, Murat 'the Magnificent'. And naturally, Alekto Sarantos was at his dazzling best, even though he was barely visible through the sea of eager women who were clamouring round him. Michela was matron of honour—her silk gown cleverly hiding the beginning of a baby bump.

With Alannah's encouragement, Niccolò had told Michela the truth about their parents' death—and the admission had brought brother and sister much closer. Because secrets were always more dangerous than the truth, as he'd learned.

Alannah shivered with pleasure as Niccolò lifted her out of the discarded wedding dress and carried her over to the bed, wearing nothing but her underwear, sheer stockings and a pair of very high, white stilettos. As he undressed her she thought about the inhibitions which had once crippled her and which now seemed like a distant memory.

Tomorrow they were flying to the island of Niccolò's birth. He had only been back to Sicily once, after his mother's death—when he had been full of youthful rage and bitterness about the rejection she had suffered at the hands of her own family. But time had mellowed him and Alannah had helped him get some perspective. His maternal grandparents were dead—but he had cousins and uncles and aunts living there. A whole new family for them to get to know. And she was excited about that, too—looking forward to a big, extended family after so many years on her own.

He moved over her, his face suddenly very serious as he brushed her hair away from her cheek. 'Thank you,' he said softly.

She took his hand and kissed it. 'For?'

'For loving me. For being you.'

For being you. He didn't want anyone else, she had come to realise. He just wanted her exactly as she was, with no changes or modifications. He didn't want to rewrite her past, or pretend it hadn't happened, because her past had made her the woman she was today. And he loved that woman.

Alannah sighed.

Just like she loved her man.

* * * * *

A CHRISTMAS BRIDE FOR THE KING

ABBY GREEN

This is for my Charlotte, whose friendship has made my life immeasurably richer in so many ways. Thelma & Louise 4 Ever. xx

PROLOGUE

THE PUNISHINGLY HOT shower Sheikh Salim Ibn Hafiz Al-Noury had just subjected himself to had done little to dispel the hollow feeling that lingered after his less than sensually satisfying encounter with a convenient lover. It wasn't her fault. She was stunning. And, what was more important, she accepted his strict no-strings rules.

He never engaged with women who didn't, because he'd built his life around an independence he'd cultivated as far back as he could remember. Distancing himself from his own family and the heavy legacy of his birth. Distancing himself from painful memories. Distancing himself from emotional entanglements or investment, which could only lead to unbearable heartbreak.

Salim and his brother, Zafir, had been bred as coldly and calculatedly as animals bred for their coats or meat. They'd been bred to inherit neighbouring kingdoms—Jandor, the home of their father, where they'd been born and brought up along with Salim's twin sister, Sara, and Tabat, their mother's ancestral home.

The two countries had been at war for hundreds of years, but a peace agreement had been brokered when their mother, the Crown Princess of Tabat, had married the new King of Jandor and they'd pledged to have their sons eventually ruling both countries in a bid to secure peace in the region.

On the death of their father over a year ago Zafir, as the eldest, had assumed his role as King of Jandor—which had always been more of a home to him than to Salim.

But Salim had yet to assume *his* role, as King of Tabat, and the pressure to do so was mounting on all sides.

He hitched a towel around his waist, irritated that his thoughts were straying in this direction. He ignored the sting of his conscience that told him it was a situation he had to deal with.

He'd managed to avoid dealing with it for this long because he'd built up a vast empire of business concerns, ranging from real estate to media and tech industries, none of which he could easily walk away from. None of which he wanted to walk away from. And yet, if he was honest with himself, he knew he'd finally achieved a level of success and security that *could* enable him to step back—if he had to.

The steam of the shower cleared and Salim caught his reflection in the mirror. He was momentarily taken off guard by the cynical weariness etched into his face. Blue eyes stood out starkly against the darkness of his skin. Stubble lined a hard jaw. Too hard.

With no sense of satisfaction he took in the aesthetically pleasing symmetry of his features, which called to mind another set of features—the feminine version of this face. Except that face was frozen in time, at eleven years old when his twin sister had died.

A part of Salim had broken irreparably that day: his heart. And with it any illusion of invincibility or a belief that the world was a benign place. He'd lost his soul-mate when Sara had died, and he never wanted to experience that kind of excoriating pain again.

For a moment the memory of his sister's lifeless form and pale face was sharp enough to make him draw a breath. Even after all this time. Nineteen years. He had avenged her death, but instead of bringing him peace it had compounded the emptiness inside him.

Salim's hands curled around the sink so tightly that his knuckles shone white through the skin. It was only a persistent ringing noise that broke him out of the moment.

He went into the bedroom of his New York penthouse apartment and saw his phone flashing on the nightstand. As he picked it up he registered who it was and immediately felt a tightening sensation in his chest, along with a familiar mix of turbulent emotions, the strongest of which was guilt. He was tempted to let the call go to voicemail, but he knew it would only be delaying the inevitable.

He answered with a curtness arising out of that mix of emotions and memories. 'Brother. How nice to hear from you.'

Zafir made a rude sound at this less than effusive greeting. 'I've been trying to contact you for weeks. *Hell*, Salim, why are you doing this? You're making it harder for everyone—including yourself.'

Salim ignored what Zafir had said and replied, 'I believe congratulations are in order. I'm sorry I didn't make the wedding.'

Zafir sighed. 'It's not as if I really expected you to come, Salim, but it would have been nice for you to meet Kat. She wants to meet you.'

His tone made the tightness in Salim's chest intensify. He'd done such a good job of pushing Zafir away for as long as he could remember that it seemed impossible to bridge the chasm now. And why did he suddenly feel the need to?

He shut down that rogue impulse and assured himself that he owed Zafir nothing—nor his new sister-in-law, who was now Queen of Jandor.

'I don't really have time to chat, Zafir. Why did you call?'

His brother's voice hardened. 'You know exactly why I'm calling. You've shirked your duties for long enough. Officials in Tabat have been waiting for over a year for you to assume your role as king—as per the terms of our father's will.'

Before Salim could react to that succinct summary of his situation, Zafir was continuing.

'Tabat is close to descending into chaos. This isn't just about you, Salim. People will get hurt if stability isn't restored. It's time for you to take responsibility. You are king, whether you like it or not.'

Salim wanted to snarl down the phone that he was the furthest thing from a king that a man could be. He'd pursued a life far from royal politics and that closed, rarefied world. He'd never asked for this role—it had been thrust upon him before he'd even been born. His brother's acceptance of the status quo was in direct contrast to Salim's rejection of it.

Before he could say anything, Zafir went on. 'You can't avoid this, Salim. It's your destiny, and if you don't face up to that destiny you'll have blood on your hands.'

Destiny. Salim's anger dissipated as he thought bleakly of their sister's destiny. Had it been her destiny to suffer unspeakable trauma and die so young?

After what had happened to his sister Salim didn't believe in destiny. He believed you made your own destiny. And that was what he had done for his whole life—as much for himself as to honour the life his sister had lost.

He looked out over the skyline of Manhattan, where the late autumn dawn was slowly breaking, bathing everything in a soft pink glow. It was beautiful, but it left him untouched.

At that moment a falcon glided on the air outside his window, majestic and deadly, its head swivelling back and forth, looking for prey. It was a long way from its natural habitat, and yet this bird of prey had adapted to city life as well as humans had.

A memory floated back, of him and Sara in the desert with their pet falcons. Sara had lifted her hand to encourage hers to fly high, teasing Salim that his was too lazy to budge itself… She'd been so carefree, innocent…

'Salim?'

His brother's voice broke the silence and a heavy weight settled in Salim's gut. Destiny or not, he knew he couldn't keep avoiding this inheritance he'd never asked for. It had to be dealt with.

'Fine,' he said grimly. 'I will give them their coronation. Let them know that I'm coming.'

And in doing so, he assured himself silently, he would sever his ties with his so-called destiny and the past for good.

CHAPTER ONE

CHARLOTTE MCQUILLAN PACED back and forth in the empty office and looked at her watch for the umpteenth time. The king, Salim Ibn Hafiz Al-Noury—or technically the king when he was crowned in three weeks—had kept her waiting for an hour now.

It was no secret that he was probably the most reluctant king in the world, having deferred his coronation for well over a year. Long after his older brother had been crowned king of neighbouring Jandor.

She might have expected as much from the *enfant terrible* of the international billionaire playboy scene.

Charlotte knew of Sheikh Salim Ibn Hafiz Al-Noury's reputation, but only in a peripheral sense. Salacious celebrity gossip magazines were anathema to her, because she'd been the focal point of a celebrity scandal at a very young age, but even she was aware of the sheikh with the outrageous good looks, near mythical virility and his ability to turn anything he touched to gold.

His playboy exploits were matched only by his ruthless reputation and his ability to amass huge wealth and success in the many business spheres he turned his attention to.

Charlotte walked over to a nearby window that looked out over a seemingly unending sea of sand under a painfully blue sky. The sun was a blazing orb and she shivered lightly in the air-conditioning, imagining how merciless that heat must be with no shade. The little taste of it she'd had walking from the plane to the sheikh's chauffeur-driven car and then into the palace had almost felled her.

With her fair, strawberry-blonde colouring, Charlotte had never been a sun-worshipper. And yet here she was. Because when the opportunity had come up to escape London in the full throes of Christmas countdown she'd jumped at it.

To say it wasn't her favourite time of the year was an understatement. She loathed Christmas, with all its glittery twinkling lights and forced festive joviality, because this was the time of year when her world had fallen apart and she'd realised that happiness and security were just an illusion that could be ripped away at any moment.

Like the Wizard of Oz, who had appeared from behind his carefully constructed façade to reveal he wasn't a wizard at all. Far from it.

And yet as she looked out over this alien view that couldn't be more removed from that London scene, she didn't feel relieved. She felt a pang. *Worse.* A yearning.

Because in spite of everything a tiny, traitorous part of her secretly ached for the kind of Christmas celebrated in cheesy movies and on cards depicting happy families and togetherness. The fact that she usually spent her Christmas Day alone, with tears coursing down her face as she watched *Miracle On 34th Street* or *It's a Wonderful Life* for the hundredth time was a shameful secret she would take to her grave.

She made a disgusted sound at herself and turned her back on the view, firmly shoving any such rogue yearnings down deep where they belonged. She distracted herself by taking in the vast expanse of the King's Royal Office—which, if the correct protocol was being observed, she should never have been allowed into without his presence. She sighed.

She could see that at one time it had been impressive, with its huge floor-to-ceiling murals depicting scenes that looked as if they'd been plucked from a book of Arabian mythology. But now they were badly faded.

Everything Charlotte had seen so far of Tabat and its eponymous capital city had an air of faded glory and neglect. But it had charmed her with its ancient winding streets, clusters of stone buildings and the river that ran all the way from the Tabat Mountains to the sea on the coast of neighbouring Jandor.

The country was rich in natural resources—oil being the most important and lucrative. But its infrastructure was in serious need of modernisation, along with myriad other aspects of the country—education, government, economy… It badly needed a leader prepared to take on the mammoth task of hauling it into the twenty-first century. Its potential was abundant and just waiting to be tapped into.

But, from the little she knew of Sheikh Al-Noury and his reputation, she didn't hold out much hope for that happening any time soon. He'd made no secret of the fact that his priorities lay with his myriad business empires in the West.

She'd been hired by his brother, King Zafir of Jandor, to advise Salim Al-Noury on international diplomacy and relations in the run-up to his coronation, but in the two weeks since she'd accepted the assignment neither the sheikh nor his people had made any effort to return Charlotte's calls or provide her with any information.

Charlotte checked her watch again. He was now well over an hour late. Feeling frustrated, and not a little irritated and tired after her journey, she walked over to where she'd put down her document case, prepared to leave and find someone who could direct her to her room. But just as she drew near to the huge doors they swung open abruptly in her face and a man walked in.

One thing was immediately and glaringly apparent. In spite of seeing his picture online, Charlotte was not remotely prepared for Sheikh Salim Ibn Hafiz Al-Noury in the flesh. For the first time in her life she was rendered speechless.

For a start he was taller than she'd expected. Much taller. Well over six feet. And his body matched that height with broad shoulders and a wide chest narrowing down to lean hips and long legs. He was a big man, and she hadn't expected him to be so physically formidable. The impression was one of sheer force and power.

Messily tousled over-long dark hair framed his exquisitely handsome face, which was liberally stubbled. His eyes were so blue they immediately reminded Charlotte of the vast sky outside—vivid and sharp. His mouth was disconcertingly sensual—a contrast to the hard angles of his body and bone structure.

A loose-fitting white shirt did little to disguise the solid mass of muscle on his chest and a tantalising glimpse of dark hair. It was tucked into very worn jodhpurs that clung to hard and well muscled thighs in a way that could only be described as provocative. Scuffed leather boots hugged his calves.

It was only then, belatedly, that Charlotte registered the very earthy and surprisingly sensual smell of horseflesh and something else—male sweat. To her utter horror she realised that she was reacting to him as if she'd taken complete leave of her senses.

He frowned. 'Mrs McQuillan?'

She nodded, only vaguely registering that he'd got her title wrong.

'You were leaving?'

His deep and intriguingly accented voice reverberated through her nerve-endings in a very distracting way.

Charlotte finally broke herself out of the disturbing inertia that was rendering her insensible. What on earth was wrong with her? It wasn't as if she hadn't seen a handsome man before. She tried to ignore the fact that she'd just made such an intense inspection of the man and shelved her unfortunate reaction to him until she could study it in private, later.

She looked him in the eye. 'I've been waiting here for over an hour, Your Majesty, I thought you weren't coming.'

Those remarkable eyes flashed with what looked like censure. 'I'm not king yet.'

He looked down, and Charlotte became conscious of her rigid grasp on her case. She forced herself to relax.

He met her eye again. 'Were you offered any refreshment?'

Charlotte shook her head. King—no, *Sheikh* Al-Noury walked back to the doorway and shouted for someone. A young boy in a long tunic and turban appeared—the same one who had shown her into the office—looking pathetically eager to please. He looked terrified, however, after the stream of rapid Arabic Sheikh Al-Noury subjected him to, and then he ran.

When Charlotte registered what he'd said she stepped forward saying heatedly, 'That was uncalled for! How was he to know to offer me anything when he only looks about twelve? Someone senior should have been here to meet me. Where are your staff?'

Sheikh Al-Noury turned around slowly. He arched a brow and leant against the doorframe, crossing his arms. Totally nonchalant and unfazed by her outburst. 'You speak Arabic?'

Charlotte nodded jerkily. 'Among numerous other languages. But that's not the point—'

He straightened from the door. 'I'm sorry. I would have been here to meet you but I got delayed at the stables, taking delivery of a new thoroughbred—a present from Sheikh Nadim Al Saqr of Merkazad. He was skittish after the journey so it took a while to settle him.'

Sheikh Al-Noury had crossed the expanse of the Royal Office before Charlotte could get her thoughts in order. The fact that his apology hadn't sounded remotely sincere was something that got lost in a haze as she found herself once again momentarily mesmerised by his sheer athletic grace. He moved like no other man she'd ever seen—all coiled muscle and barely restrained sexual magnetism. It was an assault on her senses.

He looked over his shoulder from where he was pouring dark golden liquid into a bulbous glass. 'Can I get you anything?'

Charlotte's throat suddenly felt as dry as the surrounding desert and she said, 'Just water, please, if you have it.'

He came back towards her, holding out a glass of iced water, and once again Charlotte was struck by his sheer physicality. She reached for the glass and their fingers touched. A raw jolt of electricity shot up her arm, making her accept it jerkily. She immediately raised it to her mouth to give herself something to do, feeling as if she was floundering. She didn't like it.

Sheikh Al-Noury indicated the chair from which she'd only just picked up her bag, intending to leave.

'Please, take a seat, Mrs McQuillan.'

He walked around to the other side of his desk and sat down, lifting his feet carelessly onto the desk-top and crossing them at the ankle. Charlotte's eyes grew wide at this less than respectful pose, and she forgot his offer to take a seat. Right now all he was missing was a half-naked showgirl sitting in his lap.

He swirled the drink in his glass and took a sip before looking at her and raising a brow. 'I presume from the expression on your face that I'm about to get my first lesson in diplomacy and etiquette?'

Charlotte dragged her horrified gaze away from the very battered soles of his boots. There were dark stains that looked and smelt suspiciously like animal waste, and as her gaze clashed with that painfully blue one she said frigidly, 'It is generally considered an insult of varying proportions to expose the soles of your feet to a guest anywhere in the world.'

The man did nothing for a long moment, and then he just shrugged minutely. 'Well, we are in *this* part of the world now—and, believe me, we have far more inventive ways of insulting people. Nevertheless, I will endeavour to refrain from insulting my etiquette advisor.'

He lifted his legs, which only drew Charlotte's attention to his thighs again, and then they were hidden from view under his desk. She felt the strangest twist in her belly. Almost a pang of regret. It angered her to be behaving so oddly.

That anger made her say through gritted teeth, 'I am much more than an "etiquette advisor", Sheikh Al-Noury. I am an expert in international relations and diplomacy, with a master's degree in Middle Eastern

Relations. I speak seven languages and I've just completed a successful assignment with King Alix Saint Croix, ensuring his smooth transition back onto the world stage after regaining his throne…'

Charlotte stopped and took a breath, slightly aghast at how much had just tumbled from her mouth.

Sheikh Al-Noury barely moved a muscle from his louche pose as he said, 'Mrs McQuillan—'

'And it's not *Mrs* McQuillan,' Charlotte snapped, feeling as if she was fraying from the inside out while this man remained utterly nonchalant. 'It's *Miss*.'

The sheikh's bright gaze dropped down over her upper body and back up, making Charlotte feel hot all over and yet as if she'd suddenly been found wanting. He'd obviously come to some unflattering conclusion about her single status.

He looked at her and said, with an almost infinitesimal twitching at the corner of his sensual mouth, 'Quite. Forgive me for the error. I'm afraid I'd just assumed…' He sat up straighter then, and pointed to the chair on the other side of his desk. 'Please, sit down, Miss McQuillan. You're making me nervous, looming over me like that.'

Charlotte doubted anything would make this man remotely nervous, and to her disgust felt perilously close to wanting to stamp her foot and storm out. Did he have to make her feel like an admonishing parent? And why should that be pricking at her insides like a hot poker?

Charlotte's habitual cool head was irritatingly elusive. She'd never been so aware of herself. She knew that she presented a slightly conservative front, but in her business it was paramount to appear at all times elegant and refined. Giving no cause for possible offence or provocation.

She reluctantly did as he'd bade and sat down, aware of her skirt feeling tight and the top button of her shirt digging into her throat. Clothes that had never felt restrictive before, now felt shrink-wrapped to her body.

He put the glass down on the desk and said, 'Look, your credentials are not in doubt. King Alix of Isle Saint Croix rang me himself to sing your praises. But the fact is that I did not look for your expertise. My brother hired you in spite of my protests. I would have told you before not to bother coming, but I'm afraid I got caught up in ensuring my business concerns are attended to in my absence. However, I will be more than happy to ensure your return to the UK immediately, and of course you will receive full payment in recompense.'

This man's casual disregard for who and what she was made Charlotte's hackles rise. As did his arrogant assumption that she would be so easily dismissed.

She pointed out with faux sweetness, 'As it was your brother who hired me, then I'm afraid he is the only one who has the power to terminate this contract.'

Sheikh Al-Noury immediately scowled, but it only enhanced the wickedly beautiful symmetry of his features. His gaze narrowed on her and she stopped herself from fidgeting.

'Are you seriously telling me that you would prefer to stay here in this landlocked sandpit of a country, in a city that is routinely plunged into darkness when the archaic electricity infrastructure fails, rather than be at home amongst your first-world comforts enjoying all of the festivities of the season? My coronation is due to take place a couple of days before Christmas, Miss McQuillan, and if you stay I can't guarantee that you'll make it home in time. You might not be married, but I'm sure there's someone who is expecting your…company.'

It took Charlotte a few precious seconds to assimilate everything he was saying, but what caught at her gut was the way he'd hesitated over the word *company,* as if he'd had to find a diplomatic—*ha!*—way of suggesting that there might be someone waiting for her.

Next she registered his obvious disdain for his inherited kingdom—*this landlocked sandpit of a country.* True, there was something pitilessly unrelenting about the sea of sand on all sides of this ancient city, but Charlotte had felt a quickening of something deep in her soul—an urge to go out and explore, knowing from her research and studies of this region that it hid treasures not immediately apparent.

Collecting her wits, she said coolly, 'I'm not in the habit of reneging on agreements, Sheikh Al-Noury, and it would be unprofessional in the extreme for me to walk away at this early stage. As for your kind concern about my missing Christmas, I can assure you that I have no particular desire or need to return in time for the holiday. In fact, it suits me perfectly well to be here right now.'

Salim looked at the woman on the other side of his desk—more than a little taken aback. He was used to issuing an order, or, in this case a very polite suggestion—and having it obeyed. But she was not walking out of his office as he'd fully intended—who wouldn't take pay for nothing?—instead she was sitting opposite him as straight and upright as a haughty ballet dancer, staring at him with eyes the kind of green he'd only ever seen in Scotland, on one of those ethereally misty days. Distracting. Irritating.

She wasn't remotely his type, so why was he noticing her eyes? Salim preferred his women a lot more *deshabillée,* accessible and amenable. Everything about her, from her shining cap of neatly bobbed shoulder-length hair to her pristine dark grey suit and light grey blouse, screamed control and order—constraints Salim had rebelled against for so long now that he couldn't remember a time when he *hadn't* wanted to upset the status quo.

And yet…much to his irritation…he couldn't help noticing the fact that her surprisingly lush mouth was at odds with her cool demeanour, making him wonder what other lushness might be hiding under her oh-so-prim and neat exterior.

His gaze dropped to the bow at her throat and he imagined tugging on one silken length—would her whole shirt fall open? As he watched, the silky material moved more rapidly over her chest, as if she was breathing quickly, and when Salim glanced up again her cheeks had a slight telltale flush.

He was well inured to the signs of attraction in women, but it was patently evident that this woman didn't welcome it. Which was a total novelty.

When he caught her eye again he almost felt the blast of ice along with an accusatory light. She definitely didn't like being attracted to him.

This intrigued him more than he cared to admit—as did her assertion that she didn't mind missing Christmas. But he curbed the impulse to ask her why. He avoided asking women searching questions.

Salim cursed himself and shifted in his chair to ease the sudden constriction in his pants. To find himself reacting to a woman who desired him but looked at him as if he was a naughty schoolboy was galling.

He forced his body back under control and stood up. Her gaze lingered around his chest area for a moment before rising. She stood up too—hurriedly. He had a sense that she was usually more composed—if that was possible—than she was now and that thought gave him some perverse pleasure.

'You're determined to see out your contract, then?'

She nodded. 'Yes.'

'How long did my dear brother hire you for?'

'Until the coronation takes place. He said that if you require my services after that you can extend the contract yourself.'

Salim thought to himself that as he had no intention of staying in his role as king for long that would be highly unlikely, but he desisted from sharing that information with a complete stranger.

'As you wish,' he said. 'If you really want to stay in this sand-blown place—'

'Oh, but I think it's beautiful...' She stopped, her cheeks going pink. 'I mean, from what I've seen so far. It's run down, yes, but one can see the potential.'

Salim arched a brow and ignored the pulse in his blood seeing this small glimpse of something like passion. 'Can one?'

Her green eyes flashed. Once again Salim found himself a little mesmerised by the vivid emotions crossing her face. He couldn't remember meeting a woman so lacking in artifice. And then something in him hardened. Was he losing his mind? All women wanted something from him—even this one.

Maybe she just wanted the kudos of working for him—it would certainly elevate her professional standing to be the one who had wrangled Sheikh Salim Al-Noury into accepting his crown and toeing the line like a good little king.

He thought of something and folded his arms. 'Aren't you worried that by being associated with me you'll taint your reputation?'

She tipped up her chin. 'I am here to see that that doesn't happen, Sheikh Al-Noury, and I'm very good at my job.'

For a second he stood in stunned silence, and then he couldn't stop a smile—a genuine smile—from curving his mouth upwards. It had been so long since anyone had exhibited such confidence in front of him. And a lack of awe that was as refreshing as it was slightly insulting.

She frowned. 'If you're going to make fun of me—'

Salim shook his head. 'I wouldn't dare, Miss McQuillan. I'd be afraid you'd put me over your knee and spank me for being naughty.'

The colour deepened in her cheeks, as if she was having trouble controlling her temper and Salim *almost*, but not quite, regretted goading her like this.

But then she recovered and reached for her case. She avoided his eye. 'If that's all for now, Sheikh Al-Noury, I think I'd like to settle in and get acquainted with my surroundings.'

He put out a hand. 'By all means. Let me show you to your room.'

She preceded him out of the Royal Office. She was taller than he'd initially registered. The top of her head would come to just under his chin. Her body would stand tantalisingly flush against his in heels. But if she wasn't wearing heels… Once again sexual interest flared in his groin and he scowled. She was buttoned up to within an inch of her life. Since when had he found *prim* attractive?

Charlotte was burningly aware of Sheikh Al-Noury close behind her, and it made her tense—even though she knew that he wasn't remotely interested in her in that way. She was sure he didn't taunt women he found attractive and suggest they might put him over their knee, which had caused all manner of completely inappropriate images to flood her mind.

The man was so charismatic, he could probably make an inanimate object feel something.

He led her away from the office down a long, imposing corridor. She'd only seen a handful of staff so far, which added to the surreal sense of the whole palace being in a state of arrested development.

Salim glanced at her when she'd caught up with his long-legged stride and she said, 'I'm surprised the palace is so quiet. Is there only a skeleton staff because no one has been in residence for so long?'

Sheikh Al-Noury stopped, causing Charlotte to come to a halt too. 'There is minimal staff today because it's a national holiday—don't tell me you missed that in your research?'

She *had* missed that pertinent detail, and now she felt foolish after spouting off all her qualifications.

'Don't worry,' he drawled, striding off again, 'I'll make sure someone attends to you and brings you food. Tomorrow you'll be assigned a maid—'

'That's really not necessary,' Charlotte protested as she started after him. She was aware of the customs here, but wasn't comfortable at the thought of someone waiting on her.

'It's how things are done, Ms McQuillan,' the sheikh pointed out. 'If you insist on staying then you will abide by our ways.'

Charlotte stopped for a moment, surprised that in this he seemed to be happy that customs were adhered to, but she had to keep going when he showed no signs of slowing down and was about to disappear around a corner. She wouldn't put it past him to leave her lost in this vast palace. It couldn't be more obvious that he'd prefer to be putting her on the next flight home.

She longed to be able to stop and explore as they passed intriguing-looking courtyards with colourful mosaics and ornate fountains. They rounded another corner and Charlotte jumped when a peacock appeared in their path, as nonchalant as if they were intruding on its turf, its long and vibrantly coloured tail trailing behind it.

Sheikh Al-Noury stepped around it and kept going. Charlotte felt disorientated. She'd built a picture of this man in her mind that had been based on lurid headlines:

Playboy Sheikh opens new nightclub in Monte Carlo!

Al-Noury triples fortune overnight by floating new social media messaging site!

And, while he wasn't doing much to dispel that image with his appearance or attitude, he didn't seem as...shallow as Charlotte might have expected.

They came to a set of huge double doors at the end of the corridor. Sheikh Al-Noury opened them and stood back to let her precede him. When Charlotte stepped over the threshold she sucked in a breath. This was a different palace. One that hadn't been frozen in time and left to crumble to pieces.

It was a suite containing numerous rooms, each one covered in exquisite Persian carpets. The furnishings were sumptuous and sensual—dark reds and purples. A little over the top for her tastes, but effortlessly regal. There was a private dining area, and a living room that led into a palatial en-suite bedroom dominated by a four-poster bed.

She avoided looking at that, acutely aware of the man only feet away and how he might be observing her reaction and somehow judging her. She'd never felt so conscious of being a woman before. And a woman who was lacking.

The room was pleasantly cool, thanks to the air-conditioning, and there were floor-to-ceiling windows and French doors that led out onto a private terrace, complete with a decorative swimming pool.

She turned around to face her reluctant host. 'These rooms are beautiful, but I'd be quite happy in something less…luxurious.'

He waved a dismissive hand. 'These are usually reserved for my mother's use, and they were decorated to her specifications, but as she won't be visiting any time soon you are welcome to use them.'

There was a distinctly chilly tone to his voice and Charlotte said, 'Not even for your coronation?'

Sheikh Al-Noury's face became shuttered. 'She knows she's not welcome here while I'm in residence.'

Charlotte couldn't claim much of a relationship with either of her parents, but the cold tone of Sheikh Al-Noury's voice shocked her. 'But isn't this her homeland?'

He responded curtly. 'It was.'

He backed away then, and suddenly Charlotte had an irrational fear of being left alone in this seemingly empty palace. In truth, it wasn't a totally irrational fear because she'd had plenty of experience being left to her own devices, with only a nanny and staff for company in big houses, but she refused to think of her own demons now.

She'd already revealed too much by admitting she had no desire to be at home for Christmas. Not that he'd shown much interest in why that might be. Not that she wanted him to show interest she told herself fervently. So she said nothing.

He was almost at the door when he turned back and said, 'Please, make yourself comfortable. I'll instruct someone to bring you some dinner.'

So she was to be consigned to her rooms.

But then he added, 'Do feel free to explore… I must warn you, though, that it is perilously easy to get lost in this place, so don't stray too far. The palace library is on this corridor, if you go left when you step outside.'

Just before he disappeared Charlotte blurted out, 'Sheikh Al-Noury?'

He turned around, his hand on the door. 'Yes?'

For a moment her mind went dismayingly blank at the way he so effortlessly dominated even this vast room, but she forced herself to focus and said, 'I'm not here to be a nuisance… I am actually here to try and help ease your transition into becoming king.'

She could see his jaw clench from where she stood, and he said, 'Miss McQuillan, you wouldn't be here if it had been up to me. The last thing I need is an expert in diplomacy. But you are here, and I suspect you're going to prove to be a nuisance whether you intend to or not, so you can start by calling me Salim. The way you say Sheikh Al-Noury makes me feel old.'

Before Charlotte could respond to that, or object to the way he insisted on calling *her* Miss McQuillan, as if she were a headmistress, he said, 'I'll have someone bring you some food, and I suggest that in the mean-time we stay out of each other's way.'

CHAPTER TWO

CHARLOTTE WATCHED THE door close on the most infuriating man she'd ever met, not to mention the most disturbing, and she had to quell a childish urge to hurl something at the door behind him. Instead she kicked off her shoes and paced back and forth on the sumptuous silken rugs.

She fumed. She was used to dealing with clients who thought they knew everything about international relations and diplomacy until something blew up in their faces, and then suddenly Charlotte became their most valuable asset. But she'd never encountered such downright…antipathy before.

She was patently unwelcome—and she could call him Salim but he wouldn't deign to call her Charlotte. She thought about that for a moment and felt a frisson run down her spine at the thought of his tongue wrapping itself around her name. That little frisson was humiliating, because it was glaringly obvious that he didn't view her as female—more as an asexual irritation.

Sheikh Al-Noury was affecting her in a way that she hadn't experienced before, because she was good at keeping people at a distance and yet from the first moment they'd met he'd slid under her skin with disconcerting ease.

Charlotte shucked off her jacket and undid the bow at her neck and her top button. Then, spying her bags in the bedroom near the dressing room, she set about unpacking. She found herself dwelling on the animosity the sheikh had demonstrated towards his mother. She didn't like the way it resonated within her, reminding her of her own fractured relationship with her mother, brought on by years of careless parenting after a bitter divorce.

But she diverted her mind away from wondering too much about anything personal to do with the sheikh. It wasn't her business. And the last thing she wanted to think about was her own pitiful family history.

After taking a refreshing shower in the lavish bathroom, Charlotte changed into stretchy pants and a soft long-sleeved top. Just as her stomach rumbled she heard a knock on the door. Her gut clenched as she imagined it might be him, but when she opened the door there was a young girl, with a trolley full of food and wine in an ice bucket on the other side.

She admonished herself; he'd hardly be delivering her dinner.

Charlotte stood back to let the girl in and watched as she silently laid the dining table for one and set out the food. Tantalising scents filled the air and her stomach rumbled louder. The girl scurried out again, too shy to return Charlotte's smile.

Charlotte sat down to explore what she'd been given. Balls of rice mixed with herbs. Lamb infused with spices and scented rice. Flat bread with hummus. It looked delicious and she found that she was ravenous.

She ate as dusk fell outside, not noticing it had got dark until she stood up and went to the window with her wine glass in her hand, feeling a little more settled after an unsettling day.

She opened the French doors and was surprised to find that it was much cooler than she'd expected—and then she chastised herself: basic geography, of course it got cold in the desert at night. She fetched a cashmere wrap and then went back outside, sitting on a seat, relishing the peace.

The thought of the vast expanse of empty desert surrounding her made a thrum of excitement pulse in her blood. She'd always found this part of the world fascinating, hence her choice of master's degree. The stars were so low and bright in the dark sky she imagined she could reach out and pluck one into her hand.

Tabat intrigued her.

And so does its enigmatic ruler, whispered a voice.

Charlotte scowled and took a sip of wine, telling herself that Sheikh Al-Noury—*Salim*—didn't intrigue her at all. He was thoroughly charmless and clearly reluctant to change his hedonistic existence before becoming king.

He didn't intrigue her because she knew his type all too well. As the only child of two high-profile parents, who had used her as an unwitting pawn in their bitter divorce and custody battle, she recognised the traits of a selfish person who was here under sufferance. After all, when her father had lost in the custody battle with her mother he'd always let it be known that her visits with him had been something he'd done purely out of legal obligation, not because he really cared for her, so she was in far too familiar territory.

However, she wouldn't let her own personal feelings intrude on her professional life. She'd worked too hard to separate herself from her parents and that time. She'd even changed her name, vowing to live a life much different from theirs, which was smack at the centre of the public eye.

She'd built an independent life and a reputation based on her intellect—not her name or the infamy associated with it. She had a strong desire never to be at the mercy of anyone else again, to the point that she'd instinctively avoided intimate relationships, too afraid of letting someone close enough to devastate her world as her parents had.

Diverting her mind away from her past, she assured herself that all she had to do was make sure the sheikh didn't cause an international scandal in the run-up to his coronation, which was due to take place in three weeks. And then, once the man had been crowned king, Charlotte could walk away and hopefully never see him again.

So why did she find her mind wandering back to him now? Wondering where he was in this vast and largely empty palace?

Then she cursed her naivety as a wave of embarrassment made her feel hot. He had surely not denied himself the pleasures of a mistress. A man like that? He'd left his life of excess in Europe and the States, to return to take up his rightful place, but he'd hardly have denied himself his base comforts, and sex and women were one of his most well-documented pastimes. And only the most beautiful women at that—albeit never for long.

Charlotte shook her head and stood up, returning to her suite. She told herself firmly that she couldn't care less if Sheikh Salim was entertaining a harem of mistresses right now as long as he was discreet about it.

The fact that it took her ages to fall asleep in the huge bed, only for her dreams to be populated by a mysteriously masked and robed man on a huge stallion cantering across vast desert sands, was a pure coincidence. And not disturbing in the slightest.

Not even when she had to concede when she woke the following morning that he hadn't really been mysterious at all. Not with those blue eyes.

A week later

'Sire, we are so grateful that you are here, finally. There is so much work to do in two weeks! And then, once you are king—'

Salim turned around abruptly from where he'd been trying to tune out his chief aide, stopping the man's words. They caused a sensation not unlike panic in his chest and Salim did not panic.

His aide—an old man who had known his grandfather—looked at him expectantly. Salim said tightly, 'Do whatever it is that you deem necessary, Rafa. You know more about this place than me, after all.'

The slightest flare of something in those old eyes was the only hint that his aide was not impressed that it had taken Salim so long to take up his role, or that he'd spent most of the last week out of Tabat.

Salim told himself that part of his motivation for leaving Tabat behind for a few days hadn't had anything to do with Charlotte McQuillan and her big green eyes looking at him so incisively. Not unlike the way Rafa was looking at him right now.

It had actually had to do with the secret meetings he'd set up with his legal team, and a close friend who ruled a nearby sultanate, to discuss who best to approach to take over from him as king once he'd abdicated.

The meetings hadn't gone well. The one person he

and his team had identified as a suitable prospective king had turned them down flat. A distant cousin of Salim's, Riad Arnaud.

The man was a billionaire and a respected businessman. He had ancestral links to this world and had inherited a tiny uninhabited Sheikhdom on the borders of Tabat and Jandor—a mining hub that workers commuted in and out of from nearby Jandor.

But, he was also a single father with a young daughter and he was adamant that he didn't want to turn his life upside down, thrusting her into a life of duty and service and taking her away from her home in France, where they lived.

Salim of all people had to respect his cousin's decision, after all, he knew the consequences of having choice taken away from you.

His friend Sultan Sadiq of Al-Omar had borne the brunt of Salim's frustration once his team had left.

When he'd finished extolling the potential virtues of Tabat that would be enjoyed by its next king his friend had just looked at him with an arched brow and asked mockingly, 'If it's such a hidden jewel then why are you so eager to pass it up?'

The fact that his friend's question had caused Salim to stop momentarily was not something he wanted to dwell on. Nor was the fact that it had made him recall Charlotte McQuillan's assessment that Tabat had potential. This was not his destiny and he would not be swayed.

In a bid to deflect his mind from that incident and from his conscience, which was proving to be dismayingly persistent, Salim asked, 'Miss McQuillan…where is she now?'

Rafa's eyes lit up. He was clearly anticipating that

Salim was finally ready to seek advice on becoming a good king. But Salim had far more carnal urges on his mind than discussions of diplomacy and he didn't like it. She wasn't his type.

Even with a vast desert between them he'd found the image of her green eyes staying with him, along with the provocative image of that damned silk bow tied so primly at her throat.

Rafa interrupted Salim's thoughts when he answered, 'She wanted to go sightseeing today, so I sent one of my junior assistants with her. They've gone to the *wadi* just outside the city limits.'

Salim frowned, his irritation increasing for no good reason. 'Which junior assistant went with her?'

Rafa looked nervous. 'Kdal, sire. He's one of my most trusted assistants—I assure you he'll take care of her.'

Picturing the young man's prettily handsome face and obsequious manner in his mind's eye, Salim found himself saying, 'Instruct the groom to get my horse ready.'

Charlotte was doing her best not to stand with her mouth hanging open, but it was hard in such a jaw-droppingly beautiful location. The *wadi* was just outside Tabat City—a deep river valley carved out of the earth. A sheer high wall of rock was on one side, dotted with palm trees at the base. The other side was flat and verdant, and obviously a popular beauty spot, although it was quiet today.

Kdal, her attentive guide, had explained that this *wadi* was always full of water due to the underground streams. The water looked green and all too inviting in the blazing midday heat.

Kdal was now guiding her over to where a makeshift table had been set up, under a tent that offered some much needed shade.

'We're having lunch here?' she asked, charmed by the idea, and also by the delicious smells coming from where a small cluster of rustic buildings stood.

'Yes, Miss McQuillan. We thought you'd enjoy the view. This is a well-known spot for travellers to stop and seek refreshment. I hope you don't think it's too basic...'

Charlotte was about to respond *not at all* but then suddenly Kdal disappeared from her eyeline and Charlotte looked down to see him prostrated at her feet. She was about to bend down and see if he'd fainted when she heard a sound behind her, and turned to see a mythically huge black stallion on top of which sat a man with a turban covering his head and face. He wore a long robe.

It was so reminiscent of her dreams that Charlotte wondered if she was suffering from sunstroke—and then the man swung his leg over and stepped gracefully off the horse, which snorted and gave a shake of its massive head.

All Charlotte could see, though, was the bright flash of blue eyes. Far too familiar blue eyes. *Sheikh Al-Noury.* Her pulse tripped and galloped at double-time.

He pulled down the material covering his mouth and said with a glint in his eye, 'You don't look very enthusiastic to have me join you for lunch.'

It *was* him. She wasn't dreaming.

A man appeared, seemingly from out of thin air, to lead the sheikh's stallion away, and she saw a sleek blacked out four-by-four vehicle purring to a stop nearby, presumably carrying his security detail.

Charlotte called on all her skills to recover, and said

as equably as she could, 'Well, if you recall, you told me that you believed my presence would be a nuisance and that you intended for us to stay out of each other's way—hardly leading me to suspect that you'd seek out my company.'

He didn't look remotely repentant. He looked breathtakingly gorgeous as he lazily pulled the turban off his head. Dark hair curled wildly from where it had been confined under his turban, and his jaw was even more stubbled than she remembered. He was wearing the jodhpurs again, and the long tunic did little to disguise the sheer masculine power of his body.

Charlotte hated that she was wearing pretty much the same outfit she'd been wearing the first time she'd seen him.

As if reading her mind, his gaze slipped down from her face and he asked, 'Do you own a similar shirt in every colour of the rainbow, Miss McQuillan?'

Defensively Charlotte answered, 'No, actually. But I find that in my line of work it's prudent to be smartly dressed at all times, and I'm mindful of not offending anyone by wearing anything too casual or revealing.'

His eyes met hers, and she could have sworn his mouth twitched.

'No, that wouldn't do at all.'

He gestured to the table behind them, and when she turned she saw that it was now miraculously set for two, with gleaming silverware and sparkling glasses on a white tablecloth. Kdal had disappeared, the little traitor.

'Please sit, Miss McQuillan.'

She sat down, feeling on edge, cursing Kdal for not warning her to expect the sheikh, who sat down opposite her. Even though they were out in the open air it suddenly felt claustrophobic.

Muted sounds came from the direction of the small cluster of buildings. There was an air of urgency that hadn't been there a few minutes before. The sheikh had clearly injected the *wadi* staff with adrenalin.

He took a sip of water and said, 'I'm sure you've noticed a change in the palace since the first day you arrived.'

Charlotte looked at him and had to admit, 'It's like a different place.'

When she'd woken up on her first morning and gone for an exploratory walk the place had gone from being eerily empty to buzzing with activity.

She said, 'I didn't realise the national holiday was to commemorate the anniversary of your grandfather's death. I'm sorry.'

The sheikh shrugged. 'Don't be. I hardly knew him. He died when I was a teenager.'

'So there's been a caretaker government here since then, until your father passed away?'

He nodded, and just then a waiter materialised, dressed in a pristine white tunic. The sheikh issued a stream of Arabic too fast for Charlotte to understand, and when the waiter had left he turned back to her.

'I hope you don't mind—I've ordered a few local delicacies.'

Charlotte narrowed her eyes at him across the table, suspecting strongly that this man would ride roughshod over anyone who let him. 'Actually, I prefer to order for myself, but I'm not a fussy eater.'

He sat back, that twitch at the corner of his mouth more obvious now.

'Duly noted, Miss McQuillan. Tell me, is that a Scottish name?'

He threw her with his question, and Charlotte busied herself unfolding her napkin in a bid not to let him see how easily an innocent question like that rattled her. Because it wasn't the name she'd been born with. It was her maternal grandmother's name.

'I…yes. It's Scots-Irish.' And then, before he could ask her more questions, she said, 'I had a tour of the city this morning with Kdal. He was very informative.'

She stopped when she saw something flash across the sheikh's face but it was quickly replaced with a very urbane expression, and he said, 'Please, tell me your impressions—after all, you did say that you thought it had much potential.'

Charlotte looked at him suspiciously, thinking he was mocking her, but his expression appeared innocent. Well, as innocent as a sinfully gorgeous reprobate could look.

'Well, obviously it needs a lot of work to restore it, but I found it fascinating. I had no idea how far back some of the buildings date. The mosque is breathtaking, and I hadn't expected to see a cathedral too.'

Sheikh Al-Noury took a sip of the white wine that had been poured into their glasses. 'The city has always been a multi-faith society—one of the most liberal in the region. Outside the city limits, however, the country runs on more traditional tribal lines. Tabat used to run all the way to the sea. Jahor, the capital of Jandor, was merely a military fortress until its warriors rose up and rebelled, creating a separate independent state and endless years of war. Tabat is where all the ancient treasures reside. And all the knowledge. We have a library that rivalled the one at Alexandria, in Egypt, before it was destroyed.'

Another waiter arrived with an array of food as Charlotte responded dryly, 'Yes, I've spent some time in the library this week—it's very impressive.'

The sheikh—she still couldn't think of him as *Salim*—gestured to the food. 'Please, help yourself. We don't really have a starter course.'

Charlotte felt self-conscious as she picked a little from each plate and added it to her own. She had to admit that she loved the Tabat cuisine as she tried a special bread that was baked with minced lamb, onions and tomatoes. Halloumi cheese and honey was another staple she was becoming addicted to. At this rate she'd have nothing to show for her time here except added inches to her waistline.

She watched Sheikh Al-Noury covertly from under her lashes, but he caught her looking and she could feel heat climb into her cheeks.

'You're not drinking your wine?' he observed.

She shook her head. 'I prefer not to when I'm working.'

He picked up his glass and tipped it towards her. 'I commend your professionalism. I, however, feel no similar urge to maintain appearances.' He took a healthy sip.

Feeling emboldened by his seeming determination to goad her, she said, 'I heard you have been away for most of the week.'

He put his glass down and his gaze narrowed on her. 'Yes. I was invited to the Sultan of Al-Omar's annual party in B'harani. He's an old friend.'

An image immediately sprang into her mind of the sheikh surrounded by beautiful women, and when she replied her voice sounded unintentionally sharp. 'I've heard of them… His parties are renowned for being impossible to get into, and they dominate the gossip columns for weeks afterwards, but there are never any pictures.'

'Yes,' he said, almost wistfully. 'That was in the good old days. But it's all changed now that he's a married man with children.'

'You don't approve, Sheikh Al-Noury?' Charlotte asked with faux innocence, almost enjoying herself now.

Those blue eyes pierced right through her. 'I thought I told you to call me Salim. And my friend Sadiq can do as he pleases. Every man seems to fall sooner or later.'

Charlotte ignored the little dart of emotion that surprised her, at the thought of this man falling for someone. 'Won't you have to...*fall* too? You'll be expected to take a queen and produce heirs once you are crowned king.'

Salim surveyed the woman opposite him, in another of those tantalising silk shirts with the damned bow that had haunted his dreams. Maybe she did it on purpose—projected this buttoned-up secretary image specifically to appeal to a man's desire to see her come undone.

It irritated him intensely that not one of the many beautiful women at Sadiq's party had managed to snare his interest. His old carousing friend had slapped him on the back and joked that he was becoming jaded. And then Sadiq's very pretty wife had joined them and whispered something in her husband's ear that had made him look at her so explicitly that even Salim, who was pretty unshockable, had felt uncomfortable.

When they'd made pathetically flimsy excuses and left, he'd silently wished them well in their obvious happy domesticity, while repeating his own refrain that he would never be snared like that. Because to commit oneself to another person was to risk untold pain.

When he'd lost his sister the grief had been so acute that for a long time he'd wanted to die too. After he'd passed through that dark phase and emerged on the other side he'd never wanted to love anyone again. It was simply too devastating. Loss had eaten away at his soul until there had been nothing left but a need to escape from the world that had brought him such pain and avenge his sister's death—which he had done.

Not that it had brought him any peace.

Angry to find his thoughts straying down this path, Salim said tersely in response to her question, 'No, Miss McQuillan, I won't have to *fall*.'

He felt an overwhelming urge to unsettle this woman who looked so pristine. So in control. So…unaffected.

'Because,' he said carefully, 'I have no intention of being King of Tabat for any longer than absolutely necessary.'

Shock bloomed across her expressive face, exactly as he'd expected, but it failed to bring any measure of satisfaction and that irritated Salim intensely.

She sat up. 'What do you mean? You're being crowned in two weeks—of course you'll be king.'

'Not for long,' he said grimly, regretting having said anything.

She shook her head, the shining cap of strawberry-blonde hair distracting him for a moment. She was so pale against this exotic backdrop. He imagined his darkness against her pale perfection…

'What on earth are you talking about?'

Her cut-glass tones enflamed Salim's arousal instead of dousing it. Only his friend Sadiq and his legal team knew of his plans. He shouldn't have said anything to this woman, who was still a relative stranger…and yet he relished the easing of a weight off his shoulders.

'I'm going to abdicate and ensure that a far more suitable person takes over as king in my place.' Even if the signs of finding that person weren't very encouraging.

Salim was mesmerised by the play of emotions over her face and he realised that she was quite beautiful. More beautiful for not being showy or wearing layers of make-up. She was obviously struggling to understand. He almost felt sorry for her.

'But…if you're intent on abdicating then why be crowned in the first place?'

'Because the country isn't entirely stable at the moment. There are tribal factions who want to see the city restored to a conservatism that hasn't existed for years. They've been growing stronger. If I was to walk away now it would create a vacuum, which they would use as an opportunity to storm the city and take over…there is a real danger of warfare.'

She glanced around them before whispering forcefully, 'But if you abdicate won't the same thing happen?'

Salim shook his head. 'By the time I abdicate I will ensure that whoever takes my place will be a force for good in the country. Someone who will command the respect of everyone and see the country into the future.'

She looked unimpressed and sat back, shaking her head. 'Isn't that meant to be you? Why would you do this when it's *your* destiny?'

Salim put down his napkin on the table, his skin prickling for exposing himself like this. 'You call being bred with calculated precision destiny? If it *was* destiny then my twin sister would be queen—she was born ten minutes before me—but because she was a girl and therefore deemed unsuitable, I was named the heir to the throne of Tabat.'

She looked at him, her face pale. 'You have a sister? I didn't realise...'

He curled his hand into a fist on the table and forced himself not to look away from that too-direct green gaze. 'She's dead. A long time ago.'

Charlotte felt the sheikh's—*Salim's*—tension. It crackled between them.

'I'm sorry, I didn't know... There was no mention...'

She was still reeling from what he'd just revealed about his plans as king...or non-plans. And that he'd had a sister.

'How did she die?'

Salim looked at her for a long moment, but Charlotte had the sense he wasn't seeing her. Then his focus narrowed to her again and she shivered.

'It doesn't matter how she died. She did. It's in the past now.'

But Charlotte had a very keen sense that it wasn't in the past at all. To change the subject a little, she pointed out, 'Your brother seems happy to accept his role.'

Salim's hand tightened around his napkin. 'My brother and I are very different people. I made my life far away from here. I have numerous business concerns around the world... I employ thousands of people. Are they worth any less than the people of Tabat?'

'No, of course not...but surely there is a way to run your businesses while also ruling Tabat?'

He inclined his head and his mouth tipped up slightly, as if mocking her. Charlotte felt heat rise. He was obviously finding her naive or clueless.

'I'm sure if I wanted to I could find a way, Miss McQuillan, but the truth is that I'm not prepared to make that sacrifice. Tabat deserves a committed and devoted ruler. I am not that man.'

Why? The word almost fell out of Charlotte's mouth, but she clawed it back at the last moment.

Salim sat back then, and said, 'I'm hosting a party in the palace this weekend. You are, of course, more than welcome. If you're still here.'

If you're still here.

Charlotte schooled her features, not liking the dart of hurt she felt that he was still intent on getting rid of her. 'Do you think the prospect of one of your infamous parties is enough to scare me off?'

He arched a brow. Supremely comfortable. Supremely dangerous. '*Infamous*? Please, do tell me what you've heard. I'm intrigued.'

She cursed her runaway mouth. 'That they're a byword in hedonism and last for days. The last party you hosted at an oasis in the Moroccan desert ended with several of the guests being airlifted to hospital.'

He shook his head. 'I hate to burst your righteously indignant bubble, Miss McQuillan, but contrary to what was reported the helicopter was for me, to take me to the airport in Marrakech so that I could make a meeting in Paris. Nothing more salacious than that. The party broke up a couple of days later of its own accord, and I can assure you that no one suffered anything more than sunburn and a hangover.'

Charlotte immediately felt like assuring him that she wasn't an avid follower of tabloid gossip and that she'd only read about it while researching him and Tabat, but she resisted. 'I told you, I've no intention of reneging on my contract.'

Salim shrugged and finished his wine. 'Suit yourself.'

Struggling to try and find some equilibrium again, some vague sense of being in control, Charlotte said,

'I really don't think that a similar party would go down well here—unless it's part of your plan to deliberately paint yourself in such a negative light that you think it'll make your abdication welcome.'

He considered her words for a long moment, and then said, 'Not a bad idea at all, Miss McQuillan. Are you sure you aren't in the PR field?'

Before she could answer he said, 'As much as your idea has some merit, I'm not as crass as that. The last thing I want is to portray Tabat in an unfavourable light. After all, I'm on a campaign to make it as desirable as possible. So, no, this party won't be featuring scenes of Bacchanalian debauchery, it'll be very civilised and elegant.'

Charlotte felt tight inside, and wasn't even sure where all this emotion was flowing from. 'So you're effectively advertising your kingdom to the highest bidder?'

His mouth tightened for a moment, before relaxing into its habitual sensual lines. 'Let's just say I'm taking an opportunity to showcase its allure and beauty.'

The waiter came then, and removed their plates.

When he'd left Salim sat forward and said, 'As I said, Miss McQuillan, you're more than welcome to join us. The dress code will be full evening dress.'

Charlotte could well imagine the haute couture finery at one of his parties and thought of her one very classic, but boring black evening-dress that would only reinforce whatever negative impression he'd already formed of her. She forced a fake smile. 'Unfortunately I don't have any such clothes with me. I'll have to decline your generous invitation.'

Salim stood up to leave. 'That's too bad, Miss McQuillan. I rather like the idea of seeing you dressed in something less…formal.'

That bright blue gaze dropped lazily down her body and back up again.

For a moment Charlotte couldn't breathe. A wave of heat scorched her from the inside out. And then humiliation swiftly doused the heat. Seeing her in a dress would have zero effect on him. He was mocking her. Toying with her.

She stood up unsteadily. He held out a hand to indicate that she should precede him, but when she went to move her foot slipped out of her shoe. The heel was stuck in the soft ground.

She let out a gasp and hopped on one foot, bending down to get her shoe, but before she could do so a large hand was plucking it up.

She looked at Salim, who was now straightening up and holding her very staid court shoe. It had never looked less sexy.

That burn was back inside her. Mortification mixing with awareness.

To Charlotte's shock he went down on one knee before her, and his expression was far too innocent when he looked up and said, 'Let's see if it fits, shall we?'

She was no Cinderella and he was not Prince Charming.

Her face was burning as she took a quick glance around the *wadi*. Thankfully there was no one to be seen. She looked down at Salim and hissed, 'I can put it on myself.'

He sighed. 'Miss McQuillan, I have no doubt you can put on your own shoe, but I am offering to do it for you—and, believe me, I don't make a habit of helping women dress. It's usually the reverse, so this is a novelty. Humour me.'

She would have happily strangled him right then. She

put her foot out reluctantly and waited. She tensed herself, not even sure what she was tensing herself against, and when he cupped her heel in his other hand she wobbled precariously.

Because his touch will destroy you, a small voice said.

He looked up at her and his eyes seemed to have darkened, but she told herself it was her imagination. Feeling ridiculous and exposed, she tried to pull her foot away but his hold tightened. He slowly let her heel slide into the shoe, and to Charlotte's eternal embarrassment it was the single most erotic thing she'd ever experienced. Electric tingles went all the way up her bare legs, straight to her groin. Her nipples tightened.

Just when she thought she would be free he didn't let her go. His hand was warm on her calf, and for a crazy moment Charlotte imagined it travelling up her leg to the back of her thigh, where— She abruptly pulled her foot free of Salim's hands—successfully this time—horrified at where her mind had gone. She stood back and watched as he rose fluidly to his full height.

It must be second nature for him to toy with women as if they were playthings. And none better than her—gauche, and as far from his usual women as could be possible.

'Thank you,' she said tightly. 'But it was completely unnecessary.' She picked up her bag, avoiding his eye, and made her way out from under the shade of the tented structure. Staff appeared, bowing to their future king.

Little did they know, Charlotte thought to herself.

The man who had taken the horse away reappeared now, leading the huge animal. Instinctively Charlotte moved away—but then she felt a hand on her lower back and stopped dead. Salim was beside her, wicked devilry dancing in his eyes.

'I could offer you a ride back to the palace, if you like? It's a beautiful way to see the country.'

Charlotte imagined sitting in front of him on this horse, with his hand splayed across her belly, her bottom tucked far too close between his legs, and a tsunami of fresh awareness sizzled through her body.

She moved aside jerkily, out of his reach. 'No, thank you. I'm sure Kdal isn't far away, and he will take me back.'

'As you wish, Miss McQuillan. If you change your mind about the party do let me know. I'm sure we can find something suitable for you to wear.'

Inexplicably—because right then Charlotte was telling herself that one of his parties was the last place she'd ever want to be seen—she found herself yearning to be the kind of woman who could walk into a crowded room and have this man stop in his tracks because he was so captivated by her…

She cursed herself. What was wrong with her today?

Salim did something with the stirrups on his horse, adjusting them, and then with enviably athletic ease vaulted onto the horse's back. He wound the turban back onto his head, covering all that dark hair, and just before he pulled a piece back over his mouth he said, 'See you soon, Miss McQuillan.'

And then, with a flash of those blue eyes that seared right into her, he and the horse turned in one graceful fluid motion and he was gone, leaving nothing behind but swirling dust. Just to add to Charlotte's general feeling of dishevelment and inadequacy.

It got worse when she found her way to the small but functional toilet behind the catering area and looked at herself in the cracked mirror. She groaned out loud. Her hair was frizzy from the humidity and her nose was suspiciously red.

She'd just sat through lunch with that man looking like a scarecrow. A sun-burned scarecrow.

Damn him anyway.

CHAPTER THREE

'Cassidy is far too beautiful for you, my friend.' But even as Salim said the words they rang hollow. Even though they were true.

His cousin's lover stood a few feet away, talking to a small group. She was tall and striking, with dark red hair piled high on her head. A black sheath of a dress set off her pale skin and thoroughbred curves. She was one of the world's most sought after supermodels.

Riad Arnaud, who Salim had invited to the party in a somewhat futile attempt to entice his friend to reconsider his decision regarding becoming king, responded with a distinct bite to his voice, 'She's not available.'

Salim turned to the other man, who was dressed in a classic black tuxedo, as he was, and whistled softly. 'It's not like you to be possessive. Maybe there's another reason you don't relish the thought of leaving your life in France behind to become a king. Is she different, then? Are you going to succumb to a life of domesticity, like my brother and everyone else we know?'

He couldn't quite keep his voice as light as he'd intended.

Riad made a snorting sound. 'I've paid my domestic penance, as you well know, and the only good thing to come out of that situation was my beautiful daughter.

She's all I need. I will never let another woman close enough to cause havoc in my life again—they can't be trusted.'

They both heard a small sound and turned to see Riad's lover, Cassidy, with her hand to her mouth. Clearly she'd heard everything. Her eyes were huge and very blue. She turned abruptly and walked away.

Riad cursed colourfully and Salim watched him stride after his mistress. Salim shook his head at his cousin's folly—clearly the man was more involved than he wanted to admit.

Something twisted in his gut as he took in the ceremonial ballroom where he would be crowned in two weeks. The scene before him was a glittering, sumptuous exercise in promoting Tabat as a desirable kingdom.

His staff had worked tirelessly to bring the palace up to a standard it hadn't seen in a long time. Rafa had been so pleased and excited, seeing it as proof that Salim was about to turn the country's fortunes around.

The twisting in Salim's gut intensified as his conscience bit hard and a pair of familiar green eyes came into his mind. Eyes that he couldn't get *out* of his mind.

He turned around, irritation and frustration making his skin prickle. Would she turn up? Would she wear the dress he'd sent to her room after he'd heard nothing from her?

The prickling intensified and he looked towards the main door just in time to see her arrive. As if he'd conjured her up with his sheer will to see her.

Adrenaline surged in his blood as his far too avid gaze swept her from head to toe. And, even though she'd defied him, he couldn't stop the smile curling his mouth upwards or the raging heat in his body as he stalked to where she stood, willing that green gaze that had been haunting him to meet his…

Charlotte stood inside the main door to the ballroom and instantly felt like an utter fool. *She should have put on the dress.*

The dress that had been delivered to her room earlier that day. The most exquisite dress she'd ever seen. Green silk…strapless.

She'd held it up and the material had dropped to the floor with a whisper of expensive fabric. She had imagined how it would mould to her body. Emphasising curves she didn't even have and hiding any flaws and imperfections.

She had imagined how she would feel… As if she was the kind of woman who could walk into a room and have men look at her. Desire her.

One man in particular.

As that thought had entered her head she'd let the dress fall back onto the bed, aghast at how instantly it had seduced her. Seduced her into thinking for a second that she could risk the almost certain rejection she'd face.

Sheikh Salim Al-Noury had sent her this dress to toy with her. To mock her for staying and not leaving. If she put on the dress and went to his party, no matter how ironically she did it, she would be exposing herself in a way that would make her unbearably vulnerable.

Since her father had walked away from her all those years ago, effectively cutting himself out of her life, Charlotte had shunned intimate male attention and relationships. She was too fearful of experiencing that excoriating pain again. She knew it was irrational, and that no man could hurt her unless she allowed him to, but no man had slid under her skin so immediately and effectively as this reluctant king.

So, galvanised by hurt and anger that he thought he could manipulate her so easily for his own amusement, Charlotte had stormed off to find the party. She'd collided briefly in the corridor with a tall, arrestingly handsome man who'd looked vaguely familiar, even though she was sure she'd never seen him before, but that hadn't stopped her.

And now she was here and she felt like an impetuous idiot.

She'd never seen such a glittering scene. She wasn't sure what she had expected, but it was not this restrained…elegance. Candles bathed the guests in golden light. Men were dressed in tuxedoes. Women were arrayed in stunning jewel-coloured dresses with diamonds sparkling at their throats and hands.

A string quartet played on a dais in one corner. French doors were open to a long terrace, where more people mingled, and the dusk painted the vast sky outside purple and grey.

She was used to exclusive events, but always in a peripheral sense, because she was usually working. And she'd never felt more peripheral than right now, in her very boring skirt and shirt, with her hair pulled back in a tidy bun. She looked as if she was about to take dictation.

If Salim saw her now… She flushed with self-conscious heat to think of how he'd mock her—she'd have been damned if she'd worn the dress and was damned now that she hadn't.

She was about to turn to make her escape when she saw him, cutting a swathe through the crowd and coming straight for her, his eyes locked on hers. Intense.

Too late.

Even from here she could see the glint in his eye. The faintly turned up corner of that wicked mouth. It made a total mockery of her fantasy. He'd noticed her now for all the wrong reasons.

Her heart thumped and her skin grew clammy when he came to a stop in front of her. He was breathtakingly handsome. The tuxedo moulded to his muscles and tall frame like a second skin. It lent him an air of civility that had never felt more like a token gesture. His hair was still unruly and his jaw dark with stubble. This man was wild, through and through. As wild as the desert outside.

He drawled, 'Miss McQuillan—welcome. I shouldn't be surprised that you have chosen not to wear the dress; for someone whose career is all about diplomacy you've got a surprisingly rebellious streak.'

His words landed like tiny poisonous darts. Charlotte had never felt remotely rebellious before meeting him. She refused to be made so acutely aware of how she stood out like a limp flower next to hothouse orchids.

She curled her hands into fists at her sides. 'Believe me, you bring out my worst traits. Thank you for the dress, but it wasn't necessary. I'm not here for your amusement, I'm here to do a job, and that is to help you transition from your current role to your new one, no matter how long you choose to stay in it.'

He folded his arms across that massive chest. 'Haven't you heard that all work and no play makes Miss McQuillan a very boring girl?'

Charlotte sucked in air to try and calm her racing pulse and emotions. This man shouldn't be appealing to her emotions. But he was. And that was bad. It made her feel threatened and she blurted out words before she could stop herself or think them through.

'You know,' she said, 'maybe you're right. Maybe I should just call your brother and tell him that he's wasting his money.'

She'd turned to walk away, but before she could move a hard hand clamped around her wrist. Her pulse hammered against his hand. She looked at him, recalling all too easily how his hands had felt on her the other day.

Any mockery was gone from his expression now. 'You disappoint me…admitting defeat so easily?'

Before Charlotte could say a word her eye was caught by a stunning amazon of a woman dressed in a very revealing black lace dress. She was bearing down on them with a determined look on her vaguely familiar face. At the last second Charlotte realised she was a famous actress.

Salim had looked around too, but instead of letting Charlotte go his grip tightened and he muttered something rude under his breath, quickly turning and walking away, dragging Charlotte with him.

He'd taken her into an anteroom nearby and locked the door behind him before she'd even fully registered what had happened.

He stood with his back against the door and Charlotte looked at him. The air between them was suddenly charged with electricity. She was barely aware that the room was dark and opulently furnished, with books on every wall. Some kind of private sitting room or study.

Salim looked away from her and said, 'This was my grandfather's European room. He fancied himself in part as an English gentleman.'

Charlotte dragged her gaze from the man in front of her and took in the room properly. The gleaming mahogany desk with a reading lamp. The high-backed leather chair. The tartan carpet. The massive stone fireplace, which was completely incongruous when the desert lay beyond these walls.

'He always kept it to a colder temperature in here, so that he could pretend he was in England, or Scotland, and not the Middle East.'

It might be colder, but Charlotte felt hot. Her blood was sluggish in her veins, and yet she was jittery. A disturbing mix.

She looked back at the sheikh, saying unthinkingly, 'Salim…why have we come in—?'

But he interrupted her with a triumphant, '*Finally.* I knew I'd like the way you say my name.'

He started coming closer again and she shook her head, feeling as if she was losing her grip on reality. 'I don't…don't say it any differently from anyone else's name.'

He stopped in front of her. Too close. She took a step back.

'Ah, but you do, Miss McQuillan. You say it with that slightly frosty tone that tells me I'm not behaving as I should.'

She immediately felt defensive. 'I have a name too—it's Charlotte.'

She wasn't even aware that she was still backing away until she hit a solid surface. Shelves. She was breathing as if she'd just run a mile. All she could see were those blue eyes, boring into her.

Why was he looking at her like this? Making her blood leap and her skin prickle? Making her think of illicit things?

He stopped and put a hand over her head. Their bodies were so close they were almost touching. Charlotte felt threatened, but not by him. The threat came from the thought of her reaction to him…

And then he said it. '*Charlotte.*' And something she'd been clinging on to gave way inside her like a wall crumbling.

Desperately she said, 'You really should return to your guests—they'll be wondering where you are.'

He dismissed that with a quirk of his mouth. 'They'll survive.'

Charlotte reacted to his louche arrogance and to the insidious suspicion that even now he was just toying with her for his own amusement.

'Will they? Just like the people of Tabat will *survive* once you walk away from them?'

The intensity in the air around them changed immediately, becoming even more charged.

Salim's body was full of tension, his eyes hard. 'What do you care about Tabat and its people? You've only been here a week.'

Charlotte cursed herself for reacting to him. For exposing herself. 'I know I've only been here a week, but even in that time I can see that this is a great country and that the people deserve better.'

Salim's eyes were burning now, and his mouth was a hard line. 'Can you, now?'

Challenging him like this was heady in the extreme. All her life Charlotte had lived with the repercussions of being forced to choose one parent over the other in a bid to keep the peace—something that had inevitably had disastrous consequences. She'd built a life and a career out of keeping the peace. And yet now, here, with this man, something was breaking apart inside her…something incredibly freeing.

All she could see was that he was no better than her feckless parents, who had used her as an unwitting pawn. He was using her for his own entertainment.

Riling her up. Making her imagine all sort of crazy things…making her want things. *Him.*

She looked Salim straight in the eye. 'Life is so easy for you, isn't it? No wonder you don't want to rule—it would put a serious cramp in your lifestyle and a dent in your empire. Have you *ever* had to think of anyone but yourself, Salim? Have you ever had to consider the consequences of your actions? People like you make me—'

'Enough.' Salim punctuated the harshly spoken word by taking her arms in his hands. He said it again. 'Enough, Charlotte. You've made your point.'

She couldn't breathe after the way he'd just said her name. Roughly. His hands were huge on her arms, and firm but not painful. She knew she should say *Let me go* but somehow the words wouldn't form in her mouth.

Salim's eyes were blazing down into hers and for a second she had the impression that she'd somehow…hurt him. But in the next instant any coherent thought fled, because he slammed his mouth down onto hers and all she was aware of was shocking heat, strength, and a surge of need such as she'd never experienced before.

Salim couldn't recall when he'd felt angrier—people had thrown all sorts of insults at him for years. Women who'd expected more than he'd been prepared to give. Business adversaries he'd bested. His brother. His parents. But for some reason this buttoned-up slender woman with her cool judgmental attitude was getting to him like no one else ever had.

The urge to kiss her had been born out of that anger and a need to stop her words, but also because he'd felt a hot throb of desire that had eluded him for so long he'd almost forgotten what it felt like.

Her mouth was soft and pliant under his, but on some

dim level not clouded red with lust and anger he knew it was shock—and, sure enough, after a couple of seconds he felt her tense and her mouth tighten against his.

He knew he should draw back.

If he was another man he might try to convince himself he'd only intended the kiss to be a display of power, but Salim had never drawn back from admitting his full failings. And he couldn't pull back—not if a thousand horses were tied to his body. Because he wanted her.

He'd never tasted anything as sweet or felt anything as soft and enticing as her slender form. As if his harder edges had finally found their perfect match in spite of her tension.

Salim took his hands off her arms and wrapped them around her back, pulling her closer. He moved his mouth on hers without releasing her, coaxing a response. The proximity of their bodies would leave her in no doubt as to how he felt. His rock-hard erection was pressed against her soft belly and he could feel the thrust of her breasts against his chest.

He brought up a hand and cupped her jaw, angling her face up to his, and nipped gently at her lower lip. It felt soft, cushiony and yet firm. That message went straight to his erection, making it even harder.

Time was suspended for a long moment. This was a novelty for Salim, who found his lovers were usually so eager that they had laid themselves bare for his delectation before he'd even tried to take their clothes off.

Charlotte quivered like a bow in his arms, taut and delicate, and yet with a steely strength that made his blood roar. Salim used every skill in his arsenal to seduce her. He caressed the line of her jaw and cupped the back of her head, fingers tangling in her silky hair, making it come loose from its tidy bun.

He soothed her lip where he'd just nipped her and then he felt it…like a sigh moving through her body. The tension melted and her mouth softened under his.

The sense of triumph Salim felt might have shocked him if he'd been able to analyse it. But he was too busy capitalising on this moment, and on the tiny sliver of opportunity that came when her mouth opened minutely and Salim could coax it open further so that he could taste her sweetness fully.

When his tongue touched hers an electric current shot through his blood. His arm tightened around her even more, so that she was on tiptoe, the full length of her body flush against his, thigh to thigh, chest to chest. Breathing quickened as their fused mouths tasted and drank from each other. Charlotte's arms crept up around Salim's neck and she mimicked his moves.

He had an impression of shyness, and it was mind-bendingly erotic when he was used to women who thought being aggressive equated to being sexy.

Fuelled by a rising fever, Salim moved his hand down between their bodies and cupped Charlotte's breast through the slippery material of her silk shirt. It was fuller than he'd imagined, and that sent another electric frisson straight to his groin. She gasped into his mouth and went still. He could feel the bud of her hard nipple and pinched it lightly between his fingers, drawing back for a moment, finally taking his mouth from hers.

He felt drunk. Dizzy. Her lashes were long and dark against her flushed cheeks and she was biting her lips. They were moist and swollen.

'Look at me, Charlotte.'

Her name rolled off his tongue as if he'd been saying it all his life. He could recognise now that he'd been using *Miss McQuillan* to keep her at a distance. There would be no more distance, he vowed now.

It seemed to take an age for her to open her eyes, and when she did they were dark green, like Scottish moss after a rain shower. She looked as dazed as he felt.

Without taking his gaze off hers he let his fingers find the buttons on her shirt and he started to undo them, slipping them through the holes with gratifying ease, the silky material providing no resistance.

When her shirt was open to just below her breasts Salim looked down, and the breath hissed through his teeth at the provocative sight of the voluptuous bounty. Pale swells rising from dark grey lace.

He moved her shirt aside and, feeling rough and uncouth, tugged one lace cup down. Her breast popped free, revealing the sharp point of a pink nipple.

Salim's mouth watered. He'd never felt so turned on after little more than heavy petting. He cupped her breast and flicked his thumb back and forth across her nipple, seeing how it tightened even more, the aureole beading around it.

He looked at her. 'You like that?'

Charlotte's hands were gripping his arms and the need on her face was stark enough to render words superfluous. She looked stunned.

'I've wanted to see you like this,' he heard himself say hoarsely, 'undone...since the moment I walked into my office and found you waiting like a stern headmistress. All buttoned up and disapproving.'

Unable to resist tasting her again, he closed his hand around her breast. Her nipple stabbed his palm and he claimed her mouth again...greedy, desperate...and she opened up under him like a flower, arching her body into his and pushing her breast deeper into his palm.

Salim was oblivious to everything but the raging need in his body to embed himself deep in her silky heat until finally, *finally*, he might feel a sense of peace that had eluded him for as long as he could remember.

Charlotte had had the briefest moment of sanity when she'd tried her best to resist Salim after he'd started kissing her, but her resistance and that moment of sanity had been pathetically weak and illusory.

From the moment his mouth had touched hers it had been as if he'd reached inside her and lit a fire that was only his to light. A fire she'd hadn't even known could exist, consuming her to the point that all rational thought was burnt away.

*This is what desire feels like...*whispered a voice.

No one had ever made her feel like this before. She'd been on dates, she'd kissed men, but she'd always felt unmoved. As if she was standing outside herself and watching. It had reinforced her belief that keeping her distance was a good thing.

But right here, right now, with this man…distance was the last thing she wanted. She was fully in her body for the first time, and the sensations were so acute that it was almost painful.

Salim's tongue stroked hers with a sure mastery that she could only follow, and mimic blindly. His hand gripped her breast hard, but she wanted it even harder. She wanted him to pinch her nipple again, inducing that sting of shock followed by intense pleasure.

The fact that there was a room full of strangers just feet beyond where they stood, suspended in time, was something Charlotte was only very dimly aware of. The fact that she hated everything this man represented had also receded to some shadowy place she'd weakly turned her mind from.

The stubble of Salim's short beard scratched at her jaw as his mouth trailed from the corner of her mouth and down. Even that was erotic, sending shockwaves down deep into her core. Her head fell back, too heavy, and he pressed a hot open-mouthed kiss to her neck. She felt the sting of teeth and then his tongue, soothing. She was being held up only by his arm and the wall of shelves behind her.

It took a few moments for a rhythmic noise to break through the fog in her brain. She thought it was her heartbeat, but it wasn't, and when it registered properly she froze.

Someone was knocking on the door and she heard a panicky voice, 'Sire…? *Sire*...are you in there? Please?'

The door handle rattled and Salim's head came up. His hair was mussed and his eyes were heavy-lidded. His cheeks were flushed. He looked exactly how she imagined a fallen angel would look. Wicked and sexy and innocent all at once.

But as reality seeped back a chill wind skated over Charlotte's skin. She looked down to see her blouse hanging open and one breast bared, her nipple pink and hard. There were marks on her pale skin—marks from his fingers.

Mortification drenched her as the full enormity of what had just happened sank in.

Salim finally stepped back and jerkily she pulled up her bra.

She could still feel the press of his arousal against her belly, long and hard. It was small comfort, though, to know he'd been as turned on as her…it only made her feel even more confused.

She sent up silent thanks that her hands weren't shaking as she did up her shirt buttons. The lace of her bra chafed against her sensitised nipples and the betraying damp heat between her legs told of just how seismic this man's effect on her had been.

Charlotte risked a look at Salim. His mouth was open, as if he was about to say something, but just then the doorknob rattled again and Charlotte had never felt so relieved. She did not want to discuss what had just happened. Not when she felt so raw.

The panicked-sounding voice floated through. 'Please, *sire…*'

Salim was still looking at her, and Charlotte said with rising panic, 'Shouldn't you see who that is?'

Finally Salim issued an Arabic curse under his breath and turned around and strode to the door, his movements lacking their customary grace.

When he opened the door she heard Rafa's anxious voice say, 'Sire, there is something of utmost importance I need to tell you.'

Charlotte walked over to the door on wobbly legs, and when Rafa saw her his eyes widened, telling her in no uncertain terms that she wore the marks of Salim's lovemaking like a gauche teenager. Mortified all over again, Charlotte used the opportunity to escape, sliding around Salim, careful not to come into contact with him or meet his eyes.

She muttered something incomprehensible, and didn't look left or right as she left the revellers in the ballroom behind her.

When Charlotte reached the sanctuary of her rooms, she went straight into the bathroom and looked at herself in the mirror—and gasped. It was worse than she'd thought.

Her eyes were huge and dark green. Her lips were swollen. Her cheeks were flushed and her jaw was pink from Salim's stubble. Where her jaw met her neck there was a distinctive mark and she touched it now, remembering the nipping of teeth, the soothing of a tongue. His tongue.

With trembling hands she undid her shirt again and opened it, pulling down her bra to look at her breast. The marks of his hand were still on her pale flesh, but fading. Between her legs a pulse throbbed when she thought of the firm pressure of his hand on her flesh, her nipple trapped between two fingers.

She looked back at herself and almost didn't recognise the person reflected in the mirror. This was so far removed from the sane responsible person she thought she was—not given to whims or vagaries. Or spontaneous combustion.

Her legs were still dangerously wobbly and she put her hands on the sink in order to stay upright. She had memories of seeing her parents kissing, before they'd divorced, and they had always frightened her because there had been something so animalistic about it. But when she thought of how she'd behaved just now she realised that their impulses were hers too, in spite of everything. Genes will out, no matter what.

And yet how he'd made her feel for those few moments had been the most exciting thing that had ever happened to her.

Her fingers were curled so tight around the rim of the sink that she had to uncurl them for fear of cracking the porcelain.

There was a peremptory knock on her door and immediately she felt ridiculous, mooning at herself in the mirror. She did up her shirt and tried to smooth her hair, hoping the mark on her neck wasn't too visible.

Assuming it would probably be the nice girl who was

her obligatory maid—Assa—she opened the door to find her eye level not on the face of a pretty dark-eyed girl but on a very broad chest. A very familiar chest. A chest that not long ago she'd been rubbing her breasts against like a hungry little kitten.

She looked up to see Salim, his expression stern. Immediately she asked, 'What is it?'

'May I come in?'

Charlotte would have bet money on the fact that Salim was regretting what had just happened even more than her, so she stood back and tried not to notice how her body immediately hummed in close proximity to his again.

As he walked into the room she noticed that he'd lost his jacket and bow-tie. The top button of his shirt was open. He turned around to face her while she stayed close to the door, feeling like a coward.

Charlotte desperately wanted to say something before he had a chance to let her know how much he regretted what had to be a momentary lapse in judgement.

'What happened just now…it shouldn't have. It wasn't appropriate.'

Something flickered in Salim's piercing eyes, but it was gone before she could figure out what it meant. Probably relief that she wasn't making the most of an opportunity to embed herself in his life.

But then he said, 'Is that your professional opinion?'

Charlotte swallowed. 'Personal. And professional.'

Liar.

Salim raked a hand through his hair, making it even messier. 'We'll discuss that another time, but there are more important matters to deal with first.'

Charlotte's heart flipped over at the fact that he wasn't immediately agreeing with her about the kiss, and then she registered what else he'd said. 'What matters?'

Salim's mouth firmed. 'The reason Rafa was looking for me is because he's been informed that some of the bigger tribes are planning on marching into Tabat City in a bid to assert their dominance over each other before I am crowned king. They seek to curry favour, hoping for preferential treatment once I'm in power.'

Charlotte watched Salim pace back and forth, her gaze drawn helplessly to the fluid athletic grace of his body. She struggled to keep her eyes up.

She said quietly, 'They've been waiting for a long time for a leader. Without someone to unite and guide them any rifts and grievances between the tribes will have grown bigger and more entrenched.'

'Yes.' He stopped pacing and looked at her. 'So what I have to do is go and meet them before they can come to me—do my best to unite them and inform them that there will be no preferential treatment.'

At first Charlotte thought this was the most selfless thing she'd heard him say to date, but then she thought it through. 'But when you abdicate they'll doubt any assurances you've given them.'

Salim's mouth tightened. 'I'm meeting them all separately, and then I'll invite each tribal leader to the city to negotiate an agreement before the coronation. They'll be bound by that no matter what happens. A tribe's word is very important in this country.'

Charlotte cursed herself for being naive. He wasn't doing this because he cared about his people. Clearly this was all merely a means to an end—to make sure his own agenda succeeded. His agenda to pursue a life of independence and freedom, amassing more wealth than any one person could possibly know what to do with.

She said coolly, 'Well, as you've made it very clear that I'm of no use to you, I fail to see why you're telling me about your plans.'

Salim's face was carefully expressionless. 'The last thing I want to do is stir up any trouble while I'm visiting the tribes by unwittingly insulting anyone, so it looks as if I'll have need of your expertise after all—if you'll accompany me.'

Charlotte felt no sense of triumph at this *volte face*, only a rising panic at the thought of going anywhere with him. And yet how could she refuse when this was her reason for being there?

'Very well. I'll come with you.'

His expression was inscrutable. No more teasing or mocking. She wasn't sure how to deal with this far more serious Salim.

He nodded briefly in acknowledgement of her acquiescence. 'We'll leave tomorrow morning—early—and travel to the three main tribes over the next week.'

His gaze swept her up and down then, and she had to stop herself from folding her arms defensively, hoping she'd buttoned her shirt all the way up.

'Where we're going is a lot more traditional than the city, so I'll have Assa ensure you have the right clothes.' His blue gaze seemed to pierce right through her. 'It'll be very rustic, if you think you can handle that.'

Charlotte bristled at the tone in his voice, which cast doubt on her ability to endure a trip into the wild desert regions.

'Of course I can handle it. I've travelled extensively, and in my experience nomadic tribes often offer better hospitality than some five-star hotels.'

For the first time she thought she saw a flash of humour in his eyes, but he just said, 'Good. I won't have to worry that you'll run screaming from using an outdoor latrine, then.'

'No,' Charlotte said tightly, perversely liking the fact that she was so obviously nothing like the women he was used to and yet also irritated by it.

A moment stretched between them, and then Salim moved, walking towards her, back to the door. Charlotte stepped out of his way, her whole body tingling as he got close.

He had his hand on the knob when he looked at her again. 'About what happened…'

She looked at him and wished she had something to hold on to. She held on to her words. 'I told you—it shouldn't have happened.'

'And yet it did, and we both enjoyed it. And if you know anything about me by now, Charlotte, it's that I'm not in the habit of denying myself things that make me feel good.'

He'd turned and walked out before Charlotte could come back with some pithy response.

She tried to drum up some sense of outrage at his arrogance, but how could she when only minutes ago she'd been opening up underneath his touch like a flower unfurling for the sun?

She turned from the door and ignored the vivid splash of green silk on the bed in her peripheral vision, reminding her of the man's ability to get to her. She assured herself that his interest in her was fleeting, at best, and that once they went into the desert she would there in a professional role, on much firmer ground.

She kept assuring herself of this as she finally fell into a fitful sleep that night, beset by dreams of ominous shifting sands.

CHAPTER FOUR

'*It shouldn't have happened.*' Salim waited impatiently for Charlotte to appear the following morning as dawn broke over Tabat. Her words, delivered in those cut-glass tones, still reverberated in his head. Irritating him intensely.

He was not used to women expressing regret after sharing intimacies with him. And certainly not after a kiss as explosive as the one they'd shared… But then he couldn't actually remember such an explosive moment with any woman.

Salim also had to admit—reluctantly—that he really didn't think it was a game, or a bluff designed to pique his interest. She'd meant it. In spite of the electric current that had sparked between them again as soon as he'd stepped into her room.

Her hair had still been deliciously tousled. Her lips swollen. Her shirt buttons had been done up wrong. He'd caught a glimpse of grey lace and just like that he'd become aroused all over again.

He'd resented the fact that she was the one inducing this crazy lust when he had a room full of beautiful uncomplicated women under his very roof, waiting for his attention.

But when he'd returned to the party, and been surrounded by sycophants and stunning women within minutes, he hadn't wanted any of them. And when he'd looked around and seen the elegant sheen on his guests wearing thin, he'd suddenly felt jaded and weary.

His conscience had tugged hard, and so he'd given instructions to his staff to start winding things down. He would have invited his cousin Riad to stay, but when he'd tried to call him he'd found a text message on his phone to say that Riad had already left with his mistress—something had come up at home that he had to attend to urgently.

There was movement in Salim's peripheral vision and he turned to see Charlotte approaching. His eyes widened as she came closer. She was wearing a long cream kaftan with gold edging that came to just below her knees, and beneath that she wore slim-fitting trousers in the same material. On her feet she wore low-heeled sandals.

He looked up and felt a spurt of something very disturbing when he saw that her hair was covered with a loose scarf, giving only a hint of that strawberry-blonde underneath.

He wanted to rip off the scarf, while at the same time feeling a possessive sense of satisfaction that her bright hair was hidden from other men. Impulses Salim had never ever experienced before.

There was something about her cool reserve and fresh-faced beauty that had sunk a hook inside him from the moment he'd seen her, and he knew it wouldn't let go until he'd had her.

Suddenly it was quite simple to Salim: he would bed her and she would lose her mystique, like every other woman he'd bedded.

She came to a stop a couple of feet away and put a hand to her head. 'What is it?'

Salim's voice was gruff when he said, 'You don't have to cover your head here.'

She pulled the scarf back and let it drop to her shoulders. Seeing the shining smooth cap of her hair made him remember what it had looked like after they'd kissed and his blood leapt. He had to restrain himself from perversely demanding that she cover it up again.

'Assa told me it's customary among most of the tribes for women to cover their heads.'

'Yes, and you can do it there.'

Salim's voice was curt and he saw how she flinched minutely. He cursed silently. He was on edge because of his unprecedented reaction to her, but also because he hadn't really acknowledged the possibility of meeting with the desert people of Tabat.

In the city it was easier to think of this as a business transaction—he was preparing this country to be strong so that it would flourish and thrive under new leadership. But now he would have to look into the eyes of those people, and it was as if he knew on some primal level that he was about to come face to face with himself in a way he'd never had to before.

And all under the cool green gaze of the woman looking at him now.

He opened the passenger door of the vehicle beside him. 'You'll travel with me.'

After a second when he thought she might argue Salim realised that, much as she provoked him, he found the prospect of her *not* being in close proximity to him was also unacceptable.

Eventually she moved towards the SUV and got in.

There was a flurry of activity as various bodyguards and staff finished packing away luggage and supplies in other vehicles.

Then Rafa approached Salim and bowed slightly, saying, 'Everything is ready, sire.'

Salim wanted to tell him not to bow, and not to call him sire, but he just nodded and got into the car himself, behind the steering wheel.

It was time to meet his destiny whether he liked it or not.

Charlotte could feel the tension rolling off Salim in waves and it surprised her. She'd assumed he would approach visiting the tribes with the same louche disregard with which he seemed to approach everything else. But he looked serious.

The city limits had been left far behind and there were at least three vehicles ahead of them and another three behind, carrying Rafa and Assa as well as other staff.

Nothing but endless sand stretched out all around them. Dunes rose and fell under the blinding sun and the horizon shimmered in the heat. Charlotte sent up silent thanks that they were protected by air-conditioning in the sturdy vehicle that navigated this shifting terrain easily.

Salim clearly didn't want to be making this trip. Charlotte took in his profile, which was effortlessly regal in spite of his reluctance to govern. He was wearing traditional robes, but hadn't made much more of an effort to clean up his appearance.

His hair was still wild and unruly, and Charlotte's fingers itched to see if it felt as silky and luxurious as it looked. She felt a crazy regret that she hadn't explored more when she'd had the chance. She clenched her hands into fists and ignored those itchy fingers.

But then her eye fell on his very stubbled jaw, and that made her think of how it had felt when he'd kissed her. The burn he'd left along her jaw…a physical brand. It made her wonder how it would feel on other parts of her body…

In a desperate bid to divert her mind, she asked, 'Why are you so reluctant to assume your role as king?'

His hand tightened on the wheel and the tension spiked. She thought he wasn't going to answer her when he was silent for so long, but then he said, 'I've already told you—I have numerous business concerns, thousands of employees. It's a role I never asked for or welcomed.'

'But…' Charlotte ignored the voice telling her to be quiet. 'No one asks to rule. They're born to rule.'

Salim's jaw tightened, but he kept his eyes on the road. 'That may be the case, but there's a better choice than me for Tabat.'

She assimilated what he'd just said and knew she should stay quiet but couldn't. She turned in her seat to face him. 'I don't think there is, actually. I think you know it's your destiny, and yet there's some other reason why you're so reluctant to take what's yours.'

Charlotte should have been alerted by the fact that the tension in the confined space suddenly changed and became more charged. Salim looked at her and let his eyes drift down over her body and immediately her blood sizzled.

'Believe me,' he drawled, 'I'm not reluctant to take what's mine at all.'

What's mine. He wasn't talking about Tabat. The thought that he considered her *his* was enough to render her speechless. No doubt exactly what he'd intended with this clever deflection.

Charlotte turned to face the front, locking her muscles tight against the betraying rush of arousal.

She refused to look at him for fear of what she'd see on his face. She'd learnt her lesson. She didn't care what this man's motivations were—she just wanted to get through the week unscathed.

Several hours later Salim was seated on a low chair in the tent of the local sheikh—the leader of the Rab'sah tribe. Charlotte had been right—the hospitality was so generous it was almost embarrassing. Even in spite of the cool reception Salim had received, which had been his due considering he hadn't come to visit them before now.

Their hospitality was even more overwhelming when he considered that they didn't have much. At all. There was a time when these nomadic tribes had had many riches—when they'd come into the city and bartered and sold precious gems and fat animals. But the world had marched on and left people like this behind, and it struck Salim somewhere very deeply now to see the aristocratic features and inherent pride of the tribe reduced to a mere shadow of its former self.

Charlotte wasn't in the tent, out of respect for the customs of the tribe that forbade women from attending formal meetings, and Salim welcomed the momentary space even as he hungered to lay his gaze on her.

He was still reeling from her far too perceptive observation earlier. No one had ever questioned his motives about anything before. No one had ever looked at him like that, as if trying to figure him out. Coming far too close to the bone.

So he told himself he was glad she wasn't here, and that ancient custom dictated women must be apart from the men, because he didn't care to be under her far too incisive green-eyed scrutiny as he listened to this sheikh and found himself feeling a sense of kinship that he'd never experienced before.

At dawn the following morning Charlotte was standing at the edge of the camp, watching as the sun rose in the east, slowly saturating the horizon with pink light. There was a low hum of activity behind her as the camp woke up, but there was an all-encompassing silence that surrounded her, deep and infinitely peaceful. Her instinct that she'd find the desert fascinating had been right.

'Bored yet?'

She started at the deep voice beside her and looked round to see Salim—tall and broad. He filled her vision in spite of the vast desert, and she realised that he truly fitted into this world even if he didn't want to. He was hewn from its very unforgiving landscape, from a long line of warriors.

She looked back out to the horizon, afraid he might see something of her fanciful thoughts on her face. 'I don't see how anyone could ever be bored here.'

'How did you sleep?'

In truth, she hadn't slept well. It might have been because she'd been sharing quarters with women and children, but they hadn't been the reason she'd lain awake. She'd been wondering about Salim, and about the fact that he was far more enigmatic than she'd ever anticipated.

She looked back at him and forced a bright smile. 'Like a log—and you?'

He smiled too, showing his teeth. 'Like a log.'

The hell he had. He'd spent hours alternating between ignoring his guilty conscience and battling images of this woman with her shirt undone and one pale plump breast filling his palm. That soft lush mouth under his.

The rising sun was bathing her in a warm glow. She was dressed traditionally again. Her hair peeped out from under the veil she wore. Her face was bare of make-up. He could see freckles. He couldn't remember the last time he'd seen such fresh-faced beauty.

The way she got to him made him ask caustically, 'You're not missing your home comforts too much?'

It rankled with him now that he knew she'd had to share a tent with some of the higher born women and children and yet it didn't seem to have fazed her in the slightest.

Those green eyes sparked and Salim felt an answering fire burn deep in his core. More than lust. Disturbing.

She folded her arms and faced him. 'Still trying to get rid of me?'

No way.

The strength of that assertion surprised him. He clamped his mouth shut in case it slipped out.

When he didn't respond, she said, 'Look, I told you—I've travelled. It's a privilege to spend time with people like these.' She sounded exasperated.

He'd seen her yesterday, sitting cross-legged with a group of women, smiling and conversing with them as best she could, given the differences in dialect. She'd looked utterly comfortable and graceful in spite of her dusty clothes and very basic surroundings. And they'd looked at her with awe.

She turned now and Salim's chest tightened. She'd looked so serene and peaceful standing there, watching the sunrise. He'd intruded because he'd been envious of that peace and absorption. And because he'd wanted her attention on *him*.

He put a hand on her arm and she stopped, looking at him warily. He cursed himself for not just letting her go.

'Did you want something?'

He let her arm go. 'Just to say we'll be leaving shortly.'

She nodded after a moment. 'I'll be ready.'

Salim turned back to face the desert and had an uncomfortable skin-prickling sense of foreboding that this trip was not going to pan out as he'd planned it.

At all.

By day three Charlotte was surprised at how easily she'd settled into the rhythm of moving from place to place. And at how little she missed civilisation. As they had moved deeper and deeper into the desert she'd found herself unwinding, helpless not to do so in the face of a much more primeval rhythm.

The evening was closing in over the oasis that was the current base for the Jadar tribe—one of the oldest in the region. It was where the name Jandor had come from, when this tribe's ancestors had sacked and invaded the city.

She walked through the camp back to her tent after meeting with the tribe's leaders. This tribe was different from most and run on more egalitarian lines. Women were just as much a part of important discussions as men and they didn't wear veils, so Charlotte had left hers off and relished the breeze through her hair now.

During the meetings Charlotte had been surprised at how deferential Salim had been, and how attentive. She'd expected to find herself cringing as he made his reluctance to be there known, but he'd been effortlessly respectful while also displaying an innate sense of authority that had nothing to do with arrogance.

She'd just returned to her small tent, and was unpacking her bag, appreciating the thought of her own private space for the first time in three nights, when a noise made her look round.

Assa was at the opening of the tent and she said, 'King Al-Noury would like you to join him for dinner in his tent.'

Even though he wasn't yet crowned, his people already called him king.

Charlotte's belly flipped. She'd managed to more or less avoid him since the other morning, keeping their conversation to a minimum as they travelled from place to place. But her awareness of him was increasing exponentially. Along with her confusion that he wasn't behaving as she might have expected.

What could Charlotte say? She'd been summoned by the king. 'Of course. I'll just change quickly.'

The fine desert sand seemed to get everywhere, so Charlotte availed herself of the small bathroom attached to the tent and refreshed herself and changed into a clean set of trousers and a tunic. When she re-emerged Assa was waiting to show her to Salim's tent.

Darkness had fallen over the camp and there were familiar sounds of rattling plates and utensils, fractious children crying and soothing voices.

Charlotte absorbed the nomadic atmosphere of the camp. Mouth-watering smells of cooking reminded her she hadn't eaten in a few hours. She stopped and smiled when some small children ran around her as they played a game of catch before disappearing behind one of the tents.

Strangely, because she'd never thought of herself as being remotely maternal—especially after her experiences at the hands of her self-absorbed mother and absent father—she was taken completely unawares by a pang of yearning, and when she saw Assa waiting for her outside a much larger tent, with golden light spilling out into the camp, she realised far too belatedly that she was not ready to face Salim's all too blistering blue gaze.

But, as if hearing her thoughts, Salim appeared in the entrance of the tent, easily filling the space. 'Please, come in.'

And she had to keep moving forward, pushing that alien emotion down.

When she walked into his tent her jaw dropped and she forgot everything for a moment. It was like something out of an Arabian fantasy. Luxurious floor-coverings, sumptuous soft furnishings in bright jewel colours. A dining area that wouldn't have looked out of place in a Parisian restaurant and a bed that Charlotte couldn't take her eyes off. It dominated the space and was covered in silk and satin, with muslin drapes around it, fluttering in the light breeze.

She'd never have guessed from the rest of the far more humble camp that this could exist.

'It's a bit much, isn't it?'

Charlotte managed to tear her gaze from the bed to look at Salim, who was wincing slightly. Feeling something light bubble up inside her she asked innocently, 'Not to your specifications, then?'

He looked at her and his mouth tipped up wryly. 'No.'

He gestured for her to take a seat at the dining table, and she said as she watched him take a seat opposite her, 'Let me guess—you're into stark minimalism and masculine colours? Abstract art?'

He flicked out a linen napkin. 'You say that like it's a bad thing.'

A moment shimmered between them, light and fragile, and then he said, 'You looked as if you'd just seen a ghost when you walked in—I hope that wasn't a reaction to my invitation.'

Charlotte avoided his eye for a moment, placing her own napkin on her lap. When she looked up again he was watching her with a narrowed gaze. She heard noises coming from the back of the tent, the sounds and smells of dinner. It helped to lessen the feeling of being in a lavish cocoon with this man.

She shrugged minutely. 'I just noticed something… walking through the camp. A real sense of community that you don't find in many places any more.'

Salim said, 'You do seem at home here. And I'm sure you don't need me to tell you this, but you're a natural diplomat. I've watched how you put everyone at ease and can converse equally with a sheikh or the girl washing the dishes.'

Ridiculously, Charlotte blushed at Salim's praise—even though she knew without false modesty that she was good at her job. 'Thank you. This part of the world has always been fascinating to me.'

They were interrupted by staff appearing with a tray of delicious-smelling food. When they were alone again Salim held up a bottle of red wine and said, 'May I?'

Charlotte felt as if she needed the sustenance so she nodded. He filled her glass and she took a sip.

There was a big bowl of food to be shared—Salim

explained that it was chicken mixed with couscous, spices, herbs and bread.

Charlotte filled her plate.

They ate in silence for a few minutes, both savouring the food, but then Salim sat back and said, 'So that sense of community...did you grow up in a small town?'

Charlotte's insides tensed automatically. She cursed her inability to lie and hoped he'd lose interest when she said, as perfunctorily as she could, 'No, I grew up in London. I was an only child and my parents divorced when I was young. I spent a lot of time in boarding schools and with nannies.'

'So you knew the opposite of community, then?' he observed, with a perspicacity that was as unwelcome as it was insightful.

Charlotte put down her fork and took another sip of wine, relishing the slight headiness it brought, which made her feel reckless enough to respond mockingly, 'I was a poor little rich girl. My parents were millionaires, which afforded them the luxury of having their child taken care of. But their lifestyles have never appealed to me. I wanted to make my own way. I don't depend on them for anything.'

She couldn't help the pride showing in her voice when she said that.

His gaze narrowed on her and she fought against squirming in her chair. Why did he have to look at her like that? As if he could see right through her?

'We have something in common. I never relished the cushion of my family's fortune. I also wanted to make my own way. I worked my way through college and everything I own now is mine and mine alone.'

She asked, 'Is that why you're reluctant to let it all go and become king?'

Salim was shocked he'd said so much, and that he'd felt the need to let her know that he appreciated her independence because he shared it. The sense of kinship was unsettling.

He shrugged, hiding how accurately her words had hit him. 'Perhaps it's part of it. Along with the responsibility I feel.'

He stopped there, before he let the real reasons slip out. He hadn't prepared for this as his brother had so assiduously. He'd allowed a rift to grow between them, so how could he unite a country? And how could he protect the people of Tabat when he hadn't been able to save his own sister?

Before she could ask any more far too pertinent questions, Salim asked, 'What about you? What drove you to become a diplomat and turn your back on the life of being an heiress?'

She avoided his eye for so long that he thought she wasn't going to answer, but then she looked at him and it was like a punch to his gut. There was something so...unguarded about her expression.

'It was my parents,' she said quietly. 'Their divorce was ugly. They used me as a pawn to score points off each other, but once my mother had custody she pretty much abandoned me. I realised at a young age that unconditional love and family happiness are an illusion. So I decided to distance myself as much as possible—become independent so they could never use me as a pawn again.'

Salim was a little speechless. He'd thought his parents were cold automatons, but evidently they hadn't been the only ones. 'Does your aversion to Christmas have anything to do with all that?'

Her eyes widened and her mouth opened before she'd recovered. 'How did you know?'

He shrugged, not liking how easily he'd intuited that. 'A guess. It's a time of year that evokes strong reactions, and you were pretty adamant that you didn't mind missing it.'

She glanced down at her napkin, folding it over and over. Salim wanted to put his hand over hers, but curled it into a fist to stop himself.

She stopped fidgeting and looked at him. 'They divorced just before Christmas. Days before.'

Some of the candles had gone out, making the light in the tent dimmer. The delicate lines of her face when she looked at him were in sharp relief. Her eyes were huge.

'Go on,' he said, aware of the irony. He never usually encouraged women to reveal anything more than the most superficial parts of their lives to him. But this woman intrigued him.

'Since then I've invariably spent Christmas on my own. Whenever the head of my boarding school knew I was due to spend the holiday alone, because my mother was working or abroad, they'd ask a family to take me in… I went once or twice, but no matter how welcome they made me feel it only made me more conscious of not being a part of a family.'

'What about your father?'

She shrugged. 'I only saw him a handful of times after I chose my mother to be my prime carer in the divorce.'

She smiled then, but it was tight, almost derisory.

'The really sad thing, though, is that as much as I hate Christmas, I love it too. The Christmas before the divorce was perfect. Just the three of us in a cottage in

Devon. It snowed that year, and my father dressed up as Santa Claus, and my mother showed him to me, tip-toeing away from the house as if he'd just left his gifts. It was magical…'

Charlotte's gaze focused on Salim again and she felt the blood drain from her face as she realised just how much she'd revealed. His expression was inscrutable in the flickering golden light of the candles. As if he cared about her sad tale! What was wrong with her? She never spoke of her past—not if she could help it—and certainly not with someone who made her feel so many conflicting emotions and desires.

She stood up abruptly, dropping her napkin. 'I should go to bed—it's been a long day. Thank you for dinner.'

She wanted to get out of that decadent and confined space *now.* And away from those blue eyes. She was burning up from the inside out and it wasn't just from embarrassment. It was from sitting in such close proximity to Salim's lazily coiled sexual magnetism.

Salim stood up too, putting down his own napkin. He was watching her warily, which made her feel even more exposed as she stepped away from the table.

She'd turned and was almost at the entrance to the tent when her hand was caught in a much bigger one and her heart leapt into her throat. She hadn't even heard him move, the sound muffled by the sumptuous carpets. She turned around and tried to pull her hand free, but he held it too firmly.

She could feel her pulse fluttering against his finger. 'What is it?'

Why did she sound so breathless?

Salim looked very tall and dark in the dim golden light. More like a warrior than ever.

'Don't go back to your tent, Charlotte, stay here tonight.'

Charlotte didn't even register what Salim had said for a minute. Without thinking, she responded automatically, 'But why? That's where I'm…'

And then she stuttered to a stop as comprehension started to sink in and the heat in his eyes made his meaning very explicit. Everything about his suggestion screamed *danger* to Charlotte, even as she could feel the betraying evidence of the effect he'd had on her all evening.

His finger moved back and forth on her wrist, over her pulse point. Hypnotising her. All her muscles pulled taut, and at the same time seemed to soften.

And then she thought of spilling her guts with little or no encouragement. She remembered the burn of embarrassment and it burned even more now at the thought that he might have manipulated her into opening up so he could take advantage of her emotional vulnerability.

A little voice mocked her that he wouldn't have to resort to such crude tactics, but she ignored it.

She pulled her hand free. 'You think that I'll just fall into your bed because you ask?'

A muscle ticked in his jaw. 'You know what there is between us—it's off the charts.'

The kiss.

She stiffened. 'We agreed that was a mistake…inappropriate. That it wouldn't happen again.'

He shook his head. 'No, *you* said it wouldn't happen again. But you're lying to yourself if you think you can resist this… We have amazing chemistry. We're both adults. We're never going to see each other again once the coronation is over. There's no reason why this can't happen.'

Yes, there is! A hysterical voice resounded inside Charlotte. And it was because of what he'd just said: *'We're never going to see each other again'*.

Of course they wouldn't. A woman like Charlotte would never feature in this man's life and that shouldn't matter to her. But already it did. And it shouldn't. It couldn't.

A million and one emotions landed in Charlotte's belly, the strongest of which was an intense feeling of vulnerability. He had no idea how innocent she was. Evidently he thought that telling her he wanted her was enough to have her swooning at his feet in gratitude…

Feeling very defensive, but not wanting him to see how he'd got to her, she said as coolly as she could, 'I'm afraid I don't agree with your assessment of the situation. Goodnight, Salim.'

She cringed inwardly. She sounded like an accountant.

Salim looked at her for a long moment, his expression unreadable. And then he just said, 'Very well. Goodnight, Charlotte.'

He reached past her to pull back the heavy drapes covering the entrance and the cool night-time desert breeze skated over her skin. She hated the treacherous part of her that wasn't exactly heartened to see this gentlemanly side of him. Where was the stereotypical playboy who wouldn't take no for an answer because she'd bruised his pride?

She quickly turned and fled, before she could give herself away. Before he could see how conflicted she was. No other person had ever pushed her buttons so effectively, and when she got back to her own tent she paced up and down, sensations and emotions boiling over too much to relax.

She should be feeling triumphant—she'd just turned down one of the sexiest and most arrogant men in the world. She'd stood up to him. But she hated to admit now that it felt like a hollow victory.

Eventually she did sit down on the bed and noticed vaguely that someone—Assa?—had come in and lit some lamps and turned the bed down. A far less lavish version of Salim's…where, if she'd said yes, they might be entwined right now…

She stood up again and busied herself undressing and getting ready for bed, ignoring the ache that spread through her whole body from her core.

She busied herself to avoid thinking about the real reason she'd turned Salim down: because she was still a virgin.

It was something she was subconsciously aware of but had managed to successfully ignore for a long time. She'd been so focused on her career—

She stopped, catching her reflection in the mirror over the sink where she was about to wash herself.

Her cheeks were flushed bright red and her neat shoulder-length bob was a lot less sleek than usual. She was pathetic. The reason she was a virgin had nothing to do with her career and everything to do with the fact that she was too afraid to let anyone close enough to hurt her as much as her parents had.

But when she thought about Salim's arrogant proposal just now—yes, arrogant—the last thing she'd been afraid of was getting hurt. It had been the fear of incineration if he kissed her again. The fear of exposure. And the fear of his look of incredulity if he found out how innocent she was. She doubted a man like that had ever slept with a virgin in his life.

He'd summed her up from the start as uptight. He would laugh in her face if he knew how right he was.

She'd already told Salim far too much this evening. She wasn't going to bare herself—literally—even more. He wasn't worth risking her precious independence for. *He wasn't*, she told herself fiercely as she did her best to ignore the ache, which only seemed to grow more acute.

CHAPTER FIVE

'IT LOOKS LIKE we'll have to stay here for a couple of days.'

'Oh, no—why?' Charlotte looked at Assa and felt panicky.

They'd been due to return to Tabat City the following morning, and frankly she couldn't wait to get back. The vast desert now felt as oppressive as a small confined space after enduring Salim's civil yet cool demeanour since they'd arrived at their last stop, the oasis camp of the Wahir tribe, earlier that day.

That morning, when Rafa had asked if Salim minded if he joined him in the car to discuss matters of state on the journey from Jadar, Charlotte had jumped at the opportunity to escape and had taken Rafa's place in his own transport.

The intense look Salim had sent her still made her shiver. She didn't want to know what he might have said to her if they'd been alone. She'd vowed not to be alone with him ever again.

Since they'd arrived, Salim had been in intense discussion with the Wahir tribe's leaders. Charlotte had been allowed to sit in on the meetings, concentrating hard to follow the very stylised Arabic they used. Once again she'd been surprised to note that Salim was respectful and attentive.

Assa said, 'I don't mind staying another night if we have to—it's as beautiful here as everyone said it was.'

Charlotte was pulled out of her spiralling thoughts. Assa was right: this camp was the most picturesque they'd been to yet. A beautiful green oasis with palm trees and a huge pool of clear green water.

'Why do we have to stay?'

The young girl looked at her, her dark eyes huge. 'They say a sandstorm will hit tonight, and if it does it'll take at least another day to unearth all the vehicles to travel back to Tabat.'

'Can't they avoid that happening?' Charlotte asked weakly, knowing she was being ridiculous. A meteorological event was hardly negotiable.

'We're on high ground, Miss McQuillan, but there's no escaping the power of a storm.'

Assa took an armful of Charlotte's dirty laundry—in spite of her protests that she could wash her own things—and turned at the opening of the tent.

'You'll come to the wedding later, won't you? It would be considered very rude not to as an honoured guest.'

'Of course,' Charlotte answered.

All the king's entourage had been invited to attend the wedding of the oldest daughter of the tribe's leader and Charlotte was intrigued, having never witnessed a Bedouin wedding before. There was an air of great excitement in the camp, and Charlotte had noticed that there were a lot more people there than there had been earlier.

Charlotte had every intention of making sure she stayed well out of Salim's way, and if a sandstorm hit overnight she'd be one of the first helping to unearth the vehicles in the morning.

* * *

Salim was acutely conscious of the ritual he was witnessing in a way that he might not have anticipated before embarking on this trip. Taking place in front of him was a centuries-old custom designed to bind families and neighbouring tribes together in a way that would unify them and promote peace in a place where wars had once been rife and deadly.

He was surprised at the strength of an echo inside him that recognised and accepted this on some deep level, in spite of doing his damnedest to deny that he was part of this history and culture.

Destiny. The hated word slid into his mind, but for once it didn't induce the same level of rejection as it normally did. The truth was that he came from these people. His ancestors had said these same words, more or less.

For the first time Salim felt a sense of belonging he'd never experienced before creep over him. As if ancient and invisible bindings were slowly but inexorably wrapping around him like tentacles and tying him to the life he was so determined to reject. As if *he* was a nomad who was returning home.

It was an unsettling thought, but not even that was unsettling enough to distract him from the woman who sat at his right-hand side, who had turned him down him so summarily the previous evening.

His body had started humming as soon as she'd sat down beside him, enveloping him with a delicate and tantalising scent that made him think of cool green moss and much earthier things, like tangling naked on a soft surface.

Thankfully his voluminous robe hid the near-constant state of arousal he had little control over, which irritated him greatly. Salim usually had no problem mastering his physical impulses, no matter how attractive the woman. But of course no other woman had proved so elusive.

Charlotte had studiously avoided his eye since she'd arrived, just as she'd been studiously avoiding him all day. He'd observed her earlier, talking earnestly with both the women and the men of the tribe in Arabic. The ease she felt with them and their acceptance of her made him all at once proud and yet perversely annoyed that his diplomatic expert was being so…diplomatic.

The couple in front of them were seated face to face on cushions, about to say their vows. Salim gave in to an urge too great for him to resist and looked at Charlotte. He noticed with another spurt of irritation that she was quite oblivious to him.

After the confidences she'd shared last night—that *they'd* shared—he should be the one pushing her away. And yet at every moment when she'd avoided his eye today, or evaded him, it had only fired up a primal urge to hunt her down.

Her green eyes were suspiciously shiny now, and he followed her gaze back to the young couple to see that the woman's hands were together in the prayer position and the man was placing the wedding ring over each of her fingers until he got to the ring finger.

The young man looked at the woman and said in Arabic as he slid the ring down her finger, 'I marry you, I marry you, I marry you,' as was this particular tribe's custom in marriage. Then she repeated his words and actions.

Now they were married. It was that simple.

They could be separated as easily, by saying the words *I divorce you* three times in front of the tribe leader, but from the way the young man was looking at his bride, and she back at him, this was a love match.

Salim's characteristic cynicism was curiously elusive.

Everyone stood up and started to cheer, and the happy young couple were shepherded out to their nuptial tent with great catcalling and fanfare.

Salim stood and put a hand out to help Charlotte stand. She looked up and he saw a definite glistening in those huge eyes before she dipped her head and smoothly rose, ignoring his hand.

His irritation at her dogged rejection was made sharper by the way the scene he'd just witnessed had sneaked under his well-worn guard.

Charlotte was turning to go and, incensed that she might evade him so easily, Salim caught her hand so she had to stop and look at him.

The lingering brightness in her eyes impacted on him in a way he didn't welcome. To cover it up, he drawled mockingly, 'Why, I do believe you're a romantic.'

'You're a romantic.'

Charlotte stiffened under his hand. A panicky feeling made her chest tight. The last thing she was was a romantic. She'd *told* Salim that she'd learnt her lessons young. That she had no illusions. And yet he didn't believe her because he could see how witnessing that achingly simple and yet profound ceremony just now—seeing the pretty girl with her elaborate wedding headdress and the dark kohl around her eyes—had affected Charlotte before she'd even absorbed the fullness of that revelation herself.

Avoiding him all day felt like an utterly futile exercise now. He was in her mind and under her skin.

Just then Rafa appeared at Salim's other side and,

taking advantage of his momentary distraction, Charlotte pulled her hand free and fled out of the tent behind the crowd without saying a word.

She was barely aware of the fact that the wind had started whipping up since the ceremony had started, or that there was a sense of urgency as people ran from tent to tent, shouting things to each other. She made her way instinctively to the natural pool and stood at the edge, breathing hard and trying to control her rising panic.

She wasn't a romantic. *She wasn't.*

So why had that ceremony affected her so profoundly? She knew the answer—fatally. It was rooted in that place where she still yearned for an idyllic Christmas and a happy family…

The choppy water mirrored her choppy emotions. She was still captivated, in spite of herself, by the thought that you could just look at someone and say those three words three times and it was done.

Charlotte hated it that Salim had been a witness to her moment of vulnerable revelation. Thinking of the way he'd drawled *'You're a romantic'* scored at her insides again.

She went cold all over as something else struck her—something far more threatening and disturbing. The thought of Salim telling himself that the reason she'd refused to sleep with him was because she wanted *more.*

Anger rose, whipping up inside her the way the wind was now whipping at her hair and her clothes. She turned around, galvanised by the thought of wiping that mocking look off Salim's face, and made her way back through the camp, which was now eerily empty.

Salim's tent stood tall and imposing, apart from the

camp, and she made straight for it, grabbing the heavy material covering the doorway and pulling it back to step into the space.

Immediately she was aware of the wind being muffled and a sense of stillness. Once again the tent was decadently furnished—like something from a lavish movie set. Candles threw out a golden glow, imbuing the space with warmth and luxury.

As the silence settled around her she realised she'd made a huge mistake, but before she could turn and escape she heard a sound and Salim stepped out from behind a screen on the other side of the tent.

Charlotte couldn't move.

He was naked.

Or almost naked. A tiny towel was hitched around his slim waist and his skin gleamed like burnished bronze. His hair was wet. He'd obviously just had a shower.

All Charlotte could see was the massive expanse of broad muscled chest and more ridges of muscle that led down to the towel, which did precious little to hide the very healthy bulge underneath, and then down lower to powerful thighs and strong legs.

If she'd thought he looked like a warrior before, now she realised he was a god. She was rooted to the spot, as if she'd never seen a naked man in the flesh before. Because she hadn't.

That realisation made her whirl around to leave, but in her agitation she couldn't find the opening of the tent. She was almost crying with frustration when she felt a solid presence behind her, and then a hand wrapped itself over her arm and turned her around.

She closed her eyes. Her heart was thumping so hard she felt light-headed.

'Open your eyes, Charlotte.'

With the utmost reluctance she did, and then felt a mixture of relief and regret to see that he'd thrown on a tunic. She couldn't lift her eyes higher, though, not wanting to see the expression on his face. But of course he tipped up her chin and she had no choice.

His face was harder than she'd ever seen it, those blue eyes burning. As if *he* was angry. When she was the angry one. She'd just forgotten for a moment.

She stepped back, dislodging his hold on her. She felt crowded and moved around him to gain some space.

He turned, watching her. 'Was there something you wished to discuss, Charlotte?'

She folded her arms, lifted her chin and hoped her voice wouldn't betray her. 'There was, actually. For your information, I am most certainly not a romantic. Nothing could be further from the truth.'

Salim folded his arms too, mirroring her defensive stance. 'So what was that back there? Some dust in your eye?'

He didn't believe her. She had to make him understand. 'I was six when my parents divorced. It was ugly and very public.'

He frowned. 'What do you mean? How public?'

Charlotte gave a short harsh laugh. 'As public as you can get. My father is Harry Lassiter and my mother is Louise Lassiter—she didn't change her name after the divorce.'

Salim's gaze sharpened. 'The award-winning movie director and the actress?'

Charlotte nodded. They'd both won multiple awards for the film, which had brought them together in the first place.

Salim's frown deepened. 'But you're Charlotte McQuillan.'

Her arms tightened around herself. Already she was regretting opening her mouth. What was it about this man that made him her confessor?

'I changed my name legally as soon as I turned eighteen. I took my grandmother's maiden name. I didn't want to be associated with my parents, or the most infamous divorce in the last couple of decades.'

Salim said, 'I was too young for it to be on my radar at the time, but I remember reading about it later.'

Charlotte grew hot, thinking of the lurid exposé programme that had been made about it, which was still on endless repeat on the entertainment channels. The memory of the pack of press waiting outside the courtroom was still vivid, and the awful knowledge that she'd wet herself because she'd been so upset after her father had said to her in the courtroom, *'You're no longer my daughter,'* because she'd chosen to stay with her mother.

Her tights had been stuck to her legs, damp and clammy, and she'd been sure that everyone would know her shame.

Diverting her mind from too-painful memories, she said, 'I'm just telling you this so that you'll understand why I have no illusions about romance or love.'

A sharp pain lanced her as she recalled the wedding ceremony she'd just witnessed and the well of secret emotion it had tapped into. She felt as if she'd just betrayed something precious.

Salim said, 'I couldn't agree more. My experiences might not have been the same as yours, but the end result is the same.'

Charlotte blinked at him. Bizarrely, his words didn't make her feel comforted.

He said tautly, 'My parents hated each other. You say you were a pawn—well, so were my brother and I. Born to lead two countries and keep the peace.'

Charlotte's insides twisted as she imagined growing up in that environment. 'People have been born for a lot less.'

He smiled, but it was hard. 'Yes, but they have their freedom.' And then his smile faded. 'Maybe we're not so different after all, hmm?'

Charlotte looked at Salim incredulously, thinking that they couldn't be *more* different. He was vital and arrogant, a force to be reckoned with, and she… Who was she? Someone who'd spent her life running from feeling rejected and abandoned, building a persona to protect herself from all that.

It suddenly felt very fragile. She felt exposed and raw, from those memories and from saying too much. Again.

She backed away. 'I'm sorry. I shouldn't have come here.'

'Wait. Stop.'

There was a note of command in his voice that stopped her in her tracks.

'Why did you come here this evening, really?'

Charlotte swallowed. Her skin felt tight and hot and her mouth was dry. Her heart was beating like a trapped bird against her chest.

'Just as I told you—I wanted to make sure you knew that I don't…don't have romantic notions.'

Salim moved towards her and she was rooted to the ground. 'Why is that so important?'

She swallowed again. 'I didn't want you to think

that I refused you last night because I wanted something more. I don't want more…' She stopped, her heart beating too hard and her brain fusing and stopping her words.

Because she was afraid she was lying to herself.

The wind screeched outside. Salim's eyes were like two blue flames. 'Believe me, the last thing you inspire is feelings of romance…'

Charlotte felt a pang of hurt. 'I don't?'

He shook his head. 'No. You inspire much earthier things. Dark and decadent things.'

There was still a couple of feet between them, but Charlotte felt as if Salim was touching her. The push and pull inside her was torture.

For a second she almost took a step towards him, giving in to the inexorable pull. But sanity prevailed. She was a virgin. She was no match for this man's presumably expert and voracious appetites. He would laugh at her, would ridicule her.

Before she could lose her mind completely, Charlotte blurted out, 'I'm going back to my tent.'

She turned abruptly and blindly felt for the opening of the tent, but nothing happened when she tried to open it. Panic mounted, and then she heard Salim's voice.

'We're in the middle of a sandstorm. The tent has been secured for our safety. If you were to step outside right now you'd be flayed in minutes.'

Charlotte noticed far too belatedly that the entire structure of the tent was swaying alarmingly. She dropped her hands and turned around.

Salim had a suspiciously innocent look on his face. 'Don't worry, we're quite safe. These tents are built to withstand such events.'

Charlotte almost couldn't articulate words, but she forced them out. 'So, what does that mean.?'

An unmistakable glint of something wicked in Salim's eyes replaced any hint of innocence on his handsome face. 'It means, Charlotte, that you'll have to spend the night here.'

CHAPTER SIX

CHARLOTTE TOOK A deep breath as she looked at herself in the small ornate mirror that hung—swinging precariously now—over the sink in the sectioned off bathing area of the tent. She looked wild. Her hair had been blown everywhere by the wind.

She tried to drum up a sense of horror seeing herself come so undone, but in truth when Salim had told her she'd have to stay there a very illicit sense of liberation had flowed into her blood, making it race. As if nature itself had colluded to take the angst she was feeling out of her belly and replace it with a sense of fatalism.

She couldn't keep fighting this. No matter how terrifying it was.

Salim hadn't been crass enough actually to articulate what might happen, but it throbbed in the air even now.

Just then, as if to test her, something soft and light-coloured was flicked over the screen separating her from the rest of the tent and Salim's voice floated in, far too close for comfort.

'You can use this after you wash. It'll be too big but it's all I have.'

Charlotte was about to open to her mouth to declare she didn't need to change, because she had no intention of taking off a stitch of her clothing, no matter what was going on in her head and body, but the words stuck in her throat when she found herself wondering if *he* had worn this tunic.

Weakly, she said nothing and pulled it over the screen into her hands. His scent drifted tantalisingly from the folds of material and something tugged deep in her belly—an ache that had become all too familiar since she'd met Salim.

She looked at herself in the mirror—her expression was one of someone who was hunted. Or *haunted*, to be more accurate. Haunted by her past.

It struck her then—as much as she'd done her best to move away from it—her past was still nipping at her heels, dictating everything she did. Stopping her from living fully for fear of annihilation. Rejection.

She thought she'd distanced herself from any possibility of pain, but she realised now with a sense of futility that you could never really escape pain. Unless you wanted to live half a life. And she knew now that she wanted more than that—even if it meant taking a risk.

The wind howled outside and the sense of being closed off from everything was very seductive. It whispered at her to let go of her inhibitions. It whispered at her to take a risk.

'Charlotte? Is everything all right?'

She jumped at Salim's voice and then answered quickly, 'Everything is fine. I'll be out in a minute.'

A reckless excitement filled her in that moment—a sense of seizing something vital and alive. Without really thinking about the invisible line she'd stepped over in her own mind, Charlotte stripped and stepped into the shower area, leaving her own clothes in a neat pile on a chair.

Hot water rained down over her head and body and

she tipped her face up. She couldn't help but be aware of the symbolism; she felt as if a layer of her carefully constructed persona was being washed away too.

She was in the middle of the desert in the middle of a sandstorm, sharing a tent with a man who had got under her skin and made her want more than she'd ever wanted in her life.

When she stepped out and dried herself perfunctorily with a towel cool air made her skin pop up into goosebumps. Her nipples were hard and tight. The ache deep in her core intensified.

The tunic Salim had given her fell heavily down her naked body, pooling on the ground at her feet. It had a vee neck that on him would look perfectly civilised, but on her cut right between her breasts, showing an indecent amount of flesh.

Suddenly Charlotte didn't care. It was as if she could see her habitual self stalking out of this space, still dressed in her own clothes, determined to resist at all costs, but she didn't want to be her any more. Or at least not for tonight.

The earth was being whipped into a frenzy outside, and they were separated from that awesome power by only a flimsy barrier. It intensified her growing urgency to seize the moment.

Charlotte took a breath and stepped out from behind the screen. For a second she couldn't see anything in the dimly lit space, and her very recent and nebulous bravado faltered. But then her eyes fell on the bed, and she saw the unmistakably masculine shape of Salim, sprawled in careless abandon on top of the sumptuous fabrics.

The tent around them groaned ominously, but he didn't move. Hardly breathing, Charlotte picked up the excess folds of the robe in one hand and moved forward, coming to a stop a few feet from the bed.

When her eyes had finally adjusted to the light she saw that he wasn't moving because he was asleep, his dark lashes resting on those slashing high aristocratic cheekbones. Even though he wore clothes—he'd thrown trousers on under his robe—the latent power of that impressive body was impossible to conceal.

There was something incredibly voyeuristic about watching him in this moment of rare defencelessness, but that wasn't strictly accurate because even now he exuded an air of force and control.

His leg moved slightly and Charlotte panicked, reality slamming into her like cold bucket of water. What was she doing? Had she really expected to walk out here and find him waiting for her just because he'd said, *'You'll have to spend the night here'* with that glint in his eye? Expected that he would still want her?

He was just toying with her because she was a woman unlike his other lovers—someone who intrigued him briefly. She was an idiot to think that anything fundamental had changed within her so that she was ready to throw caution to the winds, and she sent up silent thanks now that he'd never know how close she'd come to making a complete fool of herself.

She turned around to escape behind the screen, but got no further than a couple of feet when she heard Salim say, 'Where are you going?'

Salim pushed himself up to sit on the bed. Charlotte had her back to him. He'd been listening to the sounds of the shower and imagining rivulets of water running down over her slender pale body. Then he'd heard her steal softly into the tent and he'd feigned sleep, curious to see what she'd do…

But nothing had happened and when he'd opened his eyes she'd been walking away.

She slowly turned around to face him.

Salim stood up from the bed. The robe he'd given her was comically large on her slender frame, but comical was the last thing he was feeling as he took her in.

She was bathed in the golden light of the candles around her and it made her pale skin even more lustrous. Her hair was damp and curling from the shower. And when his gaze dipped down desire engulfed him in a hot wave.

He'd seen women dressed in the most provocative lingerie the world had to offer. And yet right now the woman in front of him was the most erotic vision he'd ever seen.

The vee of the robe came to just below Charlotte's breasts and did little to conceal the high, firm swells. He could see the outline of her body through the light material—where her waist dipped in and her hips flared out, her long legs and the slightly darker juncture between them.

His mouth watered at the prospect of tasting her there, feeling her come apart in his mouth…

She looked like the kind of woman he'd never slept with in his life. Like an innocent. And, as much as he knew he should turn away from her because he had no right corrupting anyone's innocence, the dark part of him wanted her too much. The dark part of him he'd spent a lifetime indulging to carve out his independence, further his ambitions and seek revenge.

Charlotte couldn't turn back now—not under Salim's hungry gaze. It emboldened her again. She felt as if he'd just touched her all over but it wasn't enough. She wanted him to touch her…properly.

She moved across the tent to stand in front of him, light-headed with what she was doing. She said, before she could stop herself, 'What you said…that I make you want earthy things, dark things… I want that too.'

Salim's gaze locked onto her mouth and she could see the colour slash across his cheeks. He lifted a hand and rubbed his thumb across her lower lip, his fingers touching her jaw. She held her breath, acutely aware of her innocence. Should she say something?

Her gut clenched.

Surely, she told herself, a man like him would hardly be sensitive enough to perceive her innocence. And there was some bizarre comfort in the fact that her first lover would be a man who wouldn't feel the need to give her platitudes or false promises.

She didn't want someone tender and caring, as she'd always believed. She craved this inferno of need and she wanted it with this man who stood head and shoulders above every other man she'd ever met.

She was under no illusions. She knew that this was a moment out of time, that they were cocooned in this tent while a storm raged outside. In their usual world and in their usual circumstances he wouldn't have looked at her twice, and she felt greedy now. Greedy to store up this moment for when they would be back in the real world.

He took his thumb off her mouth and put his hands on her arms. Blue eyes on green. 'Are you sure?'

She nodded. A faint alarm bell was ringing at his consideration, but it was too faint to be heard right now.

He brought his hands up her arms to her shoulders and slipped his fingers under the material of the robe. With gentle pressure he pushed at the robe until it slipped down her shoulders, baring them. It clung precariously to her upper arms and the slopes of her breasts for an infinitesimal moment, but when Salim exerted more pressure it fell all the way to the ground and pooled at her feet.

She was naked in front of him, more exposed than she'd ever been, but fire was burning inside her, and a hitherto unexplored sense of feminine power.

Salim's gaze dropped down over her body, slowly and thoroughly. His eyes lingered on her breasts, which she'd always felt were too small. Now they felt positively voluptuous under his inspection. And then his gaze dropped further, and the ache between her legs turned sharp and insistent.

She didn't realise she was trembling until he stepped back and started to take off his tunic, pulling it over his head and revealing that impressive chest again. With deft movements he shed his trousers and now he was naked too. Charlotte couldn't help herself. Her eyes widened as she took in the majestic virility of the man in front of her.

She felt as if something was slotting into place—as if she'd had the desire to see this visual since the moment she'd laid eyes on him but hadn't acknowledged it until now.

Her avid gaze roved over his chest and down to where a line of dark hair dissected his tautly flat belly, down to the dark hair between his legs. Her mouth went dry when she saw his erection, long and thick and very hard. He brought a hand to himself, wrapping long fingers around the column of flesh as if to contain it…and it was the most erotic thing Charlotte had ever seen.

Her heart was thumping so loud she felt sure he must be able to hear it.

'Come here…'

She looked up, dizzy. He was watching her with a hunger that might have made her nervous if she'd had any brain cells left. She stepped closer and he took his hand off himself to reach for her, pulling her even closer so they touched. She could feel his arousal between them—insistent, hard.

He wrapped his arms around her and Charlotte lifted her arms to his neck, stretching up, relishing the friction of his chest against her breasts. Their mouths came together without hesitation, breath moving from one to the other as Salim angled her head so he could access her more fully.

When their tongues touched she made a groaning sound deep in her throat. He devoured her with a mastery that left her nowhere to hide, and she didn't want to hide. She revelled in the feel of his much bigger body next to hers, revelled in his strength. Revelled in the inherent differences between them.

His hands moved up and down her back, learning her shape. One hand cupped a buttock, squeezing gently. She pressed her thighs together to try and contain the rush of liquid heat. But it was impossible when that same hand explored back up her body, over her waist and in between them, finding the underside of her breast and cupping the plump weight.

He pulled back and looked down, and her gaze followed his to see her pale flesh cupped in his dark hand. He moved his thumb over her hard nipple and she bit her lip.

Suddenly the languorous energy between them seemed to change and thicken with something much more urgent and sharp.

'I want you, Charlotte...*now*.'

She looked up at him and gulped. She'd never seen

such an intense look on his face before. His bone structure stood out in stark relief. She nodded, her whole being saying *yes* to whatever he meant.

He took her hand and led her over to the bed, pulling her down with him onto the soft, decadent surface. As decadent as her behaviour. Salim raised himself over her and pulled her arms up so that they were over her head.

He looked at her. 'Stay like that.'

Charlotte didn't think she could move even if she wanted to. She was enslaved.

He watched her for a moment, as if she might disobey him, and she said roughly, 'I'm not moving.'

He smiled—brief and infinitely wicked. Then he looked his fill of her, his gaze slow and thorough.

The fact that she could fascinate Salim—a *king!*—on any level was terrifying and heady.

His hand moved over her, causing her stomach muscles to contract. He cupped her breast again, until it pouted wantonly towards his mouth, and when he bent his head and surrounded her tight nipple with heat and moisture she clasped her hands together over her head, so tightly it hurt. It was the only thing she could do to counteract the intense spiking of pleasure.

Her back arched helplessly towards him, and when he left one breast he ministered the same brand of torture to the other one, until Charlotte was flushed and panting, her whole body pulsating with need.

He lifted his head and looked at her, his expression feral. 'You're so responsive...why do you hide all this heat under that prim uniform, hmm?'

Charlotte had no coherent answer except the one in her head that was silent. *Because I hadn't met you yet...*

His hand drifted down again, over her belly and

lower, as he said throatily, 'Let's see how responsive you really are.'

He pushed her legs apart with gentle force, and every nerve in Charlotte's body seemed to migrate to between her legs in anticipation of his touch.

She still wasn't prepared when he did touch her, experimentally at first, on the very outside of where she ached most. Teasing her.

She couldn't keep her arms up any longer, and gripped his wide shoulders as he moved over her, his weight pressing down on her as that hand explored deeper between her legs. She gasped when his fingers slipped past the folds of aching flesh and released the liquid heat she'd been so desperately trying to contain.

He went still and muttered an Arabic curse, and for a second Charlotte felt acutely vulnerable. 'What's wrong?'

He shook his head and looked slightly stunned. 'Nothing… You… I had no idea a woman like you existed…'

As he spoke he slipped a finger inside her and Charlotte's thoughts scattered. She was too overcome to analyse what he'd just said or what it might mean.

She could feel her body resisting this intrusion, but as he explored her with a gentleness that belied the man she'd thought he was she felt her body softening, opening… One finger became two, and stretched her wider, going deeper, making the tension coiling deep within her snap and sharpen, searching for some kind of release.

She moved against his hand unconsciously, a little overwhelmed with all the sensations he was arousing. He bent his head and found her breast, licking her nipple back to stinging life before sucking it deep as his fingers still touched her intimately.

His mouth moved down her body, leaving a trail of hot kisses on her damp skin, and then his hand moved from between her legs. She immediately felt bereft—until his shoulders pushed her thighs even further apart.

She looked down and gasped. 'What are you—?'

'Shh… I need to taste you…to feel you on my tongue…' His words sounded slurred, as if he was drunk.

Too overwhelmed to do anything but submit, she felt him press kisses to her upper inner thighs, the scrape of his short beard sending shivers of sensation all over her body. When his mouth got closer to the very centre of her she went very still, her entire being thinking, *No…he won't…* But he did—with a thorough explicitness that made Charlotte's eyes roll back in her head.

His tongue licked right into the centre of her body and she couldn't breathe. Or think. Or move except to try and shy away from such an overload of pleasure. But his big hands were clamped on her thighs, holding her still, and then one hand moved under one buttock, gripping her firmly and lifting her so that he could explore her more fully.

Charlotte shuddered and gasped against Salim's mouth, and there was nothing to save her from the fall that came with shocking speed and force.

Her whole body was throbbing in the aftermath of an explosive orgasm. Salim moved up her body, and when she could open her eyes again she saw there was a distinctly smug look on his face.

He said roughly, 'You don't know how much I have wanted to see you undone like this…'

In a surprisingly tender move he brushed some hair

off her face. She could feel that it was damp, but she was too sated to care what she looked like. Her legs were spread in wanton abandonment and she could feel his body against hers. Hard. Needy.

Instinctively she reached for him, wanting to know how that stiff column of flesh would feel.

She wrapped her hand around him and saw how his facial muscles tightened, felt his whole body going still as she moved it experimentally up and down. His silky skin glided over the hard shaft of flesh and it fascinated her…its inherent strength and intense vulnerability.

Charlotte looked down and saw a bead of moisture. She spread it over the thick head of his erection but he stopped her hand with his.

She looked at him, suddenly unsure, and he said, 'If you keep doing that I'll spill right here…and I need to be inside you.'

Her heart stuttered as she watched him reach for protection and roll it onto his turgid flesh. He came over her, settling his hips between her legs, widening them further. Her muscles ached, but she barely noticed when she felt her body softening and ripening again.

He braced himself over her with a powerful arm, his other hand on his own body, guiding himself to her core… But when she expected him to thrust into her body instead he bent his head and kissed her, mimicking penetration with his tongue.

Charlotte moved against him, twining her arms around his neck, so that when he did thrust between her legs it was in tandem with his mouth and tongue and it stopped her gasp of shock and soothed it all at once.

He stopped moving for a moment, letting her body get used to his thickness, and she felt the resisting wall of muscle relax infinitesimally, allowing him to slide deeper. He did—with a groan that reverberated deep inside her.

For a moment it was too much—Charlotte felt impaled, and had an instinct to push him off her—but even as she put her hands to his shoulders and looked up at him the urge to push turned into something else. An urge to wrap her legs around him and keep him there.

His eyes burned down into hers and held her captive as he started to move in a relentless rhythm, in and out. Gradually Charlotte started to feel that urgency build again, and Salim slid an arm underneath her, arching her up towards him. He found her breast and sucked her nipple deep, and the twin sensations made her blood thunder under her skin.

Charlotte could feel the climax coming, but couldn't articulate any words to stop it for fear that she wasn't ready for it… On some dim level she knew she'd never be ready, and that all she could do was submit and let it sweep her away.

And that was exactly what it did. Salim's body moved within hers and she couldn't remember a time when she'd been a single entity.

Her body gave up its fight to resist the oncoming storm and shattered into a million pieces, her muscles milking him as he plunged deeper and deeper until he finally reached his own completion and her body claimed his, holding him deep within her as the final spasms of her own climax faded, until there was nothing left but the tattered remnants of the person she'd once been.

Salim knew the sandstorm had passed because there was a sense of stillness outside the tent and the sound of muffled of voices. No doubt the men were already in recovery mode in the early dawn—unearthing anything that had been buried during the storm.

That storm might have passed, but another one raged inside him. He was sitting in a chair on the opposite side of the tent from the bed, looking at the sleeping figure there warily, as if she might jump up at any moment and bite him.

He recalled her biting him last night, in the throes of her orgasm, on his shoulder. She'd broken his skin and he'd welcomed it.

Even now he couldn't really credit what had happened. The most intensely pleasurable sexual experience of his life. And the most vanilla. Sex with a virgin. You couldn't get more vanilla than that. And yet… Salim had felt like a novice too—learning his way into a woman's body for the first time.

She'd been a virgin.

The word resounded like an echoing klaxon: *virgin, virgin.*

He'd sensed it before he'd known for sure, and he knew that in any other situation, with any other woman, he would have run a mile at the merest suggestion of innocence. But it had only fired up his libido even more.

So her cooler than cool persona wasn't just a front. Unlocking her body had only made him think of all that she'd told him about her family and her upbringing. That sense of kinship echoed inside him again—they'd both suffered at the hands of their families and built up walls high enough to keep everyone out.

But after last night those walls were in danger of tumbling down around Salim's feet. And he could only imagine how seismic it had been for Charlotte to give up her innocence.

He'd wanted to bed her because he'd wanted her

more than he'd wanted any other woman and he'd naively thought that would be enough. But he could feel a clawing, raging hunger for *more.* Much more. And... worse...he didn't just feel physical satisfaction. He'd felt an elusive sense of peace steal over him in the moments just after his explosive orgasm, when his body and Charlotte's had been joined so tightly that for a second he hadn't wanted ever to break the connection.

What was he doing?

Salim stood up as adrenalin flooded his system—the fight or flight impulse. He was an expert in letting women know not to expect more than a no-strings encounter, and yet Charlotte—with her prim silk shirt and pencil skirts and no fear of him—had burrowed so far under his skin that he had all but forgotten his own strict code of ethics. He'd wanted her that badly.

A very rare sense of disorientation made him feel dizzy for a moment. He never lost sight of what was important to him. And yet he was in danger of losing sight of a lot more. He was here in Tabat with one aim—to promote and stabilise the country for someone else to run—and yet that had been the last thing on his mind over the past few days as he'd broken bread with these tribes and had felt a mounting sense of ownership take hold.

As if hearing his inner dialogue, Charlotte moved on the bed and everything in Salim's body went still and taut. Just then there was a noise from outside the tent—a conspicuous clearing of a throat.

Salim tore his gaze from the still sleeping woman on the bed and went to the entrance. He found Rafa waiting for him.

'Sire, the storm wasn't as extensive as we feared so

we can leave this morning. But you need to speak with the elders before we go.'

Salim waited a beat and imagined Charlotte waking up, those green eyes landing on him, looking for something he wasn't prepared to give.

'Very well,' he said grimly, 'let's go.'

As he strode away from his tent he ignored the stinging of his conscience. He was just doing what he had done countless times before—walking away from a lover. This was no different and it couldn't afford to be—because he was in danger of forgetting why he was here at all.

Charlotte rose slowly through the levels of consciousness, registering aches and muscle twinges that told of a vigorous kind of activity she'd never indulged in before.

But the acute tenderness between her legs made her recall too easily and vividly what it had felt like to have Salim's powerful body thrusting deep inside hers, over and over again.

She opened her eyes with a snap, blinking in the dim light of the tent. The first thing she heard were voices from outside. The tent was empty, and when she came up on her elbows she saw her clothes laid out across the bottom of the bed.

Something curled up inside her.

What had she expected? To wake and find Salim mooning over her? Hadn't she gone to great pains to tell him she wasn't a romantic? That she just wanted dark and decadent things? And hadn't he obliged? *Thoroughly?*

She grabbed her clothes and went into the bathing area, washing quickly, avoiding her reflection in the mirror. When she re-emerged she felt a little disorientated in the empty tent. It was as if last night might have been a mirage, or a feverish erotic dream.

Suddenly Charlotte was terrified that Salim would appear before she was ready to see him, and she went to the opening of the tent, pulling back the flap of material. She saw sand piled against the surrounding tents, obviously shifted there by the storm, but it appeared not to have caused too much damage.

There was no one in the immediate vicinity and she escaped back to her own tent. When she got there she took a deep breath—but then almost jumped out of her skin when someone entered just behind her. She whirled around, her heart in her mouth. *Assa.* Her heart went back to a regular rhythm.

The girl looked distracted. 'Good—you're up, Miss McQuillan. The storm wasn't as bad as they feared, so we'll leave for Tabat City shortly. You should gather your things. The king is eager to be back before sunset.'

I bet he is, thought Charlotte, ignoring the dart of hurt that he didn't seem to be overly concerned as to her wellbeing this morning.

She got her things together and packed. The fact that he hadn't been there when she'd woken, hadn't thought to wake her, told her in no uncertain terms that she was most likely already consigned to the box where he stored regretful experiences. If the man had any regrets—which he probably didn't.

By the time the staff were loading up the vehicles Charlotte could see Salim in the distance, tall and dominant. He was speaking to the sheikh of the tribe, and then he got into his SUV and it took off ahead of the convoy, flanked by Security in their four by fours.

Rafa appeared, and to Charlotte's over-sensitive mind it seemed he looked at her with an expression of pity.

'You will travel with me, Miss McQuillan.'

She forced a smile, as if this was totally fine, and told herself that she wasn't devastated by the way Salim obviously couldn't bear to look at her. The thought that this genteel older gentleman might know what had happened was nearly too much to bear.

As they drove across the undulating desert, getting closer and closer to civilisation again, Salim's morning-after treatment of Charlotte continued to grate on her exposed nerves, even though she knew it shouldn't.

She cursed herself for having believed that something revelatory had happened last night. It had been sex. Her first sexual experience, yes. But just sex. The fact that Salim hadn't appeared even to notice that he'd been her first lover was something she shouldn't be disappointed by. After all, she'd hoped that he wouldn't notice. But the fact that he *hadn't* wasn't as easy to live with as she'd thought.

And, worse, it stung her where she was most vulnerable—where her parents had left an indelible mark of rejection and abandonment. *This* was what she'd wanted to protect herself from, and to think that she'd allowed someone close enough to rip those wounds open again was as humiliating as it was painful.

She'd deluded herself last night, thinking she could take what Salim offered and remain untouched. She'd wanted him badly enough to lie to herself.

They reached the palace in Tabat City as the sun was setting over the ancient building, bathing everything with a lush golden light, but Charlotte was oblivious to the beauty, her guts churning.

She got out of the car and stretched her cramped legs. She saw Salim in the distance, dark shades covering his eyes. He looked in her direction briefly, but then turned and strode into the palace with his retinue following behind him. He'd never looked more king-like than at that moment.

Assa appeared at Charlotte's side. 'I will draw you a bath, Miss McQuillan, and have some food brought to your room. You must be tired.'

Tired, hot and dusty. And still aching in secret places.

She followed Assa back to her room but a couple of hours later, after food and a bath, Charlotte couldn't settle.

She'd half expected—*hoped*—to see Salim appear, but since the sun had set and night had fallen over the desert outside there'd been no visitors. She felt powerless, and it was far too reminiscent of when she'd been younger, when she'd been at the mercy of her parents' whims.

She hated to think that after all she'd been through she had allowed herself to be treated so cavalierly, that somewhere in this vast crumbling palace Salim was oblivious to her turmoil.

And she hated it that she couldn't stop thinking about the fact that he was proving to be far more complex than she'd ever have given him credit for: the king who was too selfish to rule his own people and yet had conducted himself like a king for the past week.

He hadn't made love to her like a reprobate playboy last night. He'd made love to her like a man who cared more for her pleasure than his own. And yet today he'd treated her as if she didn't exist.

Nothing added up.

Galvanised by something deep inside that wouldn't rest, Charlotte changed out of the robe she wore and into plain trousers and the loose tribal shirt she'd bought from the women of the Jadar tribe. She looked at herself quickly in the mirror and grimaced at her tousled hair, but left it as it was. She couldn't remember the last time it had been sleek and neat.

Before she could stop and rationalise what she was doing, Charlotte slipped out of her room and along the long corridor that led up to Salim's private quarters. She only noticed halfway there that she was in bare feet, but didn't stop.

The palace was silent, and it was only when she reached Salim's door that she faltered. A bodyguard stood outside, but he recognised her and said in Arabic, 'Good evening, Miss McQuillan. You have a meeting with King Al-Noury?'

She nodded, crossing her fingers at the white lie.

He opened the door and let her go inside. Charlotte hadn't been to Salim's quarters before, and saw that it was a vast labyrinth of rooms. The decor was masculine and heavy. Dark. Perhaps these had been his grandfather's rooms.

She walked through the nearest door and found herself in a huge living area, with low couches dotted around coffee tables and a media centre in one corner where world news played on mute in the background.

And then her gaze landed on the tall figure standing by one of the windows. Her heart palpitated. He moved out of the shadows and into the low light of the room. His bone structure looked even more austere. He wore a white shirt and black trousers, once more the urbane Western billionaire. Albeit still with the beard and sexily messy hair.

For a second a sense of *déjà-vu* hit her as she recalled what that beard had felt like tickling her tender inner thighs. Charlotte wondered a little desperately if a man like Salim could ever be tamed?

He was holding a bulbous crystal glass in one hand and he raised it towards her, the amber liquid catching the light. 'Can I offer you a drink?'

Charlotte swallowed the dryness in her mouth. She shook her head. The last thing she needed was anything that made her feel dizzier.

'Was there something you wanted, Charlotte?'

He sounded almost bored, and not remotely surprised to see her. As if he'd been waiting for her because he knew she wouldn't be able to resist coming to him.

She cursed herself for having ever thought there might be hidden depths to him and felt her emotions bubble over.

She clenched her hands into fists at her sides. 'It's true what they say—you really are a bastard, aren't you?'

CHAPTER SEVEN

A SENSE OF *déjà-vu* hit Salim like a punch to his gut. The words she'd just uttered were words he was well used to hearing from women, but none had scored along his insides like a serrated knife before.

When he'd turned around just now, to see Charlotte standing just a few feet away, for a second he'd thought that he'd conjured her up out of the desire that was clawing at his insides, making a mockery of his determination to relegate her to a one-night aberration.

Salim couldn't stop his gaze dipping hungrily to the vee neck of the tribal shirt and the way it clung to her breasts. The material was so fine he could see she wore no bra, and his body responded forcibly to the memory of how those firm swells had felt in his hands. How they'd felt pressed against his chest as she'd arched into him. How they'd tasted under his tongue.

She *was* real, and he felt exposed.

Irritation at her ability to slide under his skin so effortlessly made him ask curtly, 'Why didn't you tell me you were a virgin?'

She blanched slightly, some of her bravado slipping. 'So you did notice?'

Salim felt grim. 'I may be a bastard but I'm also an

experienced lover, and last night was your first time, wasn't it?'

Charlotte didn't shy away from his question. She stepped forward and looked him directly in the eye. 'Yes, it was.'

As direct and forthright as ever. No games there.

'Then why me? Why now?'

Do you really want to know the answer to that? asked a voice. But it was too late.

Colour flared along her cheeks. 'Because you're the first man I've ever wanted like that. It was sex, pure and simple, Salim. Nothing more.'

He looked at her for a long moment, as if he could convince himself of the veracity of her words. They should be making him feel better, but if anything they only compounded his conflicting emotions because he doubted it was that pure and simple at all.

He felt compelled to goad her. 'When I lost my virginity I believed myself in love… For about a week, until I found my lover in bed with one of my security detail.'

Her eyes sparked at that, and she stepped forward. 'So that's why you weren't there when I woke this morning—to make sure I didn't get any ideas.'

Salim's conscience pricked hard. 'I don't *do* cosy mornings after.'

Charlotte folded her arms and it pushed the swells of her breasts up beneath the flimsy material of her shirt. Salim gritted his jaw.

'Believe me, I didn't imagine for a second that you did. I'm not in love with you, Salim, and I wasn't looking to wake up in your arms. But a little acknowledgement of what we'd shared might have been nice.'

Honesty forced him to admit, 'You deserved for your first time to be with a better man than me.'

Charlotte was stunned. The very thought of not having had that experience with this man made her go cold inside. No man would ever make her feel like that again. She knew that with fatal certainty.

She let her arms drop to her sides. 'But I wanted *you*.'

Salim's hand tightened on the glass he held. 'Because I gave you little choice. I suspected your innocence but I seduced you anyway.'

Charlotte shook her head. 'I know my own mind, Salim. I made the choice—you asked me if I was sure, don't you remember?'

'Did I?'

She nodded. 'Why would you think you're not worthy?'

His mouth tightened. He was looking at her, but not seeing her. He'd gone somewhere else.

'I've gone after what I want for so long that it's second nature for me to disregard others' opinions. That's why I won't remain as King of Tabat. If anything, this past week has proved to me even more that they deserve someone better.'

Charlotte struggled to process this. 'What are you talking about?'

Salim's gaze narrowed on hers, and for the first time she saw something raw and unguarded in those blue depths. Raw enough to make her suck in a breath.

He said, 'I've lived my life with two main objectives: to distance myself from my inheritance and family and to avenge my sister's death.'

Charlotte's chest tightened. 'Why did you have to avenge it?'

Salim made a curt gesture with his hand. 'That's not important now. What is important is that I know my limitations, and I am not prepared to be king. I haven't spent hours studying, like my brother. I've lived my life in a way that should convince people that I'm not remotely suitable. And yet they don't seem to want to accept that.'

'Because,' Charlotte said quietly, 'they see what I saw this week—a man prepared to sit down and learn about his country. You didn't need me there at all. Your destiny—whether you like to admit it or not—is in your DNA. You're a king, Salim, and your people can see that.'

There was no disguising the bleakness she saw in his eyes now. This was no playboy. This was a tortured man.

'Would you say the same if you knew I'd driven a man to his death in the name of vengeance?'

Her breath stopped. 'What do you mean?'

'I took a life for a life.'

Charlotte knew he must be talking about his sister. 'But you didn't actually…kill someone?'

He let out a short harsh laugh. 'Not with my hands, but as good as.'

Charlotte knew instinctively that whatever had happened Salim wasn't responsible in the way he obviously believed. But she guessed he wouldn't elaborate, or appreciate hearing her thoughts.

She could also see very clearly that his motives for not wanting to be King of Tabat for longer than absolutely necessary had nothing to do with his own selfish needs. It was based on something far deeper and darker.

Acting on an instinct she couldn't deny, Charlotte reached out and took the glass of alcohol out of Salim's hand. She raised it to her mouth and drained it. The liquid slid down her throat, leaving a burning fire in its wake and rushing to her head.

She put the glass down carefully on a table and looked back up at Salim. He was watching her. Emotion surged in spite of her best efforts to burn it away with the whisky.

She aimed for a wry smile, but it felt wobbly. 'You don't actually need my expertise at all—you're a natural.'

'Are you telling me you think your services are no longer required?' Salim's voice was harsh.

The rush of alcohol-induced confidence trickled away and Charlotte felt cold. 'No…that's not what I'm saying.'

'So what are you saying?'

She refused to let this austere Salim scare her away. 'Do you want me, Salim? Because if you don't that's fine. I'll leave right now.'

For a heart-stopping moment she saw the struggle on his face and in his eyes.

But then he reached for her as he said gutturally, 'Yes, damn you—yes, I want you.'

It was all she needed to hear. She reached up and put her arms around his neck, pressed her mouth to his.

Salim knew he was playing with fire, but he was incapable of resisting. Charlotte's mouth moved under his and he gave in to the dark hunger inside him—a voracious, needy hunger.

He wrapped his arms around her back and hauled her to him, feeling the length of her slender body trembling against his as he took control of the kiss and gorged on the sweetness she was offering.

Charlotte gave up trying to make any sense of anything—she just knew, as Salim started kissing her back, clearly showing her who was boss in this exchange, that she never wanted him to stop.

He'd awakened her on a sexual level but she knew very well that their time was finite. She felt that same greedy desire she had last night, to experience as much as she could.

When he pulled back from kissing her she went with him, opening her eyes, her vision blurry for a minute. He took her by the hand and led her through his rooms and into a vast bedroom, dominated by the biggest bed she'd ever seen in her life.

He stopped by the bed and let her hand go. 'I want to see you.'

Charlotte's inhibitions had been burnt away by alcohol and revelations. She had nothing left to hide behind, so she took off her clothes.

Salim's blue gaze devoured her from head to toe. Once again the thought that he could find her so compelling was unbelievable and heady. Too heady to resist.

He reached for her and pulled her close. Her hands automatically searched for his shirt buttons, undoing them unsteadily because he was pushing her hair back and pressing kisses to her neck and shoulder, the scratch of his beard sending shivers through her whole body.

Her breasts felt heavy as he cupped one in his hand, his thumb moving back and forth over her nipple. The sensations connected directly to the pulse between her legs, where she was throbbing with hot, damp need.

When he pulled back slightly his shirt was open, but still tucked in. He made short work of untucking it and pulling it off, his hands going to his belt and then his trousers, undoing them and pushing them down to the floor.

Now he wore just briefs, and they were tented over his erection. Charlotte remembered how she had felt when he'd thrust inside her...how full and stretched... She reached out instinctively and cupped a hand over him.

He said roughly, 'Take them off.'

With trembling hands she pulled them down from his lean hips and over his erection, down over powerful thighs and to the floor. She was almost kneeling at his feet now, and she stayed there.

She looked at that part of him that was so unashamedly masculine. She reached out and heard the breath hiss through his teeth as she wrapped her hand around his length, fascinated by the silky smoothness of the skin around that column of steel arising out of dark hair.

She touched the bead of moisture at its head with her thumb. She wanted to taste it and leant forward, licking with her tongue. Lust exploded inside her as the tart, salty taste impacted on her tastebuds and she wanted to taste more. She placed her mouth around him and for a heady moment felt a sense of unbelievable feminine power as she explored the bulbous head of his erection with her mouth and tongue.

But then he stepped back, out of her reach, and his hands came under her arms, lifting her up.

She immediately felt self-conscious. 'Was I doing something wrong?'

Salim shook his head, his eyes burning so bright it almost hurt to look into them. '*No.* But I need to be inside you right now more than I need your mouth on me...'

'Oh...'

Her heart thumped hard as Salim took her to the bed and she lay down. He came down beside her, all bronzed skin and rippling muscles. He put a hand on her thighs, opening them, and then placed his hand on the beating heart of her body before stroking her damp folds with his finger. She had to bite back a moan, she was so acutely sensitised.

Salim pressed his mouth to hers, his tongue tasting her explicitly before he drew back and said, 'Let it out… I want to hear you…'

As if to make her moan out loud, one finger became two and he thrust them in and out. The ache deep inside her grew tight and sharp. It was even sharper when his mouth encircled one breast and he drew her hard nipple in deep, suckling at the tingling flesh until she couldn't hold back any longer and moaned a plea into his shoulder…

Charlotte couldn't breathe. She was caught in a spiral of growing need. Blindly she searched for and found Salim's hard flesh, wrapping a hand around him, stroking up and down in an instinctive rhythm. She revelled in the way his breath hissed between his teeth and his muscles went taut.

He moved over her, dominating her easily…but in a way that made her excitement increase.

She explored with more confidence now, her hand still caressing him as she kissed his shoulder and moved her mouth down, exploring a hard nipple and administering the same torture he'd inflicted on her.

Salim reached to the side of the bed for something and donned protection. She moved so that she was under him, and his body settled between her spread legs as if this was a dance they'd done many times before. If she could think more clearly it would been scary how *right* this felt…

In silent answer to the question he hadn't even asked,

she just tilted her hips up towards him so that the blunt head of his erection was notched right against her body, a mere breath away from—

Aahhh...

She moaned as he slid in slowly, watching her face. She was surrounded by heat and sensation, but he was going too slowly, so she wrapped her legs around his waist and dug her heels into his muscular buttocks.

He huffed out a laugh and gave in to her body's demands, thrusting so deep inside her that for a long moment she couldn't breathe. And then he started to move, and her breath came back, and she was soaring, flying higher and higher, until everything went still inside her. It felt like a tiny death—and then she exploded back into life and crashed and burned…

Salim couldn't hold back a guttural curse as the powerful inner muscles of Charlotte's body drew him in so thoroughly that he couldn't keep from falling over the edge behind her.

It had been fast and furious. He'd never felt less in control of his own body. They'd touched and ignited immediately. He'd never experienced anything like it before.

It seemed to take for ever for his heart to slow down again as he lay slumped over Charlotte's body. Her legs had fallen to his sides and he could feel the aftershock ripples of her inner muscles along his length, keeping him hard.

He lifted his head and looked down. She opened her eyes slowly and something turned over in his chest. Her cheeks were flushed and her lips were swollen. Damp strands of strawberry-golden hair were stuck to her cheek. He tucked it back.

She looked as shocked as he felt—as if they'd both got caught in a sudden earthquake.

And then he became aware of his weight on her and reluctantly moved off her, going into the bathroom to take care of the protection.

He looked at himself for a moment in the mirror and felt a sense of *déjà-vu* as he recalled when he'd looked at himself a few weeks ago, just before talking with his brother Zafir. He'd felt jaded then—weary. Hollow.

Now he felt none of those things.

He felt as if he was connected to something much bigger than himself. Something just out of sight, intangible but solid.

Destiny, whispered a voice.

Salim scowled at his reflection—it was not destiny. It was just post-great-sex endorphins. His life wasn't changing—not for anything, and certainly not for great sex or because he'd found himself feeling more at home in Tabat than anywhere else he'd been in his life.

He heard a faint noise from the bedroom and went back to find Charlotte sitting on the edge of the bed, looking at him over her shoulder. Her naked back was delicate and pale, and just like that his body started coming back to life.

Her gaze dropped and widened as she took him in.

He strolled back to the bed and asked, with a bite that reflected his unwelcome post-coital thoughts, 'Were you going somewhere?'

He got onto the bed and reached for her, pulling her back towards him until she went off-balance and landed on her back.

She looked up at him, a slight wariness on her face, as if she could sense his volatile mood. 'I'm going back to my room.'

Salim smiled, and felt ruthless when he said, 'Wrong answer.'

And then he drowned out the myriad voices in his head by losing himself in her all over again.

When Charlotte woke the following morning she was relieved to find herself alone in Salim's bed. She couldn't have handled being under the scrutiny of that searing blue gaze when she felt so turned inside out.

Last night was almost too much to process. The mind-melting sex…and the revelations that had preceded it.

Salim didn't believe he was worthy of his kingdom.

He'd led her to believe that he didn't want to be king because he didn't want to give up his successful independent lifestyle. But it was so much more than that. Not to mention the fact that he believed he'd driven someone to his death.

Charlotte didn't for a second believe that was true. But *he* did.

She heard a noise and sat up in the bed in a panic, pulling the sheet up to her neck, not remotely ready to face Salim.

But it was Assa, and relief vied with embarrassment as the young girl came in, seemingly totally unfazed to find Charlotte in her king's bed.

'Miss McQuillan, the king will be leaving for Jandor soon. I've packed your bags and laid out some clothes in your room.'

Assa handed her a robe and Charlotte squeaked out, 'Jandor?'

The girl nodded. 'Yes, for the banquet dinner King Zafir is holding in Jahor palace, in honour of our king's upcoming coronation.' Assa's eyes shone with excitement as she said, 'I can't wait to see Queen Kat—they say she's even more beautiful than in her pictures.'

Charlotte smiled weakly and pulled the robe on. Of course. She'd completely forgotten about the scheduled trip to Jandor in the tumult of the past few days.

She followed Assa back to her rooms through a warren of back corridors—presumably to protect Charlotte's sullied reputation.

She tried to stop herself wondering where Salim was, or if he was even marginally as affected as she was by the previous night.

Salim was already on his private jet when she stepped on board a few hours later. He looked up and there was no discernible expression on his face. Charlotte tried not to let that intimidate her, or to feel out of her depth. She had so little experience with this kind of thing.

When she took a seat on the other side of the aisle, directed there by a steward, she realised that Salim was listening to Rafa, who was sitting opposite him and had been hidden by the seat.

Salim stared at her, and his gaze drifted down over her silk shirt and plain trousers. When he met her eyes again he arched a brow.

She'd found herself choosing from her own clothes again, even though Assa had left out a traditional tunic, because at the last minute she'd felt as if she needed some fortification. Except now all she could think was that she'd dressed like this subconsciously to provoke a reaction, and she cringed inwardly.

Rafa stood up then, collecting a sheaf of papers, and bowed to Salim before smiling at Charlotte and taking his leave.

She asked, 'Isn't he travelling with us?'

The staff were busy closing the door as Salim said, 'He's travelling separately.'

He came out of his seat then, and was buckling her belt across her lap before she could move. His hands were big against her belly as he tightened it.

He looked at her and said, *sotto voce*, 'Did you dress like that on purpose, Charlotte?'

A wave of heat scorched her insides, all the way to between her legs. She felt a spurt of something giddy and reckless. 'Maybe I did.'

His eyes flashed and his hands lingered for a moment before the plane started moving on the runway and he took his seat again.

When they were airborne, and the staff had checked if they needed anything, Salim undid his belt and held out a hand to Charlotte across the aisle.

'Come here,' he instructed.

Charlotte glanced up the plane to where the steward was keeping himself discreetly busy. She looked back at Salim and melted inside. The look on his face was one of such innate imperiousness that she couldn't understand how he didn't see it in himself.

Undoing her belt, she stood up and felt ridiculously shy. Salim took her hand in his and tugged her towards him until she all but fell into his lap.

'Salim!' she hissed, mindful of the staff.

He just smiled wickedly as he curved her body into his much harder one. Charlotte felt hot and breathless and exhilarated. His hands were in her hair, undoing the smooth chignon that Assa had created with such assiduousness earlier.

'Salim…' She trailed off weakly as her hair fell down and he ran his hands through it, mussing it up. She'd already gathered that he liked to muss her up as much as possible.

'Why do you do it?' His voice rumbled against her breasts, which were pressed against his chest.

'Do what?' she asked, feeling dizzy.

His hand was on her back now, shaping her body under her silk shirt, finding where it was tucked into her trousers and sliding underneath to find bare skin.

'Hide your true nature.'

Instantly Charlotte was tense. Her true nature was to seek order in a chaotic world by any means necessary, and to erect a façade that was becoming increasingly flimsy.

'What do you mean?' she asked warily.

He looked at her. 'You're a deeply passionate and sensual woman, Charlotte. Yet you hide behind these prim suits. You revelled in the freedom of the desert—you appreciated it in a way that most Western people would never understand. It called to something in you.'

Charlotte felt as if someone had pushed her off a cliff and she was free-falling. How was it that this man could see so much? She'd never thought of herself as passionate before…not until now. Until him. And, as for the desert, she did feel a deep affinity for it and she had no idea where it had come from.

Salim was looking at her.

She shrugged lightly, not really wanting to talk about this but unable to escape. 'I always saw passion as something selfish…showy. Fickle. My parents were passionate, and then suddenly they weren't. They detested each other.' She avoided Salim's eye, focusing on his shoulder. 'I never trusted it, or wanted to be like them.'

Salim touched a finger to her chin, forcing her to look at him. 'Well, it's too late for that. You have it in spades. Passion and sensuality. I'm amazed you've lasted this long without letting anyone see that.'

A sharp poignancy filled Charlotte then, as she wondered what might have happened if she'd never met Salim. Would she have lived her life never knowing the true depth of pleasure a man could give a woman? Never knowing the true depth of her own nature?

She said a little shakily, 'I could say the same to you. You're a far less selfish man than you'd have others believe. I think Tabat has called to you, whether you like it or not, and you can't simply go back to your life…'

She felt the tension in Salim's body as he reacted to that, but Charlotte knew she was right. He didn't like it, though. She saw the shutters come down over his expression and his eyes glittered.

'Don't let lust infuse everything—including me—with a rose-coloured glow. I'm still the same, and I want the same things. This…what's between us…will burn out. It always does.'

Charlotte felt a mix of hurt and anger. She tensed and pushed herself away from Salim as much as he would allow. 'You don't need to patronise me, I might have been a virgin, but I'm not completely innocent. I do know how these things work. My rose-tinted glasses got broken a long time ago.'

Tension simmered between them for a second, and then it changed into something hotter. The muscles in Salim's face relaxed and his hand started wandering again, sliding up her bare back under her shirt, finding the clasp of her bra and undoing it expertly before she had a chance to stop him.

And it was too late. Her blood was boiling with lust now, and not anger.

He pressed a kiss to her jaw and said, 'Good. We both know where we stand, then.'

As his wicked mouth and hands robbed her all too easily of speech and rational thought Charlotte wondered a little hysterically what she'd just agreed to—because it felt very much as if she'd just given Salim licence to toy with her for as long as it suited him.

And as for her confident assertion that her rose-tinted glasses had been broken long ago—that felt dangerously hollow now.

CHAPTER EIGHT

BY THE TIME they'd landed, and Charlotte was walking down the steps of the plane and into the blazing Jandor sunshine, she felt thoroughly mussed and extremely ill-prepared.

Just moments ago, when Charlotte had seen the car outside bearing the king's flag, she'd rounded on Salim, feeling prickly and off-centre. She'd frantically tried to repair the damage done to her clothes, hair and make-up.

'You should have warned me your brother and his wife were coming to meet us. What on earth will they think? I haven't even briefed myself on everything I need to know about them and Jandor.'

For someone who'd always prided herself on her professional decorum, she'd felt very exposed.

Salim had just looked at her with a small smile playing around his mouth. 'Charlotte, please don't take this as a criticism of your ability, which is commendable, but even you would have to admit that your professional services haven't exactly been exercised for the past couple of weeks.'

'No,' she said hotly, tucking her hair up as best she could, acutely aware of the royal entourage lining up outside the plane. 'Because for one thing you wouldn't let me do my job, and for another you proved to be far more of a natural diplomat than you'd ever like to admit.'

And distracting!

If she'd hoped to provoke a reaction it hadn't worked. Salim had just coolly stood up and watched as she'd tucked herself in.

Now, a man who was undoubtedly Salim's brother stood with a stunningly beautiful woman at the bottom of the steps.

King Zafir was of the same height and build as Salim, but where Salim's eyes were blue Zafir's were dark grey and deep-set. He had a more austere demeanour than Salim, and she could feel the tension snap between the two men as they greeted one another with the traditional clasping of the shoulders.

Queen Kat had been one of the world's most famous supermodels until she'd disappeared off the scene almost two years before. It had since transpired that she'd suffered a cataclysmic trauma when she'd been involved in an accident and had had to have her lower left leg amputated.

Not that you would know it now, as she stood tall and regal beside her husband, with a warm but concerned look in her mesmerising golden eyes as she took in the exchange between the brothers.

Then King Zafir put out his hand towards Charlotte. 'Miss McQuillan, it's a pleasure to finally meet you, and it's even more of a pleasure to see that my brother has availed himself of your considerable services and professionalism.'

Charlotte felt her face get mortifyingly hot. She sensed Salim's mocking look in her direction and took

King Zafir's hand, willing down the heat. 'It's lovely to meet you too. Call me Charlotte, please.'

Queen Kat stepped forward then, and Charlotte couldn't help but be dazzled by her beauty and the very obviously happy glow of the recently married couple.

'Charlotte, how lovely to meet you—welcome to Jahor.'

Her smile was genuine and Charlotte couldn't fail to respond in kind.

Charlotte noticed that Salim greeted his new sister-in-law with polite civility, but not much warmth. It didn't take a clairvoyant to sense that he wanted to be anywhere but here. It had been evident from his growing tension on the plane as soon as they'd entered Jandor airspace.

He said now, to his brother, 'You really didn't need to come all the way out here to meet us.'

King Zafir's jaw tightened and Charlotte felt breathless for a second at how similar the men were.

'I haven't seen you since our father's funeral. A trip to greet you at the airport was not a chore, brother.'

Salim flushed. He obviously knew he was being rude, and Charlotte had an instinct to put her hand into his, offering silent support but of course she couldn't.

Queen Kat took her by the arm. 'Come on, let's go to the palace. I'm sure you could do with some refreshment.'

Charlotte smiled and let herself be led away to the first in a fleet of cars. It appeared that she was to travel with Kat and that the brothers would travel together in the car behind. She saw that King Zafir had got into the driver's seat and Salim into the passenger one, looking stony-faced. Charlotte wondered why there was such a schism between them—surely their adverse relationship with their parents should have bonded them?

Kat chatted easily in the back of their car, and Charlotte found herself relaxing as they wound their way up the narrow streets to the palace.

She said shyly, 'Congratulations on your wedding.'

Kat smiled radiantly. 'Thank you. Sometimes I still can't believe it myself. My life has changed so utterly, and I won't lie and say that becoming queen doesn't intimidate me every day!' She scrunched up her nose. 'But, not wanting to sound too corny about it, with Zafir by my side I feel capable of pretty much anything. I just want to make him proud—and Jandor.'

It shook Charlotte to see this evidence of their loving bond up close, and she didn't think it was just newly wedded bliss. From what she recalled, the couple had been together before, but had split up before Kat's catastrophic accident and had since reunited. A little dart of what felt like envy gripped her down low in her belly, at the sight of such devotion.

They were pulling into the palace forecourt now, and Kat put a hand on Charlotte's arm, saying with a pointed look at her blouse, 'You might want to redo your buttons before we get out.'

Charlotte looked down and gasped when she realised her shirt buttons were done up haphazardly. She rectified the situation with a flaming face, and vowed silently to kill Salim for not warning her. But then she caught Kat's eye again, and saw that the woman had a sympathetic but amused look on her face.

'Don't worry, it's not that obvious. But I do know what it's like to fall for an Al-Noury man.'

Charlotte shook her head, and opened her mouth to deny it automatically—but then shut it again when words wouldn't come. A feeling of dread mixed with exhilaration infused her whole body. And a very stark revelation. She *was* falling for Salim.

It took her a second to focus on the woman looking at her so sympathetically, as if she knew exactly what had just gone through Charlotte's head.

Stunned and feeling winded, Charlotte asked, 'Is it that obvious?'

Kat's smile was knowing. 'What you were getting up to on the plane? Yes. But as for anything deeper—it's only obvious to me because your expression reminds me of how I feel when I look at my own husband.'

Someone was opening Charlotte's door now, and she took the opportunity to escape from Kat's sympathetic golden gaze.

When she was out of the car, the awe-inspiring golden magnificence of the Jahor palace distracted her from what had just transpired.

The place was a hive of activity as Kat walked her through the ornate entrance, saying, 'I know Zafir wants to talk business with Salim, so I thought we could take refreshments in the garden?'

'Please don't feel you have to entertain me,' Charlotte said quickly, acutely aware that Kat must be busy with the banquet that evening. And more acutely feeling a need to go somewhere private and quiet, where she could assimilate what had just happened.

But the queen said, with her soft American twang, 'Honestly, you'll be doing me a favour. I'm shamelessly using you as a decoy to get them to talk while they can. And I won't bring up what we just spoke of unless you do.'

Charlotte admitted defeat in the face of Kat's easy warmth and charm. She'd never been a girly girl, but for the first time she could imagine that she would like a woman like Kat as a friend.

She smiled. 'If you're sure I'm not putting you out?'

Kat took her arm again and shepherded her through the palace, past vast corridors and beautiful courtyard gardens. 'I'm sure. Now, I want to hear all about what it is exactly that you do, because it sounds totally fascinating…'

About an hour later Charlotte was even more impressed with Kat. She knew the woman was an amputee, but apart from a small but definite limp it was impossible to tell—especially when her cream and gold kaftan effectively hid any sign of a prosthetic leg.

Kat was showing her the gardens after a delicious tea, and Charlotte stopped when she saw the entrance into a walled garden where a fountain of water burbled into an exquisite pool and wild exotic flowers bloomed in every corner.

Unable to stop herself, she walked to the entrance and looked in. Kat came alongside her and Charlotte said, 'It's beautiful…so peaceful.'

Kat grimaced and stepped into the garden. Charlotte followed.

'It wasn't always like this. It was an abandoned ruin for many years…'

'Why?'

But before Kat could respond another voice, unmistakably male and familiar, cut in harshly.

'Because it shouldn't have been touched, that's why. Who the hell is responsible for this?'

Charlotte whirled around at the sudden arrival of Salim. 'Where did you come from?'

He flicked a glance at Charlotte, and she was shocked at the depth of cold anger in his eyes.

'I was looking for you.'

Queen Kat was contrite. 'Salim, I thought I was doing a good thing. I know this is where—'

He cut her off. 'You know nothing. You shouldn't have done this. You had no right.'

He'd turned and strode out of the garden again before Charlotte could take in what had just happened, his long robe billowing after him. She looked at Kat, who was obviously upset, and anger swelled at his unforgivable treatment of his sister-in-law.

Charlotte said, 'I'm so sorry, Kat, you didn't deserve that at all. I'll go after him.'

The other woman caught her hand and said, 'Please tell him I'm sorry. I thought I was doing a good thing in her memory…'

Salim knew that he had just behaved unforgivably. Charlotte's look of shock was etched into his brain. As was Kat's contrite response. His sister-in-law didn't deserve his opprobrium—but seeing what she'd done to that place had cracked something open inside him. Something raw.

Being back here was fraught enough with painful memories and reminders of how he'd turned his back on so much…on his brother—

'Salim!'

Charlotte.

Her voice stopped his self-recrimination and was like balm to a wound. As that registered fully Salim suddenly resented the fact that she'd slid so far under his skin. That she'd witnessed that moment.

He stopped and whirled around on the path to see Charlotte hurrying towards him. She stopped, her chest moving up and down enticingly under that silk blouse. She was angry.

'What on earth is wrong with you, speaking to Kat like that?'

Salim lashed out. 'I'm sorry—was that not very diplomatic? Is Queen Kat your new best friend? Perhaps you like what you see and you're fancying your chances of becoming a queen, too?'

Charlotte's face leached of colour and her green eyes stood out starkly against her pale skin. Salim felt immediate remorse.

Before she could respond he said roughly, 'I'm sorry. That was unforgivable. You didn't deserve that, and Kat didn't deserve it either.'

Still looking a little shaken, Charlotte said, 'Then why? What is that place?'

Salim looked up into the sky for a moment, drawing in a long breath, and then looked back down. 'It's where Sara died. She was on the high wall and she fell. She had a massive head injury...she died in my arms.'

Charlotte started towards him. 'Oh, Salim...'

But he held out his hand, stopping her. If she touched him he wasn't sure he wouldn't shatter completely.

She shook her head, eyes bright with an emotion that caught at Salim's chest, making it tight.

'What a tragic accident.'

Salim steeled himself. He didn't have to tell her. He didn't have to say a word. But he couldn't stop it spilling out, as if some force was compelling him.

'That's just it—it wasn't an accident. She fell off that wall deliberately. She didn't want to die but she did.' His voice had turned unbearably harsh.

Charlotte frowned, clearly not understanding. She looked so pale that Salim went over to her, taking her arm and making her sit down on a nearby stone bench.

She looked up at him. 'What are you talking about?'

Salim paced back and forth, cursing himself for having given in to the impulse to unburden himself while at the same time feeling a sense of compulsion to keep going. As if he knew this was the only way the heavy weight he bore might ever be lightened.

He stopped in front of Charlotte.

'Sara and I were always joined at the hip. We were so close we even had our own language. One week, not long after our eleventh birthday, our father was hosting an economic forum. Ambassadors from neighbouring countries were here, as well as representatives from all over the world. It was a big, prestigious event. Sara had been tasked to do some things with our mother, to help out, so we were separated during the week. I didn't notice until almost the end of the week that something was wrong. Sara was avoiding me…not talking.'

Charlotte asked quietly, 'What happened?'

'I was in the walled garden—it was our favourite place to hide and play. She came in and I knew something was wrong. I'd never seen her so subdued… Eventually she told me—' He stopped.

Charlotte stood up. 'Go on.'

Salim's jaw was tight, constricting his voice. 'It was the Italian ambassador. An oily, sleazy man. He'd taken a liking to Sara and had persuaded my mother to let her attend to him especially.'

Charlotte put a hand to her mouth, clearly jumping to a dark conclusion.

Salim continued. 'Up to that point he hadn't actually touched her, but he'd said something to scare her enough to take her clothes off, telling her he just wanted to look at her. When she told me this she couldn't even look at me. She was so ashamed. She told me how he'd kept telling her she was perfect, and that before he left he would show her how a man kissed a woman…how they touched each other…'

'Oh, Salim…'

But Salim didn't hear Charlotte's voice. He was back in that garden, his insides turning to jelly as he watched his sister—his life—transform into someone he didn't know. Someone haunted and terrified. Someone who had lost her innocence.

She'd climbed up onto the high wall in spite of his pleas and said through her tears.

'I don't want him to look at me again, and if I'm not perfect, he won't like me anymore...'

Salim's voice was toneless. 'She jumped off the wall deliberately, to try and injure herself enough so that she would no longer draw the eye of a debased man. She believed this because when our older brother broke his arm once, our parents kept him out of sight until he was healed, telling us that no-one wanted to see a prince who wasn't perfect. But she didn't just injure herself. She hit her head and died almost instantly.'

Charlotte couldn't help the tears filling her eyes. She went to Salim and took his hands. They were cold.

Her voice was thick. 'You know it wasn't your fault…'

Salim let out a curt sound and took his hands out of hers. 'Wasn't it?'

'You were her brother—not her parent.'

Salim shook his head, as if determined not to let her absolve him. 'We were twins…we had a natural affinity… But somehow I didn't pick up on what was happening.'

'You didn't tell your parents? Your brother?'

A muscle in Salim's jaw ticked. 'I couldn't speak to Zafir. Sara and I…we'd all but blocked him out as soon as we could communicate with each other. We didn't need him. We didn't need anyone. Zafir seemed very remote to us. He was older. Serious. I did try to tell my father, but he just slapped me across the face and told me never to repeat such lies again. He said that Sara was dead and nothing could be done.'

'So you've kept that awful knowledge inside you for all these years…?'

He looked at her, and she shivered at the bleakness in his eyes.

'I made it my life's mission to get away from this place that never valued Sara and go after her abuser. I did. And now he's dead.'

Charlotte said faintly, 'He's the man you mentioned before?'

Salim nodded.

She sat down again, her legs feeling weak. 'Why didn't you bring him up on child abuse charges?'

'Because too much time had passed. There was no evidence. He actually laughed in my face when I mentioned my sister. So I got him the only way I could—by ruining him. Ruining him to the point where he took his own life.'

Charlotte's heart ached. '*He* took his life, Salim. Not you—no matter what you did.'

He looked at her, and opened his mouth as if he was going to argue with her, but at that moment there was a sound of movement nearby.

Salim tensed. 'Who's there?'

Zafir, his brother, stepped onto the path from around the corner. He looked as if he'd just been punched in the gut. Evidently he'd heard everything.

He looked at Salim—haunted, stricken. 'Why didn't you tell me, Salim? I would have done anything for you… She was my sister too…'

Emotion thickened between the two men, who stood facing each other, and Charlotte discreetly stepped back and away, sensing that this was a conversation that had been a long time coming and that they didn't require an audience.

Charlotte stole back along the path, her throat tight with emotion at the thought of Salim carrying the burden of his sister's trauma on his shoulders for all this time.

She found Kat pacing a little further along the path, clearly anxious.

When she saw Charlotte she hurried to meet her. 'What's happening? Zafir went storming after Salim, even though I told him I wasn't upset. I never should have meddled in Sara's garden...'

Charlotte took her hands. 'I think you did a beautiful thing, and I think Salim will recognise that when he's calmed down. He's talking to Zafir now... Your husband should be the one to explain things to you.'

Kat looked torn, but eventually she sighed and said, 'Fine. I should go and see how preparations are going for the banquet anyway. I just hope they're not tearing lumps out of each other.'

'I don't think they are,' Charlotte said weakly, mentally crossing her fingers and already feeling for Kat when she would learn the full story later.

When they reached the palace entrance Charlotte offered to help Kat, but the woman said an emphatic *no* and got a staff member to show Charlotte to her room, so she could rest before the banquet.

When Charlotte got to her room, Assa was laying out something gold and shimmery on the bed.

Charlotte went over and touched it reverently. 'What is this?'

Assa's voice was awed. 'It's a traditional Jandori kaftan, supplied by the queen as a gift to you. It was designed by one of their most famous designers. She has left a note saying that you don't have to feel obliged to wear it tonight, but that it's yours in any case.'

It looked too beautiful to be worn…the fabric as delicate as a butterfly's wing. The queen's generosity was humbling.

Charlotte looked at Assa. 'What do you think I should do?'

Assa was incredulous. 'You *have* to wear it, Miss McQuillan, you can't insult the queen.'

Charlotte smiled, glad to feel some lightness again.

Assa was backing away. 'I've unpacked all your things, and you should rest now. I'll be back to help you dress in a couple of hours.'

Charlotte was about to protest that she didn't need help, but she didn't have the heart to curtail Assa's obvious excitement. 'Thank you, Assa.'

Alone again, Charlotte took in the luxurious yet understated surroundings of her room. This was how Tabat palace could be some day, with some loving care.

And then Salim's sneering words came back to her, when he'd accused her of wanting to be a queen. Humiliation flooded her again at the thought that he might have seen something of her feelings on her face, like Kat had, and had seen all the way into her deepest secret yearnings for unconditional love and a family.

But did she secretly fantasise about being a queen?

Charlotte walked to the window and looked out over Jahor. The thought made her feel panicky, and yet she appreciated what Kat had said about feeling capable of anything with Zafir by her side.

Charlotte didn't want to be a queen, but to be Salim's queen… That was a different and far more dangerous dream.

She turned from the window in disgust at her mind's wanderings. Salim wasn't even going to be king for long…and she could appreciate fully now just why he'd resisted so forcibly. Even if she still didn't agree with him.

Charlotte had to remind herself that she was a temporary lover. Someone who had piqued his interest for a while because she was nothing like his usual women.

He was so proud. She knew he wouldn't relish having spilled his guts to her just now. But no doubt he felt that it was excusable, because soon she would be relegated to his past while he got on with his future. With or without Tabat.

And if he *did* decide to stay on as king then he would have to choose a suitable queen. Maybe someone from one of the tribes—a high-born tribal leader's daughter. Like the young woman who'd married that man. With her gorgeous kohled eyes and elaborate headdress. They would say *I marry you* three times to each other and then they would be married…

Charlotte cursed herself when she realised where her mind was going. She decided to take a refreshing shower and stripped off, pulling on a silk robe that was hanging behind the bathroom door.

She heard a noise in the bedroom and, thinking it would be Assa, went back out, stumbling to a halt when she saw that a door she hadn't even noticed was open between her room and another. And it was dominated by the man standing there, looking a little wild and feral.

Salim.

'You left.'

Charlotte was glad to see there were no obvious signs

of a fight on his face. She wondered how the exchange had gone with his brother.

'I didn't want to intrude.'

He made a sound at that—something between a laugh and a growl. He held out a hand. 'Come here. I need you.'

His voice resonated like a sensual command, deep inside her. She walked forward, very aware of the flimsiness of the silk robe against her naked body and of Salim's blue gaze on her.

She stopped in front of him. The air crackled between them, alive and electric.

'What do you need?' she asked, slightly breathlessly.

He looked even wilder up close, and it sent a shiver of awareness over Charlotte's skin. He put his hands on her hips and pulled her right into him. She gasped when she felt the thrust of his arousal against her belly.

'I need you,' he said thickly, 'and *this*.'

And then his mouth slammed down on hers and she was sucked into an immediate vortex of white heat and lust, making her legs turn to jelly.

Any of the remaining ice around her heart, that had protected her for years, was well and truly burnt away in this conflagration. How could she deny this man the release he sought in her arms when every bit of her ached to give him that release and then selfishly take her own…?

The surge of emotion Salim had felt when he'd seen Charlotte standing there in the silky robe was too much for him to take in. The need he'd felt for her was instantaneous and urgent. The need to lose himself in her until the pain went away.

She was arching her body into his and her mouth was so soft and sweet… He couldn't hold back even if he wanted to now. It was fast and furious, but somehow he managed to navigate them so that her back was against a wall.

They didn't even make it to the bed.

Salim lifted Charlotte so that her legs were wrapped around his waist, then pulled at her robe like an animal until she was bared and he could feast on her breasts, tugging first one and then the other nipple into his mouth, their pointed tips sending his arousal levels into orbit.

He somehow managed to pull up his own robe and she reached down between feverish kisses, finding his rock-hard erection and freeing him from the confines of his trousers.

For a second, while she held his body in her hand, he pulled back and looked at her. Her eyes were wide and glazed, her cheeks flushed. Hair tousled. His chest grew tight.

He removed her hand from his shaft and with less finesse than he'd ever shown in his life he found the heart of her body, where she was slick, tight and hot, and thrust up so deep that they both stopped breathing for a long moment.

When her hips moved against his he withdrew, before slamming back in. Her muscles clenched around him and he let loose the beast inside him until their skin glistened with sweat and he had nowhere else to go but to pull out before he lost all control, to spill his seed across her belly.

He'd never done that before, because he'd never not used protection, but right now he couldn't even drum up shock or recrimination.

Charlotte was looking at him wild-eyed, her hips still

moving against him, and to his shame and mortification he realised that she hadn't climaxed.

She was biting her lip as Salim lowered her to the floor, instructing roughly as he knelt before her, 'Put your leg over my shoulder.'

She did, and Salim pushed apart the robe even more, so that her body was bare apart from the flimsy belt dissecting her belly where he'd branded her. He spread apart her thighs and laved her body, hearing her sighs and moans, feeling her fist in his hair as he plunged two fingers inside her and found the sensitive nub of her pleasure, suckling on it remorselessly until she too fell apart, screaming her release.

When she was spent, Salim rested his head against her hips and for the first time in his life felt a sense of peace so profound that it silenced all the voices in his head.

Later, at the glittering banquet, Charlotte still felt flayed. They'd made love like two animals. Except she couldn't drum up any sense of shame or humiliation. It had felt wild and strangely cathartic. As if something had been burnt clean.

Incinerated, more like.

She caught Salim's eye now, across the table, and her inner muscles clenched. His mouth tipped up slightly on one side, as if he knew exactly what she was going through. She scowled at him and looked away, trying not to think about how he'd carried her into the shower afterwards and soaped her thoroughly—so thoroughly that she'd splintered to pieces *again* while he'd watched her with an intensity that she hadn't been able to escape.

Just before she'd returned to her room he had said, 'I didn't use protection…'

Her face had flamed as she'd thought how erotic it had felt to have him spend his release on her skin.

She'd hurriedly assured him, 'It'll be fine. I'm not at a dangerous part of my cycle'.

And she wasn't, so she could be relatively sure there would be no repercussions. But it had shocked her how easily she'd forgotten about safety. And how easily a very illicit image of a small, earnest dark-haired child with blue eyes had sneaked into her imagination.

The chatter of the banquet brought Charlotte back to the present moment and panic rose inside her.

Imagining babies and being queen… She was in so much deeper than she'd appreciated.

Salim was finding it hard not to stand up and walk around the vast banquet table to where Charlotte was sitting. Her face was turned away as she spoke to someone else, and one word thrummed in his blood: *mine*.

She was a vision in a gold kaftan, her hair piled high on her head. He'd noticed several men's gazes lingering on her all evening, and it had taken all his restraint not to drag her across the table and claim her.

His body was still heavy, replete with carnal satisfaction, and yet, as ever, there was an edge of growing hunger. Already. He observed her as dispassionately as he could, feeling a little desperate at the effect she had on him, but he couldn't be objective.

It struck him then, as he took in the delicate line of her jaw and aquiline profile… She looked regal. Maybe that awareness had precipitated his taunt earlier—that she wanted to be a queen. Suddenly Salim thought of how very perfect Charlotte would be as a queen, but she would have to be someone else's, wouldn't she?

She looked up at him now, and Salim felt pinned to

the spot. So much so that he had to look away—only to catch his brother's gaze at the head of the table. He felt something tight loosen inside him. Today had marked the very fragile start of a long overdue *rapprochement* with his brother, who hadn't done anything to deserve the distance Salim had put between them.

Salim could see now that for a long time he'd blamed Zafir for not protecting Sara, even though of course it wasn't his fault. But it had been easier to do that and push him away than to admit he was terrified of loving his brother and losing him, too.

Salim stood up and tapped his glass gently with a knife, causing everyone to stop and look at him. He made a short speech of thanks to his brother and his sister-in-law, to whom he'd apologised earlier, easing his conscience slightly. Then he found his gaze gravitating back to Charlotte's green one. She was looking at him with that unwavering regard that left him no place to hide.

He said, 'I pledge here, this evening, to do my very best to ensure a secure and successful future for Tabat.'

Everyone clapped and cheered, not realising that Salim's statement had been deliberately ambiguous. Charlotte did, though, and he saw the way she avoided his eye, as if she couldn't bear to look at him.

For the first time Salim felt more than just a twinge of conscience—he felt the inexorable rise of something he'd been trying to ignore for weeks. The realisation that he really meant what he'd just said, and that there was only one person he wanted to see guide Tabat into that secure and successful future…*him*.

He hadn't given so much as a thought to finding his replacement in the last couple of weeks…as if a part of him had already accepted the inevitable.

Shock at that revelation kept him rooted to the spot as everyone around him started to get up from their tables for the second part of the evening's celebrations, and he watched Charlotte—still avoiding his eye—as she got up too and turned away.

That broke him out of his stasis and he went after her, not really knowing what he was going to say when he got to her, but knowing that she was the only person he wanted to see.

CHAPTER NINE

'DANCE WITH ME?'

Charlotte stopped in her tracks at the familiar deep voice behind her. She considered saying *no* for a second and then thought, who would she be fooling?

No one.

And yet she couldn't let him see her for a moment.

It had hurt her more than she could say when he'd made that deliberately misleading comment just now, about Tabat. It had felt like a betrayal of everything she knew he stood for and a betrayal of this last week, when he'd been so inherently respectful of his people. His actions had spoken louder than his words. But he wasn't prepared to admit that.

The fact that she was the only one who knew that he had no intention of being King of Tabat felt like the heaviest burden now.

He came into her field of vision, holding out a hand. She looked up at him reluctantly and schooled her features as best she could. But she knew it was futile when she saw how that blue gaze narrowed on her face. He still looked as thoroughly disreputable as he had when she'd first seen him, in spite of the traditional robes. Wild curling hair. Stubbled jaw. Wicked eyes and an even more wicked mouth.

She wanted very much not to let Salim lead her into the other room, where slow, sexy jazz was playing. She wanted to resist his pull because it was fatal now, and she knew he'd destroy her without even realising what he was doing.

But she found her hand reaching for his even as she cursed herself for it.

Salim led her into the other room, where there were already couples dancing. King Zafir and Queen Kat were dancing, staring deep into each other's eyes, oblivious to their guests.

Salim expertly took Charlotte into his arms and started to lead her around the floor. The fact that he was such a graceful dancer when he strived so hard to pretend he wasn't a part of this world made something snap inside her.

She pulled back and looked up. 'Did you tell your brother that you're planning on abdicating?'

Salim seemed to sense her mood, and looked at her while still managing to guide her faultlessly around the dance floor. Charlotte wondered churlishly if the man displayed mediocrity in anything at all.

'No, I haven't—not yet.'

'Well, you should,' Charlotte said tartly, 'because he will have to deal with the fall-out in Tabat, his closest neighbour.'

Charlotte focused on a point somewhere over his shoulder acutely aware of his body next to hers, making her feel hot and jittery.

His chest rumbled against hers. 'You might be interested to know that I haven't told him because I haven't made a final decision yet.'

Charlotte's feet stopped and she looked at Salim. They'd halted in the middle of the floor.

'What are you saying?'

He didn't seem remotely fazed that they'd stopped dancing and were drawing interested glances.

He arched a brow. 'I would have thought that a woman of your considerable intelligence could work that one out.'

His mocking tone bounced off her. A surge of emotion was rising. 'You're really considering becoming king…and not abdicating?'

His mouth tipped up on one side in a wry smile. 'Is that so hard for you to contemplate?'

Charlotte shook her head, barely aware that they'd started moving again. 'Not at all. I just thought you'd made up your mind.'

'Well, I haven't yet…for sure. Let's just say that I've been persuaded to look at things a little differently in the past few weeks. And after meeting the people of Tabat…seeing it with my own eyes…it's a challenge that might not be as unpalatable as I'd thought.'

Charlotte looked up at Salim, unable to stop herself from saying huskily, 'You will be a great king, Salim. You deserve to serve them, and they deserve you.'

He grimaced slightly and said, 'That remains to be seen. And first I have to go to London tomorrow, for a function. Tabat's ambassador to Europe is holding a Christmas party in my honour. Come with me?'

Charlotte's insides clenched.

Christmas. London.

She wasn't ready to leave this part of the world, or Salim, but it would be an opportunity for her to remember who she was and where she came from. Her life wasn't here, with this man.

She had to protect herself. She had to move on.

She prayed that her emotions weren't showing on

her face when she looked up and said, as nonchalantly as she could, 'Yes, I'll come with you.'

She knew now that she wouldn't return to Tabat with Salim for the coronation—she couldn't. This was his destiny. But it was not hers. And it was time to remember that.

She ducked her head and turned her face to rest a cheek on his chest as they danced. And she closed her stinging eyes.

Driving through London and seeing the festive cheer of Christmas—streets thronged with slightly crazed-looking shoppers and the bright faces of children pressed up against shop windows to see the displays better—sent Charlotte on a brutal collision course with her past.

Usually by now, or around now, she would be holed up in her apartment, blocking it all out, pretending it wasn't happening. But now she welcomed it—because she'd been in danger of losing herself completely. Losing herself in a fantasy where she belonged to a man from an exotic land, full of vast deserts and beautiful nomadic people.

But the fact was that whatever affinity she felt for his land was as much of a fabrication as this forced festive cheer. And she most certainly didn't belong to Salim, no matter how intense their lovemaking had been just hours ago, as dawn had broken and the call to prayer had sounded over the sleepy city of Jahor.

She was like a miser, grabbing hold of as much as she could before it was all ripped away from her.

Charlotte couldn't help hearing Salim's phone conversations on the plane to England. He'd made no attempt to keep them private so she'd heard him instruct his staff to set up a hub office in Tabat palace from where he could oversee everything. And then he'd informed his legal team that he would be scheduling a significant meeting in the New Year, after his coronation.

A meeting to tell them that his business would be changing dramatically? That he would be scaling back to concentrate on his royal duties because he wouldn't be abdicating after all?

The speed with which he seemed to be happy to turn his life around in another direction would have made her dizzy if she hadn't got to know him by now, and to know his capabilities.

Charlotte couldn't help thinking that if he was indeed going to be king, then he would be looking for a queen to stand by his side. To have his heirs.

That made her think of Queen Kat, and how seamlessly and effortlessly she seemed to have become a beloved fixture in her adopted country. Because she was loved.

And that was the scariest revelation of all: falling for Salim had shown Charlotte that her parents' treatment of her hadn't damaged her as irrevocably as she'd believed. Somewhere deep inside her she'd nurtured a small seed of hope, and when Salim had come along it had burst into life before she could stop it.

'We're almost there.'

Salim's voice broke Charlotte out of her reverie and she looked at him. They were inching along in traffic on a street in Mayfair, near Tabat's embassy.

He was watching her, and she schooled her features, but not before he'd evidently seen something. 'You really do hate this time of year, don't you?'

'Yes,' she said tightly, relieved that he wasn't seeing anything deeper than that.

The car drew to a stop outside a stately house with

the Tabat flag flying on a pole outside. Seeing it made Charlotte feel even more homesick for a country where she'd only spent a few weeks.

She clambered out before Salim could come around to help her, and he looked at her as she preceded him up the steps and into the house.

The house was decorated for Christmas, making Charlotte feel a disjointed mixture of rejection and yearning. She felt churlish. A huge tree dominated the hall, and the smell of mulled wine and spices infused the air. It was surprisingly homely and familiar, and it was pushing about a million of her buttons.

Salim came to stand in front of her. 'The function will take place here, in the ceremonial ballroom. I have to attend a meeting with the ambassador first—I'll collect you at seven.'

'I'm sure I can make my own way there,' Charlotte responded quickly, wanting to put some distance between them. Especially when she felt so all over the place.

A familiar steely expression settled over Salim's face. 'I'll meet you at seven.'

Charlotte saw a smartly dressed older man waiting with her bags and forced a smile. 'Fine—if you insist.'

Salim watched as Charlotte disappeared up the main staircase behind the housekeeper. He frowned. It was almost as if she'd become a different person as soon as they'd landed in London. She'd hunched in on herself, as far away from him as possible in the back of the car, looking haunted and hunted.

He felt an uncharacteristic sense of concern…a compulsion to go after her and—what…? He cursed himself. Charlotte was just a lover. Different from any lover he'd had before, but that was all.

'Sire?'

Salim turned from where he'd been staring into space—which further irritated him. He didn't stand staring into space, wondering about a lover. Mooning after her.

'Yes?'

A secretary smiled and said, 'Let me show you to the ambassador's office.'

Salim resisted the urge to slide a finger under the collar of his shirt to ease the sense of constriction as he followed the older woman.

Taking him unawares was the strength of yearning he felt to be back in Tabat and looking out over the endless desert. He'd once dismissed it as a sandpit, but he now knew that it teemed with life. Humans and animals and plants. Majestic. Beholden to none but themselves...

How had he never really appreciated that before?

When Charlotte was alone in her luxurious suite of rooms she paced back and forth in front of the window, oblivious to her surroundings or the view of a private park outside.

What was she doing?

She should have insisted on making her way back to her own apartment from the airport, and she should have let Salim know that she was terminating her contract. After all, King Zafir had all but terminated it the previous evening.

He'd pulled her aside for a moment at the banquet and said, 'Thank you for everything you've done for my brother...'

Charlotte had fought not to go puce, and he'd continued before she could come up with a suitable response.

'I think you know by now as well as I do that Salim

follows his own path and seeks help from no one. He never has. However, I just wanted to say that as far as I'm concerned you've fulfilled the terms of our agreement. If you do decide to stay for the coronation, or longer than that, it'll be an agreement between you and my brother…'

Feeling a sense of grim fatalism, Charlotte went to the wardrobe, where the housekeeper had insisted on putting away her things. She was going to pack and tell Salim that she was leaving…or, better yet, leave now before he could come and get her.

But every thought left her head when she opened the wardrobe and saw a familiar silky green gown hanging inside.

Her heart spasmed. It was the gown Salim had sent to her room to wear at his party. The one she'd refused to go to. The one where she'd confronted him and he'd kissed her.

Barely daring to breathe, she took it out and held it up. It was as stunning as she remembered, falling in a swathe of silk from under the bust. A symphony of simplicity and elegance.

Charlotte cursed Assa—she must have seen it hanging up at the back of the wardrobe in Tabat and packed it.

A very rogue desire swept over her—*one more night with Salim*. One more night to indulge in fantasy and let herself believe that this was her world and he was her man.

She could protect herself, couldn't she? She wasn't so far gone that she wouldn't be able to pick up the pieces of her life again and pretend nothing had happened…

But the tightness around her heart told her otherwise. She felt icy for a second as the memory of her father's rejection came back—but surely, she reassured herself, this was totally different? She was an adult now, and if she walked away from Salim before he ended things then she'd be in control.

Charlotte knew she didn't have the strength to walk away. Not just yet.

One more night.

Salim was still trying to compose himself. But he felt feral. He was oblivious to the people around him because he was fixated on the woman on the other side of the room, talking to a group of people whom she apparently knew.

Why isn't she by my side? he asked himself again, irrationally.

The dress she was wearing… It was the green dress he'd ordered especially for her, describing what he'd wanted, the colour and style, to an amused French stylist friend of his who had teased him.

'This one must be special if you are ordering a dress to match her eyes…normally you send in your lovers to dress themselves.'

Salim had answered defensively, 'She's not my lover…'

But his friend had just laughed and said, 'Not yet.'

He'd been right about the colour. Even from here he could see that the green made her eyes look even mossier than usual. The dress was strapless and it clung to her breasts before falling in a swathe of silk to the floor.

But what was really exercising him was the fact that he'd never seen so much of her pale flesh exposed in public before. And now *everyone* could see the freckles that dusted her shoulders and arms.

Her hair was swept to one side, and one of the tuxedoed gentlemen near her had put a hand on her bare upper back.

Salim was moving forward before he realised that someone had put a hand on *his* arm and was saying, 'Please can I have a word?'

He curbed the urge to snarl, and stopped and looked. It was a young attractive woman, with dark eyes and hair, and for some reason a cold shiver went down his spine.

He recognised her at the same moment as she said, 'Maybe you don't know me. I'm Giovanna Scozza. My father was—'

'I know who your father was,' Salim said grimly, feeling slightly sick.

She took her hand from his arm and Salim could see the shadows in her eyes. She looked nervous.

'Do you think we could talk privately for a moment?'

She didn't have to say it, but Salim heard it. *Surely you can give me that?*

'Of course.'

He did owe her this—and more.

He instructed a staff member who was hovering nearby to ensure they weren't interrupted and he took her into a private study off the main ballroom.

Charlotte's skin crawled when Peter Harper put his hand on her back—*again*. Once again she moved subtly from underneath it, automatically seeking out Salim on the other side of the room.

Something sharp lanced her when she saw that he was talking to a tall and very beautiful young woman, with dramatic black hair, olive skin and dark eyes. The woman had put her hand on his arm.

He was looking at her as if…

Charlotte's heart hitched. She'd never seen him look so arrested before, and her insides turned to water.

This was it.

He might have looked at her as if he'd wanted to devour her on the spot just moments ago, but of course it wouldn't be long before he realised what he'd been missing.

She watched as he led the young woman into another room and a uniformed staff member took up a position outside, clearly under instructions not to let anyone disturb them.

Feeling sick, Charlotte made an excuse to the people she'd been talking to—fellow diplomatic staff—and escaped the crush of the crowd to find some air, some space.

When Salim re-emerged into the main room he was still reeling. He immediately looked for a familiar strawberry-blonde head and frowned when he couldn't spot her immediately. *Where was she?*

The group of men she'd been talking to had dispersed, and Salim cursed under his breath at the thought that she was in some more private space with the one who had been touching her.

People moved out of his way with widening eyes as he cut a swathe through the room, but he was unaware of the intensity of his expression.

He thought he saw a flash of green in the far corner and followed it, finding himself at the door of another private room much like the one he'd just left.

He went inside. A fire was blazing and the room's walls were lined with shelves filled with books. There was an elaborately decorated Christmas tree in the corner, but Salim only had eyes for the slender pale figure standing near the fire, watching him.

Immediately something in him eased. Even as desire swept through him, igniting his blood.

He closed the door behind him.

For a moment he forget what had just happened as he stalked towards her. 'Who were those men you were talking to?'

Her eyes looked very dark in this low light, and the flames of the fire picked out the red hues in her hair.

'Colleagues…from the diplomatic circuit.'

'Oh? It's a circuit?'

Her eyes glittered and he could see the pulse at the base of her neck throbbing.

Her voice was tight. 'Yes, Salim, it's a circuit much like any other. Much like the one you inhabit when you return to Europe—you know, where you run into old friends…even old *lovers*?'

For a second he didn't compute, and then he remembered.

His gaze narrowed. 'You saw me talking to Giovanna?'

Charlotte shrugged minutely, hating it that she couldn't hide her emotions better. 'Is that her name?'

Salim shook his head and a smile tipped up one corner of his wicked mouth. 'I do believe you're jealous.'

Charlotte's hands clenched into fists. Yes, she was jealous—and she hated it.

Innate honestly forced her to say, 'I never asked for this, Salim. I shouldn't really care less what you do, or who with, because I'm sure you couldn't give a damn what I do.'

She let out a choked sound of anger at herself and went to go past Salim and make her escape. But he caught her with a hand on her arm.

'On the contrary. I do give a damn. I didn't like seeing that man touching you. Who was he?'

Charlotte blinked up at Salim, momentarily distracted by the feral glitter in his eyes. She told herself it was just possessiveness, nothing more. 'It was no one… Peter Harper—a diplomat with the foreign office.'

She found herself melting at the thought that he could be jealous—but then she remembered seeing him disappearing into that room with that sultry dark-haired beauty and she pushed against his chest, forcing him back.

She stepped around him and folded her arms. 'Who was *she*?'

Salim ran a hand through his hair, making it even messier. He took off his jacket, throwing it onto a chair, and then he pulled off his bow tie. He turned around and Charlotte nearly took a step back at how wild he looked. Like a caged animal.

Eventually he said, 'Giovanna Scozza. That's who she was.'

Charlotte frowned. The name was somehow familiar.

Salim's face was stark. 'She's the eldest daughter of the man who abused Sara. The man I ruined in revenge.'

Charlotte went cold in spite of the heat from the fire. 'What did she want?'

'She asked if she could speak to me and I said yes, of course.' His eyes pinned Charlotte to the spot. 'Do you know I tried to absolve myself after he died by making sure that the family were taken care of financially?' He emitted a curt laugh.

Charlotte's heart turned over. *Of course he had.* 'No, you never mentioned that. Why did she want to see you?'

Salim sighed. 'She wanted to thank me for what I'd

done… She told me that he'd been an abusive father—' He must have seen something on Charlotte's face, because he put out a hand and said, 'No, not *that*. Not with his children, at least. But he was violent to them—and their mother. It finally stopped when I went after him. But not completely. He beat their mother the day before he took his own life. She ended up in hospital. Giovanna revealed that they'd finally told him they were going to press charges against him. It was that more than anything else that made him take his own life—the thought of the shame if it got out…'

Salim looked at Charlotte and his face was leached of colour.

'She's effectively absolved me of guilt, but all I can think of now is that if I'd done something sooner then I might have spared them all—'

Charlotte stepped forward and put her hand to Salim's mouth, cutting off his words. She shook her head. 'It wasn't your responsibility, Salim. You can't blame yourself for his sick violence, just like you can't blame yourself for what happened to Sara.'

She took her hand down and stepped back, terrified that her heightened emotions might give her away. She had to be strong. Especially now.

But she couldn't help saying, 'You're free now, Salim. Free to live out your destiny.'

'Free to live out your destiny.'

Charlotte's words impacted Salim deeply. As was becoming dismayingly familiar with this woman, she had somehow managed to slide right into the heart of him and bear witness to the darkest parts of his soul without turning from him in horror.

But then she turned and walked away, to pick up her bag from a chair.

Something icy skated down Salim's spine.

When she turned around to face him again her face was a smooth mask. He might have imagined the emotion he'd seen shimmering in her eyes just now.

'Charlotte…?'

'I'm going to my room to pack.'

'But we're not leaving for Tabat till tomorrow afternoon—there's plenty of time.'

She looked straight at him. As if she was making herself do it. 'I'm not staying here.'

Salim moved towards her, ignoring the ominous feeling in his gut. 'If you hate being here this much we can leave tonight.'

She shook her head. 'It's not that. I'm not coming back to Tabat with you, Salim. Tonight or tomorrow.'

She turned to walk to the door and for a second Salim was incredulous. He wasn't even aware of moving until he was standing between her and the door, every muscle in his body taut. He didn't trust himself to touch her.

'What are you talking about, not coming back? You're working for me—or have you forgotten that pertinent detail?'

Charlotte let out a curt laugh that didn't sound like her. 'Working for you? *Now* I work for you? You know very well how to navigate in this milieu, Salim.' She waved a hand towards the noises coming from the other room. 'You really don't need my expertise. Your brother hired me, and he's released me from the contract so I'm choosing to go.'

Salim wanted to throttle his brother. 'He had no right to do that. But it doesn't matter because we've gone way beyond anything professional now. It's personal, Charlotte. '

She stepped back. Her face was flushed. She gestured between them. 'This was improbable from the start.'

Salim frowned. 'What are you talking about? We have amazing chemistry.'

'Chemistry, but that's all. How do you see this playing out, Salim?'

He didn't like the growing feeling of desperation. People obeyed him. Especially women.

But she never did, whispered a jeering voice.

He ignored it and bit out, 'I see this playing out by you coming back to Tabat with me, Charlotte.'

She shook her head. 'No, this ends here—now. If you need professional advice I can recommend someone, and as for the other…' She stopped and then said stiltedly, 'Well I'm sure you won't be alone for long.'

Salim was in uncharted territory. He knew if he touched Charlotte he could make her acquiesce in seconds, but something held him back. Some sense of self-preservation he'd never had to call on before.

'I told you I don't play games, Charlotte. If you leave here now I won't come after you. You know I want you. And I know you want me. Come back with me and we'll enjoy this for as long as it lasts.'

'I'm happy for it to end now.'

For the first time in his life Salim felt an urge to plead, or beg… And then a cold weight settled in his gut. *Not the first time.* He'd pleaded and begged with Sara, but she hadn't listened to him. She'd still left him.

The fact that he was thinking of Sara and Charlotte in the same vein was enough to make Salim take a step back.

She didn't mean that much to him. She couldn't.

It was lust. That was all. And the lust he felt for Charlotte would fade once she was out of sight and mind. Of course it would. Because that was all it was. No woman would ever make him beg again. Or feel the acute pain of grief or loss.

Salim felt cold as he said, 'You have a choice, Charlotte. Either you come back with me to Tabat and we pursue our mutual attraction to its natural end—and it *will* end—or you will never see me again.'

Charlotte had been teetering on the edge, fearing she was too weak to walk away from what Salim was offering even if it was finite. The lure to return to Tabat one final time with him had almost broken her. But then he'd said what he just had, and his words were hitting her like a million tiny pointed barbs.

It wasn't his voice she heard now—it was her father's.

'You have a choice here, Charlotte. Choose me and we leave together today. Choose your mother and you will never see me again.'

The toxic memory faded, but not the words.

She looked at Salim and felt her heart break into two pieces. She said quietly, 'Thank you for making it easy for me to walk away from you, Salim. Goodbye.'

And then she turned and left.

CHAPTER TEN

'Well, well...apparently leopards *can* change their spots!'

Charlotte's hand was clenched so tightly around her glass of champagne that she had to relax it for fear of cracking the delicate crystal. A TV screen on mute was showing the news in a corner of the private club where the Christmas party she'd been invited to was taking place.

She hadn't wanted to come. It was Christmas Eve the following day, and she'd fully intended to be deep in hibernation mode by now. But knowing that the coronation was taking place today had driven her out in a kind of desperation to prove something to herself. That she was coping. That Christmas wasn't her *bête noir.* That the fact that man she loved was getting on with his life wasn't like a knife sliding between her ribs.

But every sparkling light, every Christmas tree and every group of carol singers she'd spotted on her way here had flayed her alive. It seemed to be particularly cruel that her heartbreak was coinciding with Christmas.

She watched now, helpless not to, as King Salim Al-Noury was crowned in the main ceremonial ballroom of the Tabat palace under the avid eyes of the world, eager to see this playboy prince brought to heel.

But, as Charlotte knew only too well, Salim would never be brought to heel. He would always retain that air of wild unpredictability and it would make him a great man.

He was almost unrecognisable. His hair had been cut militarily short and he was clean-shaven. His blue eyes stood out stark against his dark olive skin.

King Zafir was there, and Queen Kat. And Charlotte recognised some of the tribal leaders. And the young couple whose marriage she had witnessed in the tent. Then she saw Rafa and Assa in the crowd and she felt like crying.

The man next to her was blissfully oblivious to her turmoil. 'Didn't you just come back from Tabat?'

Charlotte forced a smile and tore her eyes away from the TV. She looked at the man and said, 'I was there just briefly. Now, if you'll excuse me, I have to be somewhere else.'

And that somewhere else was far away from here, where she could lick her wounds. Hopefully when she emerged again it would be spring and her heart might not still be weeping.

It was Christmas Day and there was nothing but endless grey skies and crashing waves. Not a Christmas tree in sight nor a twinkling light. But it wasn't much comfort to Charlotte as she turned and made her way down the long empty beach, back towards the cottage her grandmother had owned.

She'd left it to Charlotte in her will and it was in the furthest western reaches of Ireland, with literally nothing between it and America except the Atlantic ocean.

In the end she'd come here because she'd always found solace at her grandmother's cottage, even though

Charlotte had been only four or five when she'd died. The cottage felt like a link to someone she remembered vaguely as being very maternal, and Charlotte had used it as frequently as she could over the years.

She felt tears threaten and willed them back, refusing to give in to the weakness. She'd stockpiled enough cheesy DVDs to last her a week, and food to last her at least until the shops opened again. She was planning on curling up under her duvet and not emerging until it was at least January the sixth.

She pulled the zip of her parka up as far as she could and trudged back towards the cottage behind the sand dunes. As she got closer she frowned. There was smoke coming from the chimney that she could see peeping just above the dunes. She'd cleaned out the fire from the previous night and left it set, but she was certain she hadn't lit it.

She hurried her pace, cursing herself for not locking the door. But she'd always felt so safe here. The nearest neighbour was at least three miles away.

She was breathing hard by the time she came over the dune and stumbled to a stop.

There were vehicles outside the tiny cottage. A sleek four-by-four. And a van.

She saw a man come out dressed in overalls and ran down the other side of the dune, shouting, 'Hey! What on earth is going on?'

The man stopped and looked to the doorway, where someone else had just emerged. Charlotte followed his gaze and her heart stopped dead. *Salim*. Dressed in black jeans and a snug black Puffa jacket. He looked as out of place here as an exotic animal.

Another two men and a woman emerged from the cottage, and she could see him saying something to them and shaking one of the men's hands. They got into the van and another four-by-four she hadn't seen and drove away.

Somehow, fearing she was dreaming, Charlotte made her legs work and approached the cottage. Salim didn't disappear. He looked at her steadily, but when she got close she saw lines of strain around his mouth. And his eyes.

She shook her head. 'Salim…?'

He said nothing, just stood back and gestured with a hand for her to go into the cottage. As if it was his. As if it was perfectly normal.

She could smell the peat on the fire, and the distinctive scent grounded her in reality slightly. But when she stepped through the door reality slipped out of her grasp again.

Her jaw dropped. The fire was burning merrily. The entire open-plan downstairs area was decorated with holly and ivy and strings of lights. There was a smell of mulled wine and spices. Candles were burning, sending out a soft golden glow.

Charlotte looked into the kitchen and saw the table set with linen and cutlery finer than her grandmother had ever owned. The oven was on and she smelled cooking meat. Turkey. Food was piled up on the sideboard. Vegetables, wine, cake. Dessert. Fruit.

In the corner of the living room stood a Christmas tree bedecked with lights and glittering ornaments. There was one present under the tree—a small wrapped box.

Finally, Charlotte's heart seemed to kick into action. She looked at Salim. 'What is all this? Why are you here?'

Charlotte knew fatally that if this was some grand gesture just to get her back into his bed then she wouldn't have the strength to say no…

Salim came and stood in front of her and she couldn't take her eyes off his. They were so intense. She noticed now that he was pale.

'I did it because I wanted you to have a better memory of Christmas than the one that made you hate it so much...'

Her heart lurched. She was fragile enough to crumble at the slightest thing and this was pushing her to the edge.

'You didn't have to do that just because you felt sorry for me...'

He frowned. 'Sorry for you? The last thing I feel is sorry for you.'

Charlotte wanted to ask *why* again, but she wasn't sure she wanted to hear the answer. Or she did, but she was afraid it might not be what she wanted to hear.

'But...you were just crowned.' She struggled not to let her imagination run riot. She thought of something and sucked in a breath. 'You haven't abdicated already?'

He shook his head. 'I'm not going to abdicate.'

Relief flooded Charlotte, and for a moment she couldn't speak, she felt so overcome. Finally she managed to get out, 'I'm glad you decided not to.'

'But there is one thing that would make me consider it again.'

'What?'

'I can't do this without the right queen by my side. I've always believed I didn't need anyone, but recently I met someone and the truth is that I can't live without her. I was stupid enough to think that it was a temporary thing...lust. That it would burn itself out... But I was wrong. Dead wrong.'

Charlotte wasn't breathing.

Salim turned and went over to the tree, bent down to pick up the small wrapped present.

He came back and handed it to her. 'Open your present.'

She took it, but her hands were numb with shock and she couldn't work out how to take the paper off. Salim took it out of her hands and she noticed that they were shaking slightly. He ripped the paper and the bow off and handed it back to her.

It was a velvet box. Royal blue.

She opened it. It was a ring. A stunning emerald in an antique gold setting shone up at her from white silk.

She looked at Salim, hardly daring to ask the question even though he was looking at her in a way that set her insides alight with a very dangerous flame of hope.

'What does this mean?'

He came close and cupped her face. 'It means, my beautiful Charlotte McQuillan, of the silk shirts that drove me to distraction and still do, that I love you. I should never have let you walk away from me. I panicked. I was all but begging you to come back to Tabat with me and it reminded me of begging Sara…' He stopped and swallowed.

Charlotte put a trembling hand to Salim's jaw, scarcely able to believe what she was hearing.

He went on. 'I couldn't bear the thought of watching you walk away if I begged and you said no. I was a coward. It's taken me a lifetime to learn to love again, and I tried not to love you because I'm terrified of losing you, but it's too late… I know what you meant now, when you thanked me for making it easy for you to walk away. I was making you choose, just like your father made you choose.' He shook his head. 'I'm so sorry.'

Charlotte's emotion overflowed and tears slipped down her cheeks.

She whispered, 'I used it as an excuse not to tell you how I felt. I thought it would only last until you didn't want me any more. I had to reject you first.' Before she lost her nerve she said fervently, 'I love you, Salim. Even if you only think you love me and realise later—'

He stopped her words with his mouth. His kiss was explicit and thorough and when they came up for air Charlotte was welded to Salim's body, as close as she could get with several layers of clothing in the way.

As if realising this, he kicked the front door closed and started to take off their coats, dropping them where they stood. He took her in his arms again, the lines of strain on his face disappearing.

'I love you, Charlotte McQuillan. For ever. Come back to Tabat with me and help me to make it our home. The first real home we've ever had…'

She wound her arms around his neck, emotion making her chest ache. She nodded. 'Yes, I'd like that. I'd go to the ends of the world with you.'

They kissed again, with less desperate urgency this time, as if savouring this moment.

When Salim pulled back Charlotte said with a wobbly smile, 'I saw your coronation. You looked very regal.'

He looked serious. 'I needed you there. That's when I knew I couldn't do it without you.'

Charlotte's heart flipped.

And then it flipped again when he grimaced and said, 'I'm doing this all backwards…'

He went down on one knee and looked up at her. 'Will you marry me, Charlotte McQuillan?'

Love flooded her whole body and heart, healing all the past hurts. She said fervently, 'Yes, I will.'

'Now? Here?'

Charlotte blinked. 'But how?'

He stood up. 'You saw how it's done… We can say

the words to each other. Obviously we'll get married officially, but I don't want to waste any time.'

Charlotte's vision blurred and she nodded. 'Yes, I'd like that.'

Salim let her go and dragged a throw off the couch. He spread it on the floor and put down two cushions. He knelt on one and put out a hand for Charlotte to join him. She knelt in front of him on the other cushion, heard the fire crackling in the hearth.

He took the ring out of the box and joined their hands together in the prayer position. Then with his free hand he touched the tops of their fingers with the ring saying, 'I marry you…' three times, until he came to her ring finger and slid the ring home.

Then he took another ring out of his pocket, for him, and gave it to her. Charlotte felt the intensity of the moment as she copied his words, sliding his ring onto his finger and holding it there.

Salim interlaced their fingers. 'Now we're married.'

Charlotte said emotionally, 'For better or worse.'

'In sickness and in health.'

'Till death do us part.'

A huge smile split Salim's face, making him look young and free.

He reached for her. 'Come here, Queen Al-Noury, I need to make love to my wife.'

Charlotte went willingly, and it was much, much later when they finally emerged, sated and happy, to enjoy the first of many happy Christmases together.

Christmas Day, a year later. Tabat City.

'Three—two—one—ooh!'

Charlotte's breath caught along with the crowd's as

the massive Christmas tree in Tabat City's main square sparkled and shone when a thousand tiny lights came to life against the clear dusk-filled sky.

It was stunning, and she had been deeply moved when Rafa had come to tell her that the city's councillors had decided they wanted to do this to honour their English queen's heritage and make her feel at home.

'Is this okay?'

Charlotte heard the genuine concern in her husband's voice and felt him slide an arm around her waist. She nodded and bit her lip to contain her emotion, and then said, with a small hitch in her voice, 'It's more than okay… I think your antics last year cured me of any negative associations with Christmas for ever, and now this…'

He made a harrumphing sound and said, close to her ear, 'You talk of the deeply romantic actions of a man who had never done anything like that in his life.'

Charlotte turned her head to look up at her husband and remarked with a teasing smile, 'Indeed—who knew that behind the stone-cold heart of a playboy there was a romantic dying to be set free?'

He smiled and lifted her left hand, the light glinting off the solid gold eternity ring inlaid with tiny emeralds that he'd presented her with on the birth of their daughter, Sara, three months before. A month after Zafir and Kat—now both firm friends to Charlotte—had given birth to their son, Kalim.

The crowd cheered and clapped and the bundle in Charlotte's arms started to move, making small mewling sounds. She looked down into the just-awake eyes of her daughter and her heart squeezed.

Sara's eyes were still an indeterminate colour—somewhere between blue, grey and green. Charlotte secretly hoped they'd be blue, taking after her father and the beloved aunt they'd named her for. She would be the first Queen of Tabat, if she so wished. And if she didn't wish it, then that would be ok too.

Salim had vowed to do everything in his power to ensure the rules of succession were as democratic as possible so no child of theirs would be forced to take on a role they didn't want.

Sara's garden in Jahor was now a much loved and visited site—a place of peace and contemplation for anyone who had suffered loss. In the past year Salim had done a lot of healing, together with his brother, and he'd truly come into his own. He was the beloved king, who was slowly but surely bringing his country into a new future.

He had set up a foundation to take care of all his myriad business concerns, run now by carefully hand-picked staff. And he was also setting up the first digital hub in this part of the world, determined not to let his tech investments fall by the wayside. There was an air of industry and optimism throughout Tabat now, and tourism was rocketing.

Kat had been invaluable to Charlotte—helping to ease her into the intimidating role of queen—but to her relief the people of Tabat had welcomed her with unconditional acceptance and affection. The birth of their daughter had helped unite the country even more, and Charlotte's favourite moments were those spent with the nomadic tribes out in the far reaches of the endless desert.

Salim saw the telltale brightness in his wife's eyes as she looked out over the crowd and felt an answering surge of emotion. He still couldn't believe where he was now—*who* he was. How rich his life was. And how poor it would have been if he hadn't finally embraced his destiny.

He deftly took Sara from Charlotte's arms, cradling her against his chest. His daughter gazed up at him with the unblinking trust and love that humbled him every time he looked at her.

They waved for the few more requisite minutes, and as the crowd's cheers died down and they finally started to disperse Charlotte slid her arm around his waist.

He looked down at her. She smiled. 'Home?'

Salim's heart felt so full it might burst. He nodded and said emotionally, 'Yes, *home*.'

And together they went back to their palace, savouring every moment of joy and happiness their love brought them, because they both knew the value of learning to trust and love again.

* * * * *

A BILLIONAIRE FOR CHRISTMAS

JANICE MAYNARD

For my mother, Pat Scott, who loved Christmas
as much as anyone I have ever known

One

Leo Cavallo had a headache. In fact, his whole body hurt. The drive from Atlanta to the Great Smoky Mountains in East Tennessee hadn't seemed all that onerous on the map, but he'd gravely miscalculated the reality of negotiating winding rural roads after dark. And given that the calendar had flipped only a handful of days into December, he'd lost daylight a long time ago.

He glanced at the clock on the dashboard and groaned as he registered the glowing readout. It was after nine. He still had no idea if he was even close to his destination. The GPS had given up on him ten miles back. The car thermometer read thirty-five degrees, which meant that any moment now the driving rain hammering his windshield might change over to snow, and he'd really be screwed. Jags were not meant to be driven in bad weather.

Sweating beneath his thin cotton sweater, he reached into the console for an antacid. Without warning, his brother's voice popped into his head, loud and clear.

"I'm serious, Leo. You have to make some changes. You had a heart attack, for God's sake."

Leo scowled. "A mild cardiac event. Don't be so dramatic. I'm in excellent physical shape. You heard the doctor."

"Yes, I did. He said your stress levels are off the charts. And he preached heredity. Our father died before he hit forty-two. You keep this up, and I'll be putting you in the ground right beside him..."

Leo chewed the chalky tablet and cursed when the road suddenly changed from ragged pavement to loose gravel. The wheels of his vehicle spun for purchase on the uneven surface. He crept along, straining his eyes for any signs of life up ahead.

On either side, steep hillsides boxed him in. The headlights on his car picked out dense thickets of rhododendron lining the way. Claustrophobic gloom swathed the vehicle in a cloying blanket. He was accustomed to living amidst the bright lights of Atlanta. His penthouse condo offered an amazing view of the city. Neon and energy and people were his daily fuel. So why had he agreed to voluntary exile in a state whose remote corners seemed unwelcoming at best?

Five minutes later, when he was almost ready to turn around and admit defeat, he saw a light shining in the darkness. The relief he felt was staggering. By the time he finally pulled up in front of the blessedly illuminated house, every muscle in his body ached with tension. He hoped the porch light indicated some level of available hospitality.

Pulling his plush-lined leather jacket from the backseat, he stepped out of the car and shivered. The rain had slacked off...finally. But a heavy, fog-wrapped drizzle accompanied by bone-numbing chill greeted him. For the moment, he would leave his bags in the trunk. He didn't know exactly where his cabin was located. Hopefully, he'd be able to park closer before he unloaded.

Mud caked the soles of his expensive leather shoes as he made his way to the door of the modern log structure. It looked as if it had been assembled from one of those kits that well-heeled couples bought to set up getaway homes in the mountains. Certainly not old, but neatly put together.

From what he could tell, it was built on a single level with a porch that wrapped around at least two sides of the house.

There was no doorbell that he could see, so he took hold of the bronze bear-head knocker and rapped it three times, hard enough to express his growing frustration. Additional lights went on inside the house. As he shifted from one foot to the other impatiently, the curtain beside the door twitched and a wide-eyed female face appeared briefly before disappearing as quickly as it had come.

From inside he heard a muffled voice. "Who is it?"

"Leo. Leo Cavallo," he shouted at the door. Grinding his teeth, he reached for a more conciliatory tone. "May I come in?"

Phoebe opened her front door with some trepidation. Not because she had anything to fear from the man on the porch. She'd been expecting him for the past several hours. What she dreaded was telling him the truth.

Backing up to let him enter, she winced as he crossed the threshold and sucked all the air out of the room. He was a big man, built like a lumberjack, broad through the shoulders, and tall, topping her five-foot-nine stature by at least four more inches. His thick, wavy chestnut hair gleamed with health. The glow from the fire that crackled in the hearth picked out strands of dark gold.

When he removed his jacket, running a hand through his disheveled hair, she saw that he wore a deep blue sweater along with dark dress pants. The faint whiff of his aftershave mixed with the unmistakable scent of the outdoors. He filled the room with his presence.

Reaching around him gingerly, she flipped on the overhead light, sighing inwardly in relief when the intimacy of firelight gave way to a less cozy atmosphere. Glancing down at his feet, she bit her lip. "Will you please take off your shoes? I cleaned the floors this morning."

Though he frowned, he complied. Before she could say another word, he gave her home a cursory glance, then settled his sharp gaze on her face. His übermasculine features were put together in a pleasing fashion, but the overall impression was intensely male. Strong nose, noble forehead, chiseled jaw and lips made for kissing a woman. His scowl grew deeper. "I'm tired as hell, and I'm starving. If you could point me to my cabin, I'd like to get settled for the night, Ms....?"

"Kemper. Phoebe Kemper. You can call me Phoebe." Oh, wow. His voice, low and gravelly, stroked over her frazzled nerves like a lover's caress. The faint Georgia drawl did nothing to disguise the hint of command. This was a man accustomed to calling the shots.

She swallowed, rubbing damp palms unobtrusively on her thighs. "I have a pot of vegetable beef stew still warm on the stove. Dinner was late tonight." And every night, it seemed. "You're welcome to have some. There's corn bread, as well."

The aura of disgruntlement he wore faded a bit, replaced by a rueful smile. "That sounds wonderful."

She waved a hand. "Bathroom's down the hall, first door on the right. I'll get everything on the table."

"And afterward you'll show me my lodgings?"

Gulp. "Of course." Perhaps she shouldn't have insisted that he remove his shoes. There was something about a man in his sock feet that hinted at a level of familiarity. The last thing she needed at this juncture in time was to feel drawn to someone who was most likely going to be furious with her no matter how she tried to spin the facts in a positive light.

He was gone a very short time, but Phoebe had everything ready when he returned. A single place mat, some silverware and a steaming bowl of stew flanked by corn bread and a cheerful yellow gingham napkin. "I didn't know what you wanted to drink," she said. "I have decaf iced tea, but the weather's awfully cold tonight."

"Decaf coffee would be great…if you have it."

"Of course." While he sat down and dug into his meal, she brewed a fresh pot of Colombian roast and poured him a cup. He struck her as the kind of man who wouldn't appreciate his java laced with caramel or anything fancy. Though she offered the appropriate add-ons, Leo Cavallo took his coffee black and unsweetened. No fuss. No nonsense.

Phoebe puttered around, putting things away and loading the dishwasher. Her guest ate with every indication that his previous statement was true. Apparently, he *was* starving. Two large bowls of stew, three slabs of corn bread and a handful of the snickerdoodles she had made that morning vanished in short order.

As he was finishing his dessert, she excused herself. "I'll be back in just a moment." She set the pot on the table. "Help yourself to more coffee."

Leo's mood improved dramatically as he ate. He hadn't been looking forward to going back down that road to seek out dinner, and though his cabin was supposed to be stocked with groceries, he was not much of a cook. Everything he needed, foodwise, was close at hand in Atlanta. He was spoiled probably. If he wanted sushi at three in the morning or a full breakfast at dawn, he didn't have to look far.

When he finished the last crumb of the moist, delicious cookies, he wiped his mouth with his napkin and stood up to stretch. After the long drive, his body felt kinked and cramped from sitting in one position for too many hours. Guiltily, he remembered the doctor's admonition not to push himself. Truthfully, it was the only setting Leo had. Full steam ahead. Don't look back.

And yet now he was supposed to turn himself into somebody new. Even though he'd been irritated by the many people hovering over him—work colleagues, medical professionals and his family—in his heart, he knew the level of their concern was a testament to how much he had scared them all. One moment he had been standing at the head of a large conference table giving an impassioned pitch to a group of global investors, and the next, he'd been on the floor.

None of the subsequent few minutes were clear in his memory. He recalled not being able to breathe. And an enormous pressure in his chest. But not much more than that. Shaken and disturbed by the recollection of that day, he paced the confines of the open floor plan that incorporated the kitchen and living area into a pleasing whole.

As he walked back and forth, he realized that Phoebe Kemper had created a cozy nest out here in the middle of nowhere. Colorful area rugs cushioned his feet. The floor consisted of wide, honey-colored hardwood planks polished to a high sheen.

Two comfortable groupings of furniture beckoned visitors to sit and enjoy the ambience. Overhead, a three-tiered elk antler chandelier shed a large, warm circle of light. On the far wall, built-in bookshelves flanked the stacked stone fireplace. As he scanned Phoebe's collection of novels and nonfiction, he realized with a little kick of pleasure that he was actually going to have time to read for a change.

A tiny noise signaled his hostess's return. Whirling around, he stared at her, finally acknowledging, if only to himself, that his landlady was a knockout. Jet-black hair long enough to reach below her breasts had been tamed into a single thick, smooth braid that hung forward over her shoulder. Tall and slender and long-limbed, there was nothing frail or helpless about Phoebe Kemper. Yet he could imagine many men rushing to her aid, simply to coax a smile from those lush unpainted lips that were the color of pale pink roses.

She wore faded jeans and a silky coral blouse that brought out the warm tones in her skin. With eyes so dark they were almost black, she made him wonder if she claimed Cherokee blood. Some resourceful members of that tribe had hidden deep in these mountains to escape the Trail of Tears.

Her smile was teasing. "Feel better now? At least you don't look like you want to commit murder anymore."

He shrugged sheepishly. "Sorry. It was a hell of a day."

Phoebe's eyes widened and her smile faded. "And it's about to get worse, I'm afraid. There's a problem with your reservation."

"Impossible," he said firmly. "My sister-in-law handled all the details. And I have the confirmation info."

"I've been trying to call her all day, but she hasn't answered. And no one gave me your cell number."

"Sorry about that. My niece found my sister-in-law's phone and dropped it into the bathtub. They've been scrambling to get it replaced. That's why you couldn't reach her. But no worries. I'm here now. And it doesn't look like you're overbooked," he joked.

Phoebe ignored his levity and frowned. "We had heavy rains and high winds last night. Your cabin was damaged."

His mood lightened instantly. "Don't worry about a thing, Ms. Phoebe. I'm not that picky. I'm sure it will be fine."

She shook her head in disgust. "I guess I'll have to show you to convince you. Follow me, please."

"Should I move my car closer to the cabin?" he asked as he put on his shoes and tied them. The bottoms were a mess.

Phoebe scooped up something that looked like a small digital camera and tucked it into her pocket. "No need," she said. She shrugged into a jacket that could have been a twin to his. "Let's go." Out on the porch, she picked up a large, heavy-duty flashlight and turned it on. The intense beam sliced through the darkness.

The weather hadn't improved. He was glad that Luc and Hattie had insisted on packing for him. They had undoubtedly covered every eventuality if he knew his sister-in-law. Come rain, sleet, snow or hail, he'd be prepared. But for now, everything he'd brought with him was stashed in the trunk of his car. Sighing for the lost opportunity to carry a load, he followed Phoebe.

Though he would never have found it on his own in the inky, fog-blinding night, the path from Phoebe's cabin to the next closest one was easy to pick out with the flashlight. Far more than a foot trail, the route they followed was clearly an extension of the gravel road.

His impatience grew as he realized they could have driven the few hundred feet. Finally, he dug in his heels. "I should move the car," he said. "I'm sure I'll be fine."

At that very moment, Phoebe stopped so abruptly he nearly plowed into her. "We're here," she said bluntly. "And *that* is what's left of your two-month rental."

The industrial-strength flashlight was more than strong enough to reveal the carnage from the previous night's storm. An enormous tree lay across the midline of the house at a forty-five-degree angle. The force of the falling trunk had crushed the roof. Even from this vantage point, it was clear that the structure was open to the elements.

"Good Lord." He glanced behind him instinctively, realizing with sick dismay that Phoebe's home could have suffered a similar fate. "You must have been scared to death."

She grimaced. "I've had better nights. It happened about 3:00 a.m. The boom woke me up. I didn't try to go out then, of course. So it was daylight before I realized how bad it was."

"You haven't tried to cover the roof?"

She chuckled. "Do I look like Superwoman? I know

my own limitations, Mr. Cavallo. I've called my insurance company, but needless to say, they've been inundated with claims from the storm. Supposedly, an agent will be here tomorrow afternoon, but I'm not holding my breath. Everything inside the house got soaked when the tree fell, because it was raining so hard. The damage was already done. It's not like I could have helped matters."

He supposed she had a point. But that still left the issue of where he was expected to stay. Despite his grumblings to Luc and Hattie, now that he was finally here, the idea of kicking back for a while wasn't entirely unpleasant. Perhaps he could find himself in the great outdoors. Maybe even discover a new appreciation for life, which as he so recently had found out, was both fragile and precious.

Phoebe touched his arm. "If you've seen enough, let's go back. I'm not going to send you out on the road again in this miserable weather. You're welcome to stay the night with me."

They reversed their steps as Leo allowed Phoebe to take the lead. The steady beam of light led them without incident back to his car. The porch light was still on, adding to a feeling of welcome. Phoebe waved a hand at the cabin. "Why don't you go inside and warm up? Your sister-in-law told me you've been in the hospital. I'd be happy to bring in your luggage if you tell me what you'll need."

Leo's neck heated with embarrassment and frustration. Damn Hattie and her mother-hen instincts. "I can get my own bags," he said curtly. "But thank you." He added that last bit grudgingly. Poor Phoebe had no reason to know that his recent illness was a hot-button issue for him. He was a young man. Being treated like an invalid made him nuts. And for whatever reason, it was especially important to him that the lovely Phoebe see him as a competent, capable male, and not someone she had to babysit.

His mental meanderings must not have lasted as long

as he thought, because Phoebe was still at his side when he heard—very distinctly—the cry of a baby. He whirled around, expecting to see that another car had made its way up the narrow road. But he and Phoebe were alone in the night.

A second, less palatable possibility occurred to him. He'd read that a bobcat's cry could emulate that of an upset infant's. And the Smoky Mountains were home to any number of those nocturnal animals. Before he could speculate further, the sound came again.

Phoebe shoved the flashlight toward him. "Here. Keep this. I've got to go inside."

He took it automatically, and grinned. "So you're leaving me out here alone with a scary animal stalking us?"

She shook her head. "I don't know what you're talking about."

"The bobcat. Isn't that what we're hearing?"

Phoebe laughed softly, a pleasing sensual sound that made the hair on his arms stand up even more than the odd noise had. "Despite your interesting imagination," she said with a chuckle, "no." She reached in her pocket and removed the small electronic device he had noticed earlier. Not a camera, but a monitor. "The noise you hear that sounds like a crying baby is *actually* a baby. And I'd better get in there fast before all heck breaks loose."

Two

Leo stood there gaping at her even after the front door slammed shut. It was only the realization his hands were in danger of frostbite that galvanized him into motion. In short order he found the smaller of the two suitcases he had brought. Slinging the strap across one shoulder, he then reached for his computer briefcase and a small garment bag.

Locking the car against any intruders, human or otherwise, he walked up the steps, let himself in and stopped dead in his tracks when he saw Phoebe standing by the fire, a small infant whimpering on her shoulder as she rubbed its back. Leo couldn't quite sort out his emotions. The scene by the hearth was beautiful. His sister-in-law, Hattie, wore that same look on her face when she cuddled her two little ones.

But a baby meant there was a daddy in the picture somewhere, and though Leo had only met this particular Madonna and child today, he knew the feeling in the pit of his stomach was disappointment. Phoebe didn't wear a wedding ring, but he could see a resemblance between mother and child. Their noses were identical.

Leo would simply have to ignore this inconvenient attraction, because Phoebe was clearly not available. And though he adored his niece and nephew, he was not the kind of man who went around bouncing kids on his knee and playing patty-cake.

Phoebe looked up and smiled. “This is Teddy. His full name is Theodore, but at almost six months, he hasn’t quite grown into it yet.”

Leo kicked off his shoes for the second time that night and set down his luggage. Padding toward the fire, he mustered a smile. “He’s cute.”

“Not nearly as cute at three in the morning.” Phoebe’s expression as she looked down at the baby was anything but aggravated. She glowed.

“Not a good sleeper?”

She bristled at what she must have heard as implied criticism. “He does wonderfully for his age. Don’t you, my love?” The baby had settled and was sucking his fist. Phoebe nuzzled his neck. “Most evenings he’s out for the count from ten at night until six or seven in the morning. But I think he may be cutting a tooth.”

“Not fun, I’m sure.”

Phoebe switched the baby to her left arm, holding him against her side. “Let me show you the guest room. I don’t think we’ll disturb you even if I have to get up with him during the night.”

He followed her down a short hallway past what was obviously Phoebe’s suite all the way to the back right corner of the house. A chill hit him as soon as they entered the bedroom.

“Sorry,” she said. “The vents have been closed off, but it will warm up quickly.”

He looked around curiously. “This is nice.” A massive king-size bed made of rough timbers dominated the room. Hunter-green draperies covered what might have been a large picture window. The attached bathroom, decorated in shades of sand and beige, included a Jacuzzi tub and a roomy shower stall. Except for the tiled floor in the bathroom, the rest of the space boasted the same attractive hardwood he'd seen in the remainder of the house, covered here and there by colorful rugs.

Phoebe hovered, the baby now asleep. "Make yourself at home. If you're interested in staying in the area, I can help you make some calls in the morning."

Leo frowned. "I paid a hefty deposit. I'm not interested in staying anywhere else."

A trace of pique flitted across Phoebe's face, but she answered him calmly. "I'll refund your money, of course. You saw the cabin. It's unlivable. Even with a speedy insurance settlement, finding people to do the work will probably be difficult. I can't even guesstimate how long it will be before everything is fixed."

Leo thought about the long drive from Atlanta. He hadn't wanted to come here at all. And yesterday's storm damage was his ticket out. All he had to do was tell Luc and Hattie, and his doctor, that circumstances had conspired against him. He could be back in Atlanta by tomorrow night.

But something—stubbornness maybe—made him contrary. "Where is Mr. Kemper in all this? Shouldn't he be the one worrying about repairing the other cabin?"

Phoebe's face went blank. "Mr. Kemper?" Suddenly, she laughed. "I'm not married, Mr. Cavallo."

"And the baby?"

A small frown line appeared between her brows. "Are you a traditionalist, then? You don't think a single female can raise a child on her own?"

Leo shrugged. "I think kids deserve two parents. But having said that, I do believe women can do anything they like. I can't, however, imagine a woman like you needing to embrace single parenthood."

He'd pegged Phoebe as calm and cool, but her eyes flashed. "A woman like me? What does that mean?"

Leaning his back against one of the massive bedposts,

he folded his arms and stared at her. Now that he knew she wasn't married, all bets were off. "You're stunning. Are all the men in Tennessee blind?"

Her lips twitched. "I'm pretty sure that's the most clichéd line I've ever heard."

"I stand by my question. You're living out here in the middle of nowhere. Your little son has no daddy anywhere in sight. A man has to wonder."

Phoebe stared at him, long and hard. He bore her scrutiny patiently, realizing how little they knew of each other. But for yesterday's storm, he and Phoebe would likely have exchanged no more than pleasantries when she handed over his keys. In the weeks to come, they might occasionally have seen each other outside on pleasant days, perhaps waved in passing.

But fate had intervened. Leo came from a long line of Italian ancestors who believed in the power of *destino* and *amore.* Since he was momentarily banned from the job that usually filled most of his waking hours, he was willing to explore his fascination with Phoebe Kemper.

He watched as she deposited the sleeping baby carefully in the center of the bed. The little boy rolled to his side and continued to snooze undisturbed. Phoebe straightened and matched her pose to Leo's. Only instead of using the bed for support, she chose to lean against the massive wardrobe that likely held a very modern home entertainment center.

She eyed him warily, her teeth nibbling her bottom lip. Finally she sighed. "First of all, we're not in the middle of nowhere, though it must seem that way to you since you had to drive up here on such a nasty night. Gatlinburg is less than ten miles away. Pigeon Forge closer than that. We have grocery stores and gas stations and all the modern conveniences, I promise. I like it here at the foot of the mountains. It's peaceful."

"I'll take your word for it."

"And Teddy is my nephew, not my son."

Leo straightened, wondering what it said about him that he was glad the woman facing him was a free agent. "Why is he here?"

"My sister and her husband are in Portugal for six weeks settling his father's estate. They decided the trip would be too hard on Teddy, and that cleaning out the house would be much easier without him. So I volunteered to let him stay with me until they get home."

"You must like kids a lot."

A shadow crossed her face. "I love my nephew." She shook off whatever mood had momentarily stolen the light. "But we're avoiding the important topic. I can't rent you a demolished cabin. You have to go."

He smiled at her with every bit of charm he could muster. "You can rent me *this* room."

Phoebe had to give Leo Cavallo points for persistence. His deep brown eyes were deceptive. Though a woman could sink into their warmth, she might miss entirely the fact that he was a man who got what he wanted. If he had been ill recently, she could find no sign of it in his appearance. His naturally golden skin, along with his name, told her that he possessed Mediterranean genes. And in Leo's case, that genetic material had been spun into a ruggedly handsome man.

"This isn't a B and B," she said. "I have an investment property that I rent out to strangers. That property is currently unavailable, so you're out of luck."

"Don't make a hasty decision," he drawled. "I'm housebroken. And I'm handy when it comes to changing lightbulbs and killing creepy-crawlies."

"I'm tall for a woman, and I have monthly pest control service."

"Taking care of a baby is a lot of work. You might enjoy having help."

"You don't strike me as the type to change diapers."

"Touché."

Were they at an impasse? Would he give up?

She glanced at Teddy, sleeping so peacefully. Babies were an important part of life, but it was a sad day when a grown woman's life was so devoid of male companionship that a nonverbal infant was stimulating company. "I'll make a deal with you," she said slowly, wondering if she were crazy. "You tell me why you really want to stay, and I'll consider your request."

For the first time, she saw discomfort on Leo's face. He was one of those consummately confident men who strode through life like a captain on the bridge of his ship, everyone in his life bowing and scraping in his wake. But at the moment, a mask slipped and she caught a glimpse of vulnerability. "What did my sister-in-law tell you when she made the reservation?"

A standard ploy. Answering a question with a question. "She said you'd been ill. Nothing more than that. But in all honesty, you hardly look like a man at death's door."

Leo's smile held a note of self-mockery. "Thank God for that."

Curiouser and curiouser. "Now that I think about it," she said, trying to solve the puzzle as she went along, "you don't seem like the kind of man who takes a two-month sabbatical in the mountains for any reason. Unless, of course, you're an artist or a songwriter. Maybe a novelist? Am I getting warm?"

Leo grimaced, not quite meeting her gaze. "I needed a break," he said. "Isn't that reason enough?"

Something in his voice touched her…some note of discouragement or distress. And in that moment, she felt a kinship with Leo Cavallo. Hadn't she embraced this land

and built these two cabins for that very reason? She'd been disillusioned with her job and heartbroken over the demise of her personal life. The mountains had offered healing.

"Okay," she said, capitulating without further ado. "You can stay. But if you get on my nerves or drive me crazy, I am well within my rights to kick you out."

He grinned, his expression lightening. "Sounds fair."

"And I charge a thousand dollars a week more if you expect to share meals with me."

It was a reckless barb, an attempt to get a rise out of him. But Leo merely nodded his head, eyes dancing. "Whatever you say." Then he sobered. "Thank you, Phoebe. I appreciate your hospitality."

The baby stirred, breaking the odd bubble of intimacy that had enclosed the room. Phoebe scooped up little Teddy and held him to her chest, suddenly feeling the need for a barrier between herself and the charismatic Leo Cavallo. "We'll say good night, then."

Her houseguest nodded, eyes hooded as he stared at the baby. "Sleep well. And if you hear me up in the night, don't be alarmed. I've had a bit of insomnia recently."

"I could fix you some warm milk," she said, moving toward the door.

"I'll be fine. See you in the morning."

Leo watched her leave and felt a pinch of remorse for having pressured her into letting him invade her home. But not so much that he was willing to leave. In Atlanta everyone had walked on eggshells around him, acting as if the slightest raised voice or cross word would send him into a relapse. Though his brother, Luc, tried to hide his concern, it was clear that he and Hattie were worried about Leo. And as dear as they both were to him, Leo needed a little space to come to terms with what had happened.

His first instinct was to dive back into work. But the

doctor had flatly refused to release him. This mountain getaway was a compromise. Not an idea Leo would have embraced voluntarily, but given the options, his only real choice.

When he exited the interstate earlier that evening, Leo had called his brother to say he was almost at his destination. Though he needed to escape the suffocating but well-meaning attention, he would never *ever* cause Luc and Hattie to worry unnecessarily. He would do anything for his younger brother, and he knew Luc would return the favor. They were closer than most siblings, having survived their late teen and early-adult years in a foreign land under the thumb of their autocratic Italian grandfather.

Leo yawned and stretched, suddenly exhausted. Perhaps he was paying for years of burning the candle at both ends. His medical team *and* his family had insisted that for a full recovery, Leo needed to stay away from work and stress. Maybe the recent hospital stay had affected him more than he realized. But whatever the reason, he was bone tired and ready to climb into that large rustic bed.

Too bad he'd be sleeping alone. It was oddly comforting when his body reacted predictably to thoughts of Phoebe. Something about her slow, steady smile and her understated sexuality really did it for him. Though his doctor had cleared Leo for exercise and sexual activity, the latter was a moot point. Trying to ignore the erection that wouldn't be seeing any action tonight, he reached for his suitcase, extracted his shaving kit and headed for the shower.

To Phoebe's relief, the baby didn't stir when she laid him in his crib. She stood over him for long moments watching the almost imperceptible movements of his small body as he breathed. She knew her sister was missing Teddy like crazy, but selfishly, Phoebe herself was looking forward to having someone to share Christmas with.

Her stomach did a little flip as she realized that Leo might be here, as well. But no. Surely he would go home at the holidays and come back to finish out his stay in January.

When she received the initial reservation request, she had researched Leo and the Cavallo family on Google. She knew he was single, rich and the CFO of a worldwide textile company started by his grandfather in Italy. She also knew that he supported several charities, not only with money, but with his service. He didn't need to work. The Cavallo vaults, metaphorically speaking, held more money than any one person could spend in a lifetime. But she understood men like Leo all too well. They thrived on challenge, pitting themselves repeatedly against adversaries, both in business and in life.

Taking Leo into her home was not a physical risk. He was a gentleman, and she knew far more about him than she did about many men she had dated. The only thing that gave her pause was an instinct that told her he needed help in some way. She didn't need another responsibility. And besides, if the cabin hadn't been demolished, Leo would have been on his own for two months anyway.

There was no reason for her to be concerned. Nevertheless, she sensed pain in him, and confusion. Given her own experience with being knocked flat on her butt for a long, long time, she wouldn't wish that experience on anyone. Maybe she could probe gently and see why this big mountain of a man, who could probably bench-press more than his body weight, seemed lost.

As she prepared for bed, she couldn't get him out of her mind. And when she climbed beneath her flannel sheets and closed her eyes, his face was the image that stayed with her through the night.

Three

Leo awoke when sunlight shining through a crack in the drapes hit his face. He yawned and scrubbed his hands over his stubbly chin, realizing with pleased surprise that he had slept through the night. Perhaps there was something to this mountain retreat thing after all.

Most of his stuff was still in the car, so he dug out a pair of faded jeans from his overnight case and threw on his favorite warm cashmere sweater. It was a Cavallo product… of course. The cabin had an efficient heat system, but Leo was itching to get outside and see his surroundings in the light of day.

Tiptoeing down the hall in case the baby was sleeping, he paused unconsciously at Phoebe's door, which stood ajar. Through the narrow crack he could see a lump under the covers of a very disheveled bed. Poor woman. The baby must have kept her up during the night.

Resisting the urge to linger, he made his way to the kitchen and quietly located the coffeepot. Phoebe was an organized sort, so it was no problem to find what he needed in the cabinet above. When he had a steaming cup brewed, strong and black, he grabbed a banana off the counter and went to stand at the living room window.

Supposedly, one of his challenges was to acquire the habit of eating breakfast in the morning. Normally, he had neither the time nor the inclination to eat. As a rule, he'd be at the gym by six-thirty and at the office before eight. After that, his day was nonstop until seven or later at night.

He'd never really thought much about his schedule in the past. It suited him, and it got the job done. For a man in his prime, *stopping to smell the roses* was a metaphor for growing old. Now that he had been admonished to do just that, he was disgruntled and frustrated. He was thirty-six, for God's sake. Was it really time to throw in the towel?

Pulling back the chintz curtains decorated with gamboling black bears, he stared out at a world that glistened like diamonds in the sharp winter sun. Every branch and leaf was coated with ice. Evidently, the temperatures had dropped as promised, and now the narrow valley where Phoebe made her home was a frozen wonderland.

So much for his desire to explore. Anyone foolish enough to go out at this moment would end up flat on his or her back after the first step. *Patience, Leo. Patience.* His doctor, who also happened to be his racquetball partner on the weekends, had counseled him repeatedly to take it easy, but Leo wasn't sure he could adapt. Already, he felt itchy, needing a project to tackle, a problem to solve.

"You're up early."

Phoebe's voice startled him so badly he spun around and managed to slosh hot coffee over the fingers of his right hand. "Ouch, damn it."

He saw her wince as he crossed to the sink and ran cold water over his stinging skin.

"Sorry," she said. "I thought you heard me."

Leo had been lost in thought, but he was plenty alert now. Phoebe wore simple knit pj's that clung to her body in all the right places. The opaque, waffle-weave fabric was pale pink with darker pink rosebuds. It faithfully outlined firm high breasts, a rounded ass and long, long legs.

Despite his single-minded libido, he realized in an instant that she looked somewhat the worse for wear. Her long braid had frayed into wispy tendrils and dark smudges underscored her eyes.

"Tough night with the baby?" he asked.

She shook her head, yawning and reaching for a mug in the cabinet. When she did, her top rode up, exposing an inch or two of smooth golden skin. He looked away, feeling like a voyeur, though the image was impossible to erase from his brain.

After pouring herself coffee and taking a long sip, Phoebe sank into a leather-covered recliner and pulled an afghan over her lap. "It wasn't the baby this time," she muttered. "It was me. I couldn't sleep for thinking about what a headache this reconstruction is going to be, especially keeping track of all the subcontractors."

"I could pitch in with that," he said. The words popped out of his mouth, uncensored. Apparently old habits were hard to break. But after all, wasn't helping out a fellow human being at least as important as inhaling the scent of some imaginary rose that surely wouldn't bloom in the dead of winter anyway? Fortunately, his sister-in-law wasn't around to chastise him for his impertinence. She had, in her sweet way, given him a very earnest lecture about the importance of not making work his entire life.

Of course, Hattie was married to Luc, who had miraculously managed to find a balance between enjoying his wife and his growing family and at the same time carrying his weight overseeing the R & D department. Luc's innovations, both in fabric content and in design, had kept their company competitive in the changing world of the twenty-first century. Worldwide designers wanted Cavallo textiles for their best and most expensive lines.

Leo was happy to oblige them. For a price.

Phoebe sighed loudly, her expression glum. "I couldn't ask that of you. It's my problem, and besides, you're on vacation."

"Not a vacation exactly," he clarified. "More like an involuntary time-out."

She grinned. "Has Leo been a naughty boy?"

Heat pooled in his groin and he felt his cheeks redden. He really had to get a handle on this urge to kiss her senseless. Since he was fairly sure that her taunt was nothing more than fun repartee, he refrained from saying what he really thought. "Not naughty," he clarified. "More like too much work and not enough play."

Phoebe swung her legs over the arm of the chair, her coffee mug resting on her stomach. For the first time he noticed that she wore large, pink Hello Kitty slippers on her feet. A less seductive female ensemble would be difficult to find. And yet Leo was fascinated.

She pursed her lips. "I'm guessing executive-level burnout?"

Her perspicacity was spot-on. "You could say that." Although it wasn't the whole story. "I'm doing penance here in the woods, so I can see the error of my ways."

"And who talked you into this getaway? You don't seem like a man who lets other people dictate his schedule."

He refilled his cup and sat down across from her. "True enough," he conceded. "But my baby brother, who happens to be part of a disgustingly happy married couple, thinks I need a break."

"And you listened?"

"Reluctantly."

She studied his face as though trying to sift through his half-truths. "What did you think you would do for two months?"

"That remains to be seen. I have a large collection of

detective novels packed in the backseat of my car, a year of *New York Times* crossword puzzles on my iPad and a brand-new digital camera not even out of the box yet."

"I'm impressed."

"But you'll concede that I surely have time to interview prospective handymen."

"Why would you want to?"

"I like keeping busy."

"Isn't that why you're here? To be *not* busy? I'd hate to think I was causing you to fall off the wagon in the first week."

"Believe me, Phoebe. Juggling schedules and workmen for your cabin repair is something I could do in my sleep. And since it's not my cabin, there's no stress involved."

Still not convinced, she frowned. "If it weren't for the baby, I'd never consider this."

"Understood."

"And if you get tired of dealing with it, you'll be honest."

He held up two fingers. "Scout's honor."

"In that case," she sighed, "how can I say no?"

Leo experienced a rush of jubilation far exceeding the appropriate response to Phoebe's consent. Only at that moment did he realize how much he had been dreading the long parade of unstructured days. With the cabin renovation to give him focus each morning, perhaps this rehabilitative exile wouldn't be so bad.

Guiltily, he wondered what his brother would say about this new turn of events. Leo was pretty sure Luc pictured him sitting by a fire in a flannel robe and slippers reading a John Grisham novel. While Leo enjoyed fiction on occasion, and though Grisham was a phenomenal author, a man could only read so many hours of the day without going bonkers.

Already, the idleness enforced by his recent illness had

made the days and nights far too long. The doctor had cleared him for his usual exercise routine, but with no gym nearby, and sporting equipment that was useless in this environment, it was going to require ingenuity on his part to stay fit and active, especially given that it was winter.

Suddenly, from down the hall echoed the distinct sound of a baby who was awake and unhappy.

Phoebe jumped to her feet, nearly spilling her coffee in the process. “Oh, shoot. I forgot to bring the monitor in here.” She clunked her mug in the sink and disappeared in a flash of pink fur.

Leo had barely drained his first cup and gone to the coffeepot for a refill when Phoebe reappeared, this time with baby Teddy on her hip. The little one was red-faced from crying. Phoebe smoothed his hair from his forehead. “Poor thing must be so confused not seeing his mom and dad every morning when he wakes up.”

“But he knows you, right?”

Phoebe sighed. “He does. Still, I worry about him day and night. I’ve never been the sole caregiver for a baby, and it’s scary as heck.”

“I’d say you’re doing an excellent job. He looks healthy and happy.”

Phoebe grimaced, though the little worried frown between her eyes disappeared. “I hope you’re right.”

She held Teddy out at arm’s length. “Do you mind giving him his bottle while I shower and get dressed?”

Leo backed up half a step before he caught himself. It was his turn to frown. “I don’t think either Teddy or I would like that. I’m too big. I scare children.”

Phoebe gaped. Then her eyes flashed. “That’s absurd. Wasn’t it you, just last night, who was volunteering to help with the baby in return for your keep?”

Leo shrugged, feeling guilty but determined not to show it. “I was thinking more in terms of carrying dirty diapers out to the trash. Or if you're talking on the phone, listening to the monitor to let you know when he wakes up. My hands are too large and clumsy to do little baby things."

"You've never been around an infant?"

"My brother has two small children, a boy and a girl. I see them several times a month, but those visits are more about kissing cheeks and spouting kudos as to how much they've grown. I might even bounce one on my knee if necessary, but not often. Not everyone is good with babies."

Little Teddy still dangled in midair, his chubby legs kicking restlessly. Phoebe closed the distance between herself and Leo and forced the wiggly child to Leo's chest. "Well, you're going to learn, because we had a deal."

Leo's arms came up reflexively, enclosing Teddy in a firm grip. The wee body was warm and solid. The kid smelled of baby lotion and some indefinable nursery scent that was endemic to babies everywhere. "I thought becoming your renovation overseer got me off the hook with Teddy."

Phoebe crossed her arms over her chest, managing to emphasize the fullness of her apparently unconfined breasts. "*It. Did. Not.* A deal is a deal. Or do I need a written contract?"

Leo knew when he was beaten. He'd pegged Phoebe as an easygoing, Earth Mother type, but suddenly he was confronted with a steely-eyed negotiator who would as soon kick him to the curb as look at him. "I'd raise my hands in surrender if I were able," he said, smiling, "But I doubt your nephew would like it."

Phoebe's nonverbal response sounded a lot like *humph.* As Leo watched, grinning inwardly, she quickly prepared a serving of formula and brought it to the sofa where Leo sat with Teddy. She handed over the bottle. "He likes it sitting up. Burp him halfway through."

"Yes, ma'am."

Phoebe put her hands on her hips. “Don’t mock me. You’re walking on thin ice, mister.”

Leo tried to look penitent, and also tried not to take note of the fact that her pert nipples were at eye level. He cleared his throat. “Go take your shower,” he said. “I’ve got this under control. You can trust me.”

Phoebe nibbled her bottom lip. “Yell at my bedroom door if you need me.”

Something about the juxtaposition of *yell* and *bedroom door* and *need* rekindled Leo’s simmering libido. About the only thing that could have slowed him down was the reality of a third person in the cabin. Teddy. Little innocent, about-to-get-really-hungry Teddy.

“Go,” Leo said, taking the bottle and offering it to the child in his lap. “We’re fine.”

As Phoebe left the room, Leo scooted Teddy to a more comfortable position, tucking the baby in his left arm so he could offer the bottle with his right hand. It was clear that the kid was almost capable of feeding himself. But if he dropped the bottle, he would be helpless.

Leo leaned back on the comfy couch and put his feet on the matching ottoman, feeling the warmth and weight of the child, who rested so comfortably in his embrace. Teddy seemed content to hang out with a stranger. Presumably as long as the food kept coming, the tyke would be happy. He did not, however, approve when Leo withdrew the bottle for a few moments and put him on his shoulder to burp him.

Despite Teddy’s pique, the new position coaxed the desired result. Afterward, Leo managed to help the kid finish the last of his breakfast. When Teddy sucked on nothing but air, Leo set aside the bottle and picked up a small, round teething ring from the end table flanking the sofa. Teddy chomped down on it with alacrity, giving Leo the opportunity to examine his surroundings in detail.

He liked the way Phoebe had furnished the place. The

cabin had a cozy feel that still managed to seem sophisticated and modern. The appliances and furniture were top-of-the-line, built to last for many years, and no doubt expensive because of that. The flooring was high-end, as well.

The pale amber granite countertops showcased what looked to be handcrafted cabinetry done in honey maple. He saw touches of Phoebe's personality in the beautiful green-and-gold glazed canister set and in the picture of Phoebe, her sister and Teddy tacked to the front of the fridge with a magnet.

Leo looked down at Teddy. The boy's big blue eyes stared up at him gravely as if to say, *What's your game?* Leo chuckled. "Your auntie Phoebe is one beautiful woman, my little man. Don't get me in trouble with her and you and I will get along just fine."

Teddy's gaze shifted back to his tiny hands covered in drool.

Leo was not so easily entertained. He felt the pull of Atlanta, of wondering what was going on at work, of needing to feel in control…at the helm. But something about cuddling a warm baby helped to freeze time. As though any considerations outside of this particular moment were less than urgent.

As he'd told Phoebe, he wasn't a complete novice when it came to being around kids. Luc and Hattie adopted Hattie's niece after they married last year. The little girl was almost two years old now. And last Valentine's Day, Hattie gave birth to the first "blood" Cavallo of the new generation, a dark-haired, dark-eyed little boy.

Leo appreciated children. They were the world's most concrete promise that the globe would keep on spinning. But in truth, he had no real desire to father any of his own. His lifestyle was complicated, regimented, full. Children deserved a healthy measure of their parents' love and attention. The Cavallo empire was Leo's baby. He knew on any given day what the financial bottom line was. During hard financial times, he wrestled the beast that was their investment and sales strategy and demanded returns instead of losses.

He was aware that some people called him hard…unfeeling. But he did what he did knowing how many employees around the world depended on the Cavallos for their livelihoods. It irked the hell out of him to think that another man was temporarily sitting in his metaphorical chair. The vice president Luc had chosen to keep tabs on the money in Leo's absence was solid and capable.

But that didn't make Leo feel any less sidelined.

He glanced at his watch. God in heaven. It was only ten-thirty in the morning. How was he going to survive being on the back burner for two months? Did he even want to try becoming the man his family thought he could be? A balanced, laid-back, easygoing guy?

He rested his free arm across the back of the sofa and closed his eyes, reaching for something Zen. Something peaceful.

Damn it, he didn't want to change. He wanted to go home. At least he had until he met Phoebe. Now he wasn't sure what he wanted.

Hoping that the boy wasn't picking up on his frustration and malcontent thoughts, Leo focused on the only thing capable of diverting him from his problems. Phoebe. Tall, long-legged Phoebe. A dark-haired, dark-eyed beauty with an attitude.

If Phoebe could be lured into an intimate relationship, then this whole recuperative escape from reality had definite possibilities. Leo sensed a spark between them. And he was seldom wrong about things like that. When a man had money, power and reasonably good looks, the female sex swarmed like mosquitoes. That wasn't ego speaking. Merely the truth.

As young men in Italy, he and Luc had racked up a number of conquests until they realized the emptiness of being wanted for superficial reasons. Luc had finally found his soul mate in college. But things hadn't worked out, and it had been ten years before he achieved happiness with the same woman.

Leo had never even made it that far. Not once in his life had he met a female who really cared about who he was as a person. Would-be "Mrs. Cavallos" saw the external trappings of wealth and authority and wanted wedding rings. And the real women, the uncomplicated, good-hearted ones, steered clear of men like Leo for fear of having their hearts broken.

He wasn't sure which category might include Phoebe Kemper. But he was willing to find out.

Four

Phoebe took her time showering, drying her hair and dressing. If Leo wasn't going to live up to his end of the bargain, she wanted to know it now. Leaving Teddy in his temporary care was no risk while she enjoyed a brief respite from the demands of surrogate parenthood. Despite Leo's protestations to the contrary, he was a man who could handle difficult situations.

It was hard to imagine that he had been ill. He seemed impervious to the things that lesser mortals faced. She envied him his confidence. Hers had taken a serious knock three years ago, and she wasn't sure if she had ever truly regained it. A younger Phoebe had taken the world by storm, never doubting her own ability to craft outcomes to her satisfaction.

But she had paid dearly for her hubris. Her entire world had crumbled. Afterward, she had chosen to hide from life, and only in the past few months had she finally begun to understand who she was and what she wanted. The lessons had been painful and slow in coming.

Unfortunately, her awakening had also made her face her own cowardice. Once upon a time she had taken great pleasure in blazing trails where no other women had gone.

Back then, she would have seen a man like Leo as a challenge, both in business and in her personal life.

Smart and confident, she had cruised through life, never realizing that on any given day, she—like any other human being—was subject to the whims of fate. Her perfect life had disintegrated in the way of a comet shattering into a million pieces.

Things would never be as they were. But could they be equally good in another very different way?

She took more care in dressing than she did normally. Instead of jeans, she pulled out a pair of cream corduroy pants and paired them with a cheery red scoop-necked sweater. Christmas was on the way, and the color always lifted her mood.

Wryly acknowledging her vanity, she left her hair loose on her shoulders. It was thick and straight as a plumb line. With the baby demanding much of her time, a braid was easier. Nevertheless, today she wanted to look nice for her guest.

When she finally returned to the living room, Teddy was asleep on Leo's chest, and Leo's eyes were closed, as well. She lingered for a moment in the doorway, enjoying the picture they made. The big, strong man and the tiny, defenseless baby.

Her chest hurt. She rubbed it absently, wondering if she would always grieve for what she had lost. Sequestering herself like a nun the past few years had given her a sort of numb peace. But that peace was an illusion, because it was the product of not living.

Living hurt. If Phoebe were ever going to rejoin the human race, she would have to accept being vulnerable. The thought was terrifying. The flip side of great love and joy was immense pain. She wasn't sure the first was worth risking the prospect of the last.

Quietly she approached the sofa and laid a hand on Leo's

arm. His eyes opened at once as if he had perhaps only been lost in thought rather than dozing. She held out her arms for the baby, but Leo shook his head.

"Show me where to take him," he whispered. "No point in waking him up."

She led the way through her bedroom and bathroom to a much smaller bedroom that adjoined on the opposite side. Before Teddy's arrival she had used this space as a junk room, filled with the things she was too dispirited to sort through when she'd moved in.

Now it had been tamed somewhat, so that half the room was full of neatly stacked plastic tubs, while the other half had been quickly transformed into a comfy space for Teddy. A baby bed, rocking chair and changing table, all with matching prints, made an appealing, albeit temporary, nursery.

Leo bent over the crib and laid Teddy gently on his back. The little boy immediately rolled to his side and stuck a thumb in his mouth. Both adults smiled. Phoebe clicked on the monitor and motioned for Leo to follow her as they tiptoed out.

In the living room, she waved an arm. "Relax. Do whatever you like. There's plenty of wood if you feel up to building us a fire."

"I told you. I'm not sick."

The terse words had a bite to them. Phoebe flinched inwardly, but kept her composure. Something had happened to Leo. Something serious. Cancer maybe. But she was not privy to that information. So conversation regarding the subject was akin to navigating a minefield.

Most men were terrible patients. Usually because their health and vigor were tied to their self-esteem. Clearly, Leo had been sent here or had agreed to come here because he needed rest and relaxation. He didn't want Phoebe hovering or commenting on his situation. Okay. Fine. But she was still going to keep an eye on him, because whatever had given him a wallop was serious enough to warrant a two-month hiatus from work.

That in itself was telling. In her past life, she had interacted with lots of men like Leo. They were alpha animals, content only with the number one spot in the pack. Their work was their life. And even if they married, familial relationships were kept in neatly separated boxes.

Unfortunately for Phoebe, she possessed some of those same killer instincts…or she had. The adrenaline rush of an impossible-to-pull-off business deal was addictive. The more you succeeded, the more you wanted to try again. Being around Leo was going to be difficult, because like a recovering alcoholic who avoided other drinkers, she was in danger of being sucked into his life, his work issues, whatever made him tick.

Under no circumstances could she let herself be dragged back into that frenzied schedule. The world was a big, beautiful place. She had enough money tucked away to live simply for a very long time. She had lost herself in the drive to achieve success. It was better now to accept her new lifestyle.

Leo moved to the fireplace and began stacking kindling and firewood with the precision of an Eagle Scout. Phoebe busied herself in the kitchen making a pot of chili to go with sandwiches for their lunch. Finally, she broke the awkward silence. "I have a young woman who babysits for me when I have to be gone for a short time. It occurred to me that I could see if she is free and if so, she could stay here in the house and watch Teddy while you and I do an initial damage assessment on the other cabin."

Leo paused to look over his shoulder, one foot propped on the raised hearth. "You sound very businesslike about this."

She shrugged. "I used to work for a big company. I'm accustomed to tackling difficult tasks."

He lit the kindling, stood back to see if it would catch, and then replaced the fire screen, brushing his hands together to remove the soot. "Where did you work?"

Biting her lip, she berated herself inwardly for bringing up a subject she would rather not pursue. "I was a stockbroker for a firm in Charlotte, North Carolina."

"Did they go under? Is that why you're here?"

His was a fair assumption. But wrong. "The business survived the economic collapse and is expanding by leaps and bounds."

"Which doesn't really answer my question."

She grimaced. "Maybe when we've known each other for more than a nanosecond I might share the gory details. But not today."

Leo understood her reluctance, or he thought he did. Not everyone wanted to talk about his or her failures. And rational or not, he regarded his heart attack as a failure. He wasn't overweight. He didn't smoke. Truth be told, his vices were few, perhaps only one. He was type A to the max. And type A personalities lived with stress so continuously that the condition became second nature. According to his doctor, no amount of exercise or healthy eating could compensate for an inability to unwind.

So maybe Leo was screwed.

He joined his hostess in the kitchen, looking for any excuse to get closer to her. "Something smells good." *Smooth, Leo. Real smooth.*

Last night he had dreamed about Phoebe's braid. But today…wow. Who knew within that old-fashioned hairstyle was a shiny waterfall the color of midnight?

Phoebe adjusted the heat on the stove top and turned to

face him. "I didn't ask. Do you have any dietary restrictions? Any allergies?"

Leo frowned. "I don't expect you to cook for me all the time I'm here. You claimed that civilization is close by. Why don't I take you out now and then?"

She shot him a pitying look that said he was clueless. "Clearly you've never tried eating at a restaurant with an infant. It's ridiculously loud, not to mention that the chaos means tipping the server at least thirty percent to compensate for the rice cereal all over the floor." She eyed his sweater. "I doubt you would enjoy it."

"I know kids are messy." He'd eaten out with Luc and Hattie and the babies a time or two. Hadn't he? Or come to think of it, maybe it was always at their home. "Well, not that then, but I could at least pick up a pizza once a week."

Phoebe smiled at him sweetly. "That would be lovely. Thank you, Leo."

Her genuine pleasure made him want to do all sorts of things for her…and *to* her. Something about that radiant smile twisted his insides in a knot. The unmistakable jolt of attraction was perhaps inevitable. They were two healthy adults who were going to be living in close proximity for eight or nine weeks. They were bound to notice each other sexually.

He cleared his throat as he shoved his hands into his pockets. "Is there a boyfriend who won't like me staying here?"

Again, that faint, fleeting shadow that dimmed her beauty for a moment. "No. You're safe." She shook her head, giving him a rueful smile. "I probably should say yes, though. Just so you don't get any ideas."

He tried to look innocent. "What ideas?" All joking aside, he was a little worried about having sex for the first time since… Oh, hell. He had a hard time even saying it in his head. Heart attack. There. He wasn't afraid of two stupid words.

The doctor had said *no restrictions,* but the doctor hadn't seen Phoebe Kemper in a snug crimson sweater. She reminded Leo of a cross between Wonder Woman and Pocahontas. Both of whom he'd fantasized about as a preteen boy. What did that say about his chances of staying away from her?

She shooed him with her hands. "Go unpack. Read one of those books. Lunch will be ready in an hour."

Leo enjoyed Phoebe's cooking almost as much as her soft, feminine beauty. If he could eat like this all the time, maybe he wouldn't skip meals and drive through fast-food places at nine o'clock at night. Little Teddy sat in his high chair playing with a set of plastic keys. It wasn't time for another bottle, so the poor kid had to watch the grown-ups eat.

They had barely finished the meal when Allison, the babysitter, showed up. According to Phoebe, she was a college student who lived at home and enjoyed picking up extra money. Plus, she adored Teddy, which was a bonus.

Since temperatures had warmed up enough to melt the ice, Leo went out to the car for his big suitcase, brought it in and rummaged until he found winter gear. Not much of it was necessary in Atlanta. It did snow occasionally, but rarely hung around. Natives, though, could tell hair-raising stories about ice storms and two-week stints without power.

When he made his way back to the living room, Allison was playing peekaboo with the baby, and Phoebe was slipping her arms into a fleece-lined sheepskin jacket. Even the bulky garment did nothing to diminish her appeal.

She tucked a notepad and pen into her pocket. "Don't be shy about telling me things you see. Construction is not my forte."

"Nor mine, but my brother and I did build a tree house once upon a time. Does that count?"

He followed her out the door, inhaling sharply as the icy wind filled his lungs with a jolt. The winter afternoon enwrapped them, blue-skied and damp. From every corner echoed the sounds of dripping water as ice gave way beneath pale sunlight.

Lingering on the porch to take it all in, he found himself strangely buoyed by the sights and sounds of the forest. The barest minimum of trees had been cleared for Phoebe's home and its mate close by. All around them, a sea of evergreen danced in the brisk wind. Though he could see a single contrail far above them, etched white against the blue, there was little other sign of the twenty-first century.

"Did you have these built when you moved here?" he asked as they walked side by side up the incline to the other cabin.

Phoebe tucked the ends of her fluttering scarf into her coat, lifting her face to the sun. "My grandmother left me this property when she died a dozen years ago. I had just started college. For years I held on to it because of sentimental reasons, and then much later…"

"Later, what?"

She looked at him, her eyes hidden behind dark sunglasses. Her shoulders lifted and fell. "I decided to mimic Thoreau and live in the woods."

Phoebe didn't expand on her explanation, so he didn't push. They had plenty of time for sharing confidences. And besides, he was none too eager to divulge all his secrets just yet.

Up close, and in the unforgiving light of day, the damage to the cabin was more extensive than he had realized. He put a hand on Phoebe's arm. "Let me go first. There's no telling what might still be in danger of crumbling."

They were able to open the front door, but just barely. The tree that had crushed the roof was a massive oak, large enough around that Leo would not have been able to encircle it with his arms. The house had caved in so dramatically that the floor was knee-deep in rubble—insulation, roofing shingles, branches of every size and, beneath it all, Phoebe's furnishings.

She removed her sunglasses and craned her neck to look up at the nonexistent ceiling as she followed Leo inside. "Not much left, is there?" Her voice wobbled a bit at the end. "I'm so grateful it wasn't *my* house."

"You and me, both," he muttered. Phoebe or Teddy or both could have been killed or badly injured…with no one nearby to check on them. The isolation was peaceful, but he wasn't sure he approved of a defenseless woman living here. Perhaps that was a prehistoric gut feeling. Given the state of the structure in which they were standing, however, he did have a case.

He just didn't have any right to argue it.

Taking Phoebe's hand to steady her, they stepped on top of and over all the debris and made their way to the back portion of the cabin. The far left corner bedroom had escaped unscathed…and some pieces of furniture in the outer rooms were okay for the moment. But if anything were to be salvaged, it would have to be done immediately. Dampness would lead to mildew, and with animals having free rein, further damage was a certainty.

Phoebe's face was hard to read. Finally she sighed. "I might do better to bulldoze it and start over," she said glumly. She bent down to pick up a glass wildflower that had tumbled from a small table, but had miraculously escaped demolition. "My friends cautioned me to furnish the rental cabin with inexpensive, institutional stuff that would not be a big deal to replace in case of theft or carelessness on the part of the tenants. I suppose I should have listened."

"Do you have decent insurance?" He was running the numbers in his head, and the outcome wasn't pretty.

She nodded. "I don't remember all the ins and outs of the policy, but my agent is a friend of my sister's, so I imagine he made sure I have what I need."

Phoebe's discouragement was almost palpable.

"Sometimes things work out for a reason," he said, wanting to reassure her, but well aware that she had no reason to lean on him. "I need something to do to keep me from going crazy. You have a baby to care for. Let me handle this mess, Phoebe. Let me juggle and schedule the various contractors. Please. You'd be doing me a favor."

Five

Phoebe was tempted. So tempted. Leo stood facing her, legs planted apart in a stance that said he was there to stay. Wearing an expensive quilted black parka and aviator sunglasses that hid his every emotion, he was an enigma. Why had a virile, handsome, vigorous male found his way to her hidden corner of the world?

What was he after? Healing? Peace? He had the physique of a bouncer and the look of a wealthy playboy. Had he really been sick? Would she be committing a terrible sin to lay this burden on him from the beginning?

"That's ridiculous," she said faintly. "I'd be taking advantage of you. But I have to confess that I find your offer incredibly appealing. I definitely underestimated how exhausting it would be to take care of a baby 24/7. I love Teddy, and he's not really a fussy child at all, but the thought of adding all this…" She flung out her arm. "Well, it's daunting."

"Then let me help you," he said quietly.

"I don't expect you to actually do the work yourself."

He pocketed his sunglasses and laughed, making his rugged features even more attractive. "No worries there. I'm aware that men are known for biting off more than they can chew, but your cabin, or what's left of it, falls into the category of catastrophe. That's best left to the experts."

She stepped past him and surveyed the large bed with the burgundy-and-navy duvet. "This was supposed to be your room. I know you would have been comfortable here." She turned to face him. "I'm sorry, Leo. I feel terrible about shortchanging you."

He touched her arm. Only for a second. The smile disappeared, but his eyes were warm and teasing. "I'm pretty happy where I ended up. A gorgeous woman. A cozy cabin. Sounds like I won the jackpot."

"You're flirting," she said, hearing the odd and embarrassingly breathless note in her voice.

His gaze was intent, sexy…leaving no question that he was interested. "I've been admonished to stop and smell the roses. And here you are."

Removing her coat that suddenly felt too hot, she leaned against the door frame. The odd sensation of being inside the house but having the sunlight spill down from above was disconcerting. "You may find me more of a thorn. My sister says that living alone up here has made me set in my ways." It was probably true. Some days she felt like a certified hermit.

Once a social animal comfortable at cocktail parties and business lunches, she now preferred the company of chipmunks and woodpeckers and the occasional fox. Dull, dull, dull…

Leo kicked aside a dangerously sharp portion of what had been the dresser mirror. "I'll take my chances. I've got nowhere to go and nobody to see, as my grandfather used to say. You and Teddy brighten the prospect of my long exile considerably."

"Are you ever going to tell me why you're here?" she asked without censoring her curiosity.

He shrugged. “It’s not a very interesting story…but maybe…when it’s time.”

“How will you know?” This odd conversation seemed to have many layers. Her question erased Leo’s charmingly flirtatious smile and replaced it with a scowl.

“You’re a pain in the butt,” he said, the words a low growl.

“I told you I’m no rose.”

He took her arm and steered her toward the front door. “Then pretend,” he muttered. “Can you do that?”

Their muted altercation was interrupted by the arrival of the insurance agent. The next hour was consumed with questions and photographs and introducing Leo to the agent. The two men soon had their heads together as they climbed piles of rubble and inspected every cranny of the doomed cabin.

Phoebe excused herself and walked down the path, knowing that Allison would be ready to go home. As she opened the door and entered the cabin, Teddy greeted her with a chortle and a grin. Envy pinched her heart, but stronger still was happiness that the baby recognized her and was happy to see her.

Given Phoebe’s background, her sister had been torn about the arrangement. But Phoebe had reassured her, and eventually, her sister and brother-in-law gave in. Dragging a baby across the ocean was not an easy task in ideal circumstances, and facing the disposal of an entire estate, they knew Teddy would be miserable and they would be overwhelmed.

Still, Phoebe knew they missed their small son terribly. They used FaceTime to talk to him when Phoebe went into town and had a decent phone signal, and she sent them constant, newsy updates via email and texts. But they were so far away. She suspected they regretted their decision to leave him. Probably, they were working like fiends to take care of all the estate business so they could get back to the U.S. sooner.

When Allison left, Phoebe held Teddy and looked out the window toward the other cabin. Leo and the insurance agent were still measuring and assessing the damage. She rubbed the baby's back. "I think Santa has sent us our present early, my little man. Leo is proving to be a godsend. Now all I have to do is ignore the fact that he's the most attractive man I've seen in a long, long time, and that he makes it hard to breathe whenever I get too close to him, and I'll be fine."

Teddy continued sucking his thumb, his long-lashed eyelids growing heavy as he fought sleep.

"You're no help," she grumbled. His weight was comfortable in her arms. Inhaling his clean baby smell made her womb clench. What would it be like to share a child with Leo Cavallo? Would he be a good father, or an absent one?

The man in question burst through the front door suddenly, bringing with him the smell of the outdoors. "Honey, I'm home." His humor lightened his face and made him seem younger.

Phoebe grinned at him. "Take off your boots, *honey*." She was going to have to practice keeping him at arm's length. Leo Cavallo had the dangerous ability to make himself seem harmless. Which was a lie. Even in a few short hours, Phoebe had recognized and assessed his sexual pull.

Some men simply oozed testosterone. Leo was one of them.

It wasn't just his size, though he was definitely a bear of a man. More than that, he emanated a gut-level masculinity that made her, in some odd way, far more aware of her own carnal needs. She would like to blame it on the fact that they were alone together in the woods, but in truth, she would have had the same reaction to him had they met at the opera or on the deck of a yacht.

Leo was a man's man. The kind of male animal who caught women in his net without even trying. Phoebe had thought herself immune to such silly, pheromone-driven impulses, but with Leo in her house, she recognized an appalling truth. She needed sex. She wanted sex. And she had found just the man to satisfy her every whim.

Her face heated as she pretended to be occupied with the baby. Leo shed his coat and pulled a folded piece of paper from his pocket. "Here," he said. "Take a look. I'll hold the kid."

Before Phoebe could protest, Leo scooped Teddy into his arms and lifted him toward the ceiling. Teddy, who had been sleepy only moments before, squealed with delight. Shaking her head at the antics of the two males who seemed in perfect accord, Phoebe sank into a kitchen chair and scanned the list Leo had handed her.

"Ouch," she said, taking a deep breath for courage. "According to this, I was probably right about the bulldozer."

Leo shook his head. "No. I realize the bottom line looks bad, but it would be even worse to build a new cabin from the ground up. Your agent thinks the settlement will be generous. All you have to provide is an overabundance of patience."

"We may have a problem," she joked. "That's not my strong suit."

Teddy's shirt had rucked up. Leo blew a raspberry against the baby's pudgy, soft-skinned stomach. "I'll do my best to keep you out of it. Unless you want to be consulted about every little detail."

Phoebe shuddered. "Heavens, no. If you're foolish enough to offer me the chance to get my property repaired without my lifting a finger, then far be it from me to nitpick."

Teddy wilted suddenly as Leo cuddled him. What was it about the sight of a big, strong man being gentle with a baby that made a woman's heart melt? Phoebe told herself she shouldn't be swayed by such an ordinary thing, but she couldn't help it. Seeing Leo hold little Teddy made her insides mushy with longing. She wanted it all. The man. The baby. Was that too much to ask?

Leo glanced over at her, hopefully not noticing the way her eyes misted over.

"You want me to put him in his bed?" he asked.

"Sure. He takes these little forty-five-minute catnaps on and off instead of one long one. But he seems happy, so I go with the flow."

Leo paused in the hallway. "How long have you had him?"

"Two weeks. We've settled into a routine of sorts."

"Until I came along to mess things up."

"If you're fishing for compliments, forget it. You've already earned your keep, and it hasn't even been twenty-four hours yet."

He flashed her a grin. "Just think how much you'll love me when you get to know me."

Her knees went weak, and she wasn't even standing. "Go put him down, Leo, and behave."

He kissed the baby's head, smiling down at him. "She's a hard case, kiddo. But I'll wear her down."

When Leo disappeared from sight, Phoebe exhaled loudly. She'd been holding her breath and hadn't even realized it. Rising to her feet unsteadily, she went from window to window closing the curtains. Darkness fell early in this mountain *holler,* as the old generation called it. Soon it would be the longest night of the year.

Phoebe had learned to dread the winter months. Not just the snow and ice and cold, gray days, but the intense loneliness. It had been the season of Christmas one year when she lost everything. Each anniversary brought it all back. But even before the advent of Leo, she had been determined to make this year better. She had a baby in the house. And now a guest. Surely that was enough to manufacture holiday cheer and thaw some of the ice that had kept her captive for so long.

Leo returned, carrying his laptop. He made himself at home on the sofa. "Do you mind giving me your internet password?" he asked, opening the computer and firing it up.

Uh-oh. "Um…" She leaned against the sink for support. "I don't have internet," she said, not sure there was any way to soften that blow.

Leo's look, a cross between horror and bafflement, was priceless. "Why not?"

"I decided I could live my life without it."

He ran his hands through his hair, agitation building. His neck turned red and a pulse beat in his temple. "This is the twenty-first century," he said, clearly trying to speak calmly. "*Everybody* has internet." He paused, his eyes narrowing. "This is either a joke, or you're Amish. Which is it?"

She lifted her chin, refusing to be judged for a decision that had seemed entirely necessary at the time. "Neither. I made a choice. That's all."

"My sister-in-law would never have rented me a cabin that didn't have the appropriate amenities," he said stubbornly.

"Well," she conceded. "You're right about that. The cabin I rent out has satellite internet. But as you saw for yourself, everything was pretty much demolished, including the dish."

She watched Leo's good humor evaporate as he absorbed the full import of what she was saying. Suddenly he pulled his smartphone from his pocket. "At least I can check email with this," he said, a note of panic in his voice.

"We're pretty far back in this gorge," she said. "Only one carrier gets a decent signal and it's—"

"Not the one I have." He stared at the screen and sighed. "Unbelievable. Outposts in Africa have better connectivity than this. I don't think I can stay somewhere that I have to be out of touch from the world."

Phoebe's heart sank. She had hoped Leo would come to appreciate the simplicity of her life here in the mountains. "Is it really that important? I have a landline phone you're welcome to use. For that matter, you can use *my* cell phone. And I do have a television dish, so you're welcome to add the other service if it's that important to you." If he were unable to understand and accept the choices she had made, then it would be foolish to pursue the attraction between them. She would only end up getting hurt.

Leo closed his eyes for a moment. "I'm sorry," he said at last, shooting her a look that was half grimace, half apology. "It took me by surprise, that's all. I'm accustomed to having access to my business emails around the clock."

Was that why he was here? Because he was *too* plugged in? Had he suffered some kind of breakdown? It didn't seem likely, but she knew firsthand how tension and stress could affect a person.

She pulled her cell phone from her pocket and crossed the room to hand it to him. "Use mine for now. It's not a problem."

Their fingers brushed as she gave him the device. Leo hesitated for a moment, but finally took it. "Thank you," he said gruffly. "I appreciate it."

Turning her back to give him some privacy, she went to the kitchen to rummage in the fridge and find an appealing dinner choice. Now that Leo was here, she would have to change her grocery buying habits. Fortunately, she had chicken and vegetables that would make a nice stir-fry.

Perhaps twenty minutes passed before she heard a very ungentlemanly curse from her tenant. Turning sharply, she witnessed the fury and incredulity that turned his jaw to steel and his eyes to molten chocolate. “I can’t believe they did this to me.”

She wiped her hands on a dish towel. “What, Leo? What did they do? Who are you talking about?”

He stood up and rubbed his eyes with the heels of his hands. “My brother,” he croaked. “My black-hearted, devious baby brother.”

As she watched, he paced, his scowl growing darker by the minute. “I’ll kill him,” he said with far too much relish. “I’ll poison his coffee. I’ll beat him to a pulp. I’ll grind his wretched bones into powder.”

Phoebe felt obliged to step in at that moment. “Didn’t you say he has a wife and two kids? I don’t think you really want to murder your own flesh and blood…do you? What could he possibly have done that’s so terrible?”

Leo sank into an armchair, his arms dangling over the sides. Everything about his posture suggested defeat. “He locked me out of my work email,” Leo muttered with a note of confused disbelief. “Changed all the passwords. Because he didn’t trust me to stay away.”

“Well, it sounds like he knows you pretty well, then. ’Cause isn’t that exactly what you were doing? Trying to look at work email?”

Leo glared at her, his brother momentarily out of the crosshairs. “Whose side are you on anyway? You don’t even know my brother.”

“When you spoke of him earlier…he and your sister-in-law and the kids…I heard love in your voice, Leo. So that tells me he must love you just as much. Following that line of reasoning, he surely had a good reason to do what he did.”

A hush fell over the room. The clock on the mantel ticked loudly. Leo stared at her with an intensity that made the hair on the back of her neck stand up. He was pissed. Really angry. And since his brother wasn't around, Phoebe might very well be his default target.

She had the temerity to inch closer and perch on the chair opposite him. "Why would he keep you away from work, Leo? And why did he and your sister-in-law send you here? You're not a prisoner. If being with me in this house is so damned terrible, then do us both a favor and go home."

Six

Leo was ashamed of his behavior. He'd acted like a petulant child. But everything about this situation threw him off balance. He was accustomed to being completely in charge of his domain, whether that be the Cavallo empire or his personal life. It wasn't that he didn't trust Luc. He did. Completely. Unequivocally. And in his gut, he knew the business wouldn't suffer in his absence.

Perhaps that was what bothered him the most. If the company he had worked all of his adult life to build could roll along just fine during his two-month hiatus, then what use was Leo to anyone? His successes were what he thrived on. Every time he made an acquisition or increased the company's bottom line, he felt a rush of adrenaline that was addictive.

Moving slot by slot up the Fortune 500 was immensely gratifying. He had made more money, both for the company and for himself, by the time he was thirty than most people earned in a lifetime. He was damned good at finance. Even in uncertain times, Leo had never made a misstep. His grandfather even went so far as to praise him for his genius. Given that eliciting a compliment from the old dragon was as rare as finding unicorn teeth, Leo had been justifiably proud.

But without Cavallo…without the high-tech office…without the daily onslaught of problems and split-second decisions…who was he? Just a young man with nowhere to go and nothing to do. The aimlessness of it all hung around his neck like a millstone.

Painfully aware that Phoebe had observed his humiliating meltdown, he stood, grabbed his coat from the hook by the door, shoved his feet in his shoes and escaped.

Phoebe fixed dinner with one ear out for the baby and one eye out the window to see if Leo was coming back. His car still sat parked out front, so she knew he was on foot. The day was warm, at least by December standards. But it *was* possible to get lost in these mountains. People did it all the time.

The knot in her stomach eased when at long last, he reappeared. His expression was impossible to read, but his body language seemed relaxed. "I've worked up an appetite" he said, smiling as if nothing had happened.

"It's almost ready. If we're lucky we'll be able to eat our meal in peace before Teddy wakes up."

"He's still asleep?"

She nodded. "I can never predict his schedule. I guess because he's still so small. But since I'm flexible, I'm fine with that."

He held out a chair for her and then joined her at the table. Phoebe had taken pains with the presentation. Pale green woven place mats and matching napkins from a craft cooperative in Gatlinburg accentuated amber stoneware plates and chunky handblown glass goblets that mingled green and gold in interesting swirls.

She poured each of them a glass of pinot. "There's beer in the fridge if you'd prefer it."

He tasted the wine. "No. This is good. A local vintage?"

"Yes. We have several wineries in the area."

Their conversation was painfully polite. Almost as awkward as a blind date. Though in this case there was nothing of a romantic nature to worry about. No *will he* or *won't he* when it came time for a possible good-night kiss at the front door.

Even so, she was on edge. Leo Cavallo's sexuality gave a woman ideas, even if unintentionally. It had been a very long time since Phoebe had kissed a man, longer still since she had felt the weight of a lover's body moving against hers in urgent passion. She thought she had safely buried those urges in her subconscious, but with Leo in her house, big and alive and so damned sexy, she was in the midst of an erotic awakening.

Like a limb that has gone to sleep and then experienced the pain of renewed blood flow, Phoebe's body tingled with awareness. Watching the muscles in his throat as he swallowed. Inhaling the scent of him, warm male and crisp outdoors. Inadvertently brushing his shoulder as she served him second helpings of chicken and rice. Hearing the lazy tempo of his speech that made her think of hot August nights and damp bodies twined together beneath a summer moon.

All of her senses were engaged except for taste. And the yearning to do just that, to kiss him, swelled in her chest and made her hands shake. The need was as overwhelming as it was unexpected. She fixated on the curve of his lips as he spoke. They were good lips. Full, but masculine. What would they feel like pressed against hers?

Imagining the taste of his mouth tightened everything inside her until she felt faint with arousal. Standing abruptly, she put her back to him, busying herself at the sink as she rinsed plates and loaded the dishwasher. Suddenly, she felt him behind her, almost pressing against her.

"Let me handle cleanup," he said, the words a warm breath of air at her neck. She froze. Did he sense her jittery nerves, her longing?

She swallowed, clenching her fingers on the edge of the counter. "No. Thank you. But a fire would be nice." She was already on fire. But what the heck…in for a penny, in for a pound.

After long seconds when it seemed as if every molecule of oxygen in the room vaporized, he moved away. "Whatever you want," he said. "Just ask."

Leo was neither naive nor oblivious. Phoebe was attracted to him. He knew, because he felt the same inexorable pull. But he had known her for barely a day. Perhaps long enough for an easy pickup at a bar or a one-night stand, but not for a relationship that was going to have to survive for a couple of months.

With a different woman at another time, he would have taken advantage of the situation. But he was at Phoebe's mercy for now. One wrong move, and she could boot him out. There were other cabins…other peaceful getaways. None of them, however, had Phoebe. And he was beginning to think that she was his talisman, his lucky charm, the only hope he had of making it through the next weeks without going stark raving mad.

The fire caught immediately, the dry tinder flaming as it coaxed the heavier logs into the blaze. When he turned around, Phoebe was watching him, her eyes huge.

He smiled at her. "Come join me on the sofa. We're going to be spending a lot of time together. We might as well get to know each other."

At that very moment, Teddy announced his displeasure with a noisy cry. The relief on Phoebe's face was almost comical. "Sorry. I'll be back in a minute."

While she was gone, he sat on the hearth, feeling the heat

from the fire sink into his back. Beneath his feet a bearskin pelt covered the floor. He was fairly certain it was fake, but the thick, soft fur made him imagine a scenario that was all too real. Phoebe…nude…her skin gilded with firelight.

The vivid picture in his mind hardened his sex and dried his mouth. Jumping to his feet, he went to the kitchen and poured himself another glass of wine. Sipping it slowly, he tried to rein in his hunger. Something might develop during this time with Phoebe. They could become friends. Or even more than that. But rushing his fences was not the way to go. He had to resist the temptation to bring sex into the picture before she had a chance to trust him.

Regardless of Phoebe's desires, or even his own, this was a situation that called for caution. Not his first impulse, or even his last. But if he had any hope of making her his, he'd bide his time.

His mental gyrations were interrupted by Phoebe's return. "There you are," he said. "I wondered if Teddy had kidnapped you."

"Poopy diaper," she said with a grimace. She held the baby on her hip as she prepared a bottle. "He's starving, poor thing. Slept right through dinner."

Leo moved to the sofa and was gratified when Phoebe followed suit. She now held the baby as a barricade between them, but he could wait. The child wasn't big enough to be much of a problem.

"So tell me," he said. "What did you do with yourself before Teddy arrived?"

Phoebe settled the baby on her lap and held the bottle so he could reach it easily. "I moved in three years ago. At first I was plenty busy with decorating and outfitting both cabins. I took my time and looked for exactly what I wanted. In the meantime, I made a few friends, mostly women I met at the gym. A few who worked in stores where I shopped."

"And when the cabins were ready?"

She stared down at the baby, rubbing his head with a wistful smile on her face. He wondered if she had any clue how revealing her expression was. She adored the little boy. That much was certain.

"I found someone to help me start a garden," she said. "Buford is the old man who lives back near the main road where you turned off. He's a sweetheart. His wife taught me how to bake bread and how to can fruits and vegetables. I know how to make preserves. And I can even churn my own butter in a pinch, though that seems a bit of a stretch in this day and age."

He studied her, trying to get to the bottom of what she wasn't saying. "I understand all that," he said. "And if I didn't know better, I'd guess you were a free spirit, hippie-commune, granola-loving Earth Mother. But something doesn't add up. How did you get from stockbroker to this?"

Phoebe understood his confusion. None of it made sense on paper. But was she willing to expose all of her painful secrets to a man she barely knew? No…not just yet.

Picking her words carefully, she gave him an answer. Not a lie, but not the whole truth. "I had some disappointments both personally and professionally. They hit me hard…enough to make me reconsider whether the career path I had chosen was the right one. At the time, I didn't honestly know. So I took a time-out. A step backward. I came here and decided to see if I could make my life simpler. More meaningful."

"And now? Any revelations to report?"

She raised an eyebrow. "Are you mocking me?"

He held up his hands. "No. I swear I'm not. If anything, I have to admire you for being proactive. Most people simply slog away at a job because they don't have the courage to try something new."

"I wish I could say it was like that. But to be honest,

it was more a case of crawling in a hole to hide out from the world."

"You don't cut yourself much slack, do you?"

"I was a mess when I came here."

"And now?"

She thought about it for a moment. No one had ever asked her straight-out if her self-imposed exile had borne fruit. "I think I have a better handle on what I want out of life. And I've forgiven myself for mistakes I made. But do I want to go back to that cutthroat lifestyle? No. I don't."

"I know this is a rude question, but I'm going to ask it anyway. What have you done for money since you've been out of work?"

"I'm sure a lot of people wonder that." She put the baby on her shoulder and burped him. "The truth is, Leo. I'm darned good at making money. I have a lot stashed away. And since I've been here, my weekly expenses are fairly modest. So though I can't stay here forever, I certainly haven't bankrupted myself."

"Would you say your experience has been worth it?"

She nodded. "Definitely."

"Then maybe there's hope for me after all."

Phoebe was glad to have Teddy as a buffer. Sitting with Leo in a firelit room on a cold December night was far too cozy. But when Teddy finished his bottle and was ready to play, she had no choice but to get down on the floor with him and let him roll around on the faux bearskin rug. He had mastered flipping from his back to his tummy. Now he enjoyed the increased mobility.

She was truly shocked when Leo joined them, stretching out on his right side and propping his head on his hand. "How long 'til he crawls?"

"Anytime now. He's already learned to get his knees up under him, so I don't think it will be too many more weeks." Leo seemed entirely relaxed, while Phoebe was in danger of hyperventilating. Anyone watching them might assume they were a family…mom, dad and baby. But the truth was, they were three separate people who happened to be occupying the same space for the moment.

Teddy was her nephew, true. But he was on loan, so to speak. She could feed him and play with him and love him, but at the end of the day, he wasn't hers. Still, what could it hurt to pretend for a while?

She pulled her knees to her chest and wrapped her arms around her legs. Ordinarily, she would have lain down on her stomach and played with Teddy at his level. But getting horizontal with Leo Cavallo was not smart, especially since he was in touching distance. She'd give herself away, no doubt. Even with a baby between them, she couldn't help thinking how nice it would be to spend an unencumbered hour with her new houseguest.

Some soft music on the radio, another bottle of wine, more logs on the fire. And after that…

Her heartbeat stuttered and stumbled. Dampness gathered at the back of her neck and in another, less accessible spot. Her breathing grew shallow. She stared at Teddy blindly, anything to avoid looking at Leo. Not for the world would she want him to think she was so desperate for male company that she would fall at his feet.

Even as she imagined such a scenario, he rolled to his back and slung an arm across his face. Moments later, she saw the steady rise and fall of his chest as he gave in to sleep.

Teddy was headed in the same direction. His acrobatics had worn him out. He slumped onto his face, butt in the air, and slept.

Phoebe watched the two males with a tightness in her chest that was a combination of so many things. Yearning for what might have been. Fear of what was yet to come.

Hope that somewhere along the way she could have a family of her own.

Her sleepless night caught up with her, making her eyelids droop. With one wary look at Leo to make sure he was asleep, she eased down beside her two companions and curled on her side with Teddy in the curve of her body. Now she could smell warm baby and wood smoke, and perhaps the faint scent of Leo's aftershave.

Closing her eyes, she sighed deeply. She would rest for a moment….

Seven

Leo awoke disoriented. His bed felt rock-hard, and his pillow had fallen on the floor. Gradually, he remembered where he was. Turning his head, he took in the sight of Phoebe and Teddy sleeping peacefully beside him.

The baby was the picture of innocence, but Phoebe… He sucked in a breath. Her position, curled on her side, made the neckline of her sweater gape, treating him to an intimate view of rounded breasts and creamy skin. Her hair tumbled around her face as if she had just awakened from a night of energetic sex. All he had to do was extend his arm and he could stroke her belly beneath the edge of her top.

His sex hardened to the point of discomfort. He didn't know whether to thank God for the presence of the kid or to curse the bad timing. The strength of his desire was both surprising and worrisome. Was he reacting so strongly to Phoebe because he was in exile and she was the only woman around, or had his long bout of celibacy predisposed him to want her?

Either way, his hunger for her was suspect. It would be the height of selfishness to seduce her because of boredom or propinquity. Already, he had taken her measure. She was loving, generous and kind, though by no means a pushover.

Even with training in what some would call a nonfeminine field, she nevertheless seemed completely comfortable with the more traditional roles of childcare and homemaking.

Phoebe was complicated. That, more than anything else, attracted him. At the moment a tiny frown line marked the space between her brows. He wanted to erase it with a kiss. The faint shadowy smudges beneath her eyes spoke of her exhaustion. He had been around his brother and sister-in-law enough to know that dealing with infants was harrowing and draining on the best of days.

He also knew that they glowed with pride when it came to their children, and he could see in Phoebe the same self-sacrificial love. Even now, in sleep, her arms surrounded little Teddy, keeping him close though he was unaware.

Moving carefully so as not to wake them, he rolled to his feet and quietly removed the screen so he could add wood to the smoldering fire. For insurance, he tossed another handful of kindling into the mix and blew on it gently. Small flames danced and writhed as he took a medium-size log and positioned it across the coals.

The simple task rocked him in an indefinable way. How often did he pause in his daily schedule to enjoy something as elemental and magical as an honest-to-God wood fire? The elegant gas logs in his condo were nothing in comparison.

As he stared into the hearth, the temperature built. His skin burned, and yet he couldn't move away. Phoebe seemed to him more like this real fire than any woman he had been with in recent memory. Energetic…messy… mesmerizing. Producing a heat that warmed him down to his bones.

Most of his liaisons in Atlanta were brief. He spent an enormous amount of time, perhaps more than was warranted, growing and protecting the Cavallo bottom line. Sex was good and a necessary part of his life. But he had never been tempted to do what it took to keep a woman in his bed night after night.

Kneeling, he turned and looked at Phoebe. Should he wake her up? Did the baby need to be put to bed?

Uncharacteristically uncertain, he deferred a decision. Snagging a pillow from the sofa, he leaned back against the stone hearth, stretched out his legs and watched them sleep.

Phoebe awoke slowly, but in no way befuddled. Her situation was crystal clear. Like a coward, she kept her eyes closed, even though she knew Leo was watching her. Apparently, her possum act didn't fool him. He touched her foot with his. "Open your eyes, Phoebe."

She felt at a distinct disadvantage. There was no graceful way to get up with him so close. Sighing, she obeyed his command and stared at him with as much chutzpah as she could muster. Rolling onto her back, she tucked her hands behind her head. "Have I brought a voyeur into my home?" she asked with a tart bite in her voice. It would do no good to let him see how much he affected her.

Leo yawned and stretched, his eyes heavy-lidded. "It's not my fault you had too much wine at dinner."

"I did not," she said indignantly. "I'm just tired, because the baby—"

"Gotcha," he said smugly, his eyes gleaming with mischief.

She sat up and ran her hands through her hair, crossing her legs but being careful not to bump Teddy. "Very funny. How long was I out?"

He shrugged. "Not long." His hot stare told her more clearly than words what he was thinking. They had rocketed from acquaintances to sleeping partners at warp speed. It was going to be difficult to pretend otherwise.

Her breasts ached and her mouth was dry. Sexual tension

shimmered between them like unseen vines drawing them ever closer. The only thing keeping them apart was a baby.

A baby who was her responsibility. That reality drew her back from the edge, though the decision to be clear-headed was a painful one. "I think we'll say good-night," she muttered. "Feel free to stay up as long as you like. But please bank the fire before you go to bed."

His gaze never faltered as she scooped up Teddy and gathered his things. "We have to talk about this," he said, the blunt words a challenge.

It took a lot, but she managed to look him straight in the eyes with a calm smile. "I don't know what you mean. Good night, Leo."

At two o'clock, he gave up the fight to sleep. He was wired, and his body pulsed with arousal, his sex full and hard. Neither of which condition was conducive to slumber. The *New York Times* bestseller he had opened failed to hold his attention past the first chapter. Cursing as he climbed out of his warm bed to pace the floor, he stopped suddenly and listened.

Faintly, but distinctly, he heard a baby cry.

It was all the excuse he needed. Throwing a thin, gray wool robe over his navy silk sleep pants, he padded into the hall, glad of the thick socks that Hattie had packed for him. Undoubtedly she had imagined him needing them if it snowed and he wore his boots. But they happened to be perfect for a man who wanted to move stealthily about the house.

In the hallway, he paused, trying to locate his landlady. There was a faint light under her door, but not Teddy's. The kid cried again, a fretful, middle-of-the-night whimper. Without weighing the consequences, Leo knocked.

Seconds later, the door opened a crack. Phoebe peered

out at him, her expression indiscernible in the gloom. “What’s wrong? What do you want?”

Her stage whisper was comical given the fact that Teddy was clearly awake.

“You need some backup?”

“I’m fine.” She started to close the door, but he stuck his foot in the gap, remembering at the last instant that he wasn’t wearing shoes.

She pushed harder than he anticipated, and his socks were less protection than he expected. Pain shot up his leg. He groaned, jerking backward and nearly falling on his ass. Hopping on one foot, he pounded his fist against the wall to keep from letting loose with a string of words definitely not rated for kid ears.

Now Phoebe flung the door open wide, her face etched in dismay. “Are you hurt? Oh, heavens, of course you are. Here,” she said. “Hold him while I get ice.”

Without warning, his arms were full of a squirmy little body that smelled of spit-up and Phoebe’s light floral scent. “But I…” He followed her down the hall, wincing at every step, even as Teddy’s grumbles grew louder.

By the time he made it to the living room, Phoebe had turned on a couple of lamps and filled a dish towel with ice cubes. Her fingers curled around his biceps. “Give me the baby and sit down,” she said, sounding frazzled and irritated, and anything but amorous. She pushed him toward the sofa. “Put your leg on the couch and let me see if you broke anything.”

Teddy objected to the jostling and cried in earnest. Leo lost his balance and flopped down onto the sofa so hard that the baby’s head and Leo’s chin made contact with jarring force.

“Damn it to hell.” He lay back, half-dazed, as Phoebe plucked Teddy from his arms and sat at the opposite end of the sofa. Before he could object, she had his leg in her lap and was peeling off his sock.

When slim, cool fingers closed around the bare arch of his foot, Leo groaned again. This time for a far different reason. Having Phoebe stroke his skin was damned arousing, even if he was in pain. Her thumb pressed gently, moving from side to side to assess the damage.

Leo hissed, a sharp involuntary inhalation. Phoebe winced. "Sorry. Am I hurting you too badly?"

She glanced sideways and her eyes grew big. His robe had opened when he lost his balance. Most of his chest was bare, and it was impossible to miss the erection that tented his sleep pants. He actually saw the muscles in her throat ripple as she swallowed.

"It feels good," he muttered. "Don't stop."

But Teddy shrieked in earnest now, almost inconsolable.

Phoebe dropped Leo's foot like it was a live grenade, scooting out from under his leg and standing. "Put the ice on it," she said, sounding breathless and embarrassed. "I'll be back."

Phoebe sank into the rocker in Teddy's room, her whole body trembling with awareness. The baby curled into her shoulder as she rubbed his back and sang to him quietly. He wasn't hungry. She had given him a bottle barely an hour ago. His only problem now was that his mouth hurt. She'd felt the tiny sharp edge of a tooth on his bottom gum and knew it was giving him fits. "Poor darling," she murmured. Reaching for the numbing drops, she rubbed a small amount on his sore mouth.

Teddy sucked her fingertip, snuffled and squirmed, then gradually subsided into sleep. She rocked him an extra five minutes just to make sure. When he was finally out, she laid him in his crib and tiptoed out of the room.

Her bed called out to her. She was weaving on her feet,

wrapped in a thick blanket of exhaustion. But she had told Leo she would come back. And in truth, nothing but cowardice could keep her from fulfilling that promise.

When she returned to the living room, it was filled with shadows, only a single lamp burning, though Leo had started another fire in the grate that gave off some illumination. He was watching television, but he switched it off as soon as she appeared. She hovered in the doorway, abashed by the sexual currents drawing her to this enigma of a man. "How's the foot?"

"See for yourself."

It was a dare, and she recognized it as such. Her legs carried her forward, even as her brain shouted, *Stop. Stop.* She wasn't so foolish this time as to sit down on the sofa. Instead, she knelt and removed the makeshift ice pack, setting it aside on a glass dish. Leo's foot was bruising already. A thin red line marked where the sharp corner of the door had scraped him.

"How does it feel?" she asked quietly.

Leo sat up, wincing, as he pulled his thick wool sock into place over his foot and ankle. "I'll live."

When he leaned forward with his forearms resting on his knees, he was face-to-face with her. "Unless you have an objection," he said, "I'm going to kiss you now." A lock of hair fell over his forehead. His voice was husky and low, sending shivers down her spine. The hour was late, that crazy time when dawn was far away and the night spun on, seemingly forever.

She licked her lips, feeling her nipples furl tightly, even as everything else in her body loosened with the warm flow of honey. "No objections," she whispered, wondering if he had woven some kind of spell over her while she was sleeping.

Slowly, gently, perhaps giving her time to resist, he cupped her cheeks with his hands, sliding his fingers into her hair and massaging her scalp. His thumbs ran along her jawline, pausing when he reached the little indentation beneath her ear.

"God, you're beautiful," he groaned, resting his forehead against hers. She could feel the heat radiating from his bare chest. All on their own, her hands came up to touch him, to flatten over his rib cage, to explore miles of warm, smooth skin. Well-defined pectoral muscles gave way to a thin line of hair that led to a flat belly corded with more muscles.

She felt drunk with pleasure. So long…it had been so long. And though she had encountered opportunities to be intimate with men during the past three years, none of them had been as tempting as Leo Cavallo. "What are we doing?" she asked raggedly, almost beyond the point of reason.

He gathered handfuls of her hair and played with it, pulling her closer. "Getting to know each other," he whispered. His mouth settled over hers, lips firm and confident. She opened to him, greedy for more of the hot pleasure that built at the base of her abdomen and made her shift restlessly.

When his tongue moved lazily between her lips, she met it with hers, learning the taste of him as she had wanted to so badly, experimenting with the little motions that made him shudder and groan. He held her head tightly now, dragging her to him, forcing her neck to arch so he could deepen the kiss. He tasted of toothpaste and determination.

Her hands clung to his wrists. "You're good at this," she panted. "A little too good."

"It's you," he whispered. "It's you." He moved down beside her so that they were chest to chest. "Tell me to stop, Phoebe." Wildly he kissed her, his hands roving over her back and hips. They were so close, his erection pressed into her belly.

She was wearing her usual knit pajamas, nothing sexy about them. But when his big hands trespassed beneath the elastic waistband and cupped her butt, she felt like a desirable woman. It had been so long since a man had touched her. And this wasn't just any man.

It was Leo. Big, brawny Leo, who looked as if he could move mountains for a woman, and yet paradoxically touched her so gently she wanted to melt into him and never leave his embrace. "Make love to me, Leo. Please. I need you so much…."

He dragged her to her feet and drew her closer to the fireplace. Standing on the bearskin rug, he pulled her top over her head. As he stared at her breasts, he cradled one in each hand, squeezing them carefully, plumping them with an expression that made her feel wanton and hungry.

At last looking at her face, he rubbed her nipples lightly as he kissed her nose, her cheeks, her eyes. His expression was warmly sensual, wickedly hot. "You make a man weak," he said. "I want to do all sorts of things to you, but I don't know where to start."

She should have felt awkward or embarrassed. But instead, exhilaration fizzed in her veins, making her breathing choppy. His light touch was not enough. She twined her arms around his neck, rubbing her lower body against his. "Does this give you any ideas?"

Eight

Leo was torn on a rack of indecision. Phoebe was here… in his arms…willing. But some tiny shred of decency in his soul insisted on being heard. The timing wasn't right. *This* wasn't right.

Cursing himself inwardly with a groan of anguish for the effort it took to stop the train on the tracks, he removed her arms from around his neck and stepped back. "We can't," he said. "I won't take advantage of you."

Barely able to look at what he was saying no to, he grabbed her pajama top and thrust it toward her. "Put this on."

Phoebe obeyed instantly as mortification and anger colored her face. "I'm not a child, Leo. I make my own decisions."

He wanted to comfort her, but touching her again was out of the question. An explanation would have to suffice. He hoped she understood him. "A tree demolished one of your cabins. You're caring for a teething baby, who has kept you up big chunks of the past two nights. Stress and exhaustion are no basis for making decisions." He of all people should know. "I don't want to be that man you regret when the sun comes up."

She wrapped her arms around her waist, glaring at him with thinly veiled hurt. "I should toss you out on your ass," she said, the words holding a faint but audible tremor.

His heart contracted. "I hope you won't." There were things he needed to tell her before they became intimate, and if he wasn't ready to come clean, then he wasn't ready to have sex with Phoebe. He hurt just looking at her. With her hair mussed and her protective posture, she seemed far younger than he knew her to be. Achingly vulnerable.

She lifted her chin. "We won't do this again. You keep to yourself, and I'll keep my end of the bargain. Good night, Leo." Turning on her heel, she left him.

The room seemed cold and lonely in her absence. Had he made the most colossal mistake of his life? The fire between the two of them burned hot and bright. She was perfection in his arms, sensual, giving, as intuitive a lover as he had ever envisaged.

Despite his unfilled passion, he knew he had done the right thing. Phoebe wasn't the kind of woman who had sex without thinking it through. Despite her apparent willingness tonight to do just that, he knew she would have blamed both herself and him when it was all over.

What he wanted from her, if indeed he had a chance of ever getting close to her again, was trust. He had secrets to share. And he suspected she did, as well. So he could wait for the other, the carnal satisfaction. Maybe….

Phoebe climbed into her cold bed with tears of humiliation wetting her cheeks. No matter what Leo said, tonight had been a rejection. What kind of man could call a halt when he was completely aroused and almost at the point of penetration? Only one who wasn't fully involved or committed to the act of lovemaking.

Perhaps she had inadvertently stimulated him with her foot massage. And maybe the intimacy of their nap in front of the fire had given him a buzz. But in the end, Phoebe simply wasn't who or what he wanted.

The fact that she could be badly hurt by a man she had met only recently gave her pause. Was she so desperate? So lonely? Tonight's debacle had given her some painful truths to examine.

But self-reflection would have to wait, because despite her distress, she could barely keep her eyes open....

Leo slept late the next morning. Not intentionally, but because he had been up much of the night pacing the floor. Sometime before dawn he had taken a shower and pleasured himself, but it had been a hollow exercise whose only purpose was to allow him to find oblivion in much-needed sleep.

The clock read almost ten when he made his way to the front of the house. He liked the open floor plan of the living room and kitchen, because it gave fewer places for Phoebe to hide.

Today, however, he was dumbstruck to find that she was nowhere in the house. And Teddy's crib was empty.

A twinge of panic gripped him until he found both of them out on the front porch chatting with the man who had come to remove the enormous fallen oak tree. When he stepped outside, Phoebe's quick disapproving glance reminded him that he had neither shaved nor combed his hair.

The grizzled workman who could have been anywhere from fifty to seventy saluted them with tobacco-stained fingers and headed down the lane to where he had parked his truck.

"I'm sorry," Leo said stiffly. "I was supposed to be handling this."

Phoebe's lips smiled, but her gaze was wintry. "No problem. Teddy and I dealt with it. If you'll excuse me, I have to get him down for his morning nap."

"But I—"

She shut the door in his face, leaving him out in the cold…literally.

He paused on the porch to count to ten, or maybe a hundred. Then, when he thought he had a hold on his temper, he went back inside and scavenged the kitchen for a snack to hold him until lunch. A couple of pieces of cold toast he found on a plate by the stove would have to do. He slathered them with some of Phoebe's homemade strawberry jam and sat down at the table. When Phoebe returned, he had finished eating and had also realized that he needed a favor. Not a great time to ask, but what the heck.

She ignored him pointedly, but he wasn't going to let a little cold shoulder put him off. "May I use your phone?" he asked politely.

"Why?"

"I'm going to order a new phone from your carrier since mine is virtually useless, and I also want to get internet service going. I'll pay the contract fees for a year, but when I leave you can drop it if you want to."

"That's pretty expensive for a short-term solution. It must be nice to be loaded."

He ground his teeth together, reminding himself that she was still upset about last night. "I won't apologize for having money," he said quietly. "I work very hard."

"Is it really that important to stay plugged in? Can't you go cold turkey for two months?" Phoebe was pale. She looked at him as if she would put him on the first plane out if she could.

How had they become combatants? He stared at her until her cheeks flushed and she looked away. "Technology and business are not demons," he said. "We live in the information age."

"And what about your recovery?"

"What about it?"

"I got the impression that you were supposed to stay away from business in order to rest and recuperate."

"I can do that and still have access to the world."

She took a step in his direction. "Can you? Can you really? Because from where I'm standing, you look like a guy who is determined to get what he wants when he wants it. Your doctor may have given you orders. Your brother may have, as well. But I doubt you respect them enough to really do what they've asked."

Her harsh assessment hit a little too close to home. "I'm following doctor's orders, I swear. Though it's really none of your business." The defensive note in his voice made him cringe inwardly. Was he honestly the ass she described?

"Do what you have to do," she said, pulling her phone from her pocket and handing it to him. Her expression was a mix of disappointment and resignation. "But I would caution you to think long and hard about the people who love you. And why it is that you're here."

At that moment, Leo saw a large delivery truck pull up in front of the cabin. Good, his surprise had arrived. Maybe it would win him some brownie points with Phoebe. And deflect her from the uncomfortable subject of his recuperation.

She went to the door as the bell rang. "But I didn't order anything," she protested when the man in brown set a large box just inside the door.

"Please sign here, ma'am," he said patiently.

The door slammed and Phoebe stared down at the box as if it possibly contained dynamite.

"Open it," Leo said.

Phoebe couldn't help being a little anxious when she tore into the package. It didn't have foreign postage, so it was not from her sister. She pulled back the cardboard flaps and stared in amazement. The box was full of food—an expensive ham, casseroles preserved in freezer packs, desserts, fresh fruit, the list was endless.

She turned to look at Leo, who now lay sprawled on the sofa. "Did you do this?"

He shrugged, his arms outstretched along the back of the couch. "Before I lost my temper yesterday about my work email, I scrolled through my personal messages and decided to contact a good buddy of mine, a cordon bleu chef in Atlanta who owes me a favor. I felt bad about you agreeing to cook for me all the time, so I asked him to hook us up with some meals. He's going to send a box once a week."

Her mind reeled. Not only was this a beautifully thoughtful gesture, it was also incredibly expensive. She stared at the contents, feeling her dismal mood slip away. A man like Leo would be a lovely companion for the following two months, even if all he wanted from her was friendship.

Before she could lose her nerve, she crossed the room, leaned down and kissed him on the cheek. His look of shock made her face heat. "Don't worry," she said wryly. "That was completely platonic. I merely wanted to say thank-you for a lovely gift."

He grasped her wrist, his warm touch sending ripples of heat all the way up her arm. "You're welcome, Phoebe. But of course, it's partially a selfish thing. I get to enjoy the bounty, as well." His smile could charm the birds off the trees. In repose, Leo's rugged features seemed austere, even intimidating. But when he smiled, the force of his charisma increased exponentially.

Feeling something inside her soul ease at the cessation of hostilities, she returned the smile, though she pulled away and put a safe distance between them. It was no use being embarrassed or awkward around Leo. She wasn't so heartless as to throw him out, and truthfully, she didn't want to. Teddy was a sweetheart, but having another adult in the house was a different kind of stimulation.

Suddenly, she remembered what she had wanted to ask Leo before last night when everything ended so poorly. "Tell me," she said. "Would you object to having Christmas decorations in the house?"

"That's a strange segue, but why would I object?" he asked. "I'm not a Scrooge."

"I never thought you were, but you might have ethnic or religious reasons to abstain."

"No problems on either score," he chuckled. "Does this involve a shopping trip?"

"No. Actually, I have boxes and boxes of stuff in the attic. When I moved here, I wasn't in the mood to celebrate. Now, with Teddy in the house, it doesn't seem right to ignore the holiday. I wasn't able to take it all down on my own. Do you mind helping? I warn you…it's a lot of stuff."

"Including a tree?"

She smiled beseechingly. "My old one is artificial, and not all that pretty. I thought it might be fun to find one in the woods."

"Seriously?"

"Well, of course. I own thirty acres. Surely we can discover something appropriate."

He lifted a skeptical eyebrow. *"We?"*

"Yes, we. Don't be so suspicious. I'm not sending you out in the cold all on your own. I have one of those baby carrier things. Teddy and I will go with you. Besides, I don't think men are the best judge when it comes to locating the perfect tree."

"You wound me," he said, standing and clutching his chest. "I have excellent taste."

"This cabin has space limitations to consider. And admit it. Men always think bigger is better."

"So do women as a rule."

His naughty double entendre was delivered with a straight face, but his eyes danced with mischief. Phoebe knew her cheeks had turned bright red. She felt the heat. "Are we still talking about Christmas trees?" she asked, her throat dry as the Sahara.

"You tell me."

"I think you made yourself pretty clear last night," she snapped.

He looked abashed. "I never should have let things go that far. We need to take baby steps, Phoebe. Forced proximity makes for a certain intimacy, but I respect you too much to take advantage of that."

"And if *I* take advantage of you?"

She was appalled to hear the words leave her mouth. Apparently her libido trumped both her pride and her common sense.

Leo's brows drew together in a scowl. He folded his arms across his broad chest. With his legs braced in a fighting stance, he suddenly seemed far more dangerous. Today he had on old jeans and a cream wool fisherman's sweater.

Everything about him from his head to his toes screamed wealth and privilege. So why hadn't he chosen some exclusive resort for his sabbatical? A place with tennis courts and spas and golf courses?

He still hadn't answered her question. The arousal swirling in her belly congealed into a small knot of embarrassment. Did he get some kind of sadistic kick out of flirting with women and then shutting them down?

"Never mind," she said, the words tight. "I understand."

He strode toward her, his face a thundercloud. "You don't understand a single damn thing," he said roughly. Before she could protest or back up or initiate any other of a dozen protective moves, he dragged her to his chest, wrapped one arm around her back and used his free hand to anchor her chin and tip her face up to his.

His thick-lashed brown eyes, afire with emotion and seemingly able to peer into her soul, locked on hers and dared her to look away. “Make no mistake, Phoebe,” he said. “I want you. And Lord willing, I’m going to have you. When we finally make it to a bed—or frankly any flat surface, ’cause I’m not picky—I’m going to make love to you until we’re both too weak to stand. But in the meantime, *you’re* going to behave. *I’m* going to behave. Got it?”

Time stood still. Just like in the movies. Every one of her senses went on high alert. He was breathing hard, his chest rising and falling rapidly. When he grabbed her, she had braced one hand reflexively on his shoulder, though the idea of holding him at bay was ludicrous. She couldn’t manage that even if she wanted to. His strength and power were evident despite whatever illness had plagued him.

Dark stubble covered his chin. He could have been a pirate or a highwayman or any of the renegade heroes in the historical novels her sister read. Phoebe was so close she could inhale the warm scent of him. A great bear of a man not long from his bed.

She licked her lips, trembling enough that she was glad of his support. “Define *behave.*” She kissed his chin, his wrist, the fingers caressing her skin.

Leo fought her. Not outwardly. But from within. His struggle was written on his face. But he didn’t release her. Not this time.

The curse he uttered as he gave in to her provocation was heartfelt and earthy as he encircled her with both arms and half lifted her off her feet. His mouth crushed hers, taking…giving no quarter. His masculine force was exhilarating. She was glad she was tall and strong, because it gave her the ability to match him kiss for kiss.

Baby steps be damned. She and Leo had jumped over miles of social convention and landed in a time of desperation, of elemental reality. Like the prehistoric people who had lived in these hills and valleys centuries before, the base human instinct to mate clawed its way to the forefront, making a mockery of soft words and tender sentiments.

This was passion in its most raw form. She rubbed against him, desperate to get closer. “Leo,” she groaned, unable to articulate what she wanted, what she needed. “Leo…”

Nine

He was lost. Months of celibacy combined with the uncertainty of whether his body would be the same after his attack walloped him like a sucker punch. In his brain he repeated a frenzied litany. *Just a kiss. Just a kiss, just a kiss...*

His erection was swollen painfully, the taut skin near bursting. His lungs had contracted to half capacity, and black dots danced in front of his eyes. Phoebe felt like heaven in his arms. She was feminine and sinfully curved in all the right places, but she wasn't fragile. He liked that. No. Correction. He loved that. She kissed him without apology, no half measures.

Her skin smelled like scented shower gel and baby powder. This morning her hair was again tamed in a fat braid. He wrapped it around his fist and tugged, drawing back her head so he could nip at her throat with sharp love bites.

The noise she made, part cry, part moan, hit him in the gut. He lifted her, grunting when her legs wrapped around his waist. They were fully clothed, but he thrust against her, tormenting them both with pressure that promised no relief.

Without warning, Phoebe struggled to get away from him. He held her more tightly, half crazed with the urge to take her hard and fast.

She pushed at his chest. "Leo. I hear the baby. He's awake."

Finally, her breathless words penetrated the fog of lust that chained him. He dropped her to her feet and staggered backward, his heart threatening to pound through the wall of his chest.

Afraid of his own emotions, he strode to the door where his boots sat, shoved his feet into them, flung open the door and left the cabin, never looking back.

Phoebe had never once seen Teddy's advent into her life as anything but a blessing. Until today. Collecting herself as best she could, she walked down the hall and scooped him out of his crib. "Well, that was a short nap," she said with a laugh that bordered on hysteria. Teddy, happy now that she had rescued him, chortled as he clutched her braid. His not-so-nice baby smell warned her that he had a messy diaper, probably the reason he had awakened so soon.

She changed him and then put him on a blanket on the floor while she tidied his room. Even as she automatically carried out the oft-repeated chores, her mind was attuned to Leo's absence. He had left without a coat. Fortunately, he was wearing a thick sweater, and thankfully, the temperature had moderated today, climbing already into the low fifties.

She was appalled and remorseful about what had happened, all of it her fault. Leo, ever the gentleman, had done his best to be levelheaded about confronting their attraction amidst the present situation. But Phoebe, like a lonely, deprived spinster, had practically attacked him. It was no wonder things had escalated.

Men, unless they were spoken for—and sometimes not even then—were not physically wired to refuse women who threw out such blatant invitations. And that's what

Phoebe had done. She had made it abysmally clear that she was his for the taking.

Leo had reacted. Of course. What red-blooded, straight, unattached male wouldn't? *Oh, God.* How was she going to face him? And how did they deal with this intense but ill-timed attraction?

A half hour later she held Teddy on her hip as she put away the abundance of food Leo's chef friend had sent. She decided to have the chimichangas for lunch. They were already prepared. All she had to do was thaw them according to the directions and then whip up some rice and salad to go alongside.

An hour passed, then two. She only looked out the window a hundred times or so. What if he was lost? Or hurt? Or sick? Her stomach cramped, thinking of the possibilities.

Leo strode through the forest until his legs ached and his lungs gasped for air. It felt good to stretch his physical limits, to push himself and know that he was okay. Nothing he did, however, erased his hunger for Phoebe. At first he had been suspicious of his immediate fascination. His life had recently weathered a rough patch, and feminine companionship hadn't even been on his radar. That was how he rationalized his response to Phoebe, even on the day they'd met.

But he knew it was more than that. She was a virus in his blood, an immediate, powerful affliction that was in its own way as dangerous as his heart attack. Phoebe had the power to make his stay here either heaven or hell. And if it were the latter, he might as well cut and run right now.

But even as he thought it, his ego *and* his libido shouted a vehement *hell, no.* Phoebe might be calling the shots as his landlady, but when it came to sex, the decision was already made. He and Phoebe were going to be lovers. The only question was when and where.

His head cleared as he walked, and the physical exertion gradually drained him to the point that he felt able to go back. He had followed the creek upstream for the most part, not wanting to get lost. In some places the rhododendron thickets were so dense he was forced to climb up and around. When he finally halted, he was partway up the mountainside. To his surprise, he could see a tiny section of Phoebe's chimney sticking up out of the woods.

Perhaps Luc had been right. Here, in an environment so antithetical to Leo's own, he saw himself in a new light. His world was neither bad nor good in comparison to Phoebe's. But it was different.

Was that why Phoebe had come here? To get perspective? And if so, had she succeeded? Would she ever go back to her earlier life?

He sat for a moment on a large granite boulder, feeling the steady pumping of his heart. Its quiet, regular beats filled him with gratitude for everything he had almost lost. Perhaps it was the nature of humans to take life for granted. But now, like the sole survivor of a plane crash, he felt obliged to take stock, to search for meaning, to tear apart the status quo and see if it was really worthy of his devotion.

Amidst those noble aspirations, he shamefully acknowledged if only to himself that he yearned to be back at his desk. He ran a billion-dollar company, and ran it well. He was Leo Cavallo, CFO of a textile conglomerate that spanned the globe. Like a recovering addict, his hands itched for a fix…for the pulse-pumping, mentally stimulating, nonstop schedule that he understood so intimately.

He knew people used *workaholic* as a pejorative term, often with a side order of pitying glances and shakes of the head. But, honest to God, he didn't see anything wrong with having passion for a job and doing it well. It irritated the hell out of him to imagine all the balls that were being dropped in his absence. Not that Luc and the rest of the team weren't as smart as he was…it wasn't that.

Leo, however, gave Cavallo his everything.

In December, the prep work began for year-end reports. Who was paying attention to those sorts of things while Leo was AWOL? It often became necessary to buy or sell some smaller arms of the business for the appropriate tax benefit. The longer he thought about it, the more agitated he became. He could feel his blood pressure escalating.

As every muscle in his body tensed, he had to force himself to take deep breaths, to back away from an invisible cliff. In the midst of his agitation, an inquisitive squirrel paused not six inches from Leo's boot to scrabble in the dirt for an acorn. Chattering his displeasure with the human who had invaded his territory, the small animal worked furiously, found the nut and scampered away.

Leo smiled. And in doing so, felt the burden he carried shift and ease. He inhaled sharply, filling his lungs with clean air. As a rule, he thrived on the sounds of traffic and the ceaseless hum of life in a big city. Yet even so, he found himself noticing the stillness of the woods. The almost imperceptible presence of creatures who went about their business doing whatever they were created to do.

They were lucky, Leo mused wryly. No great soul-searching for them. Merely point A to point B. And again. And again.

He envied them their singularity of purpose, though he had no desire to be a hamster on a wheel. As a boy, his teachers had identified him as gifted. His parents had enrolled him in special programs and sent him to summer camps in astrophysics and geology and other erudite endeavors.

All of it interested and engaged him, but he never quite fit in anywhere. His size and athletic prowess made him a target of suspicion in the realm of the nerds, and his academic successes and love for school excluded him from the jock circle.

His brother became, and still was, his best friend. They squabbled and competed as siblings did, but their bond ran deep. Which was why Leo was stuck here, like a storybook character, lost in the woods. Because Luc had insisted it was important. And Leo owed his brother. If Luc believed Leo needed this time to recover, then it was probably so.

Rising to his feet and stretching, he shivered hard. After his strenuous exercise, he had sat too long, and now he was chilled and stiff. Suddenly, he wanted nothing more than to see Phoebe. He couldn't share his soul-searching and his minor epiphanies with her, because he hadn't yet come clean about his health. But he wanted to be with her. In any way and for any amount of time fate granted him.

Though it was not his way, he made an inward vow to avoid the calendar and to concentrate on the moment. Perhaps there was more to Leo Cavallo than met the eye. If so, he had two months to figure it out.

Phoebe couldn't decide whether to cry or curse when Leo finally came through the door, his tall, broad silhouette filling the doorway. Her giddy relief that he was okay warred with irritation because he had disappeared for so long without an explanation. Of course, if he had been living in his own cabin, she would not have been privy to his comings and goings.

But this was different. He and Phoebe were cohabiting. Which surely gave her some minimal rights when it came to social conventions. Since she didn't have the guts to chastise him, her only choice was to swallow her pique and move forward.

As he entered and kicked off his muddy boots, he smiled sheepishly. "Have you already eaten?"

"Yours is warming in the oven." She returned the smile

but stayed seated. It wasn't necessary to hover over him like a doting housewife. Leo was a big boy.

Teddy played with a plastic straw while Phoebe enjoyed a second cup of coffee. As Leo joined her at the table, she nodded at his plate. "Your friend is a genius. Please thank him for me. Though I'm sure I'll be ruing the additional calories."

Leo dug into his food with a gusto that suggested he had walked long and hard. "You're right. I've even had him cater dinner parties at my home. Makes me very popular, I can tell you."

As he finished his meal, Phoebe excused herself to put a drooping Teddy down for his nap. "I have a white noise machine I use sometimes in his room, so I think we'll be able to get the boxes down without disturbing him," she said. "And if he takes a long afternoon nap like he sometimes does, we can get a lot of the decorating done if you're still up for it."

Leo cocked his head, leaning his chair back on two legs. "I'm definitely *up* for it," he said, his lips twitching.

She couldn't believe he would tease about their recent insanity. "That's not funny."

"You don't have to tell me." He grinned wryly. "I realize in theory that couples with young children have sex. I just don't understand how they do it."

His hangdog expression made Phoebe burst into laughter, startling Teddy, who had almost fallen asleep on her shoulder. "Well, you don't have to worry about it," she said sharply, giving him a look designed to put him in his place. "All I have on the agenda this afternoon is decking the halls."

Leo had seldom spent as much time alone with a woman as he had with Phoebe. He was beginning to learn her expressions and to read them with a fair amount of accuracy.

When she reappeared after settling the baby, her excitement was palpable.

"The pull-down steps to the attic are in that far corner over there." She dragged a chair in that direction. "I'll draw the cord and you get ready to steady the steps as they come down."

He did as she asked, realizing ruefully that this position put him on eye level with her breasts. Stoically, he looked in the opposite direction. Phoebe dragged on the rope. The small framed-off section of the ceiling opened up to reveal a very sturdy set of telescoping stairs.

Leo grabbed the bottom section and pulled, easing it to the floor. He set his foot on the first rung. "What do you want me to get first?"

"The order doesn't really matter. I want it all. Except for the tree. That can stay. Here," she said, handing him a flashlight from her pocket. "I almost forgot."

Leo climbed, using the heavy flashlight to illuminate cobwebs so he could swat them away. Perhaps because the cabin was fairly new, or maybe because Phoebe was an organized sort, her attic was not a hodgepodge of unidentified mess. Neatly labeled cardboard cartons and large plastic tubs had been stacked in a tight perimeter around the top of the stairs within easy reach.

Some of the containers were fairly heavy. He wondered how she had managed to get them up here. He heard a screech and bent to stick his head out the hole. "What's wrong?"

Phoebe shuddered. "A spider. I didn't think all this stuff would have gotten so icky in just three years."

"Shall I stop?"

She grimaced. "No. We might as well finish. I'll just take two or three showers when we're done."

He tossed her a small box that was light as a feather. In neat black marker, Phoebe had labeled *Treetop Angel*

When she caught it, he grinned at her. "I'd be glad to help with that body check. I'll search the back of your hair for creepy-crawlies."

"I can't decide if that's revolting or exciting. Seems like you made a similar offer when you were convincing me to let you stay. Only then, you promised to kill *hypothetical* bugs."

"Turns out I was right, doesn't it?" He returned to his task, his body humming with arousal. He'd never paid much attention to the holidays. But with Phoebe, suddenly all the chores surrounding Christmas took on a whole new dimension.

By the time he had brought down the last box and stored away the stairs, Phoebe was elbows-deep into a carton of ornaments.

She held up a tiny glass snowman. "My grandmother gave me this when I was eight."

He crouched beside her. "Is she still alive?"

"No. Sadly."

"And your parents?" He was close enough to brush his lips across the nape of her neck, but he refrained.

Phoebe sank back on her bottom and crossed her legs, working to separate a tangle of glittery silver beads. "My parents were hit by a drunk driver when my sister and I were in high school. A very kind foster family took us in and looked after us until we were able to graduate and get established in college."

"And since then?"

"Dana and I are very close."

"No significant others in your past?"

She frowned at the knot that wouldn't give way. "What about your family, Leo?"

He heard the unspoken request for privacy, so he backed off. "Oddly enough, you and I have that in common. Luc and I were seventeen and eighteen when we lost our parents. Only it was a boating accident. My father loved his nautical toys, and he was addicted to the adrenaline rush of speed. We were in Italy visiting my grandfather one spring break. Dad took a friend's boat out, just he and my mom. On the way back, he hit a concrete piling at high speed as they were approaching the dock."

"Oh, my God." Her hands stilled. "How dreadful."

He nodded, the memory bleak even after all this time. "Grandfather insisted on having autopsies done. My mother wasn't wearing a life jacket. She drowned when she was flung into the water. I took comfort in the fact that she was probably unconscious when she died, because she had a severe head wound."

"And your father?"

Leo swallowed. "He had a heart attack. That's what caused him to lose control of the boat." Repeating the words stirred something dark and ugly in his gut. To know that he was his father's son had never pained him more than in the past few months.

Phoebe put a hand on his arm. "But wasn't he awfully young?"

"Forty-one."

"Oh, Leo. I'm so very sorry."

He shrugged. "It was a long time ago. After the funerals, Grandfather took Luc and I back to Italy to live with him. He insisted we attend college in Rome. Some would say we were lucky to have had such an education, but we were miserable for a long time. Our grief was twofold, of course. On top of that, Grandfather is not an easy man to love." He hesitated for a moment. "I don't tell many people that story, but you understand what it feels like to have the rug ripped out from under your feet."

"I do indeed. My parents were wonderful people. They always encouraged Dana and me to go for any goal we wanted. Never any question of it being *too hard* or *not a girl thing.* Losing them changed our lives."

Silence fell like a pall. Leo tugged at her braid. "Sorry. I didn't mean to take us down such a dismal path."

She rested her head against his hand. "It's hard not to think of family at this time of year, especially the ones we've lost. I'm glad you're here, Leo."

Ten

She wasn't sure who initiated the intimate contact. Their lips met briefly, sweetly. The taste of him was as warm and comfortable as a summer rain. She felt the erotic river of molten lava hidden just beneath the surface, but as if by unspoken consent, the kiss remained soft and easy.

Leaning into him, she let herself be bolstered by his strength. One big arm supported her back. He was virile and sexy. She couldn't be blamed for wanting more. "Leo," she muttered.

All she said was his name, but she felt the shudder that ran through him. "What?" he asked hoarsely. "What, Phoebe?"

A million different answers hovered at the tip of her tongue. *Undress me. Touch my bare skin. Make love to me.* Instead, she managed to be sensible. "Let me put some music on to get us in the mood for decorating."

"I *am* in the mood," he grumbled. But he smiled when he said it and kissed the tip of her nose. Then he sobered. "To be absolutely clear, I want you in my bed, tonight, Phoebe. When the little man is sound asleep and not likely to interrupt us."

His eyes were dark chocolate, sinful and rich and designed to make a woman melt into their depths. She stared at him, weighing the risks. As a financial speculator, she played hunches and often came out on top. But taking Leo as a lover was infinitely more dangerous.

He was here only for a short while. And though Phoebe had made peace with her demons and embraced her new lifestyle, she was under no illusions that Leo had done the same. He was anxious to return home. Coming to the mountains had been some sort of penance for him, a healing ritual that he accepted under protest.

Leo would never be content to stagnate. He had too much energy, too much life.

She touched his cheek, knowing that her acquiescence was a forgone conclusion. "Yes. I'd like that, too. And I'm sorry that we can't be more spontaneous. A new relationship should be hot and crazy and passionate." *Like this morning when you nearly took me standing up.* Her pulse tripped and stumbled as her thighs tightened in remembrance.

Leo cupped her hand to his face with one big palm. "It will be, Phoebe, darlin'. Don't you worry about that."

To Phoebe's surprise and delight, the afternoon became one long, drawn-out session of foreplay. Leo built a fire so high and hot they both had to change into T-shirts to keep cool. Phoebe found a radio station that played classic Christmas songs. She teased Leo unmercifully when she realized he never remembered any of the second verses, and instead made up his own words.

Together, they dug out a collection of balsam-scented candles, lit them and set them on the coffee table. During the summer, the trapped heat in the attic had melted the wax a bit, so the ones that were supposed to be Christmas trees looked more like drunken bushes.

Phoebe laughed. "Perhaps I should just throw them away."

Leo shook his head. "Don't do that. They have *character.*"

"If you say so." She leaned down and squinted at them. "They look damaged to me. Beyond repair."

"Looks can be deceiving."

Something in his voice—an odd note—caught her attention. He was staring at the poor trees as if all the answers to life's great questions lay trapped in green wax.

What did Leo Cavallo know about being damaged? As far as Phoebe could see, he was at the peak of his physical strength and mental acuity. Sleek muscles whispered of his ability to hold a woman…to protect her. And in a contest of wits, she would need to stay on her toes to best him. Intelligence crackled in his eyes and in his repartee.

Leo was the whole package, and Phoebe wanted it all.

Gradually, the room was transformed. With Leo's assistance, Phoebe hung garland from the mantel and around the doorways, intertwining it with tiny white lights that sparkled and danced even in the daytime. She would have preferred fresh greenery. But with a baby to care for and a cabin to repair, she had to accept her limits.

Leo spent over an hour tacking silver, green and gold snowflakes to the ceiling. Far more meticulous than she would have been, he measured and arranged them until every glittering scrap of foil was perfectly placed. The masculine satisfaction on his face as he stood, neck craned, and surveyed his handiwork amused her, but she was quick to offer the appropriate accolades.

In addition to the misshapen candles, the coffee table now sported a red wool runner appliquéd in reindeer. The *Merry Christmas* rug she remembered from her home in Charlotte now lay in front of a new door. The kitchen table boasted dark green place mats and settings of Christmas china.

At long last, Leo flopped down on the sofa with a groan. “You *really* like Christmas, don’t you?”

She joined him, curling into his embrace as naturally as if they were old friends. “I lost the spirit for a few years, but with Teddy here, this time I think it will be pretty magical.” Weighing her words, she finally asked the question she had been dying to have him answer. “What about you, Leo? Your sister-in-law made your reservation for two months. But you’ll go home for the holidays, won’t you?”

Playing lazily with the ends of her braid, he sighed. “I hadn’t really thought about it. Many times in the past six or eight years, Luc and I flew to Italy to be with Grandfather for Christmas. But when Luc and Hattie married the year before last, Grandfather actually came over here, though he swore it wouldn’t be an annual thing, because the trip wore him out. Now, with two little ones, I think Luc and Hattie deserve their own family Christmas.”

“And what about you?”

Leo shrugged. “I’ll have an invitation or two, I’m sure.”

“You could stay here with Teddy and me.” Only when she said the words aloud did she realize how desperately she wanted him to say yes.

He half turned to face her. “Are you sure? I wouldn’t want to intrude.”

Was he serious? She was a single woman caring for a baby that wasn’t hers in a lonely cabin in the woods. “I think we can make room,” she said drily. Without pausing to think of the ramifications, she ran a hand through his thick hair. The color, rich chestnut shot through with dark gold, was far too gorgeous for a man, not really fair at all.

Leo closed his eyes and leaned back, a smile on his face, but fine tension in his body. “That would be nice…” he said, trailing off as though her gentle scalp massage was making it hard to speak.

She put her head on his chest. With only a thin navy

T-shirt covering his impressive upper physique, she could hear the steady *ka-thud, ka-thud, ka-thud* of his heart. "Perhaps we should wait and see how tonight goes," she muttered. "I'm out of practice, to be honest." Better he know now than later.

Moving so quickly that she never saw it coming, he took hold of her and placed her beneath him on the sofa, his long, solid frame covering hers as he kissed his way down her throat. One of his legs lodged between her thighs, opening her to the possibility of something reckless. She lifted her hips instinctively. "Don't stop," she pleaded.

He found her breasts and took one nipple between his teeth, wetting the fabric of her shirt and bra as he tormented her with a bite that was just short of pain. Fire shot from the place where his mouth touched her all the way to her core. Shivers of pleasure racked her.

Suddenly, Leo reared back, laughing and cursing.

Blankly, she stared up at him, her body at a fever pitch of longing. "What? Tell me, Leo."

"Listen. The baby's awake."

When a knock sounded at the door minutes later, Leo knew he and Phoebe had narrowly escaped embarrassment on top of sexual frustration. She was out of sight tending to Teddy, so Leo greeted the man at the door with a smile. "Can I help you?"

The old codger in overalls looked him up and down. "Name's Buford. These sugared pecans is from my wife. She knowed they were Miss Phoebe's favorite, so she made up an extra batch after she finished the ones for the church bazaar. Will you give 'em to her?"

Leo took the paper sack. "I'd be happy to. She's feeding the baby a bottle, I think, but she should be finished in a moment. Would you like to come in?"

"Naw. Thanks. Are you the fella that was going to rent the other cabin?"

"Yes, sir, I am."

"Don't be gettin' any ideas. Miss Phoebe's pretty popular with the neighbors. We look out fer her."

"I understand."

"You best get some extra firewood inside. Gonna snow tonight."

"Really?" The afternoon sunshine felt more like spring than Christmas.

"Weather changes quicklike around here."

"Thanks for the warning, Buford."

With a tip of his cap, the guy ambled away, slid into a rust-covered pickup truck and backed up to turn and return the way he had come.

Leo closed the door. Despite feeling like a sneaky child, he unfolded the top of the sack and stole three sugary pecans.

Phoebe caught him with his hand in the bag…literally. "What's that?" she asked, patting Teddy on the back to burp him.

Leo chewed and swallowed, barely resisting the urge to grab another handful of nuts. "Your farmer friend, Buford, came by. How old is he anyway?"

"Buford is ninety-eight and his wife is ninety-seven. They were both born in the Great Smoky Mountains before the land became a national park. The house Buford and Octavia now live in is the one he built for her when they married in the early 1930s, just as the Depression was gearing up."

"A log cabin?"

"Yes. With a couple of rambling additions. They still used an actual outhouse up until the mid-eighties when their kids and grandkids insisted that Buford and Octavia were getting too old to go outside in the dead of winter to do their business."

"What happened then?"

"The relatives chipped in and installed indoor plumbing."

"Good Lord." Leo did some rapid math. "If they married in the early thirties, then—"

"They'll be celebrating their eightieth anniversary in March."

"That seems impossible."

"She was seventeen. Buford one year older. It happened all the time."

"Not their ages. I mean the part about eighty years together. How can anything last that long?"

"I've wondered that myself. After all, even a thirty-five-year marriage is becoming harder to find among my peers' parents."

Leo studied Phoebe, trying to imagine her shoulders stooped with age and her beautiful skin lined with wrinkles. She would be lovely still at sixty, and even seventy. But closing in on a hundredth birthday? Could any couple plan on spending 85 percent of an entire life looking at the same face across the breakfast table every morning? It boggled the mind.

Somehow, though, when he really thought about it, he *was* able see Phoebe in that scenario. She was strong and adaptable and willing to step outside her comfort zone. He couldn't imagine ever being bored by her. She had a sharp mind and an entertaining sense of humor. Not to mention a body that wouldn't quit.

Leo, himself, had never fallen in love even once. Relationships, good ones, took time and effort. Until now, he'd never met a woman capable of making him think long term.

Phoebe was another story altogether. He still didn't fully understand the decision that had brought her to the mountains, but he planned on sticking around at least long enough to find out. She intrigued him, entertained him and aroused him. Perhaps it was their isolation, but he felt a connection that transcended common sense and entered the realm of the heart. He was hazy about what he wanted from her in the long run. But tonight's agenda was crystal clear.

He desired Phoebe. Deeply. As much and as painfully as a man could hunger for a woman. Barring any unforeseen circumstances, she was going to be his.

To Phoebe's eyes, Leo seemed to zone out for a moment. She didn't feel comfortable demanding an explanation, not even a joking "Penny for your thoughts." Instead, she tried a distraction. "Teddy is fed and dry and rested at the moment. If we're going to get a tree, the time is right."

Leo snapped out of his fog and nodded, staring at the baby. "You don't think it will be too cold?"

"I have a snowsuit to put on him. That should be plenty of insulation for today. I'll get the two of us ready. If you don't mind going out to the shed, you can get the ax. It's just inside the door."

"You have an ax?" He was clearly taken aback.

"Well, yes. How else would we cut down a tree?"

"But you told me you haven't had a Christmas tree since you've been here. Why do you need an ax?"

She shrugged. "I split my own wood. Or at least I did in the pre-Teddy days. Now I can't take the chance that something might happen to me and he'd be in the house helpless. So I pay a high school boy to do it."

"I'm not sure how wise it is for you to be so isolated and alone. What if you needed help in an emergency?"

"We have 911 access. And I have the landline phone in addition to my cell. Besides, the neighbors aren't all that far away."

"But a woman on her own is vulnerable in ways a man isn't."

She understood what he wasn't saying. And she'd had those same conversations with herself in the beginning. Sleeping had been difficult for a few months. Her imagination had run wild, conjuring up rapists and murderers and deviants like the Unabomber looking for places to hide out in her neck of the woods.

Eventually, she had begun to accept that living in the city carried the same risks. The only difference being that they were packaged differently.

"I understand what you're saying," Phoebe said. "And yes, there have been nights, like the recent storm for instance, when I've questioned my decision to live here. But I decided over time that the benefits outweigh the negatives, so I've stayed."

Leo looked as if he wanted to argue the point, but in the end, he shook his head, donned his gear and left.

It took longer than she expected to get the baby and herself ready to brave the outdoors. That had been the biggest surprise about keeping Teddy. Everything about caring for him was twice as complicated and time-consuming as she had imagined. Finally, though, she was getting the hang of things, and already, she could barely remember her life without the little boy.

Eleven

It was the perfect day for an excursion. Since men were still working at the cabin removing the last of the tree debris and getting ready to cover the whole structure with a heavy tarp, Phoebe turned in the opposite direction, walking side by side with Leo back down the road to a small lane which turned off to the left and meandered into the forest.

She had fastened Teddy into a sturdy canvas carrier with straps that crisscrossed at her back. Walking was her favorite form of exercise, but it took a quarter mile to get used to the extra weight on her chest. She kept her hand under Teddy's bottom. His body was comfortable and warm nestled against her.

Leo carried the large ax like it weighed nothing at all, when Phoebe knew for a fact that the wooden-handled implement was plenty heavy. He seemed pleased to be out of the house, whistling an off-key tune as they strode in amicable silence.

The spot where she hoped to find the perfect Christmas tree was actually an old home site, though only remnants of the foundation and the chimney remained. Small weather-roughened headstones nearby marked a modest family cemetery. Some of the writing on the stones was still legible, including several that read simply, Beloved Baby. It pained her to think of the tragic deaths from disease in those days.

But she had suffered more than her share of hurt. She liked to think she understood a bit of what those families had faced.

Leo frowned, seeing the poignant evidence of human lives loved and lost. "Does this belong to you?" The wind soughed in the trees, seeming to echo chattering voices and happy laughter of an earlier day.

"As much as you can own a graveyard, I guess. It's on my property. But if anyone ever showed up to claim this place, I would give them access, of course. If descendants exist, they probably don't even know this is here."

One of the infant markers caught his attention. "I can't imagine losing a child," he said, his expression grim. "I see how much Luc and Hattie love their two, and even though I'm not a parent, sometimes it terrifies me to think of all the things that happen in the world today."

"Will you ever want children of your own?" Her breath caught in her throat as she realized that his answer was very important to her.

He squatted and brushed leaves away from the base of the small lichen-covered stone. "I doubt it. I don't have the time, and frankly, it scares the hell out of me." Looking up at her, his smile was wry. But despite the humor, she realized he was telling the absolute truth.

Her stomach tightened in disappointment. "You're still young."

"The business is my baby. I'm content to let Luc carry on the family lineage."

Since she had no answer to that, the subject lapsed, but she knew she had been given fair warning. Not from any intentional ultimatum on Leo's part. The problem was, Phoebe had allowed her imagination to begin weaving fantasies. Along the way, her heart, once broken but well on the way to recovery, had decided to participate.

The result was an intense and sadly dead-end infatuation with Leo Cavallo.

She stroked Teddy's hair, smiling to see the interest he demonstrated in his surroundings. He was a happy, inquisitive baby. Since the day he was born, she had loved him terribly. But this time alone, just the two of them, and now with Leo, had cemented his place in her heart. Having to return him to his parents was going to be a dreadful wrench. The prospect was so dismal, she forced the thought away. Much more of this, and she was going to start quoting an infamous Southern belle. *I'll think about that tomorrow.*

Leo stood and stretched, rolling his shoulders, the ax on the ground propped against his hip. "I'm ready. Show me which one."

"Don't be silly. We have to make a careful decision."

"This is the world's biggest Christmas tree farm. I'd say you won't have too much trouble. How about that one right there?" He pointed at a fluffy cedar about five feet tall.

"Too small and the wrong variety. I'll know when I see it."

Leo took her arm and steered her toward a grouping of evergreens. "Anything here grab your fancy?"

She and Leo were both encased in layers of winter clothes. But she fancied she could feel the warmth of his fingers on her skin. A hundred years ago, Leo would have worked from dawn to dusk, providing for his family. At night, when the children were asleep in the loft, she could see him making love to his wife on a feather tick mattress in front of the fire. Entering *her,* Phoebe, with a fire, a passion he had kept banked during the daylight hours. Saving those special moments of intimacy for the dark of night.

Wishing she could peel out of her coat, she stripped off her gloves and removed her scarf. The image of a more primitive Leo was so real, her breasts ached for his touch. She realized she had worn too many clothes. The day was warm for a winter afternoon. And thoughts of Leo's expertise in bed made her feel as if she had a fever.

She cleared her throat, hoping he wouldn't notice the hot color that heated her neck and cheeks. "Give me a second." Pretending an intense interest in the grouping of trees, she breathed deeply, inhaling the scent of the fresh foliage. "This one," she said hoarsely, grabbing blindly at the branches of a large Fraser fir.

At her back, Leo stood warm and tall. "I want you to have your perfect Christmas, Phoebe. But as the voice of reason I have to point out that your choice is a little on the big side." He put his hands on her shoulders, kissing her just below the ear. "If it's what you want, though, I'll trim it or something."

She nodded, her legs shaky. "Thank you."

He set her aside gently, and picked up the ax. "Move farther back. I don't know how far the wood chips will fly."

Teddy had dozed off, his chubby cheeks a healthy pink. She kept her arms around him as Leo notched the bottom of the tree trunk and took a few practice chops. At the last minute, he shed his heavy parka, now clad above the waist in only a thermal weave shirt, green to match his surroundings.

It was ridiculous to get so turned on by a Neanderthal exhibition of strength. But when Leo took his first powerful swing and the ax cut deeply into the tree, Phoebe felt a little faint.

Leo was determined to make Phoebe happy. The trunk of this particular fir was never going to fit into a normal-size tree stand. He'd have to cobble something together with a large bucket and some gravel. Who knew? At the moment, his first task was to fell the sucker and drag it home.

At his fifth swing, he felt a twinge in his chest. The feeling was so unexpected and so sharp, he hesitated half a second, long enough for the ax to lose its trajectory and land out of target range. Now, one of the lower branches was about two feet shorter than it had been.

Phoebe, standing a good ten feet away, called out to him. "What's wrong?"

"Nothing," he said, wiping his brow with the back of his hand. Tree chopping was damned hard work. Knowing that her eyes were on him, he found his stride again, landing four perfect strikes at exactly the same spot. The pain in his chest had already disappeared. Probably just a muscle. His doctor had reassured him more than once that Leo's health was perfect. Trouble was, when a man had been felled by something he couldn't see, it made him jumpy.

Before severing the trunk completely, he paused before the last swing and tugged the tree to one side. The fragrance of the branches was alluring. Crisp. Piquant. Containing memories of childhood days long forgotten. Something about scent leaped barriers of time and place.

Standing here in the forest with sap on his hands and his muscles straining from exertion, he felt a wave of nostalgia. He turned to Phoebe. "I'm glad you wanted to do this. I remember Christmases when I begged for a real tree. But my dad was allergic. Our artificial trees were always beautiful—Mom had a knack for that—but just now, a whiff of the air brought it all back. It's the smell of the holidays."

"I'm glad you approve," she said with a charming grin. Standing as she was in a splash of sunlight, her hair glistened with the sheen of a raven's wing. The baby slept against her breast. Leo wondered what it said about his own life that he envied a little kid. Phoebe's hand cradled Teddy's head almost unconsciously. Every move she made to care for her sister's child spoke eloquently of the love she had for her nephew.

Phoebe should have kids of her own. And a husband. The thought hit him like a revelation, and he didn't know why it was startling. Most women Phoebe's age were looking to settle down and start families. But maybe she wasn't. Because, clearly, she had hidden herself away like the unfortunate heroine in Rapunzel's castle. Only in Phoebe's case, the incarceration was voluntary.

Why would a smart, attractive woman isolate herself in an out-of-the-way cabin where her nearest neighbors were knocking on heaven's door? When was the last time she'd had a date? Nothing about Phoebe's life made sense, especially since she had admitted to working once upon a time in a highly competitive career.

A few thin clouds had begun to roll in, dropping the temperature, so he chopped one last time and had the satisfaction of hearing the snap that freed their prize. Phoebe clapped softly. "Bravo, Paul Bunyan."

He donned his coat and lifted an eyebrow. "Are you making fun of me?"

She joined him beside the tree and reached up awkwardly to kiss his cheek, the baby tucked between them. "Not even a little. You're my hero. I couldn't have done this on my own."

"Happy to oblige." Her gratitude warmed him. But her next words gave him pause.

"If we eat dinner early, we can probably get the whole thing decorated before bedtime."

"Whoa. Back up the truck. I thought we had *plans* for bedtime." He curled a hand behind her neck and stopped her in her tracks by the simple expedient of kissing her long and slow. Working around the kid was a challenge, but he was motivated.

Phoebe's lashes fluttered downward as she leaned into him. "We do," she whispered. The fact that she returned his kiss was noteworthy, but even more gratifying was her enthusiasm. She went up on tiptoes, aligned their lips perfectly and kissed him until he shuddered and groaned. "Good Lord, Phoebe."

She smoothed a strand of hair behind his ear, her fingers warm against his chilled skin. "Are you complaining, Mr. Cavallo?"

"No," he croaked.

"Then let's get crackin'."

Even though Phoebe carried a baby, and had been for some time, Leo was equally challenged by the difficulty of dragging the enormous tree, trunk first, back to the house. He walked at the edge of the road in the tall, dead grass, not wanting to shred the branches on gravel. By the time they reached their destination, he was breathing hard. "I think this thing weighs a hundred pounds."

Phoebe looked over her shoulder, her smile wickedly teasing. "I've seen your biceps, Leo. I'm sure you can bench-press a single measly tree." She unlocked the front door and propped it open. "I've already cleared a spot by the fireplace. Let me know if you need a hand."

Phoebe couldn't remember the last time she'd had so much fun. Leo was a good sport. Chopping down the large tree she had selected was not an easy task, but he hadn't complained. If anything, he seemed to get a measure of satisfaction from conquering *O Tannenbaum.*

Phoebe unashamedly used Teddy as a shield for the rest of the day. It wasn't that she didn't want to be alone with Leo. But there was something jarring about feeling such wanton, breathless excitement for a man when she was, at the same time, cuddling a little baby.

It would probably be different if the child were one they shared. Then, over Teddy's small, adorable head, she and Leo could exchanges smiles and loving glances as they remembered the night they created this precious bundle of joy. With no such scenario in existence, Phoebe decided her feelings were fractured…much like the time she'd had a high school babysitting job interrupted by the arrival of her boyfriend. That long-ago night as a sixteen-year-old, it had been all she could do to concentrate on her charges.

Almost a decade and a half later, with Leo prowling the interior of the cabin, all grumpy and masculine and gorgeous, she felt much the same way. Nevertheless, she focused on entertaining her nephew.

Fortunately, the baby was in an extremely good mood. He played in his high chair while Phoebe threw dinner together. Thanks to the largesse of Leo's buddy—which Leo no doubt cofunded—it was no trouble to pick and choose. Chicken Alfredo. Spinach salad. Fruit crepes for dessert. It would be easy to get spoiled by having haute cuisine at her fingertips with minimal effort. She would have to resist, though. Because, like Leo's presence in her life, the four-star meals were temporary.

Leo, after much cursing and struggling, and with a dollop of luck, finally pronounced himself satisfied with the security of their Christmas pièce de résistance. After changing the baby's diaper, Phoebe served up two plates and set them on the table. "Hurry, then. Before it gets cold."

Leo sat down with a groan. "Wouldn't matter to me. I'm starving."

She ended up sitting Teddy in his high chair and feeding him his bottle with one hand while she ate with the other. At the end of the meal, she scooped Teddy up and held him out to Leo. "If you wouldn't mind playing with him on the sofa for a little while, I'll clean up the kitchen, and we can start on the tree."

A look of discomfort crossed Leo's face. "I'm more of an observer when it comes to babies. I don't think they like me."

"Don't be silly, Leo. And besides, you did offer to help with Teddy when I let you stay. Remember?"

He picked up his coat. "Buford says it's going to snow tonight. I need to move half of that pile of wood you have out by the shed and stack it on the front porch. If it's a heavy snow, we might lose power." Before Phoebe could protest, he bundled up in his winter gear and was gone.

Phoebe felt the joy leach out of the room. She wanted Leo to love Teddy like she did, but that was silly. Leo had his own family, a brother, a sister-in-law, a niece, a nephew and a grandfather. Besides, he'd been pretty clear about not wanting kids. Some people didn't get all warm and fuzzy when it came to infants.

Still, she felt a leaden sense of disappointment. Leo was a wonderful man. Being squeamish about babies was hardly a character flaw.

She put Teddy back in the high chair. "Sorry, kiddo. Looks like it's you and me on KP duty tonight. I'll be as quick as I can, and then I'll read you a book. How about that?"

Teddy found the loose end of the safety strap and chewed it. His little chortling sounds and syllables were cute, but hardly helpful when it came to the question of Leo.

Tonight was a big bridge for Phoebe to cross. She was ready. She wanted Leo, no question. But she couldn't help feeling anxiety about the future. In coming to the mountains, she had learned to be alone. Would agreeing to be Leo's lover negate all the progress she had made? And would ultimately losing him—as she surely would—put her back in that dark place again?

Even with all her questions, tonight's outcome was a forgone conclusion. Leo was her Christmas present to herself.

Twelve

Leo pushed himself hard, carrying five or six heavy logs at a time. He took Buford's warning seriously, but the real reason he was out here was because staying in the cabin with Phoebe was torture. It was one thing to casually say, "We'll wait until bedtime." It was another entirely to keep himself reined in.

Every time she bent over to do something with the baby or to put something in the oven, her jeans cupped a butt that was the perfect size for a man's hands to grab hold of. The memory of her naked breasts lodged in his brain like a continuous, R-rated movie reel.

Earlier, he had called Luc, explaining the isolation of Phoebe's cabin and promising to stay in touch. His new phone should arrive in the morning, and the satellite internet would be set up, as well. By bedtime *tomorrow* night, Leo would be plugged in, all of his electronic devices at his fingertips. A very short time ago, that notion would have filled him with satisfaction and a sense of being on track. Not today. Now he could think of nothing but taking Phoebe to bed.

When he had a healthy stack of logs tucked just outside the front door in easy reach, he knew it was time to go in and face the music. His throat was dry. His heart pounded far harder than warranted by his current task. But the worst part was his semipermanent erection. He literally ached all over…wanting Phoebe. *Needing* her with a ferocious appetite that made him grateful to be a man with a beating heart.

He told himself he was close to having everything he craved. All he had to do was make it through the evening. But he was jittery with arousal. Testosterone charged through his bloodstream like a devil on his shoulder. Urging him on to stake a claim. Dismissing the need for gentleness.

Phoebe was his for the taking. She'd told him as much. A few more hours, and everything he wanted would be his.

Phoebe moved the portable crib into the living room near the fireplace, on the opposite side from the tree. Her hope was that Teddy would amuse himself for a while. He'd been fed, changed, and was now playing happily with several of his favorite teething toys.

When Leo came through the door on a blast of cold air, her stomach flipped. She'd given herself multiple lectures on remaining calm and cool. No need for him to know how agitated she was about the evening to come. Her giddiness was an odd mixture of anticipation and reservation.

Never in her life had she been intimate with a man of whom she knew so little. And likewise, never had she contemplated sex with someone for recreational purposes. She and Leo were taking advantage of a serendipitous place and time. Neither of them made any pretense that this was more. No passionate declarations of love. No tentative plans for the future.

Just sex.

Did that cheapen what she felt for him?

As he removed his coat and boots, she stared. The look in his eyes was hot and predatory. A shiver snaked down her spine. Leo was a big man, both in body and in personality. His charisma seduced her equally as much as his honed, masculine body.

She licked her lips, biting the lower one. "Um…there's hot chocolate on the stove. I made the real stuff. Seemed appropriate."

He rubbed his hands together, his cheeks ruddy from the cold. "Thanks."

The single syllable was gruff. Phoebe knew then, beyond the shadow of a doubt, that Leo was as enmeshed in whatever was happening between them as she was. The knowledge settled her nerves. She had been afraid of seeming gauche or awkward. Leo's intensity indicated that he was perhaps as off balance as she felt.

As he poured his drink, she expected him to come sit on the sofa. Instead, he lingered in the kitchen. She dragged a large red plastic tub nearer the tree. "If you'll do the lights, I'll sort through the ornaments and put hangers on them so that part will go quickly."

He set his mug in the sink. "Lights?"

She shot him an innocent look. "It's the man's job. Always."

"And if there were no man around?"

"I'd have to handle it. But I'm sure the tree would not look nearly as pretty."

Finally, he joined her, his body language somewhat more relaxed. "You are so full of it," he said with a fake glower as he bent and picked up the first strand. "You realize, don't you, that many people buy pre-lit trees these days."

"True." She plugged in the extension cord and handed him the end. "But not live ones. Think how proud you're going to be when we're finished, how satisfied with a job well done."

Tugging her braid, he deliberately brushed the backs of his fingers down her neck. "I'm a long way from satisfied."

His chocolate-scented breath was warm on her cheek. If she turned her head an inch or two, their lips would meet.

She closed her eyes involuntarily, her body weak with longing. Leo had to know what he was doing to her. And judging by the smirk on his face when she finally managed to look at him, he was enjoying her discomfiture.

Turnabout was fair play. "Good things come to those who wait," she whispered. She stroked a hand down the middle of his rib cage, stopping just above his belt buckle.

Leo sucked in a sharp breath as his hands clenched on her shoulders. "Phoebe…"

"Phoebe, what?" Toying with the hem of his shirt, she lifted it and touched his bare skin with two fingertips. Teasing him like this was more fun than she could have imagined. Her long-buried sensual side came out to play. Taking one step closer so that their bodies touched chest to knee, she laid her cheek against him, hearing the steady, though rapid, beat of his heart.

Between them, she felt the press of his erection, full and hard, at her stomach. For so long she had hidden from the richness of life, afraid of making another tragic misstep. But one lesson she had learned well. No matter how terrible the mistake and how long the resultant fall, the world kept on turning.

Leo might well be her next blunder. But at least she was living. Feeling. Wanting. Her emotions had begun to thaw with the advent of Teddy. Leo's arrival in the midst of her reawakening had been fortuitous. Six months ago, she would not have had the courage to act on her attraction.

Now, feeling the vestiges of her grief slide into the realm of the past, her heart swelled with joy in the realization that the Phoebe Kemper she had once known was still alive. It had been a long road. And she didn't think she would ever want to go back and reclaim certain remnants of that woman's life.

But she was ready to move forward. With Leo.

He set her away from him, his expression strained. "Give me the damn lights."

Leo was at sixes and sevens, his head muddled with a million thoughts, his body near crippled with desire. Fortunately for him, Phoebe was the meticulous sort. There were no knots of wire to untangle. Every strand of lights had been neatly wrapped around pieces of plywood before being stored away. He sensed that this Christmas decorating ritual was far more important to Phoebe than perhaps he realized. So despite his mental and physical discomfort, he set his mind to weaving lights in amongst the branches.

Phoebe worked nearby, unwrapping tissue-wrapped ornaments, discarding broken ones, tending to Teddy now and again. Music played softly in the background. One tune in particular he recognized. He had always enjoyed the verve and tempo of the popular modern classic by Mariah Carey. But not until this exact minute had he understood the songwriter's simple message.

Some things were visceral. It was true. He needed no other gift but Phoebe. When a man was rich enough to buy anything he wanted, the act of exchanging presents took on new meaning. He had always given generously to his employees. And he and Luc knew each other well enough to come up with the occasional surprise gift that demonstrated thought and care.

But he couldn't remember a Christmas when he'd been willing to strip the holiday down to its basic component. Love.

His mind shied away from that thought. Surely a man of his age and experience and sophistication didn't believe in love at first sight. The heart attack had left him floundering, grasping at things to stay afloat in a suddenly changing world. Phoebe was here. And it was almost Christmas.

He wanted her badly. No need to tear the situation apart with questions.

He finished the last of the lights and dragged one final tub over to the edge of the coffee table so he could sit and sift through the contents. Though the tree was large, he wasn't sure they were going to be able to fit everything on the limbs.

Spying a small, unopened green box, he picked it up and turned it over. Visible through the clear plastic covering was a sterling sliver rocking horse with the words *Baby's First Christmas* engraved on the base. And a date. An old date. His stomach clenched.

When he looked up, Phoebe was staring at the item in his hands, her face ashen. Cursing himself for not moving more quickly to tuck it out of sight, he stood, not knowing what to say. A dozen theories rushed through his mind. But only one made sense.

Tears rolled from Phoebe's huge pain-darkened eyes, though he was fairly certain she didn't know she was crying. It was as if she had frozen, sensing danger, not sure where to run.

He approached her slowly, his hands outstretched. "Phoebe, sweetheart. Talk to me."

Her eyes were uncomprehending…even when she wiped one wet cheek with the back of her hand.

"Let me see it," she whispered, walking toward the tub of ornaments.

He put his body in front of hers, cupping her face in his hands. "No. It doesn't matter. You're shaking." Wrapping his arms around her and holding her as tightly as he could, he tried to still the tremors that tore through her body cruelly.

Phoebe never weakened. She stood erect, not leaning into him, not accepting his comfort. He might as well have been holding a statue. At last, he stepped back, staring into her eyes. "Let me get you a drink."

"No." She wiped her nose.

Leo reached into his pocket for a handkerchief and handed it to her. He was torn, unsure if talking about it would make things better or worse. As he stood there, trying to decide how to navigate the chasm that had opened at his feet, the fraught moment was broken by a baby's cry.

Phoebe whirled around. "Oh, Teddy. We were ignoring you." She rushed to pick him up, holding him close as new tears wet her lashes. "It's your bedtime, isn't it, my sweet? Don't worry. Aunt Phoebe is here."

Leo tried to take the boy. "You need to sit down, Phoebe." He was fairly certain she was in shock. Her hands were icy cold and her lips had a blue tinge.

Phoebe fought him. "No. You don't like babies. I can do it."

The belligerence in her wild gaze shocked him, coming as it did out of nowhere. "I never said that." He spoke softly, as though gentling a spooked animal. "Let me help you."

Ignoring his plea, she exited the room, Teddy clutched to her chest. He followed the pair of them down the hall and into the baby's nursery cum storage room. He had never seen this door open. Phoebe always used her own bedroom to access Teddy's.

She put the child on the changing table and stood there. Leo realized she didn't know what to do next.

Quietly, not making a fuss, he reached for the little pair of pajamas hanging from a hook on the wall nearby. The diapers were tucked into a cheerful yellow plastic basket at the boy's feet. Easing Phoebe aside with nothing more than a nudge of his hip, he unfastened what seemed like a hundred snaps, top and bottom, and drew the cloth up over Teddy's head. Teddy cooed, smiling trustingly as Leo stripped him naked. The baby's skin was soft, his flailing arms and legs pudgy and strong.

The diaper posed a momentary problem, but only until Leo's brain clicked into gear and he saw how the assembly worked. Cleaning the little bottom with a baby wipe, he gave thanks that he was only dealing with a wet diaper, not a messy one.

Phoebe hadn't moved. Her hands were clenched on the decorative edge of the wooden table so hard that her knuckles were white.

Leo closed up the diaper, checked it for structural integrity, and then held up the pajamas. He couldn't really see much difference between these pj's and the daytime outfits the kid wore, but apparently there was one. This piece of clothing was even more of a challenge, because the snaps ran from the throat all the way down one leg. It took him three tries to get it right.

Through it all, Phoebe stood unaware. Or at least it seemed that way.

Cradling the child in one arm, Leo used his free hand to steer Phoebe out of the room. "You'll have to help me with the bottle," he said softly, hoping she was hearing him.

Her brief nod was a relief.

Leo installed Phoebe in a kitchen chair. Squatting in front of her, he waited until her eyes met his. "Can you hold him?"

She took the small, squirmy bundle and bowed her head, teardrops wetting the front of the sleeper. "I have a bottle ready," she said, the words almost inaudible. "Put it in a bowl of hot water two or three times until the formula feels warm when you sprinkle it on your wrist."

He had seen her perform that task several times, so it was easy to follow the instructions. When the bottle was ready, he turned back to Phoebe. Her grip on Teddy was firm. The child was in no danger of being dropped. But Phoebe had ceased interacting with her nephew.

Leo put a hand on her shoulder. "Would you like to feed him, or do you want me to do it? I'm happy to."

Long seconds ticked by. Phoebe stood abruptly, handing him the baby. "You can. I'm going to my room."

He grabbed her wrist. "No. You're not. Come sit with us on the sofa."

Thirteen

Phoebe didn't have the emotional energy to fight him. Leo's gaze was kind but firm. She followed him to the living room and sat down with her legs curled beneath her. Leo sat beside her with Teddy in his arms. Fortunately, Teddy didn't protest the change in leadership. He took his bottle from Leo as if it were an everyday occurrence.

Despite the roaring fire that Leo had built, which still leaped and danced vigorously, she felt cold all over. Clenching her jaw to keep her teeth from chattering, she wished she had thought to pick up an afghan. But the pile neatly folded on the hearth was too far away. She couldn't seem to make her legs move.

Trying to distract her thoughts, she studied Leo out of the corner of her eye. The powerful picture of the big man and the small baby affected her at a gut-deep level. Despite Leo's professed lack of experience, he was doing well. His large hands were careful as he adjusted Teddy's position now and again or moved the bottle to a better angle.

Beyond Leo's knee she could see the abandoned ornaments. But not the little green box. He must have shoved it out of sight beneath the table. She remembered vividly the day she'd purchased it. After leaving her doctor's office, she was on her way back to work. On a whim, she stopped by the mall to grab a bite of lunch and to walk off some of her giddy euphoria.

It was September, but a Christmas shop had already opened its doors in preparation for the holidays. On a table near the front, a display of ornaments caught her eyes. Feeling crazily joyful and foolishly furtive, she picked one out and paid for it.

Until this evening she had suppressed that memory. In fact, she didn't even realize she had kept the ornament and moved it three years ago.

Leo wrapped an arm around her shoulders, pulling her closer to his side. "Lean on me," he said.

She obeyed gladly, inhaling the scent of his aftershave and the warm "man" smell of him. Gradually, lulled by the fire and the utter security of Leo's embrace, she closed her eyes. Pain hovered just offstage, but she chose not to confront it at the moment. She had believed herself to be virtually healed. As though all the dark edges of her life had been sanded away by her sojourn in the woods.

How terribly unfair to find out it wasn't true. How devastating to know that something so simple could trip her up.

Perhaps because the afternoon and evening had been so enjoyable, so delightfully *homey,* the harshness of being thrust into a past she didn't want to remember was all the more devastating.

Teddy drained the last of the bottle, his little eyelashes drooping. Leo coaxed a muffled burp from him and then put a hand on Phoebe's knee. "Is it okay for me to lay him down? Anything I need to know?"

"I'll take him," she said halfheartedly, not sure if she could make the effort to stand up.

He squeezed her hand. "Don't move. I'll be right back."

She stared into space, barely even noticing when he returned and began moving about the kitchen with muffled sounds. A few minutes later he handed her a mug of cocoa. She wrapped her fingers around the warm stoneware, welcoming the heat against her frozen skin.

Leo had topped her serving with whipped cream. She sipped delicately, wary of burning her tongue.

He sat down beside her and smiled. "You have a mustache," he teased. Using his thumb, he rubbed her upper lip. Somewhere deep inside her, regret surfaced. She had ruined their sexy, fun-filled evening.

Leo appeared unperturbed. He leaned back, his legs outstretched, and propped his feet on the coffee table. With his mug resting against his chest, he shot her a sideways glance. "When you're ready, Phoebe, I want you to tell me the story."

She nodded, her eyes downcast as she studied the pale swirls of melted topping in the hot brown liquid. It was time. It was beyond time. Even her sister didn't know all the details. When the unthinkable had happened, the pain was too fresh. Phoebe had floundered in a sea of confused grief, not knowing how to claw her way out.

In the end, her only choice had been to wait until the waves abated and finally receded. Peace had eventually replaced the hurt. But her hard-won composure had been fragile at best. Judging by today, she had a long way to go.

Leo got up to stoke the fire and to add more music to the stereo. She was struck by how comfortable it felt to have him in her cabin, in her life. He was an easy man to be with. Quiet when the occasion demanded it, and drolly amusing when he wanted to be.

He settled back onto the couch and covered both of them with a wool throw. Fingering the cloth, he wrinkled his nose. "We should burn this," he said with a grin. "Imported fabric, cheap construction. I could hook you up with something far nicer."

"I'll put it on my Christmas list." She managed a smile,

not wanting him to think she was a total mental case. "I'm sorry I checked out on you," she muttered.

"We're all entitled now and then."

The quiet response took some of the sting out of her embarrassment. He was being remarkably patient. "I owe you an explanation."

"You don't *owe* me anything, sweet Phoebe. But it helps to talk about it. I know that from experience. When our parents were killed, Grandfather was wise enough to get us counseling almost immediately. We would never have shown weakness to him. He was and still is a sharp-browed, blustering tyrant, though we love him, of course. But he knew we would need an outlet for what we were feeling."

"Did it work?"

"In time. We were at a vulnerable age. Not quite men, but more than boys. It was hard to admit that our world had come crashing down around us." He took her hand. She had twisted one piece of blanket fringe so tightly it was almost severed. Linking their fingers, he raised her hand to his lips and kissed it. "Is that what happened to you?"

Despite her emotional state, she was not above being moved by the feel of his lips against her skin. Hot tears stung her eyes, not because she was so sad, but in simple recognition of his genuine empathy. "You could say that."

"Tell me about your baby."

There was nothing to be gained from denial. But he would understand more if she began elsewhere. "I'll go back to the beginning if you don't mind."

"A good place to start." He kissed her fingers again before tucking her hand against his chest. The warmth of him, even through his clothing, calmed and comforted her.

"I told you that I was a stockbroker in Charlotte."

"Yes."

"Well, I was good, really good at my job. There were a half dozen of us, and competition was fierce. Gracious for the most part, but inescapable. I had a knack for putting together portfolios, and people liked working with me, because I didn't make them feel stupid or uninformed about their money. We had a number of very wealthy clients with neither the time nor the inclination to grow their fortunes, so we did it for them."

"I'm having a hard time reconciling *killer* Phoebe with the woman who bakes her own bread."

His wry observation actually made her laugh. "I can understand your confusion. Back then I focused on getting ahead in my profession. I was determined to be successful and financially comfortable."

"Perhaps because losing your parents left you feeling insecure in so many other ways."

His intuitive comment was impressive. "You should hang out a shingle," she said. "I'm sure people would pay for such on-the-mark analysis."

"Is that sarcasm I hear?"

"Not at all."

"I can't take too much credit. You and I have more in common than I realized. Getting the foundations knocked out from under you at a time when most young people are getting ready to step out into the big wide world breeds a certain distrust in the system. Parents are supposed to help their children with the shift into adulthood."

"And without them, everything seems like a scary gamble at best."

"Exactly. But there's more, isn't there?"

She nodded, fighting the lump in her throat. "I was engaged," she croaked. "To another broker. We had an ongoing battle to see who could bring in the most business. I thought we were a team, both professionally *and* personally, but it turns out I was naive."

"What happened?"

Taking a deep breath, she ripped off the Band-Aid of her

old wound and brought it all back to life…to ugly life. “We had plans to get married the following year, but no specific date. Then—in the early fall—I found out I was pregnant.”

“Not planned, I assume?”

“Oh, gosh, no. I assumed that motherhood, if it ever rolled around, was sometime *way* in the future. But Rick and I—that was his name—well…once we got over the shock, we started to be happy about it. Freaked-out, for sure. But happy nevertheless.”

“Did you set a date then for a wedding?”

“Not at first. We decided to wait a bit, maybe until we knew the sex of the baby, to tell our coworkers. I thought everything was rocking along just fine, and then Rick began dropping subtle and not-so-subtle hints that I should think about taking a leave for a while.”

“Why? It wasn't a physically demanding job, was it?”

“No. But he kept bringing up the stress factor. How my intensity and my long hours could be harmful to the baby. At first, I was confused. I honestly didn't see any problem.”

“And was there?”

“Not the one he was trying to sell to me. But the truth was, Rick knew he could be top dog at the company if I were gone. And even when I came back after maternity leave, he would have made so much progress that I would never catch up.”

“Ouch.”

She grimaced. “It was a nasty smack in the face. We had a huge fight, and he accused me of being too ambitious for my own good. I called him a sexist pig. Things degenerated from there.”

“Did you give the ring back?”

“How could I? Even if I now knew that my fiancé was a jerk, he was the father of my baby. I decided I had no choice but to make it work. But no matter how hard I tried, things only got worse.”

"Did you have an abortion?"

Leo's quiet query held no hint of judgment, only a deep compassion. From where he was standing, that assumption made perfect sense.

She swallowed. The trembling she had managed to squelch started up again. "No. I wanted the baby by then. Against all odds. I was three and a half months along, and then…" Her throat tightened. Leo rubbed her shoulder, the caress comforting rather than sexual.

"What happened, Phoebe?"

Closing her eyes, she saw the moment as if it had been yesterday. "I started bleeding at work one day. Terribly. They rushed me to the hospital, but I lost the baby. All I could think about when I was lying in that bed, touching my empty belly, was that Rick had been right."

"You were young and healthy. I can't imagine there was a reason you shouldn't have been working."

"That's what my doctor said. She tried to reassure me, but I wasn't hysterical. Just cold. So cold. They told me the baby had developed with an abnormality. I would never have carried it to term. One of those random, awful things."

She didn't cry again. The emptiness was too dry and deep for that…a dull, vague feeling of loss.

Leo lifted her onto his lap, turning her sideways so her cheek rested on his chest. His arms held her tightly, communicating without words his sympathy and his desire to comfort her. He brushed a stray hair from her forehead. "I'm so sorry, Phoebe."

She shrugged. "Lots of people lose babies."

"But usually not a fiancé at the same time. You lost everything. And that's why you came here."

"Yes. I was a coward. I couldn't bear people staring at me with pity. And with Rick still working at the company, I knew I was done. My boss wasn't happy about it. I think he would have liked to fire Rick and keep me, but you can't terminate a guy for being a selfish, self-absorbed bastard."

"I would have." The three words encompassed an icy intensity that communicated his anger toward a man he had never met. "Your boss shouldn't have been so spineless. You were good at your job, Phoebe. If you had stayed, you might have recovered from your loss much sooner. The work would have been a healthy distraction. Perhaps even fulfilling in a new way."

Here was the crux of the matter. "The thing is," she said slowly. "I have my doubts. Looking back, I can see that I had all the makings of a workaholic. It's bad enough when a man falls into that trap. But women are traditionally the caregivers, the support system for a spouse or a family. So even though the doctor told me I had done nothing wrong, I felt as if I had betrayed my child by working nonstop."

Leo's arms tightened around her, his chest heaving in a startled inhalation. "Good Lord, Phoebe. That's totally irrational. You were an unencumbered woman on the upswing of your career. Female pioneers have fought for decades so you could be exactly where you were."

"And yet we still have battles within the sisterhood between stay-at-home moms and those who work outside the home. I've seen both groups sneer at each other as though one choice is more admirable than the other."

"I'll give you that one. In reality, though, I assume women work for many reasons. Fulfillment. Excitement. Or in some cases, simply to put food on the table."

"But it's about balance, Leo. And I had none. It's not true that women can have it all. Life is about choices. We only have twenty-four hours in a day. That never changes. So if I don't learn how to fit *work* into a box of the appropriate size, I don't know that I'll ever be able to go back."

"That's it, then? You're never going to be employed

again? Despite the fact that you've been gifted with financial talents and people skills?"

"I'd like to have a family someday. And even more importantly, find peace and contentment in the way I live my life. Is that so wrong?"

"How are you supposed to accomplish that by hiding out? Phoebe, you're not doing what you're good at…and borrowing a baby from your sister isn't exactly going after what you want."

"I don't know if I'm ready yet. It sounds like a cliché, but I've been trying to find myself. And hopefully in the process learning something about balance."

"We all have to live in the real world. Most of the life lessons I've learned have come via failure."

"Well, that's depressing."

"Not at all. You have to trust yourself again."

"And if I crash and burn?"

"Then you'll pick yourself up and start over one more time. You're more resilient than you think."

Fourteen

Leo was more bothered by Phoebe's soul-searching than he should have been. Her self-evaluation proved her to be far more courageous than he was in facing up to painful truths. But in his gut, he believed she was missing the bigger picture. Phoebe had clearly excelled in her previous career. And had loved the work, even with overt competition...perhaps *because* of it.

She was lucky to have had the financial resources to fund her long sabbatical. In the end, though, how would she ever know if it was time to leave the mountains? And what if she decided to stay? She had proved her independence. And in her eyes and in her home he saw peace. Did that mean she couldn't see herself finding happiness—and perhaps a family—anywhere but here?

He played with her hair, removing the elastic band that secured her braid. Gently, he loosened the thick ropes, fanning out the dark, shiny tresses until they hung down her back, covering his hand in black silk. Holding her in his arms as a friend and not a lover was difficult, but he couldn't push her away.

Phoebe saw herself as a coward, but that was far from the truth. Though she had been at the top of her game, she had wanted the baby that threatened to disrupt her life. Even in the face of disappointment, knowing that her fiancé was not the man she thought he was, she had been prepared to work at the relationship so they could be a family.

Leo admired her deeply.

Her eyes were closed, her breathing steady. It had been a long, busy day, and an emotional one for her. Leo knew their timing was off. Again. Even with Teddy sleeping soundly, Phoebe was in no shape to initiate a sexual relationship with a new partner. Perhaps if they had been a couple for a long time, Leo could have used the intimacy of sex to comfort and reassure her. As it was, his role would have to be that of protector.

A man could do worse when it came to Phoebe Kemper.

He stood, prepared to carry her to her room. Phoebe stirred, her long lashes lifting to reveal eyes that were still beautiful, though rimmed in red. "What are you doing?"

"You need to be in bed. Alone," he clarified, in case there was any doubt about his intentions.

She shook her head, a stubborn expression he had come to know all too well painting her face with insistence. "I want to sleep in here so I can see the tree. I'll keep the monitor with me. You go on to bed. I'm fine."

He nuzzled her nose with his, resisting the urge to kiss her. Her aching vulnerability held him back. "No," he said huskily. "I'll stay with you." He set her on her feet and went to his room to get extra blankets and a pillow. The bearskin rug in front of the fire would be a decent enough bed, and from there, he'd be able to keep the fire going. He brushed his teeth and changed into his pajama pants and robe.

By the time he returned, Phoebe had made the same preparations. It was colder tonight. Instead of her knit pj's, she had donned a high-necked flannel nightgown that made her look as if she had stepped right out of the pages of *Little*

House on the Prairie. The fabric was pale ivory with little red reindeer cavorting from neck to hemline.

The old-fashioned design should have made her look as asexual as a nun. But with her hair spilling around her shoulders and her dark eyes heavy-lidded, all Leo could think about was whether or not she had on panties beneath that fortress of a garment.

If the utilitarian cloth and enveloping design was meant to discourage him, Phoebe didn't know much about men. When the castle was barricaded, the knights had to fight all the harder to claim their prize.

She clutched a pillow to her chest, her cheeks turning pink. "You don't have to stay with me. I'm okay…really."

"What if I want to?" The words came out gruffer than he intended.

Her eyes widened. He could swear he saw the faint outline of pert nipples beneath the bodice of her nightwear. She licked her lips. "You've been very sweet to me, Leo. I'm sorry the night didn't go the way we planned. But maybe it's for the best. Perhaps we were rushing into this."

"You don't want me?" He hadn't meant to ask it. Hated the way the question revealed his need.

Phoebe's chin wobbled. "I don't know. I mean, yes. Of course I want you. I think that's painfully obvious. But we're not…"

"Not what?" He took the pillow from her and tossed it on the couch. Gathering her into his arms, he fought a battle of painful scale. It seemed as if he had wanted her for a lifetime. "Only a fool would press you now…when you've dealt with so much tonight. But make no mistake, Phoebe. I'm going to have you. No matter how long the wait." He stroked his hands down her back, pulling her hips to his, establishing once and for all that she was *not* wearing underwear.

Had he detected any resistance at all on her part, he

would have been forced to release her. But she melted into him, her body warm and soft and unmistakably feminine through the negligible barrier of her gown. He had belted his robe tightly before leaving his bedroom, not wanting to give any appearance of carnal intent.

To his intense shock and surprise, a small hand made its way between the thin layers of cashmere and found his bare chest. Within seconds his erection lifted and thickened. His voice locked in his throat. He was positive that if he spoke, the words would come out wrong.

Phoebe's hand landed over his heart and lingered as if counting the beats. Could she hear the acceleration? Did she feel the rigidity of his posture? He gulped, his breathing shallow and ragged. There was no way she could miss his thrusting sex, even through her pseudo armor.

The woman in his arms sighed deeply. "You should go to your room," she whispered. "The floor will be too hard."

"I'll manage." He thrust her away, hoping the maneuver wasn't as awkward as it felt. Turning his back, he added logs to the fire and then prepared his makeshift bed.

In his peripheral vision he saw Phoebe ready the sofa with a pile of blankets and her own pillow. When she sat down, removed her slippers and swung her legs up onto the couch, he caught one quick glimpse of bare, slender thighs. *Holy hell.*

A shot of whiskey wouldn't come amiss, but Phoebe's fridge held nothing stronger than beer. Quietly, keeping a wide perimeter between himself and temptation, he went about the cabin turning off lights. Soon, only the glow of the fire and the muted rainbow colors of the tree illuminated the room.

He checked the lock on the front door and closed a gap in the drapes. When he could think of nothing else as a distraction, he turned reluctantly and surveyed the evocative scene Phoebe's love of Christmas had created. Even the most hardened of "Scrooge-ish" hearts surely couldn't resist the inherent emotion.

Peace. Comfort. Home. All of it was there for anyone with eyes to see. Had his luxurious condo in Atlanta ever been as appealing?

Phoebe's eyes were closed, a half smile on her lips. She lay like a child with one hand tucked beneath her cheek. He didn't know if she was already asleep or simply enjoying the smell of the outdoors they had managed to capture in a tree. Perhaps it was the sound of the fire she savored, the same life-affirming heat that popped and hissed as it had for generations before.

Exhaustion finally overrode his lust-addled brain and coaxed him toward sleep. He fashioned his bed in front of the hearth and climbed in. It wasn't the Ritz-Carlton, but for tonight, there was nowhere he would rather be. After no more than five minutes, he realized that his robe was going to be far too warm so close to the fire.

Shrugging out of it, he tossed it aside and lay back in the covers with a yawn. A month ago if anyone had told him he'd be camping out on a hard floor in dangerous proximity to a fascinating woman he wanted desperately, he'd have laughed. Of course, he would have had a similar reaction if that same someone had told him he'd have a heart attack at thirty-six.

He had to tell Phoebe the truth about why he had come to the Smoky Mountains…to her cabin in the woods. She had bared her soul to him. Perhaps tomorrow he would find the opportunity and the words to reveal the truth. The prospect made him uneasy. He hated admitting weakness. Always had. But his pride should not stand in the way of his relationship to a woman he had come to respect as much or more than he desired her.

He shifted on the furry pallet, searching for a position that was comfortable. With Phoebe in the same room, he didn't even have the option of taking his sex in hand and finding relief. Hours passed, or so it seemed, before he slept....

Phoebe jerked awake, her heart pounding in response to some unremembered dream. It took her several seconds to recognize her surroundings. In the next instant, she glanced at the baby monitor. Reassurance came in the form of a grainy picture. Teddy slept in his usual position.

Sighing shakily as adrenaline winnowed away, she glanced at the clock on the far wall. Two in the morning. The fire burned brightly, so Leo must have been up tend-ng to it recently. The room was warm and cozy. Despite her unaccustomed bed and the late hour, she felt momen-tarily rested and not at all sleepy.

Warily, she lifted her head a couple of inches, only enough to get a clear view of Leo over the top of the coffee able. Her breath caught at the picture he made. Sprawled on his back on the bearskin rug, he lay with one arm flung outward, the other bent and covering his eyes.

He was bare-chested. Firelight warmed skin that was deep gold dusted with a hint of dark hair that ran down the midline of his rib cage. Smooth muscles gave definition to torso that was a sculptor's dream.

Arousal swam in her veins, sluggish and sweet, washing way any vestige of sadness from earlier in the evening. A wave of yearning tightened her thighs. Moisture gathered in er sex, readying her for his possession. Leo would never ave made a move on her this evening in light of what she ad shared with him.

Which meant that Phoebe had to take the initiative.

Telling herself and her houseguest that intimacy between hem wasn't a good idea was as realistic as commanding he moon not to rise over the mountain. She *wanted* Leo. he trembled with the force of that wanting. It had been aeons since she had felt even the slightest interest in a man longer still since she had paid any attention to the sexua needs of her body.

It was foolish to miss this chance that might never com her way again. Leo was not only physically appealing, h was also a fascinating and complex man. She was draw to him with a force that was as strong as it was unexpected Some things in life couldn't be explained. Often in her ol life, she had picked stocks based on hunches. Nine time out of ten she was right.

With Leo, the odds might not be as good. Heartbrea and loss were potential outcomes. But at this barren tim in her life, she was willing to take that chance.

Before she could change her mind, she drew her gow up and over her head. Being naked felt wanton and wicked particularly in the midst of winter. Too long now she ha bundled herself up in every way…mentally…emotionall It was time to face life and be brave again.

She knelt beside him and sat back on her haunches, ma veling at the beauty of his big, elegant body. His navy slee pants hung low on his hips, exposing his navel. The tangl of bedding, blankets and all, reached just high enough t conceal his sex. Though she was pushing her limits, sh didn't quite have the courage to take a corner of the shee and pull.

Would he reject her, citing her emotional distress an bad timing? Or was Leo's need as great as hers? Did h want her enough to ignore all the warning signs and go fo it regardless of possible catastrophe?

There was only one way to find out. Slipping her han beneath the blanket, she encountered silk warmed by hi skin. Carefully, she stroked over the interesting mound th was his sex. She had no more than touched him when h began to swell and harden.

Fifteen

Leo was having the most amazing dream. One of Phoe-
e's hands touched him intimately, while the other moved
ightly over his chest, toying with his navel, teasing his
ipples with her thumb. He groaned in his sleep, trying
ot to move so the illusion wouldn't shatter.

He sensed her leaning over him, her hair brushing his
hest, his shoulders, his face, as she found his mouth. The
iss tasted sweet and hot. Small, sharp teeth nipped his bot-
om lip. He shuddered, bound in thrall to a surge of arousal
hat left him weak and gasping for breath. His chest heaved
s he tried to pull air into his lungs.

His heart pounded like the hooves of a racehorse in the
ast turn. For a split second, a dash of cold fear dampened
is enthusiasm. He hadn't had sex since his heart attack. All
nedical reassurances to the contrary, he wasn't sure what
vould happen when he was intimate with a woman. His
and—and the process of self-gratification—he trusted.
Vould the real deal finish him off?

But this was a dream. No need for heartburn. He laughed
nwardly at his own pun. Nothing mattered but hanging
nto the erotic fantasy and enjoying it until the end.

He felt Phoebe slide his loose pants down his legs and

over his feet. In the next second she was up on her knee straddling him. Grabbing one smooth, firm thigh, h tugged, angling her leg over his shoulder so he could plea sure her with his mouth. When he put his tongue at he center and probed, he shot from the realm of slumber t delicious reality in a nanosecond. The taste of Phoebe' sweet, hot sex was all too authentic.

His hands cupped her ass to hold her steady, even as hi brain struggled to catch up. "Phoebe?" The hoarse wor was all he could manage. Blinking to clear his sleep-fogge eyes, he looked up and found himself treated to the visio of soft, full breasts half hidden in a fall of silky black hai Curvy hips nipped into a narrow waist.

Phoebe's wary-eyed gaze met his. She licked her lips uncertainty in every angle of her body. "I didn't ask," sh said, looking delightfully guilty.

"Trust me, honey. There's not a man living who woul object. But you should have woken me up sooner. I don' want to miss anything." He loved the fact that she had take the initiative in their coming together, because it told hin she was as invested in this madness as he was. He scoote his thumb along the damp crevice where her body wa pink and perfect. When he concentrated on a certain spot Phoebe moaned.

Inserting two fingers, he found her swollen and wet *Sweet Lord.* The driving urge he had to take her wildly an immediately had to be subdued in favor of pleasuring suc an exquisite creature slowly. Making her yearn and bur and ultimately reach the same razor-sharp edge of arousa on which he balanced so precariously.

"Put your hair behind your shoulders," he commanded Phoebe lifted her arms and obeyed.

"Link your hands behind your back."

A split second of hesitation and then compliance. Th

docile acquiescence gave him a politically incorrect rush of elation. She was his. She was his.

Watching her face for every nuance of reaction, he played with her sex…light, teasing strokes interspersed with firmer pressure. Her body bloomed for him, the spicy scent of her making him drunk with hunger. Keeping his thumb on the little bud that encompassed her pleasure center, he entered her with three fingers this time, stretching her sheath.

Phoebe came instantly, with a keening cry. He actually felt the little flutters inside her as she squeezed. Imagining what that would feel like on his shaft made him dizzy.

When the last ripple of orgasm released her, he sat up, settling Phoebe in his lap and holding her tightly. His eager erection bumped up against her bottom. Her thighs were draped over his, her ankles linked at his back.

Emotions hit him hard and fast. The one he hadn't anticipated was regret. Not for touching her, never that. But sorrow that they hadn't met sooner. And fear that she would be dismissive of their intimacy because their time together had been so brief.

He waited as long as he could. At least until her breathing returned to normal. Then he pulled back and searched her face. "Don't think for a minute that we're almost done. That was only a tiny prelude. I'm going to devote myself to making you delirious with pleasure."

Her smile was smug. "Been there, done that, bought the T-shirt."

Leo knew that if things were to progress he had to get up. But knowing and doing were two different matters. "Can I ask you a very important question, my Phoebe?"

She rested her forehead on his shoulder. "Ask away."

"If I go fetch a bushel of condoms, will you change your mind about this while I'm gone?"

He felt her go still. "No." The voice was small, but the sentiment seemed genuine.

"And if Teddy wakes at an inopportune moment, will that be an excuse? Or even a sign from the universe that we should stop?"

She lifted her head, her eyes searching his. For what? Encouragement? Sincerity? "If that happens," she said slowly, "we'll settle him back to sleep and pick up where we left off."

"Good." He told himself to release her. Until he rustled up some protection, he couldn't take her the way he wanted to. But holding her like this was unutterably sweet. A real conundrum, because he couldn't ever remember feeling such a thing with another lover. This mix of shivering need and overwhelming tenderness.

Phoebe smiled. "Shall I go get them?"

He shook his head. "No. Just give me a minute." The actual fire had died down, and he needed to take care of that, as well.

While he sat there, desperately trying to find the will to stand up, Phoebe reached behind her bottom and found his shaft, giving it a little tug. The teasing touch was almost more than he could stand. The skin at the head was tight and wet with fluid that had leaked in his excitement.

Her fingers found the less rigid part of his sex and massaged him gently. "Don't. Ah, God, don't," he cried. But it was too late. He came in a violent climax that racked him with painful, fiery release. Gripping Phoebe hard enough to endanger her ribs, he groaned and shuddered, feeling the press of her breasts against his chest.

In the pregnant silence that followed, the witch had the temerity to laugh. "Perhaps we should quit while we're ahead. I don't think you're going to make it down the hall anytime soon."

He pinched her ass, gasping for breath. "Impertinent hussy."

"Well, it's true. I suppose I should have thought through all the ramifications before I jumped your bones."

"You *were* a tad eager," he pointed out, squeezing her perfectly plump butt cheeks.

Phoebe wriggled free and wrapped a blanket around her shoulders. "Go, Leo. Hurry. I'm getting cold."

Dragging himself to his feet, he yawned and stretched. Just looking at her had his erection bobbing hopefully again. *Down, boy.* He removed the fire screen, threw on a couple of good-size logs and poked the embers until they blazed up again. "Don't go anywhere," he ordered. "I'll be right back."

Phoebe watched him walk away with stars in her eyes. This was bad. This was very bad. Leo in the buff was one spectacular sight. Aside from his considerable *assets,* the view from the rear was impressive, as well. Broad shoulders, trim waist, taut buttocks, nicely muscled thighs. Even his big feet were sexy.

Despite everything they had done in the last forty-five minutes, her body continued to hum with arousal. She still couldn't believe she had stripped naked and attacked him in his sleep. That was something the old Phoebe might have done. But only if the man in question were Leo. He had the ability to make a woman throw caution to the wind.

She tidied the pile of bedding and smoothed out the wrinkles. Just like a cavewoman preparing for the return of her marauding spouse. It struck her as funny that Leo really had provided food for her. Not by clubbing anything over the head, but still…

Now that he was gone, she felt a bit bashful. She had seen the size of his sex. Wondering how things would fit together made her nipples furl in anticipation.

His return was rapid and startling. From his hand dangled a long strip of connected condom packages. She licked her lips. "I don't think the night is that long."

Dropping down beside her, he bit her shoulder. "Trust me, sweetheart."

He took her chin in his hand, the lock of hair falling across his forehead making him look younger and more carefree. "I'm thinking we'll go hard and fast the first time and then branch out into variations."

As he cupped her breast, her eyelids fluttered shut all of their own accord. Despite the fact that he had paraded nude through the house, his skin was as warm as ever. She burrowed closer. "Merry Christmas to me," she muttered.

"Look at me, Phoebe."

When she obeyed, she saw that every trace of his good humor had fled. His face was no more than planes and angles, painted by firelight to resemble an ancient king. Eyes so dark they appeared black. Still he held her chin. "I'm looking," she quipped with deliberate sass. "What am I supposed to see?" His intensity aroused and agitated her, but she wouldn't let him know how his caveman antics affected her. Not yet.

He flipped her onto her back without warning, her brief fall cushioned by the many-layered pallet. Instead of answering her provocative question, he *showed* her. Kneeling between her thighs, he yanked a single packet free, ripped it open with his teeth and extracted the contents. Making sure she watched him—by the simple expedient of locking her gaze to his—he rolled the condom over his straining erection.

She doubted he meant for her to see him wince. But the evidence of his arousal lit a fire low in her belly. Leo was in pain. Because of her. He wanted her so badly his hands were shaking. That meant he was more vulnerable than she had imagined. And knowing she was not the only one falling apart calmed her nerves.

Clearly, Leo did not see her as one in a line of faceless women. Whatever their differences in lifestyle, or world view, or even sexual experience, tonight was special.

She grabbed his wrist. “Tell me what you’re going to do to me.” She breathed the words on a moan as his legs tangled with hers and he positioned the head of his sex at her opening.

Still he didn’t smile. His expression was a mask of frayed control…jaw clenched, teeth ground together. “I’m going to take you, my sweet. To heaven and back.”

At the first push of his rigid length, she lost her breath. Everything in the room stood still. Her body strained to accommodate him. Though she was more than ready, she had been celibate a long time, and Leo was a big man.

He paused, though the effort brought beads of perspiration to his forehead. “Too much?” he asked, his voice raw.

“No.” She concentrated on relaxing, though everything inside her seemed wound tight. “I want all of you.”

Her declaration made him shudder as though the mental picture was more stimulating than the actual joining of their flesh. Steadily, he forced his way in. Phoebe felt his penetration in every inch of her soul. She knew in that instant that she had been deceiving herself. Leo was more than a mere fling. He was the man who could make her live again.

When he was fully seated, he withdrew with a hoarse shout and slammed into her, making her grab the leg of the coffee table as a brace. “I don’t want to hurt you,” he rasped.

“Then don’t stop, Leo. I can handle whatever you have to give.”

Sixteen

Leo was out of control. In some sane corner of his mind, he knew it. But Phoebe…God, Phoebe…she milked the length of him every time he withdrew, and on the downstroke arched her back, taking him a centimeter deeper with each successive thrust.

Her legs had his waist in a vise. Her cloud of night-dark hair fanned out around them. He buried his face in it at one point, stilling his frantic motions, desperately trying to stave off his release. She smelled amazing. Though he couldn't pinpoint the fragrance, he would have recognized her scent in a pitch-black room.

Her fingernails dug into his back. He relished the stinging discomfort…found his arousal ratcheting up by a degree each time she cried out his name and marked his flesh.

But nothing prepared him for the feel of her climax as she tightened on his shaft and came apart in release. He held her close, feeling the aftershocks that quivered in her sex like endless ripples of sensation.

When he knew she was at peace, he lost it. Slamming into her without finesse or reason, he exploded in a white-hot flash of lust. He lost a few seconds in the aftermath, his mouth dry and his head pounding.

Barely conscious, he tried to spare her most of his weight. He had come twice in quick succession, and his brain was muddled, incredulous that he wanted her still.

Phoebe stirred restlessly. "We should get some sleep." Her words were barely audible, but he caught the inference.

No way. She wasn't leaving him. No way in hell. Rolling onto his side, he scooped her close, spooning her with a murmur of satisfaction. Though her soft bottom pressed into the cradle of his thighs, his arousal was a faint whisper after two incredible climaxes. The need he felt was more than physical.

Her head pillowed on his arm, he slept.

He couldn't mark the moment consciousness returned, but he knew at once that he was alone. Sunlight peeked in around the edges of the drapes, the reflection strangely bright. He could hear the furnace running, and although the fire had long since burned out, he was plenty warm.

Sitting up with a groan, he felt muscle twinges that came from a night of carnal excess. Thinking about it made him hard. He cursed, well aware that any repeat of last night's sexual calisthenics was hours in the future.

Phoebe had put away all the bedding she had used on the sofa. But on the kitchen counter he saw a pot of coffee steaming. He stood up, feeling as if he'd been on a weekend bender. Grabbing his robe that had gotten wedged beneath the edge of the sofa, he slid his arms into the sleeves and zeroed in on the life-saving caffeine.

After two cups he was ready to go in search of his landlady. He found her and Teddy curled up on Phoebe's bed reading books. She sat up when she saw him, her smile warm but perhaps tinged with reserve. "I hope we didn't wake you."

He put his hands on top of the door frame and stretched

hard, feeling the muscles loosen bit by bit. "I didn't hear a thing. Has he been up long?"

"An hour maybe. I gave him his bottle in here."

They were conversing like strangers. Or perhaps a married couple with nothing much to say.

He sat down on the edge of the bed and took her hand. "Good morning, Phoebe."

Hot color flushed her cheeks and reddened her throat. "Good morning."

He dragged her closer for a scorching kiss. "It sure as hell is."

That surprised a laugh from her, and immediately he felt her relax. "Have you looked outside?" she asked.

He shook his head. "No. Why? Did it snow?"

She nodded. "We got three or four inches. Buford's grandson will plow the driveway by midmorning. I know you were expecting some deliveries."

Shock immobilized him. It had been hours since he had checked his email on Phoebe's phone or even sent his brother a text. Never in his adult life could he remember going so long without his electronic lifelines. Yet with Phoebe, tucked away from the world, he had gradually begun to accept the absence of technology as commonplace.

Not that she was really rustic in her situation. She had phones and television. But beyond that, life was tech-free. He frowned, not sure he was comfortable with the knowledge that she had converted him in a matter of days. It was the sex. That's all. He'd been pleasantly diverted. Didn't mean he wanted to give up his usual M.O. on a permanent basis.

Smiling to cover his unease, he released her. "I'm going to take a shower. I can play with the kid after that if you want to clean up."

* * *

Phoebe watched him go, her heart troubled. Something was off, but she couldn't pinpoint it. Maybe nothing more than a bad case of *morning after.*

By the time both adults were clean and dressed, the sound of a tractor echoed in the distance. Soon the driveway was passable, and in no time at all, vehicles began arriving. A truck dealing with Leo's satellite internet. The express delivery service with his new phone. A large moving van that somehow managed to turn and back up to the damaged cabin.

With the felled tree completely gone now, a small army of men began carrying out everything salvageable to place into storage until the repairs were complete. Leo didn't even linger for breakfast. He was out the door in minutes, wading into the midst of chaos…coordinating, instructing, and generally making himself indispensable. Phoebe wasn't sure what she would have done without his help. If she had not been laden with the responsibility of Teddy, she would have managed just fine. But caring for a baby and trying to deal with the storm damage at the same time would have made things extremely difficult.

She was amazed that she could see a difference in the baby in two weeks. He was growing so quickly and his personality seemed more evident every day. This morning he was delighting himself by blowing bubbles and babbling nonsense sounds.

After tidying the kitchen, Phoebe picked him up out of his high chair and carried him over to the tree. "See what Leo and I did, Teddy? Isn't it pretty?" The baby reached for an ornament, and she tucked his hand to her cheek. "I know. It isn't fair to have so many pretty baubles and none of them for you to play with."

Teddy grabbed a strand of her hair that had escaped her braid and yanked. She'd been in a hurry that morning after her shower and had woven her hair in its usual style with less than her usual precision. It was beginning to be clear to her why so many young mothers had simple hairstyles. Caring for an infant didn't leave much time for primping.

In another half hour Teddy would be ready for a nap. Already his eyes were drooping. After last night's excess, Phoebe might try to sneak in a few minutes of shut-eye herself. Thinking about Leo made her feel all bubbly inside. Like a sixteen-year-old about to go to prom with her latest crush.

Even in the good days with her fiancé, sex had never been like that. Leo had devoted himself to her pleasure, proving to her again and again that she had more to give and receive. Her body felt sensitized…energized…eager to try it all over again.

She walked the baby around the living room, humming Christmas carols, feeling happier than she had felt in a long time.

When the knock sounded at the front door, she looked up in puzzlement. Surely Leo hadn't locked himself out. She had made sure to leave the catch undone when he left. Before she could react, the door opened and a familiar head appeared.

"Dana!" Phoebe eyed her sister with shock and dismay. "What's wrong? Why are you here?"

Leo jogged back to the cabin. He was starving, but more than that, he wanted to see Phoebe. He didn't want to give her time to think of a million reasons why they shouldn't be together. When he burst through the front door, he ground to a halt, immediately aware that he had walked into a tense situation. He'd seen an unfamiliar car outside, but hadn't paid much attention, assuming it belonged to one of the workmen.

Phoebe's eyes met his across the room. For a split second, he saw into her very soul. Her anguish seared him, but the moment passed, and now her expression seemed normal. She smiled at him. "You're just in time. My sister, Dana, arrived unexpectedly. Dana, this is Leo."

He shook hands with the other woman and tried to analyze the dynamic that sizzled in the room. Dana was a shorter, rounder version of her sister. At the moment, she seemed exhausted and at the point of tears.

Phoebe held Teddy on her hip. "What are you doing here, Dana? Why didn't you let me know you were coming? I would have picked you up at the airport. You look like you haven't slept in hours."

Dana plopped onto the sofa and burst into tears, her hands over her face. "I knew you would try to talk me out of it," she sobbed. "I know it's stupid. I've been on a plane for hours, and I have to be back on a flight at two. But I couldn't spend Christmas without my baby. I thought I could, but I can't."

Leo froze, realizing at once what was happening. Phoebe…dear, beautiful, strong Phoebe put whatever feelings she had aside and went to sit beside her sister. "Of course you can't. I understand. Dry your eyes and take your son." She handed Teddy over to his mother as though it were the most natural thing in the world.

Leo knew it was breaking her heart.

Dana's face when she hugged her baby to her chest would have touched even the most hardened cynic. She kissed the top of his head, nuzzling the soft, fuzzy hair. "We found a lady in the village who speaks a little English. She's agreed to look after him while we work."

Phoebe clasped her hands in her lap as if she didn't know what to do with them. "How are things going with your father-in-law's estate?"

Dana made a face. "It's a mess. Worse than we thought. So stressful. The house is chock-full of junk. We have to go through it all so we don't miss anything valuable. I know it doesn't make sense to take Teddy over there, but if I can just have him in the evenings and be able to see him during the day when we take breaks, I know I'll feel so much better."

Phoebe nodded. "Of course you will."

Dana grabbed her sister's wrist. "You don't know how much we love you and appreciate all you've done for Teddy. I have an extra ticket on standby if you want to come back with me…or even in a day or two. I don't want you to be alone at Christmas, especially because it was that time of year when you lost—" She clapped her hand over her mouth, her expression horrified. "Oh, God, honey. I'm sorry. I'm exhausted and I don't know what I'm saying. I didn't mean to mention it."

Phoebe put an arm around the frazzled woman and kissed her cheek. "Take a deep breath, Dana. Everything's fine. I'm fine. If you're really on such a time crunch, let's start packing up Teddy's things. He'll nap in the car while you drive."

Phoebe paused in the back hallway, leaning against the wall and closing her eyes. Her smile felt frozen in place. Leo wasn't fooled. She could see his concern. But the important thing was for Dana not to realize what her unexpected arrival had done to Phoebe's plans for a cozy Christmas.

In less than an hour from start to finish, Dana came and went, taking Teddy with her. The resultant silence was painful. The only baby items left behind were the high chair in the kitchen and the large pieces of furniture in Teddy's room. Without asking, Leo took the high chair, put it in with the other stuff and shut the door. Phoebe watched him, her heart in pieces at her feet.

When he returned, she wrapped her arms around her

waist, her mood as flat as a three-day-old helium balloon. "I knew he wasn't my baby."

"Of course you did."

Leo's unspoken compassion took her close to an edge she didn't want to face. "Don't be nice to me or I may fall apart."

He grinned, taking her in his arms and resting his cheek on her head. "I'm very proud of you, Phoebe."

"For what?"

"For being such a good sister and aunt. For not making Dana feel guilty. For doing what had to be done."

"I was looking forward to Christmas morning," she whispered, her throat tight with unshed tears. "His presents are all wrapped." She clung to Leo, feeling his warm presence like a balm to her hurting spirit.

He squeezed her shoulders. "I have an idea to cheer you up."

She pulled back to look at him, only slightly embarrassed that her eyes were wet. "Having recently participated in some of your ideas, I'm listening," she said.

He wiped the edge of her eye with his thumb. "Get your mind out of the gutter, Ms. Kemper. I wanted to propose a trip."

"But you just arrived."

Putting a finger over her lips, he drew her to the sofa and sat down with her, tucking her close to his side. "Let me get it all out before you interrupt."

Phoebe nodded. "Okay."

"You asked me earlier about my plans for Christmas, and I had pretty much decided to stay here with you and Teddy. But I did feel a twinge of sadness and guilt to be missing some things back home. This weekend is the big Cavallo Christmas party for all our employees and their families. We have it at Luc's house. I'd like you to go with me."

She opened her mouth to speak, but he shushed her.

"Hear me out," he said. "I have an older friend who retired from Cavallo ten years ago, but he likes to keep busy. So now and again when the need arises, he does jobs for me. I know he would jump at the chance to come up here and oversee your cabin renovation. I trust him implicitly. He could stay in my room if it's okay with you. What do you think?"

"So I'm allowed to speak now?" She punched his ribs.

He inclined his head. "You have my permission."

"Where would *I* stay?"

"You mean in Atlanta?"

She nodded. "Yes."

"I was hoping you'd be at my place. But I can put you up at a nice hotel if you'd rather do that."

She scooted onto his lap, facing him, her hands on his shoulders. "But what about all my decorations and the tree?"

He pursed his lips. "Well, we could replicate the ambience at my place. You *do* like decorating. But I was also thinking that maybe you and I could come back here in time for Christmas Eve. Just the two of us. I know it won't be the same without Teddy, so if that's a bad idea, you can say so."

Seventeen

Leo held his breath, awaiting her answer. The fact that she felt comfortable enough with him to be sitting as she was reassured him. Last night a noticeable dynamic between them had shifted. She felt a part of him now. In ways he couldn't quite explain.

It had killed him to know she was so hurt this morning. Yet in the midst of her pain, she had handled herself beautifully, never once letting her sister realize how much Phoebe had been counting on Christmas with her nephew. By Phoebe's own admission, this was the first time in three years she had felt like celebrating. Yet when everything seemed to be going her way, she was blindsided by disappointment and loss.

Not a tragedy or a permanent loss, but deeply hurtful nevertheless.

Phoebe ran her fingers across his scalp, both hands… messing up his hair deliberately. "Do I have to decide now?"

"You mean about Christmas Eve?"

"Yes."

"I think that can wait. But does that mean you'll go with me?"

"I suppose I'll need a fancy dress." She traced the outer edges of his ears, making him squirm restlessly.

"Definitely. Is that a problem?" Holding her like this was a torment he could do without at the moment. He heard too much activity going on outside to be confident of no interruptions. When she slid a hand inside his shirt collar, he shivered. His erection was trapped uncomfortably beneath her denim-clad butt.

"No problem at all," she said breezily, unfastening the top two buttons of his shirt. "I have a whole closet full of nice things from my gainfully employed days."

"Define nice…."

She kissed him softly, sliding her tongue into his mouth and making him crazy. "Backless," she whispered. "Not much of a front. Slit up the leg. How does that sound?"

He groaned. "Lord, have mercy." He wasn't sure if he was talking about the dress or about the way her nimble fingers were moving down his chest. "Phoebe," he said, trying to sound more reasonable and less desperate. "Was that a *yes?*"

She cupped his face in her hands, her expression suddenly sweet and intense. "Thank you, Leo. You've saved Christmas for me. As hard as it was to say goodbye to little Teddy, you're the only other male of my acquaintance who could make me want to enjoy the season. So yes. I'd love to go with you to Atlanta."

He had to talk fast, but he managed to convince her they should leave that afternoon. Already he was fantasizing about making love to her in his comfy king-size bed. Last night's spontaneous lunacy had been mind-blowing, but there was something to be said for soft sheets and a firm mattress. Not to mention the fact that he wanted to wine and dine her and show her that the big city had its own appeal.

When she finally emerged from her bedroom, he stared.

Phoebe had one large suitcase, two smaller ones and a garment bag.

He put his hands on his hips, cocking his head. "You did understand that this was a *brief* visit…right?"

She was hot and flushed and wisps of hair stood out from her head like tiny signals saying, *Don't mess with me!* Dumping the bags at his feet, she wiped her forehead with the back of her hand. "I want to be prepared for any eventuality."

He nudged the enormous bag with his toe. "The NASA astronauts weren't *this* prepared," he joked. But inside he was pleased that the sparkle was back in her eyes. "Anything else I should know about? You do know I drive a Jag."

Phoebe smiled sweetly. "We could take my van."

He shuddered theatrically. "Leo Cavallo has a reputation to uphold. No, thank you."

While Phoebe went through the cabin turning off lights and putting out fresh sheets and towels, Leo studied the phone he had ordered. No point in taking it with him. He would only need it if he came back. If. Where had that thought come from? His reservation was fixed until the middle of January with a possible two-week extension.

Simply because he and Phoebe were going to make an appearance at the Christmas party didn't mean that his doctor and Luc were going to let him off the hook. He was painfully aware that he still hadn't told Phoebe the truth. And the reasons were murky.

But one thing stood out. Vanity. He didn't want her to see him as weak or broken. It was a hell of a thing to admit. But would she think of him differently once she knew?

By the time the car was loaded and they had dropped off the keys at Buford's house, Leo was starving. In blissful disregard of the calendar date, Phoebe had packed a picnic. To eat in the car, she insisted.

Instead of the way he had come in before, Phoebe suggested another route. "If you want to, we can take the scenic route, up over the mountains to Cherokee, North Carolina, and then we'll drop south to Atlanta from there. The road was closed by a landslide for a long time, but they've reopened it."

"I'm game," he said. "At least this time it will be daylight."

Phoebe giggled, tucking her legs into the car and waiting for him to shut the door. "You were so grumpy that night."

"I thought I was never going to get here. The rain and the fog and the dark. I was lucky I didn't end up nose deep in the creek."

"It wasn't that bad."

He shook his head, refusing to argue the point. Today's drive, though, was the complete opposite of his introduction to Phoebe's home turf. Sun shone down on them, warming the temperatures nicely. The winding two-lane highway cut through the quaint town of Gatlinburg and then climbed the mountain at a gentle grade. The vistas were incredible. He'd visited here once as a child, but it had been so long ago he had forgotten how peaceful the Smokies were… and how beautiful.

The trip flew by. Part of the time they talked. At other moments, they listened to music, comparing favorite artists and arguing over the merits of country versus pop. If driving to Tennessee had initially seemed like a punishment, today was entirely the opposite. He felt unreasonably lucky and blessed to be alive.

As they neared the city, he felt his pulse pick up. This was where he belonged. He and Luc had built something here, something good. But what if the life he knew and loved wasn't right for Phoebe?

Was it too soon to wonder such a thing?

All day he had been hyperaware of her…the quick flash of her smile, her light flowery scent, the way she moved her hands when she wanted to make a point. He remained in a state of constant semi-arousal. Now that they were almost at their destination, he found himself subject to a surprising agitation.

What if Phoebe didn't like his home?

She was silent as they pulled into the parking garage beneath his downtown high-rise building and slowed to a halt beside the kiosk. "Hey, Jerome," he said, greeting the stoop-shouldered, balding man inside the booth with a smile. "This is where we get out, Phoebe." He turned back to Jerome. "Do you mind asking one of the boys to unload the car and bring up our bags?"

"Not at all, Mr. Cavallo. We'll get them right up."

Leo took Phoebe's elbow and steered her toward the elevator, where he used his special key to access and press the penthouse button. "Jerome's a retired army sergeant. He runs this place with an iron fist."

Phoebe clutched her purse, her expression inscrutable. Because the video camera in this tiny space was recording everything they said, Leo refrained from personal chitchat. He preferred to keep his private life private.

Upstairs, they stepped out into his private hallway. He generally took the recessed lighting and sophisticated decor for granted, but Phoebe looked around with interest. Once inside, he tossed his keys on a console table and held out a hand. "Would you like the tour?"

Phoebe felt like Alice in Wonderland. To go from her comfortable though modest cabin to this level of luxury was the equivalent of situational whiplash. She had realized on an intellectual level that Leo must be wealthy. Though she hadn't known him personally before he arrived on her doorstep, she was well aware of the Cavallo empire and the pricey goods it offered to high-end consumers. But somehow, she hadn't fully understood *how* rich Leo really was.

The floors of his penthouse condo, acres of them it seemed, were laid in cream-colored marble veined with gold. Expensive Oriental rugs in hues of cinnamon and deep azure bought warmth and color to what might otherwise have been too sterile a decorating scheme.

Incredible artwork graced the walls. Some of the paintings, to Phoebe's inexperience gaze, appeared to be priceless originals. Two walls of the main living area were made entirely of glass, affording an unparalleled view of Atlanta as far as the eye could see. Everything from the gold leaf–covered dome of the Capitol building to the unmistakable outline of Stone Mountain in the far distance.

A variety of formal armchairs and sofas were upholstered in either pale gold velvet or ecru leather. Crimson and navy pillows beckoned visitors to sit and relax. Overhead, a massive modern chandelier splayed light to all corners of the room.

Undoubtedly, all of the fabrics were of Italian Cavallo design. Phoebe, who had always adored vivid color and strong statements in decor, fell in love with Leo's home immediately. She turned in a circle. "I'm speechless. Should I take off my shoes?"

He stepped behind her, his hands on her shoulders. Pushing aside her hair, left loose for a change, he kissed her neck just below her ear. "It's meant to be lived in. May I say how glad I am that you're here?"

She turned to face him, wondering if she really knew him at all. At her old job, she had earned a comfortable living. But in comparison to all this, she was a pauper. How did Leo know she was not interested in him for his money? Unwilling to disclose her unsettling thoughts, she linked her arms around his neck. "Thank you for inviting me."

She tugged at his bottom lip with the pad of her thumb. "Surely there are bedrooms I should see."

His eyes darkened. "I didn't want to rush you."

Her hand brushed the front of his trousers. "I've noticed this fellow hanging around all day."

The feel of her slim fingers, even through the fabric of his pants, affected him like an electric shock. "Seems to be a permanent condition around you."

"Then I suppose it's only fair if I offer some…um…"

His grin was a wicked flash of white teeth. "While you're thinking of the appropriate word, my sweet," Leo said, scooping her into his arms, "I could show you my etchings."

She tweaked his chin. "Not in here, I presume?"

"Down the hall." He held her close to his chest, his muscular arms bearing her weight as if she were no more than a child.

Being treated like Scarlett O'Hara seemed entirely appropriate here in the Peach State. Leo's power and strength seduced her almost as much as the memory of last night's erotic play. "The sofa is closer," she whispered, noting the shadow of his stubble and the way his golden-skinned throat moved when he spoke huskily.

He nodded his head, hunger darkening his eyes. "I like the way you think." He kissed her cheek as he strode across the room.

"No one knows you're home, right?"

"Correct."

"And there's no one else on this floor?"

He shook his head, lowering her onto the soft cushions. "No."

"So I can be as loud as I like?"

He stared at her in shock as her outrageous taunt sank in. "Good God Almighty." Color crept from his throat to his hairline. "I thought you were a sweet young thing when I first met you. But apparently I was wrong."

"Never judge a book by its cover, Mr. Cavallo." She ripped her sweater off over her head. "Please tell me you have some more of those packets."

Leo seemed fixated on the sight of her lace-covered breasts, but he recovered. "Damn it." His expression leaned toward desperation.

"What's wrong?"

"All of our luggage is downstairs."

"Your bathroom. Here?"

"Well, yes, but somebody will be coming up that elevator any moment now."

"Leo..." she wailed, not willing to wait another second. "Call them back. Tell them we're in the shower."

"Both of us?" He glanced at the door and back at her, frustration a living, breathing presence between them. An impressive erection tented his slacks. "It won't be long. Fifteen minutes tops."

The way she felt at the moment, five minutes was too long. She wanted Leo. Now.

Fortunately for both of them, a quiet chime sounded, presumably a doorbell, though it sounded more like a heavenly harp. Leo headed for the entrance and stared back at her. "You planning on staying like that?"

Her jaw dropped. She was half naked and the doorknob was turning in Leo's hand. With a squeak, she clutched her sweater to her breasts and ran around the nearest wall, which happened to conceal the kitchen. Not even bothering to envy the fabulous marble countertops and fancy appliances, she listened with bated breath as Leo conversed with the bellman. At long last, she heard the door close, and the sound of footsteps.

As she hovered amidst gourmet cookware and the scent of unseen spices, Leo appeared. “He’s gone.” In his hand he held a stack of condoms. “Is this what you wanted?”

Eighteen

Leo had never particularly considered his kitchen to be a sexy place. In truth, he spent little time here. But with Phoebe loitering half naked, like a nymph who had lost her way, he suddenly began to see about a zillion possibilities.

He leaned a hip against the counter. “Take off the rest of your clothes.” Would she follow his lead, or had he come on too strong?

When perfect white teeth mutilated her bottom lip, he couldn’t decide if she was intending to drive him crazy by delaying or if she was perhaps now a bit shy. Without responding verbally, she tugged off her knee-length boots and removed her trim black slacks. The only article of clothing that remained, her tiny panties, was a perfect match to her blush-pink bra.

“The floor is cold,” she complained as she kicked aside the better part of her wardrobe.

His hands clenched the edge of the counter behind him. Lord, she was a handful. And gorgeous to boot. “You’re not done,” he said with far more dispassion than he felt.

Phoebe thrust out her bottom lip and straightened her shoulders. “I don’t know why you have to be so bossy.”

“Because you like it.” He could see the excitement building in her wide-eyed stare as she reached behind her back and unfastened her bra. It fell to the floor like a wispy pink cloud. Though she hesitated for a brief moment, she continued disrobing, stepping out of her small undies with all the grace of a seasoned stripper.

She twirled the panties on the end of her finger. "Come and get me."

He literally saw red. His vision hazed and he felt every molecule of moisture leach from his mouth. Quickly, with razor-sharp concentration that belied the painful ache in his groin, he assessed the possibilities. Beside the refrigerator, some genius architect had thought to install a desk that matched the rest of the kitchen. The marble top was the perfect height for what Leo had in mind.

Forget the sofa or the bedroom or any other damned part of his house. He was going to take her here.

He could barely look at Phoebe without coming apart at the seams. Young and strong and healthy, she was the epitome of womanhood. Her dark hair fell over one shoulder, partially veiling one raspberry nipple. "You're beautiful, Phoebe."

The raw sincerity in his strained voice must have told her that the time for games was over. Surprised pleasure warmed her eyes. "I'm glad you think so." She licked her lips. "Do you plan on staying over there forever?"

"I don't know," he said in all seriousness. "The way I feel at the moment, I'm afraid I'll take you like a madman."

Her lips curved. "Is that a bad thing?"

"You tell me." Galvanized at last into action by a yearning that could no longer be denied, he picked her up by the waist and sat her on the desk. Phoebe yelped when the cold surface made contact with her bottom, but she exhaled on a long, deep sigh as the sensation subsided.

He ripped at his zipper and freed his sex. He was as hard as the marble that surrounded them, but far hotter. Sheathing himself with fumbling hands, he stepped between her legs. "Prop your feet on the desk, honey."

Phoebe's cooperation was instant, though her eyes rounded when she realized what he was about to do.

He positioned himself at the opening of her moist pink sex and shoved, one strong thrust that took him all the way. He held her bottom for leverage and moved slowly in and out. Phoebe's arms linked around his neck in a stranglehold. Her feet lost their purchase and instead, she linked her ankles behind his waist.

It would be embarrassing if she realized that his legs were trembling and his heart was doing weird flips and flops that had nothing to do with his recent health event. Phoebe made him forget everything he thought was important and forced him to concentrate on the two of them. Not from any devious machinations on her part, but because she was so damned cute and fun.

Even as he moved inside her, he was already wondering where they could make love next. Heat built in his groin, a monstrous, unstoppable force. "I'm gonna come," he groaned.

She had barely made a sound. In sudden dismay, he leaned back so he could see her face. "Talk to me, Phoebe." Reaching down, he rubbed gently at the swollen nub he'd been grazing again and again with the base of his sex. When his fingers made one last pass, Phoebe arched her back and cried out as she climaxed. Inside, her body squeezed him with flutters that threatened to take off the top of his head because the feeling was so intense.

With his muscles clenched from head to toe, he held back his own release so he could relish every moment of her shuddering finale. As she slumped limp in his embrace, he cursed and thrust wildly, emptying himself until he was wrung dry. With one last forceful thrust, he finished, but as he did, his forehead met the edge of the cabinet over Phoebe's head with enough force to make him stagger backward.

"Hell..." His reverse momentum was halted by the large island in the center of the kitchen. He leaned there, dazed.

Phoebe slid to her feet. "Oh, Leo. You're bleeding." Her face turned red, and she burst out laughing. Mortification and remorse filled her eyes in addition to concern, but she apparently couldn't control her mirth, despite the fact that he had been injured in battle.

Okay. So it *was* a little funny. His lips quirking, he put a hand to his forehead and winced when it came away streaked in red. "Would you please put some clothes on?" he said, trying not to notice the way her breasts bounced nicely when she laughed.

Phoebe rolled her eyes. "Take them off. Put them on. You're never satisfied."

He looked down at his erection that was already preparing for duty. "Apparently not." When she bent over to step into her underwear and pants, it was all he could do not to take her again.

Only the throbbing in his head held him back. When she was decent, he grimaced. "We're going to a party tomorrow night. How am I going to explain this?"

Phoebe took his hand and led him toward the bedrooms. "Which one is yours?" she asked. When he pointed, she kept walking, all the way to his hedonistic bathroom. "We'll put some antibiotic ointment on it between now and then. Plus, there's always makeup."

"Great. Just great."

She opened the drawer he indicated and gathered the needed supplies. "Sit on the stool."

He zipped himself back into his trousers, more to avoid temptation than from any real desire to be dressed. "Is this going to hurt?"

"Probably."

The truth was the truth. When she moistened a cotton ball with antiseptic and dabbed at the cut, it stung like fire. He glanced in the mirror. The gash, more of a deep scrape really, was about two inches long. And dead in the center of his forehead. Now, every time he saw his reflection for the next week or so, all he would remember was debauching Phoebe in his kitchen.

She smeared a line of medicated cream along the wound and tried covering it with two vertical Band-Aids. Now he looked like Frankenstein.

Their eyes met in the large mahogany-framed mirror. Phoebe put a hand over her mouth. "Sorry," she mumbled. But she was shaking all over, and he wasn't fooled. Her mirth spilled out in wet eyes and muffled giggles.

"Thank God you didn't go into nursing," he groused. He stood up and reached for a glass of water to down some ibuprofen. "Are you hungry, by any chance?" The kitchen episode had left him famished. Maybe it was the subliminal message in his surroundings.

Phoebe wiped her eyes and nodded. "That picnic food was a long time ago."

"In that case, let me show you to your room and you can do whatever you need to do to get ready. The place I want to take you is intimate, but fairly casual. You don't really have to change if you don't want to. But I'll drag your three dozen suitcases in there to be on the safe side."

Phoebe wasn't sure what to think about the opulent suite that was apparently hers for the duration of her visit. It was amazing, of course. Yards of white carpet. French country furniture in distressed white wood. A heavy cotton bedspread that had been hand embroidered with every wildflower in the world. And a bathroom that rivaled Leo's. But in truth, she had thought she would be sleeping with him.

Nevertheless, when Leo disappeared, she wasted no time

in getting ready. She took a quick shower, though she made sure to keep her hair dry. It had grown dramatically in three years, far longer than she had ever worn it. Once wet, it was a pain to dry. She brushed it quickly and bound it loosely at the back of her neck with a silver clasp.

Given Leo's description of their destination, she chose black tights and black flats topped with a flirty black skirt trimmed at the hem in three narrow layers of multicolored chiffon. With a hot-pink silk chemise and a waist-length black sweater, she looked nice, but not too over-the-top.

She had forgotten how much fun it was to dress up for a date. Fastening a silver chain around her neck, she fingered the charm that dangled from it. The letter *P* was engraved on the silver disc in fancy cursive script. Her mother's name had started with the same letter as Phoebe's. And Phoebe had decided that if her baby was a girl, she wanted to name her Polly. An old-fashioned name maybe, but one she loved.

It was hard to imagine ever being pregnant again. Would she be terrified the entire nine months? The doctor had insisted there was no reason her next pregnancy shouldn't be perfectly normal. But it would be hard, so hard, not to worry.

Pregnancy was a moot point now. There was no man in her life other than Leo. And the two of them had known each other for no time at all. Even if the relationship were serious—which it definitely was not—Leo wasn't interested in having kids. It hadn't been difficult to pick up on that.

He clearly loved his niece and nephew, and he had been great with Teddy. But he was not the kind of guy to settle for home and hearth. Running the Cavallo conglomerate required most of his devotion. He loved it. Was proud of it. And at the level of responsibility he carried, having any substantive personal life would be tricky.

His brother, Luc, seemed to have mastered the art of balance, from what Leo had said. But maybe Luc wasn't quite as single-mindedly driven as his intense brother.

When she was content with her appearance, she returned to the living room. Leo was standing in front of the expanse of glass, his hands clasped behind his back. He turned when he heard her footsteps. "That was quick."

He looked her over from head to toe. "I'll be the envy of every guy in the restaurant."

She smiled, crossing the room to him and lightly touching his forehead. "You okay?"

"A little headache, but I'll live. Are you ready?"

She nodded. "Perhaps we should stop by a pharmacy and grab some tiny Band-Aids so you don't scare children."

"Smart-ass." He put an arm around her waist and steered her toward the door.

"I'm serious."

"So am I…."

Nineteen

After a quick stop for medical supplies, they arrived at a small bistro tucked away in the heart of downtown Atlanta. The maître d' recognized Leo and escorted them to a quiet table in the corner. "Mr. Cavallo," he said. "So glad to see you are well."

An odd look flashed across Leo's face. "Thank you. Please keep our visit quiet. I hope to surprise my brother tomorrow."

"At the Christmas party, yes?" The dumpy man with the Italian accent nodded with a smile. "My nephew works in your mail room. He is looking forward to it."

"Tell him to introduce himself if he gets a chance."

Leo held Phoebe's chair as she was seated and then joined her on the opposite side of the table. He handed her a menu. "I have my favorites, but you should take a look. They make everything from scratch, and it's all pretty amazing."

After they ordered, Phoebe cocked her head and stared at him with a smile. "Does everyone in Atlanta know who you are?"

"Hardly. I'm just the guy who writes the checks."

"Modest, but suspect."

"It's true," he insisted. "I'm not a player, if that's what you're thinking."

"You don't have the traditional little black book full of names?"

"My phone is black. And a few of the contacts are women."

"That's not an answer."

"I'll plead the Fifth Amendment."

Phoebe enjoyed the dinner immensely. Leo was wearing a beautiful navy-and-gray tweed blazer with dark slacks. Even battle-scarred, he was the most impressive man in the room. Despite his size, he handled his fragile wineglass delicately, his fingers curled around the stem with care.

Thinking about Leo's light touch made Phoebe almost choke on a bite of veal. When she had drained her water glass and regained her composure, Leo grinned. "I don't know what you were thinking about, but your face is bright red."

"You're the one with the sex injury," she pointed out.

"Fair enough." His lips twitched, and his gaze promised retribution later for her refusal to explain.

On the way home, it started to rain. Phoebe loved the quiet swish of the wipers and the fuzzy glow of Christmas decorations in every window. Leo turned down a side street and parked at the curb. He stared through the windshield, his expression oddly intent, his hands clenched on the steering wheel.

"What is it?" she asked. "What's wrong?"

He glanced at her, eyes hooded. "Nothing's *wrong.* Would you mind if we go up to my office?"

She craned her neck, for the first time seeing the Cavallo name on the building directory. "Of course not." He was acting very strangely.

Leo exited the car, opened an umbrella and came around the car to help her out. Fortunately her shoes were not expensive, because her feet tripped through the edge of a puddle as they accessed the sidewalk.

She shivered while he took a set of keys from his pocket and opened the main door. The plate glass clunked shut behind them. "Over there," Leo said. Again, using his private keys, they entered a glossy-walled elevator.

Phoebe had seen dozens of movies where lovers used a quick ride to sneak a passionate kiss. Leo clearly didn't know the plot, because he leaned against the wall and studied the illuminated numbers as they went higher and higher. Cavallo occupied the top twelve floors.

When they arrived at their destination, Phoebe was not surprised to see all the trappings of an elite twenty-first-century business. A sleek reception area decorated for the season, secretarial cubicles, multiple managerial offices and, at the far end of the floor on which they entered, an imposing door with Leo's name inscribed on a brass panel.

Another key, another entry. They skirted what was obviously the domain of an executive assistant and walked through one last door.

Leo stopped so suddenly, she almost ran into his back. She had a feeling he had forgotten her presence. He moved forward slowly, stopping to run a hand along the edge of what was clearly *his* desk. The top was completely bare, the surface polished to a high sheen.

Leo turned to her suddenly, consternation on his face. "Make yourself comfortable," he said, pointing to a leather chair and ottoman near the window. "That's where I like to sit when I have paperwork to read through. I won't be long."

She did as he suggested, noting that much like his sophisticated home, his place of business, arguably the epicenter of his life, had two transparent walls. The dark, rainy night beyond the thick glass was broken up by a million pinpoints of light, markers of a city that scurried to and fro.

As she sat down and propped her feet on the ottoman,

she relaxed into the soft, expensive seat that smelled of leather and Leo's distinctive aftershave. The faint aroma made her nostalgic suddenly for the memory of curling up with him on her sofa, enjoying the Christmas tree and watching the fire.

Leo prowled, tension in the set of his shoulders. He opened drawers, shuffled papers, flicked the leaves of plants on the credenza. He seemed lost. Or at the very least confused.

Hoping to give him the semblance of privacy, she picked up a book from the small table at her elbow. It was a technical and mostly inaccessible tome about third-world economies. She read the first two paragraphs and turned up her nose. Not exactly escape reading.

Next down the pile was a news magazine. But the date was last month's, and she was familiar with most of the stories. Finally, at the bottom, was a collection of Sunday newspapers. Someone had taken great care to stack them in reverse order. Again, they were out of date, but that same someone had extracted the "Around Town" section of the most recent one and folded it to a story whose accompanying photograph she recognized instantly. It was Leo.

Reading automatically, her stomach clenched and her breathing grew choppy. No. This had to be a mistake.

She stood up, paper in her hand, and stared at him. Disbelief, distress and anger coursed through her veins in a nauseating cocktail. "You had a heart attack?"

Leo froze but turned around to face her, his shoulders stiff and his whole body tensed as if facing an enemy. "Who told you that?"

She threw the paper at him, watching it separate and rain down on the thick pile carpet with barely a sound. "It's right there," she cried, clutching her arms around her waist. Prominent Atlanta Businessman Leo Cavallo, Age 36, Suffers Heart Attack. "My God, Leo. Why didn't you tell me?"

He opened his mouth to speak, but she interrupted him with an appalled groan. "You carried wood for me. And chopped down a tree. I made you drag heavy boxes from the attic. Damn it, Leo, how could you not tell me?"

"It wasn't that big a deal." His expression was blank, but his eyes burned with an emotion she couldn't fathom.

She shivered, her mind a whirl of painful thoughts. He could have died. He could have died. He could have died. And she would never have known him. His humor. His kindness. His incredibly sexy and appealing personality. His big, perfect body.

"Trust me," she said slowly. "When a man in his thirties has a heart attack, it's a big freaking deal."

He shoved his hands into his pockets, the line of his mouth grim. "I had a very mild heart attack. A minor blockage. It's a hereditary thing. I'm extraordinarily healthy. All I have to do now is keep an eye on certain markers."

As she examined the days in the past week, things kept popping up, memories that made her feel even worse. "Your father," she whispered. "You said he had a heart attack. And that's why the boat crashed."

"Yes."

"That's it. Just *yes?* Did it ever occur to you when you were screwing me that your medical history was information I might have wanted to know? Hell, Leo, I gave you every intimate detail of my past and you couldn't be bothered to mention something as major as a heart attack?" She knew she was shouting and couldn't seem to stop. Her heart slammed in her chest.

"I've never heard you curse. I don't like it."

"Well, that's just too damn bad." She stopped short, appalled that she was yelling like a shrew. Hyperventilation threatened. "That's why you came to my cabin, isn't it? I thought maybe you'd had a bad case of the flu. Or complications from pneumonia. Or even, God forbid, a mental breakdown of some sort. But a heart attack…" Her legs gave out, and she sank back into the chair, feeling disappointed and angry and, beneath it all, so scared for him. "Why didn't you tell me, Leo? Why couldn't you trust me with the truth? Surely I deserved that much consideration."

But then it struck her. He hadn't shared the intimate details of his illness with her because she didn't matter. The bitter realization sat like a stone in her stomach. Leo had kept his secrets, because when all was said and done, Phoebe was nothing more than a vacation romance of sorts. Leo wasn't serious about any kind of a future with her. He fully planned to return to his old life and take up where he left off. As soon as his doctor gave permission.

He came to her then, sat on the ottoman and put a hand on her leg. "It wasn't something I could easily talk about, Phoebe. Try to understand that. I was a young man. One minute I was standing in a room, doing my job, and the next I couldn't breathe. Strangers were rushing me out to an ambulance. It was a hellish experience. All I wanted to do was forget."

"But you didn't want to come to the mountains."

"No. I didn't. My doctor, who happens to be a good friend, and my brother, who I consider my *best* friend, gave me no choice. I was supposed to learn how to control my stress levels."

She swallowed, wishing he wasn't touching her. The warmth of his hand threatened to dissolve the fragile hold she had on her emotions. "We had *sex,* Leo. To me, that's pretty intimate. But I can see in retrospect that I was just a piece of your convalescent plan, not dictated by your doctor friend, I'm sure. Did it even cross your mind to worry about *that?*"

He hesitated, and she knew she had hit a nerve.

She saw him swallow. He ran a hand through his hair, unintentionally betraying his agitation. "The first time I was with you…in that way, I hadn't had sex since my heart attack. And to be honest, not for several months before that. Do you want me to tell you I was scared shitless? Is that going to make you feel better?"

She knew it was the nature of men to fear weakness. And far worse was having someone witness that vulnerability. So she even understood his angry retort to some extent. But that didn't make her any less despairing. "You haven't taken any of this seriously, have you, Leo? You think you're invincible and that your exile to Tennessee was just a momentary inconvenience. Do you even want to change your ways?" Coming to the office tonight said louder than words what he was thinking.

"It's not that easy."

"Nothing important ever is," she whispered, her throat almost too tight for speech. She stood up and went to the window, blinking back tears. If he couldn't admit that he needed a life outside of work, and if he couldn't be honest with himself *or* with her, then he wasn't ready for the kind of relationship she wanted.

In that moment, she knew that any feeble hope she had nurtured for intimacy with Leo, even in the short term, was futile. "May we leave now?" she asked, her emotions at the breaking point. "I'm tired. It's been a long day."

Twenty

Leo knew he had hurt Phoebe. Badly. But for the life of him, he couldn't see a way to fix things. She disappeared into her room as soon as they got home from his office. The next day, they barely spoke. He fooled around on the internet and watched MSNBC and CNN, particularly the financial pundits.

Being in his office last night had unsettled him. The room had been cold and clinically clean, as if the last occupant had died and the desk was awaiting a new owner.

Somehow he'd thought he might get some kind of revelation about his life if he could stand where he'd once stood. As though in the very air itself he would be able to make sense of it all.

If he had gone straight home from the restaurant, he and Phoebe would no doubt have spent the night in bed dreaming up one way after another to lose themselves in pleasure.

Instead, his impulsive action had ruined everything.

He didn't blame her for being upset. But if he had it to do over again, he still wouldn't have told her about his heart attack. It wasn't the kind of news a man shared with the woman he wanted to impress.

And there it was. He wanted to impress Phoebe. With

his intellect, his entrepreneurial success, his life in general. As if by comparison she could and would see that her hermitlike retreat was not valid. That she was the one with lessons to learn.

As he remembered his brief time in Phoebe's magical mountain home, suddenly, everything clicked into focus. The reason his office had seemed sterile and empty last night was not because Leo had been gone for several weeks. The odd feelings he had experienced were a reluctant recognition of the difference between his work domain and the warm, cheerful home Phoebe had created.

In the midst of her pain and heartbreak, she hadn't become a bitter, angry woman. Instead, she had stretched her wings. She'd had the courage to step out in faith, trusting that she would find the answers she needed. Her solitude and new way of life had taught her valuable lessons about what was important. And she'd been willing to share her wisdom with Leo. But he had been too arrogant to accept that her experience could in any way shed light on his own life.

What a jackass he had been. He had lied to her by omission and all along had been patronizing about her simple existence. Instead of protecting his macho pride, he should have been begging her to help him make a new start.

He *needed* to find balance in his life. His brother, Luc, had managed that feat. Surely Leo could follow his example. And even beyond that, Leo needed Phoebe. More than he could ever have thought possible. But by his selfish actions, he had lost her. Perhaps forever. It would take every ounce of genius he possessed to win back her trust.

The magnitude of his failure was humbling. But as long as there was life, there was hope.

At his request, she consented to stay for the party. He knew she had booked a flight home for the following morning, because he had eavesdropped unashamedly at her door while she made the reservation.

When she appeared in the foyer at a quarter 'til seven that evening, his heart stopped. But this time he recognized the interruption. A lightning bolt of passion or lust or maybe nothing more complicated than need shattered his composure.

She wore a dress that many women would avoid for fear they couldn't carry it off. The fabric was red. An intense crimson that spoke for itself. And Phoebe hadn't been teasing when she described it. Cut low in the back and the front and high on the leg, it fit her as if it had been created with exactly her body in mind.

Stiletto heels in matte black leather put her almost on eye level with him. As equals.

Her hair was stunning. She had braided two tiny sections from the front and wound them at her crown. The rest cascaded in a sleek fall halfway down her back. On her right upper arm she wore a three-inch wide hammered silver band. Matching earrings dangled and caught the light.

He cleared his throat. "You look sensational."

"Thank you." Her expression was as remote as the Egyptian queen she resembled.

He had hoped tonight to strengthen the connection between them by showing her a slice of his life. His family. His employees. The way the company was built on trust and integrity. But now there was this chasm between Phoebe and him.

He hated the emotional distance, but he would use their physical attraction to fight back, to get through to her, if he had to. She had accused him of not taking his recovery seriously, but by God, he was serious now. His future hung in the balance. Everything he had worked for up until this point was rendered valueless. Without Phoebe's love and trust, he had nothing.

* * *

Fortunately his brother's home was close…on West Paces Ferry Road, an old and elegant established neighborhood for Atlanta's wealthy and powerful. But Luc and Hattie had made their home warm and welcoming amidst its elegant personality, a place where children could run and play, though little Luc Jr. was still too small for that.

Leo handed the keys of his Jag to the attendant and helped Phoebe out of the car. The college kid's eyes glazed over as he caught a glimpse of Phoebe's long, toned legs. Glaring at the boy, Leo wrapped her faux fur stole around her shoulders and ushered her toward the house.

Every tree and bush on the property had been trimmed in tiny white lights. Fragrant greenery festooned with gold bows wrapped lampposts and wrought-iron porch rails.

Phoebe paused on the steps, taking it all in. "I love this place," she said simply. "It feels like a classy Southern lady."

"Luc and Hattie will probably be at the door greeting their guests, but perhaps we can sit down with them later and catch up." The timing was off. Phoebe was leaving in the morning, and their relationship was dead in the water, but he still wanted her to meet his brother.

As it turned out, Leo was correct. His dashing brother took one look at Leo and wrestled him into a long bear hug that brought tears to Phoebe's eyes. Leo's sister-in-law wore the very same expression as she watched the two men embrace. Both brothers wore classic formal attire, and in their tuxes, they were incredibly dashing, almost like old film stars with their chiseled features.

Luc shook Phoebe's hand as they were introduced. "I wasn't sure Leo was going to come back for the holidays, or even if he should. I'm happy to see he has such a lovely woman looking after him."

Leo's jaw tightened, though his smile remained. "Phoebe's my date, not my nurse."

Phoebe saw from Luc's abashed expression that he knew he had stepped in it. Hattie whispered something in his ear, and he nodded.

Other people crowded in behind them, but Leo lingered for a moment longer. "Can we see the kids?"

Hattie touched his cheek, her smile warm and affectionate. "We have them asleep upstairs with a sitter, but you're welcome to take a peek." She smiled at Phoebe. "Leo dotes on our babies. Lord help us when he has some of his own. I've never known a man with a softer heart."

"Hey," Luc said, looking indignant. "I'm standing right here."

Hattie kissed his cheek. "Don't worry, sweetheart. I'll always love you best."

On the cloud of laughter that followed, Leo and Phoebe moved into the thick of the party. It was soon clear to her that Leo Cavallo was popular and beloved. Despite his reputation as a hard-hitting negotiator in the boardroom, everyone under Luc's roof treated Leo not only with respect, but with genuine caring and concern.

After an hour, though, she sensed that his patience was wearing thin. Perhaps he hadn't anticipated the many questions about his recovery. At any rate, she recognized his growing tension. She hated the unmistakable awkwardness between them as the evening progressed, but despite her hurt, she couldn't stop wanting to help him. Even if he couldn't be hers, she wanted him to be happy.

In a lull between conversations, she touched his arm. "Do you want to go upstairs and see your niece and nephew?"

He nodded, relief in his harried gaze.

Luc and Hattie's home was far different than Leo's, but spectacular in its own right. Phoebe experienced a frisson of envy for the couple who had created such a warm and nurturing family environment. The little girl's room was done in peach and cream with Disney fairies. The baby boy's nursery sported a delightful zoo animal theme.

Leo stroked his nephew's back and spoke to him softly, but he stayed the longest in Deedee's room. His eyes were somber as he watched the toddler sleep. "She's not their biological child, you know. When Hattie's sister died, Hattie took her baby to raise, and then after the wedding, Luc and Hattie adopted her."

"Has your brother been married long?"

"Less than two years. He and Hattie were pretty serious back in college. The relationship didn't work out, but they were lucky enough to find their way back to each other."

Phoebe stared at Leo's bent head as he sat carefully on the corner of the bed and touched his niece's hand. He took her tiny fingers in his and brought them to his lips. It would have been clear to a blind man that Leo was capable of great love and caring. He felt about these two little ones the way Phoebe did about Teddy.

He turned his head suddenly and caught her watching him, probably with her heart in her eyes. "Will you take a walk with me?" he asked gravely.

"Of course."

Tiny flurries of snow danced around them when they exited the back of the house. Leo had retrieved her wrap, but even so, the night was brisk. In the center of the upper terrace a large, tiled fire pit blazed with vigor, casting a small circle of warmth. Other than the old man adding logs now and again, Leo and Phoebe were alone. Apparently no one else was eager to brave the cold.

A wave of sadness, deep and poignant, washed over Phoebe. If only she and Leo had met under other circumstances. No pain and heartache in her past. No devastating illness in his. Just two people sharing a riveting attraction.

They could have enjoyed a sexual relationship that might have grown into something more.

Now, they stood apart, when only twenty-four hours ago, give or take, Leo had been turning her world upside down with his lovemaking. Their recent fight echoed in her mind. She had accused Leo of not wanting to change, but wasn't she just as cowardly? She had gone from one extreme to the other. Workaholic to hermit. Such a radical swing couldn't be considered balance at all.

In the faces of the crowd tonight, she saw more than the bonhomie of the season. She saw a kinship, a trust that came from working side by side. That was what she had given up, and she realized that she missed it. She missed all of it. The hard challenges, the silly celebrations, the satisfaction of a job well done.

So lost in her thoughts was she, that she jumped when Leo took her by the shoulders and turned her to face him. Again, as at her cabin, firelight painted his features. His eyes were dark, unfathomable. "I have a proposition for you, Phoebe, so hear me out before you say anything."

Her hands tightened on her wrap. "Very well." A tiny piece of gravel had found its way into her shoe. And she couldn't feel her toes. But not even a blizzard could have made her walk away.

He released her as though he couldn't speak freely when they were touching. She thought she understood. Passion had flared so hot and so quickly between them when they first met, its veracity was suspect given the length of their acquaintance.

"First of all," he said quietly, "I'm sorry I didn't tell you about the heart attack. It was an ego thing. I didn't want you to think less of me."

"But I…" She bit her lip and stopped, determined to listen as he had requested.

He ran a hand across the back of his neck. "I was angry

and bitter and confused when I met you. I'd spent a week at the hospital, a week here at Luc's, and then to top it all, they exiled me to Tennessee."

"Tennessee is a very nice state," she felt bound to point out.

A tiny smile flickered across his lips. "It's a lovely state, but that's not the point. I looked at you and saw a desirable woman. You had your hang-ups. We all do. But I didn't want you to look too closely at mine. I wanted you to see me as a strong, capable man."

"And I did."

"But you have to admit the truth, Phoebe. Last night in my office. You stared at me and saw something else." The defeat in his voice made her ill with regret.

"You don't understand," she said, willing him to hear her with an open mind. "I was upset, yes. It terrified me that you had been in such a dangerous situation. And I was angry that you didn't trust me enough to share that with me. But it never changed the way I saw you. If you felt that, then you were wrong."

He paced in silence for several long minutes. She wondered if he believed her. Finally, he stopped and lifted a hand to bat away the snowflakes that were increasing in size and frequency. "We jumped too far ahead," he said. "I want to say things to you that are too soon, too serious."

Her heart sank, because she knew he was right. "So that's it?" she asked bleakly. "We just chalk this up to bad timing and walk away?"

"Is that what you want?" He stood there…proud, tall and so alone her heart broke for him.

"No. That's not what I want at all," she said, daring to be honest with so much at stake. "So if you have a plan, I'm listening."

He exhaled noisily as if he'd been holding his breath. "Well, okay, then. Here it is. I propose that we go back to your place and spend Christmas Eve together when it rolls around. I'll stay with you for the remainder of the time I have reserved and work on learning how not to obsess about business."

"Is that even possible?" She said it with a grin so he would know she was teasing. Mostly.

"God, I hope so. Because I want you in my life, Phoebe. And you deserve a man who will not only make a place for you, but will put you front and center."

One hot tear rolled down her cheek. "Is there more?"

"Yes. And this is the scary part. At the end of January, assuming we haven't killed each other or bored each other to death, I want you to come back to Atlanta and move in with me…as my fiancée. Not now," he said quickly. "As of this moment, we are simply a man and a woman who are attracted to each other."

"Very attracted," Phoebe agreed, her heart lifting to float with the snowflakes.

She took a step in his direction, but he held up a hand. "Not yet. Let me finish."

His utter seriousness and heartfelt sincerity gave her hope that what had begun as a serendipitous fling might actually have substance and a solid foundation. Cautious elation fluttered inside her chest. But she kept her cool… barely. "Go on."

"I'm not criticizing you, Phoebe, but you have to admit—you have issues with balance, too. Work is valid and important. But when you left Charlotte, you cut off that part of yourself."

She grimaced, feeling shame for the holier-than-thou way she had judged his life. "You're right. I did. But I'm not sure how to step back in the opposite direction."

A tiny smile lifted the corners of his mouth. "When we get back to Atlanta, I want you to work for Cavallo. I could use someone with your experience and financial instincts.

Not only that, but it would make me very happy for us to share that aspect of who we are. I understand why you ran away to the mountains. I do. And I strongly suspect that knowing each of us, we'll need your cabin as an escape when work threatens to become all-encompassing."

Anxiety dampened her burgeoning joy. "I'm afraid, Leo. I messed things up so badly before."

He shook his head. "You had a man who didn't deserve you and you lost your baby, a miscarriage that was one of those inexplicable tragedies of life. But it's time to live again, Phoebe. I want that for both of us. It's not wrong to have a passion for work. But we can keep each other grounded. And I think together we can find that balance and peace that are so important." He paused. "There's one more thing."

She was shaking more on the inside than she was on the outside. Leo was so confident, so sure. Could she take another chance at happiness? "What is it?" she asked.

At last, he took her in his arms, warming her with his big, solid frame. He cupped her cheeks in his hands, his gaze hot and sweet. "I want to make babies with you, Phoebe. I thought my life was great the way it was. But then I had the heart attack, and I met you, and suddenly I was questioning everything I had ever known about myself. Watching you with Teddy did something to me. And now tonight, with Luc and Hattie's babies upstairs asleep, I see it all clearly. You and I, Phoebe, against all odds…we have a shot at the brass ring. Having the whole enchilada. I think you were wrong about that, my love. I think with the right person, life can be just about perfect."

He bent his head and took her mouth in a soft, firm kiss that was equal parts romance and knee-weakening passion. "Will you be my almost-fiancée?" he whispered, his voice hoarse and ragged. His hands slid down the silky fabric of her dress all the way to her hips. Dragging her closer still, he buried his face in her neck. She could feel him trembling.

Emotions tumbled in her heart with all the random patterns of the snowflakes. She had grieved for so long, too long in fact. Cowardice and the fear of being hurt again had constrained her equally as much as Leo's workaholic ways had hemmed him in.

The old man tending the fire had gone inside, probably to get warm. Phoebe gasped when Leo used the slit in her skirt to his advantage, placing a warm palm on her upper thigh. His fingers skated perilously close to the place where her body ached for him.

Teasing her with outrageous caresses, he nibbled her ear, her neck, the partially exposed line of her collarbone. "I need an answer, my love. Please."

Heat flooded her veins, negating the winter chill. Her body felt alive, spectacularly alive. Leo held her tightly, as if he were afraid she might run. But that was ludicrous, because there was no place she would rather be.

She gave herself a moment to say goodbye to the little child she would never know. So many hopes and dreams she had cherished had been ripped away. But the mountains had taught her much about peace, and in surviving, she had been given another chance. A wonderful, exciting, heart-pounding second chance.

Laying her cheek against Leo's crisp white shirt, feeling the steady beat of his wonderfully big heart, she nodded. "Yes, Leo Cavallo. I believe I will."

Epilogue

Leo paced the marble floor, his palms damp. "Hurry, Phoebe. They'll be here in a minute." He was nervous about his surprise, and if Phoebe lollygagged too much longer, it would be ruined. He gazed around his familiar home, noting the addition this year of a gigantic Christmas tree, its branches heavy with ornaments. In the chandelier overhead, tiny clumps of mistletoe dangled, tied with narrow red velvet ribbons.

His body tightened and his breath quickened as he recalled the manner in which he and Phoebe had christened that mistletoe, making love on the rug beneath. In truth, they had christened most of his condo in such a way. Including a repeat of what he liked to call "the kitchen episode."

He tugged at his bow tie, feeling much too hot all of a sudden.

At long last, his beloved wife appeared, her usual feminine stride hampered by a certain waddling movement. She grimaced. "This red dress makes me look like a giant tomato."

He pulled her in close for a kiss, running his hand over the fascinating swell of her large abdomen. "Red is my new favorite color. And besides, it's Christmas." Feeling the life growing inside his precious Phoebe tightened his throat and wet his eyes. So many miracles in his life. So much love.

She returned the kiss with passion. The force that drew them together in the beginning had never faded. In fact, it grew deeper and more fiery with each passing month.

This evening, though, they were headed for a night out on the town with Luc and Hattie. Dinner, followed by a performance of *The Nutcracker*.

Phoebe rubbed her back. "I hope I'm going to fit into a seat at the theater."

He grinned broadly. "Quit fishing for compliments. You know you're the sexiest pregnant woman in the entire state. But sit down, my love. I have something I want to give you before they get here."

Phoebe eased into a comfy armchair with a grimace. "It's five days 'til Christmas."

"This is an *early* present."

From his jacket pocket he extracted a ruby velvet rectangle. Flipping it open, he handed it to her. "I had it made especially for you."

Phoebe took the box from him and stared. Inside, nestled on a bed of black satin, was an exquisite necklace. Two dozen or more tiny diamond snowflakes glittered with fire on a delicate platinum chain. She couldn't speak for the emotion that threatened to swamp her with hormonal tears.

Leo went down on one knee beside her, removed the jewelry from the box and gently fastened it around her neck.

She put a hand to her throat, staring at his masculine beauty, feeling the tangible evidence of his boundless, generous love. "Thank you, Leo. It's perfect."

He wrapped a hand in her hair and fingered it. "I could have waited until our anniversary. But tonight is special to me. It was exactly a year ago that you stood in the snow and gave me a new life. A wonderful life."

Running one hand through his hair, she cupped his neck with the other and pulled him back for another kiss. "Are you channeling Jimmy Stewart now?" she teased, her heart full to bursting.

He laid a hand on her round belly, laughing softly when their son made an all too visible kick. "Not at all, my dear Phoebe. I'm merely counting my blessings. And I always count you twice."

* * * * *

LET'S TALK

Romance

For exclusive extracts, competitions and special offers, find us online:

facebook.com/millsandboon

@MillsandBoon

@MillsandBoonUK

Get in touch on 01413 063232

For all the latest titles coming soon, visit

millsandboon.co.uk/nextmonth